BBC

DOCTOR WHO

THE SILENT STARS GO BY ✻ TOUCHED BY AN ANGEL

POLICE PUBLIC CALL BOX

BBC

DOCTOR WHO

THE SILENT STARS GO BY ✳ TOUCHED BY AN ANGEL

Dan Abnett   Jonathan Morris

BBC
BOOKS

1 3 5 7 9 10 8 6 4 2

BBC Books, an imprint of Ebury Publishing
20 Vauxhall Bridge Road, London SW1V 2SA

BBC Books is part of the Penguin Random House group of companies
whose addresses can be found at global.penguinrandomhouse.com

Penguin
Random House
UK

Doctor Who is a BBC Wales production for BBC One
Executive producers: Steven Moffat and Brian Minchin

Doctor Who: Touched by an Angel first published by BBC Books in 2011
Doctor Who: The Silent Stars Go By first published by BBC Books in 2011

www.eburypublishing.co.uk

A CIP catalogue record for this book is available
from the British Library

ISBN 978 1 849 90980 8

Editorial director: Albert DePetrillo
Series consultant: Justin Richards
Project editor: Steve Tribe
Production: Alex Goddard

Printed and bound in China by Toppan Leefung

CONTENTS

BBC

DOCTOR WHO

THE SILENT STARS GO BY

Dan Abnett

For George Mann

O little town of Bethlehem
How still we see thee lie
Above thy deep and dreamless sleep
The silent stars go by
Yet in thy dark streets shineth
The everlasting Light
The hopes and fears of all the years
Are met in thee tonight

~ 'O Little Town of Bethlehem',
a song of Earth before

Vesta got up early that morning, before Guide's Bell rang to mark the start of labour, before the sun had come up and brought heat and full light. She got dressed in the dark, in woollens, and skirts both under and over, and a cap, and two shawls. She had gloves that Bel had sewn for her. It was very cold. She could feel the red in her cheeks and nose, and the water in her eyes, and she could see the white smoke of her breath in the gloom.

It was a biting cold, a bad cold. It was a cold that had a threat to it, not a promise, no matter what Bill Groan and the others said. Winter was supposed to go away, not come worse. Eighteen years Vesta had been alive, and she had never seen a white winter until the last three, each one whiter than the one before.

When she took her coat off the peg, her hands were numb despite her gloves. The twilight of dawn, a grey light made brighter by the snow, was creeping into the back hallway. By it, she found her boots, and the little pot and tie of heathouse flowers she had laid out the night before. She found the pole too, a pruning hook, strong and almost two metres long. It wasn't the season for pruning, but she'd left

7

it ready too because Bel had said it was good to know how deep snow was before you walked on it. Snow changed the landscape, and filled holes up. You could fall, or vanish, or turn an ankle and lie out of help's way so long you'd freeze.

They had all been told not to go out alone, especially early or late, but that was just worry. There had always been stories of things lurking up in the woods. They were stories made up to frighten children. Vesta had things to do. Some old dog bothering the herds wouldn't bother her.

She saw her name on the label above her peg. *Harvesta Flurrish*. Next to it, Bel's name. Next to that, an empty peg. Bel was not one for sentiment: she was older and she was clever. However, Vesta Flurrish could not let the day go unmarked.

Chaunce Plowrite had make them all metal cleats for their boots. Bill Groan, the Elect, gave Chaunce permission to make them out of leftover shipskin, and there wasn't much of that remaining. Vesta had hoped, when she woke, she wouldn't need to use them.

But she did.

Snow had come again in the night, overlaying the snow from the days before. Everything had a soft curved edge to it.

In the yard, the sky was night blue, the colour of Bel's eyes. First light, and clear all the way to the stars. The rooftops and chimneys of Beside, bearded with snow, were black against the blue, and so were the bare trees beyond, and the great rising plateaus of the Firmers. The plumes of steam coming from the vents on the tops of the Firmers were luminous white against the cobalt blue. They were catching the earliest rays of sunlight because they were so much higher up than anything else.

Vesta turned on her solamp, and hung it from her pole. Then she started to walk, her metal cleats crunching, her pruning pole probing the snow cover, one hand holding up the hem of her overskirts. A dog barked in the yard. In the byre behind the Flurrish house, the cattle were lowing.

She followed the North Lane out of Beside, past the well and up towards Would Be, which lay in the shadow of Firmer Number Two.

It was slow going. It was hard work striding over ground that sank under you. Vesta's legs began to ache. She stopped to rest for a minute and looked down at the streams that fed the autumn mills. They were frozen like glass in that stilled place between night and morning.

By the time she reached Would Be, she knew she would not manage to get back to Beside before Guide's Bell rang and called them to work. She resolved to work on after nightchime to make up. Vesta also knew that the people of the plantnation community would excuse her. They would allow her an hour or so, once a year.

Would Be was quiet. The trees were like silent figures with snowy caps. Autumn had taken their leaves, but winter was bowing their black branches and trunks. Vesta's solamp was beginning to flutter, its charge worn out, but it was getting lighter by the minute. The blue sky and the white snow were both tinged with pink from the sun-to-be.

As she walked along, in the quiet, she felt for one moment that someone was following her. But it was just the stillness, and her imagination.

The memory yard was in the centre of Would Be, a place chosen years ago as a quiet bit of earth. Patience was said to be the greatest virtue of all Morphans, and those who lay here were the most patient of all. Simple stones marked each burial spot, each one marked with a name, as clear as the labels above the pegs in the back hall of the Flurrish house.

There were Flurrishes here. Years of them, laid out and remembered, mixed up with all the other Morphan families. Vesta's mum had gone away long ago, before Vesta was really old enough to know her. She lay here, and Vesta always said a friendly hello to her stone.

But Vesta had come for her dad, Tyler Flurrish, gone four years, taken by a fever. He'd seen the colder seasons coming, and fretted about it with his kin, but he hadn't lived to see the actual snow and ice. Vesta wondered if he felt it there in the ground, across his grave like a numbing blanket. He would have worried too much, about his daughters Vesta and Bel, and about the future that awaited them.

Vesta crouched by the grave and brushed the snow off the stone so she could read the name there. She took out the flowers she had brought, and set them in the jar on his plot. It would have been his birthday, so she wished him a happy one, and then talked to him a little about the work and how things were.

Far away, down in Beside, Guide's Bell chimed.

Vesta bowed her head and said a few words to Guide, and asked Guide to look after her dad. Then she got up to make her way back.

The stars were still out. Over in the west, behind the bare silhouettes of the trees, one seemed to be moving.

Vesta stopped to watch. There had been talk of stars moving. Even Bel said she had seen one do it. Many said it was a bad omen, signifying the coming danger of the cold, but it was a mystery too. Stars weren't supposed to slide silently past in the darkness of a winter dawn.

Moving slowly, making no sound, it disappeared behind a stand of trees. Vesta hurried along to see if she could catch another glimpse of it.

That's when she saw the tracks.

She almost walked across them. They were so deep in the snow, they held shadow and looked as black as pitch. They cut straight through the heart of Would Be from the north, running away towards Firmer Number Three.

They were the biggest footprints she'd ever seen, bigger than even Jack Duggat would make, with his work boots and his metal cleats on and everything. And it wasn't just the size of the prints – the stride length was also huge.

Vesta stared for a moment. She thought hard, trying to explain what she could see. She wondered if they were footprints that had begun to melt, thus exaggerating their size.

But they were fresh. The snow was only a few hours old, and there had not yet been enough day to start to thaw it. No one was out except her, not this far north of the town. The tracks were clean cut. She could see where the heel and the toe pads had cut.

A giant had walked through the silent woods, and not long ago. If she had left her dad's grave just a few minutes earlier, she would have met it. It would have come right across her path.

Vesta Flurrish was really scared. Her hands were trembling, and it wasn't from the cold. Beside seemed a long way away: too far to reach quickly, too far to run to, too far to call to. She didn't even want to cross the tracks to run for home. That felt like the wrong thing to do, as if the giant might feel her path crossing his, and turn back for her.

She turned and began to run back towards the memory yard. At that moment, with the sun still not even risen, by her father's side seemed the safest place to be.

But there was something waiting for her in the trees, something with a deep, gurgling growl like a dog being throttled, something with red eyes that caught the gleam of the early light.

Something bred to kill.

CHAPTER 1
IN THE BLEAK MIDWINTER

'That,' said Amy, unable to disguise a slight note of surprise, 'was a perfect landing.'

'I thank you for noticing,' replied the Doctor. He beamed, and flipped a row of console switches to their 'off' positions with the flourish of a maestro organist shutting down his Wurlitzer after a career-defining performance.

'Then why are we leaning?' asked Rory.

'Leaning?' asked the Doctor, polishing the glass in the console dials with a handkerchief.

'Over,' said Rory. 'To one side.'

'We're not,' said the Doctor.

'Stand up straight,' said Amy.

They all did. They all looked at themselves in relation to the guard rail uprights.

'Ah,' said the Doctor.

'That *is* lean-y,' he conceded.

'Perhaps not as perfect as I first imagined,' he added.

'"Lean-y"?' asked Amy.

'Well, lean-*ish* at the very least,' replied the Doctor, sliding down the handrail of the stairs to reach the TARDIS main deck.

'We're allowed to make up words now, are we?' asked Rory.

'I thought that was well established,' said Amy.

'Look, it doesn't matter,' said Rory, following Amy down the control room stairs. 'It wasn't a complaint, the leaning thing.'

'Lean-*ish*,' the Doctor and Amy corrected him together.

'Whatever,' said Rory. 'It wasn't a complaint. I wasn't complaining. Lean all you like. I just want to check that we're in the right place. We can be *leaning* in the right place. That's fine. As long as we're *in* the right place. *Are* we in the right place?'

The Doctor stopped at the TARDIS door, turned to face Rory, and placed a reassuring hand on his shoulder. He peered into Rory's eyes.

'Rory Williams Pond,' said the Doctor.

'Not my actual name,' said Rory.

'Rory Williams Pond, did I not promise to get you back home for Christmas?'

'Yes.'

'Back home to Earth for Christmas?'

'Yes. Directly to Leadworth, near Gloucester f—'

'Ub-bub-bub-bub!' the Doctor chided. 'Specifics, mere specifics. Home for Christmas, that was the deal, right?'

'Yes,' Rory agreed.

'Doesn't the margin for interpretation seem huge now?' Amy asked him. She was pulling on wellies and a duffel coat. 'I mean, he's not even guaranteeing a street address, so *which* Christmas he's talking about becomes a bit vague too.'

'Oh, I hadn't even considered that,' groaned Rory.

'Home for Christmas is what I promised,' declared the

Doctor. 'Home for Christmas is what I will deliver, even if there has to be some leaning involved.'

He looked at Amy.

'Duffel, Pond?'

She was buttoning the toggles.

'Hello? Christmas? Leadworth? Chilly?' she replied.

'Good point,' said the Doctor. He looked thoughtful and twiddled his bow tie, as though it doubled as a thermostatic control.

'I had a fur coat somewhere,' he reflected. 'Big fur coat. Very warm. I wonder where that went?'

Amy glanced at Rory. 'Just the cardy, then?'

'Yes,' he said, zipping it up.

'*That's* your level of confidence?'

'You can't be disappointed if you don't get your hopes up,' said Rory.

The Doctor opened the doors. A breath of cold air touched their faces, just a gentle gust as though someone had opened an upright freezer.

'Wow,' said Amy.

'There, oh ye of little faith,' smiled the Doctor. He took a deep breath. 'You can almost smell the sleigh bells jingling.'

They went outside into perfect, virgin snow that was half a metre deep. The sky was a peerless blue, and the sun had a fiercely bright clarity. Around them, the woodland was silent and sculptural with snow.

'That's beautiful,' said Amy, gazing and smiling.

'Christmas-y, isn't it?' the Doctor agreed.

'Christmas-*ish*,' said Amy.

'It's great,' said Rory. 'I don't think it's Leadworth, but it's great.'

'Of course it's Leadworth,' said Amy. 'It's that bit of wood outside Leadworth. You know. That bit of wood?'

'Really?' asked Rory. 'Listen.'

'To what?' she asked.

'Just listen.'

They listened.

'I don't hear anything,' Amy said.

Rory nodded significantly with his eyes narrowed.

'That doesn't prove anything,' said Amy.

'No traffic? No… birds?' Rory asked.

'It's early,' said Amy. 'It's Christmas Day.'

'It's not that early. Look at the sun.'

'The roads are closed because of the snow.'

'There's not that much snow.'

'It's Leadworth *before there was traffic*,' said Amy.

'So, not the *right* Leadworth, then,' said Rory.

Amy stomped over to the Doctor, kicking up swirls of snow with her wellies.

'Tell him we're in the right place!' she insisted.

The Doctor was examining the TARDIS. The blue police box was perched on the thick snow cover, tilted by the drift so that it stood at a slight angle to the vertical.

'That explains the lean,' said the Doctor. 'We didn't land on the flat. Never mind. It's quite rakish. I'd say that was, in fact, lean-*esque*.'

'Tell him we're in the right place,' she repeated.

The Doctor turned to them.

'Oh, we're definitely in the right place!' he declared. 'Definitely! This is the right place! We're slap bang in the middle of Christmas. Christmas is all around us! Xmas marks the spot! Can't you feel it? Can't you sense it? It's all mince pies and brandy butter, and candied peel and

16

anxious turkeys! It's tinsel and carols, and baubles and egg nog! It's—'

'Is it Christmas, in Leadworth, on Earth, in 2011?' asked Rory.

The Doctor held up a thoughtful finger, and pursed his lips. He looked from side to side.

'Let's find out,' he decided, and strode off.

'If it isn't,' the Doctor called back to them over his shoulder, 'and I'm just saying "if", *if* it isn't, then the TARDIS has at least transported us to the most Christmas-y Christmas-ness in the whole universe, which is really quite something, and doesn't deserve any kind of criticism whatsoever!'

'Making it all up as he goes along,' Rory said to Amy as they scampered to keep up.

'Or *business as usual*, as it's also known,' she replied.

They began to ascend a slope through the trees. The glare of sunlight off the untouched snow was so bright they had to squint. It was hard going. Amy slipped and almost fell over. Rory chuckled so much, he did fall over. He slithered a bit too. Amy laughed, and gave him a hand to hoist him up. The Doctor kept straight on up the slope, swinging his lanky arms for balance, cheerfully singing 'I Saw Three Ships Come Sailing In'.

'Come on!' he shouted encouragingly. 'As a canon!'

'We can't even stand up,' Amy shouted back, 'let alone manage a three-part harmony!'

'Come up here! Come on!' the Doctor cried.

They joined him at the top of the rise. The view spread out below them, bright in the sunlight: woodland and fields, hills, mountains, a glorious snowscape, peaceful and still, entirely serene.

'That's pretty stunning,' said Amy.

'It is,' Rory agreed. 'It really is. It's not Leadworth, of course.'

'No,' said the Doctor.

'Unless Leadworth looked like this in, I don't know, the ninth century?' said Rory.

'With those mountains?' asked Amy.

'So, in fairness, it's not even Leadworth-*ish*, is it?' asked Rory.

'Yeah, but look at the pretty,' said the Doctor.

They were forced to agree that the pretty was really very pretty, and they looked at it admiringly for a while.

'Is that a village down there?' asked Amy.

'There's something very strange about those mountains,' said Rory.

'Village?' asked the Doctor.

'Down there, through the trees,' replied Amy, pointing. 'There, you see? I dunno, about a mile away?'

'I think you're right,' said the Doctor.

'The mountains,' said Rory, shielding his eyes from the glare. 'Very odd.'

'Yes,' said the Doctor. 'That's because they're not mountains. I don't think they're mountains, anyway. Come on!' He set off down the slope.

'Where are you going?' Amy called after him.

'What do you mean, you don't think they're mountains?' asked Rory.

'We're going to visit that village!' the Doctor announced. 'I mean, since we're here! We might get a lovely Christmas-y welcome! That'd be worth the trip, wouldn't it?'

Rory and Amy looked at each other and then back at the Doctor.

'What did you mean?' Rory repeated. 'Are you saying they're mountain-*ish*?'

'Come on!' the Doctor cried, stretching out his arms as he strode down the bank. 'Fill your lungs! Ahhhh! Taste that fresh air! Work up an appetite for all that Christmas pud!'

Amy shook her head and set off after the Doctor. Rory paused for a moment and zipped his cardigan right up to the top.

'You know what?' he said. 'It really is ever so cold.'

'Come on!' called Amy.

'It's all right for you, duffel coat,' said Rory. 'I mean, it is very pretty, it really is. But it's cold and it's very… dead. There's nothing around. It's so still and quiet and… bleak.'

The Doctor spun on his heels and pointed at Rory dramatically.

'Exactly! And a bleak midwinter, cruel frost notwithstanding, is exactly the vicinity in which you'd expect to find a really Christmas-y Christmas! So let's do that very thing!'

'Could I go back and get a coat first?' asked Rory. 'Please? It's really cold. And if this is the most Christmas-y Christmas to end all Christmases, I'd like to enjoy it and not be all dead of frostbite.'

'He *is* turning blue,' said Amy.

'I'll just be two minutes,' said Rory. 'Promise.'

The Doctor smiled.

'Of course. We'll wait right here. We'll be enjoying the view. Because it is, as you'll agree, magnificent.'

He took the TARDIS key out of his pocket and threw it to Rory.

Rory caught it neatly and held up both index fingers.

'Two minutes,' he repeated, and ran off down the rise behind him.

Amy and the Doctor turned to stare at the beautiful scenery again. The sun was very bright. Amy turned her mittened hand into a peak over her eyes.

'What did you mean about those mountains?' she asked.

'Just thinking aloud,' said the Doctor.

There was a long pause.

'Will he be all right?' she asked.

'He's only popped back to get a coat.'

'We should have gone with him,' she said.

'I think he can manage a coat.'

Amy glanced at him.

'We should have stayed together,' she said. 'Don't tut. We don't know where we are, and we just separated. I'm all right with you, but he's on his own. Which one of us is going to get into trouble and need rescuing? Come on, answer me that?'

The Doctor lowered his chin and turned cautiously to meet her look.

'Are you suggesting,' he asked, 'we could be setting ourselves up for some unnecessary shouting and running about later on?

Amy nodded.

'All right, we'll go and keep him company,' said the Doctor. They turned to head back over the slope after Rory.

And came to a dead stop.

Half a dozen men were standing at the top of the rise in front of them. They were dressed in several layers of heavy, dark clothes, proof against the cold. They wore hoods and mittens and cleated snow boots, and carried hefty farm tools: rakes, hoes and forks. Amy couldn't help noticing how grim and wary the men looked. How *intent*.

'Is this the lovely Christmas-y welcome you were looking for?' Amy whispered.

The Doctor looked a little uneasy. He regarded the heavy farm tools that were being aimed at them in a manner that unpleasantly suggested spears.

He spread his arms in an open, friendly gesture and took a step forward.

'Hoe hoe hoe?' he tried.

CHAPTER 2
LET NOTHING YOU DISMAY

Rory stepped out of the TARDIS, pulling on a pair of thick gloves to go with the parka he'd borrowed. He carefully locked the TARDIS door behind him.

'Amy?' he called, setting off in the direction they had been walking. 'Doctor?'

It was definitely the right way. He could see the three tracks of footprints, plus the fourth he'd left doubling back. The snow cover was perfect. Apart from their footprints, not an inch of it had been disturbed.

'Amy? Doctor?'

Rory made his way back to the rise where they had enjoyed the view. He stopped. There was no sign of his wife or the Doctor.

Rory wasn't especially worried at first. He was used to this. It was the kind of thing that happened a lot. People wandered off or got distracted. People didn't wait for you where they said they'd wait (which was rubbish of them, in his opinion, because he'd once waited in more or less the same place for a couple of thousand years). Sometimes, people noticed more interesting things going on around the corner while you were looking the other way. And that was before you considered the equally likely idea that the Doctor and Amy might be behind some trees nearby, skilfully constructing snowballs with which to greet him.

'Amy?'

Rory started to hunt around. He thought about scrunching together a pre-emptive snowball of his own.

He saw the tracks, the footprints of the Doctor and Amy, running a little way down the slope and back. On the top of the rise, was a mass of footprints that had arrived from the left along the line of the hill and apparently departed the same way.

Rory registered the very first twinge of worry.

'There's a perfectly reasonable explanation,' Rory told himself. 'They've met some nice people and gone off with them. Some… carol singers. They've gone carolling.'

He didn't stop to examine the logic holes in that statement. He set off after the footprints. He'd been gone ten minutes at most. How far could they have got?

After a few minutes' walk, it became evident that 'far enough to be out of sight' was the basic answer to that. Rory felt a little bit more worry. The heavy parka and the effort of tramping through the snow was actually making him feel a little warm. He stopped and took stock.

'Amy? Doctor?'

The bare trees with their heavy burdens of snow echoed his calls back to him.

Something moved.

Rory saw figures up ahead. He stepped forward, starting to smile in relief, ready to scold them for leaving him behind.

He froze in his tracks. His newborn smile froze too.

It wasn't the Doctor. It wasn't Amy. It wasn't any nice

friendly people they might have met along the way, either.

Rory knew that a snowball wasn't really going to cut it in the circumstances. He realised he needed to hide, very well and *very* quickly.

He skipped right past worry and went straight to feeling properly, deeply scared.

'Who in Guide's name are they?' asked Bill Groan.

Old Winnowner shook her head. 'They're not faces I ever knew, Elect,' she said. Winnowner Cropper was the oldest Morphan in Beside, the last of her generation. She was also the wisest of Bill Groan's councillors. If anyone knew, Bill Groan reasoned, it would be her.

'Bet they'll be from one of the other plantnations, Elect,' said Samewell.

Bill Groan looked at the young man. Samewell Crook saw the good side in everything. Bill Groan had an uneasy feeling that there wasn't much of a good side to anything just now.

'They don't look like Morphans,' said Bel Flurrish. Her voice was small and hard, as though it was huddling from the cold inside her.

'They have all kind of different fashions,' said Samewell. 'In Seeside, they have real hats. I heard that. Guide's truth.'

'We haven't had wellwishers at the festival for three years,' said Old Winnowner. 'Not since the ice started coming.'

'Well, they're making an effort this year, then, aren't they?' said Samewell.

'They're not wearing hats,' said Bel.

'Jack Duggat's party found them over at the top end of Would Be,' said Bill Groan.

'Then maybe they can say where my sister is,' said Bel.

Jack Duggat's men, their farm tools hefted like the weapons the old martials carried in Guide's books of Earth before, were leading the two visitors into the main yard. Quite a crowd of folk who were not labouring or searching had come out of their houses to watch.

One of the two strangers was tall and alert, smiling and looking at everything around him. He reminded Bel Flurrish of an inquisitive cockerel, walking comb-up into everything, heedless of its own safety. There was something in his openness that slightly reassured her. A person whose face could hold that kind of expression was not, in her opinion, a person who could do harm to another person.

The second visitor was a girl. She looked cautious, but there was a strength in her. She had red hair. Bel had never seen red hair. She'd never seen anything like it, except in Guide's books. How could something that had only ever been known of on Earth before find its way to Hereafter?

'I want to talk to them, Elect,' said Bel.

'I think you'll find it's my job,' said Bill Groan.

'I think you'll find it's my sister,' Bel replied.

Bill Groan was the elected leader of the Beside plantnation. He was a good man, with dark hair and a beard that had started to show grey the first year the winter wore white. He looked at Bel, right into her hard, angry eyes.

'You know I'm taking this serious, Arabel,' he said. 'Your sister disappearing is a Cat A matter. And now these strangers arrive? It's a concern. But there's a process. I got to do this right.'

'Then I want to be present,' she said. 'Guide help me, I deserve to be present.'

Bill glanced at Old Winnowner, saw the tiny nod she made, and told Bel Flurrish *yes*.

'Take them on into the assembly,' he told Jack Duggat.

The tall visitor heard him say this, and turned towards Bill Groan with a smile.

'Hello, I'm the Doctor!' he announced, stepping towards Bill. A hoe and a pitching fork crossed in front of him to block his way. 'Oh, dear!' he said, recoiling from the heavy wooden shafts. 'I think there's been a bit of a misunderstanding. I really do. Are you in charge? I'd love to go out and come back in again. You know? Start over! How would that be?'

'That's a funny accent, Elect,' Winnowner said, sidelong, to Bill Groan.

'Indeed.'

The Doctor and Amy watched the locals muttering about them.

'You're freaking them out, and *they've* got the pointy forks,' Amy whispered to the Doctor.

'Yes, they have,' he mused. 'Am I?'

'You really are,' said Amy. 'Could we just play along for now?'

She was shivering slightly, her arms folded tight across her chest. 'On the bright side, they might take us in the warm before they stab us to death with gardening implements.'

The leader of the community council beckoned, and the two visitors were escorted across the snowy yard into the assembly. Firebuckets had been lit, and the solamps turned on. The hall was warm and brown: worn wood beams and seats, polished from years of use and care, floorboards gleaming from a history of footsteps. The nails and pegs that had been used in the building of the assembly were made of shipskin.

Amy stood as close to one of the sputtering firebuckets as she could, basking. She took off her mittens. They were looped inside the sleeves of her duffel coat on a piece of elastic.

The Doctor looked around. He gazed up at the beamed roof. He looked at the circular inlays of metal patterning the worn wooden floor, the metal seams in the beams and ceiling posts.

'This is old,' he said. 'Beautifully made.'

Amy watched him. He crouched down beside one of the wooden guard rails that surrounded the open space they had been led into. He ran an appreciative fingertip along it, like an antiques expert.

'Those nails,' he murmured.

Amy raised her eyebrows. 'The nails matter? Really? Now? Do they *really*?'

The Doctor stood up. 'They might,' he said.

'Rory's out there. On his own. Looking for us,' said Amy. 'Can we get a move on, and persuade them to let us go?'

Jack Duggat's men took up a guard position at the assembly doors. Some Morphans filed in and took their seats. Bill Groan and other plantnation council members sat in the semicircle of chairs at the head of the chamber.

'Who are you?' Bill Groan asked.

'I'm the Doctor,' said the Doctor.

'You're a doctor?' asked Old Winnowner. 'Of what? Physic? Medicine?'

'All sorts of things,' said the Doctor.

There was a murmur. The council conferred.

'This is Amy Pond,' said the Doctor.

'An honest Morphan name,' noted Chaunce Plowrite.

'Thank you,' said Amy. 'I think.'

'Is she your wife?' asked Old Winnowner.

'Oh no!' declared the Doctor.

'No need to sound so outraged. I *could* be,' Amy hissed at him. 'I'm not, though,' she said to the council.

'We're all kind of friends, really,' said the Doctor. 'It's very informal. We don't stand on ceremony, do we, Pond?'

'Almost never,' said Amy.

'But this is a more formal occasion,' the Doctor went on, pointing an expressive, flexible forefinger at Bill Groan. 'And you're in charge of this community, aren't you?'

'It's been my honour to serve Beside as Nurse Elect of the council for eight years,' said Bill Groan. 'It's not a burden I take lightly, as these people know.'

'Of course not, of course not,' said the Doctor. 'And *Nurse*, such an interesting word. From the Latin, *nutricius*, person who nourishes. Nurse as in nursery, as in a place where plants and animals are fostered and bred.'

The council members started talking to each other animatedly.

'What are you doing?' Amy asked the Doctor, sidling up to him and whispering through the fixed grin she was aiming towards the council.

'Just establishing some context,' he replied. 'Nurse Elect. It's a high-status title. A leader. He's the chap with the beard.'

'They've all got beards, Doctor,' said Amy.

'Be fair. *She* hasn't.'

'Wait,' said Amy. 'That bloke's job title derives from Latin? How?'

'The usual way.'

'But Rory was right. This isn't Leadworth,' she whispered. 'This isn't even Earth. So how can they have a Latin name for something?'

'Wherever we are, it's Earth-*ish*,' said the Doctor. 'Very Earth-ish, in fact. My guess is it's getting more Earth-ish with every passing day. And these people are very much human.'

'Why are we wasting time with this chit-chat?' Bel Flurrish asked, her voice louder than any other in the hall. The place fell quiet. She stood up from her seat in the congregation, and glared at the council and the three visitors.

'Come now, Arabel,' said Bill Groan.

'As Guide is my witness, Elect,' said Bel, 'you're just chattering while time runs away. Why don't you ask them a proper question?'

'Oh, good idea!' said the Doctor enthusiastically. 'I like getting down to the nitty-gritty. Like what?'

Bel glowered at him, not at all warmed by his charm.

'Like where do you actually come from? You're not from Beside, so which plantnation are you from?'

Amy looked at the Doctor. 'Plant *nation*?' she mouthed.

The Doctor pulled a face and shrugged in a slightly convulsive way.

'That's... hard to answer, Bel,' he said.

'Really?' asked Bel. 'I wouldn't have thought it was. There are only three plantnations on Hereafter, so it's not difficult to choose.'

'Ah,' said the Doctor. 'Next?'

'Very well,' said Bel. 'What have you done with my sister?'

CHAPTER 3
IF THOU KNOWST
THY TELLING

'I think we should try to smooth things out,' said the Doctor, opening his hands in a gentle, calming gesture. He turned slowly so that, one by one, he caught the eye of everyone in the assembly and shared a moment of his reassuring smile.

He fixed his gaze on Jack Duggat. Jack Duggat was a big man, tallest of all the Beside Morphans, and the hoe in his fists was big too. It looked substantial enough to skewer a humpback whale.

'I'm going to reach into my pocket and take something out, all right?' the Doctor told Jack.

Jack Duggat hesitated. The Doctor began to slide a hand into his tweed jacket.

'Careful!' Amy whispered.

'Tell *him* that,' replied the Doctor. He produced the travel pass wallet that contained his psychic paper, and showed it to Jack Duggat. 'I think that clears things up,' he said.

'It says he's from Seeside,' Jack Duggat announced, studying the wallet. 'It says he's come to wish us well for the season, as is traditional, and extend the hand of friendship from Seeside Plantnation. It also says he is here

31

to offer expertise and assistance.'

Bill Groan rose to his feet.

'On behalf of the Beside Plantnation, I welcome you then as friends at this time of festival,' he said. 'I'm sorry we mistook you. These are troubled times.'

'I can tell,' said the Doctor.

'Wait,' said Jack Duggat. 'There is one thing.'

'What's that, Jack?' asked Bill Groan.

'You know it yourself, Elect,' said Jack. 'I haven't got my letters. I can't read. So how come I'm reading this?' He held the wallet out. No one seemed to want to touch it.

'Obviously, I can explain that,' the Doctor began.

Old Winnowner got up and came down to the front. She took the wallet from Jack Duggat's massive hand and looked at it.

'It is a letter,' she said. 'Guide help me, just like Jack said. A letter from the Nurse Elect of Seeside. It looks… genuine.'

'How could I read it?' asked Jack, sounding distressed.

Old Winnowner looked at Bill Groan in horror.

'Unguidely!' she breathed.

'I'm sure—' Bill began.

'It's unguidely, Elect!' Winnowner said. 'It's conjury! You know what Guide teaches us about conjury!'

'It's a Cat A wrong,' said Chaunce Plowrite.

'I know it is,' said Bill Groan heavily. 'Jack, take them to the compter and lock them in while we work out what to do.'

'It's… it's just paper,' said the Doctor, looking rather wrong-footed. 'It's just an innocent trick—'

'Conjury tricks,' said Old Winnowner. 'See, he admits it.'

The men began to jostle Amy and the Doctor away.

32

Amy glared meaningfully at him. 'I can't take you anywhere,' she said.

The compter was a cell under the assembly hall. Earth-cut steps led down into a cold, artificial cave lit by a couple of solamps. A firebucket had been stoked. The cell had a cage wall with a sliding door. The bars were made of dull, bluish metal. The interior of the cell was a sawdust floor furnished with a bench and a soil-pot.

Jack Duggat locked them in and went back up the steps jangling the keys.

Amy sat down on the bench.

'Great,' she said.

The Doctor grinned at her. He flipped out his sonic screwdriver.

'A lock,' he said. 'I can do locks. They're easy-peasy. Easier than trying to bluff a hall full of frightened people.'

'Why are they frightened?' asked Amy.

'Because we're strange,' he said. 'And anyway, wouldn't you be if you'd never seen a proper winter before?'

Amy shrugged.

'OK, open the lock,' she invited. 'Then what? We've got to get past all those blokes with pitchforks. If we're lucky, maybe they'll light torches and form a mob to chase us back to our castle.'

'You're upset,' said the Doctor. 'I can see that.'

'Top marks to you,' she replied. 'I'm worried about Rory. He'll be worried about me. About us. He could be walking into anything.'

Bel stared fiercely at the Nurse Elect of Beside. 'Just like that, Bill Groan? Just like that? You lock them up? You don't even ask the questions you should ask?'

'He will, Arabel,' said old Winnowner.

'I will,' Bill Groan agreed. He was thinking hard and studying the stranger's wallet. Part of him was worried that its unguideliness might rub off and contaminate him, but it was too intriguing to set aside. The letter contained in the wallet was exactly the sort of letter that he would have issued as Nurse Elect of Beside. It bore Guide's stamp, and the crest of the Hereafter plantnations. It was the very form of words he would compose. It even looked like his handwriting.

'Perhaps it is real. Perhaps they are who they say they are,' said Bel.

'It's not real,' said Bill Groan.

'Then they could have took it!' snapped Bel. 'Took it from some poor Seesider who was coming here with good intentions. Took it, and left him for dead in a ditch—'

'It's not real!' Bill snapped back. 'Jack could read it, remember?'

'So stop looking at it, and go and—'

'Arabel Flurrish!' Bill Groan exclaimed. 'Take yourself back to your seat!'

'Go ask them where my sister is!' Bel shouted.

'I know you're worried, Arabel, but you show some common courtesy,' said Bill Groan. He looked back at the wallet and his voice grew smaller. 'The stars, and the cold, and now this,' he said. 'Guide help me, I don't know what to do. Nothing like this has ever happened to us. I don't even know how to start to think about it.'

'It's conjury,' said Winnowner softly. 'It's a blight of conjury that's brought the harsh winter upon us, and those two strangers are the cause. It's their doing.'

'I don't believe in conjury,' said Bill.

'It's their work,' said Winnowner. 'A blight of conjury.'

'No,' said Bill, shaking his head.

'Did you see her hair?' asked Chaunce. 'I never seen hair like that before.'

'The colour of blood,' said Jack Duggat.

'Not blood,' murmured Samewell Crook.

Bill Groan looked at Old Winnowner. Her brow was furrowed with concern like an acre after the plough, but her thin smile was trying to reassure him.

'What if it is conjury?' he asked. 'What if it is an unguidely thing?'

'Then Guide will show us what to do,' the old woman said. 'Chapter and verse, we'll find the passage that applies to our situation, and follow Guide's words, and be delivered. Like we always are with all things.'

Bill didn't look convinced. He turned the wallet over in his hand, thoughtfully.

'But Jack, who I've known since we were boys, he could read the words of this when he can't read a word otherwise,' he said. 'That's something that should not happen. It should not be possible, not under Guide's laws. And if it's something to which Guide's laws do not apply, how do we fight that?'

Bel Flurrish held out her hand.

'Can I see it, please, Elect?' she asked.

Bill Groan hesitated. Old Winnowner looked particularly dubious. After a moment, he handed the wallet to Bel.

She looked at its outside first, turning it around and around before opening it.

'Oh,' she said.

'What?' asked Bill.

Bel was staring at the open wallet. Words didn't seem to want to form.

'It's—' she began.

'It's highly convincing, isn't it?' asked Bill Groan.

Bel closed the wallet and handed it back to the Nurse Elect. 'Yes, it is,' she said. 'Please, Elect. Please go down and ask them about my sister. The day is passing and night is coming again.'

'I will, Bel, as soon as I have discussed what best to do.'

'Don't delay, Elect!' Bel said in despair.

'I will consult the council,' Bill replied. 'An hour, no more. Just so I know what to do in the face of further conjury. Then I will get some answers out of them.'

Bill Groan asked the council to take their seats again, and they quickly fell to talking.

Bel Flurrish watched for a while, fidgeting and anxious. When she could bear it no more, she got up.

Everyone was too busy discussing the issue to notice her slip out of the back of the assembly.

Rory ran.

He was running about as fast as he'd ever run in his life. He was certainly running as fast as he had ever run in heavy snow. More than once, the soft depth of it took his feet out from under him, or stole away his balance, and he went sprawling.

Each time, he got up and started running again.

He had no idea where he was running to. He had no idea which way the TARDIS was any more. All he knew for certain was which direction he was running *from*.

There had been something quite dreadful about the figures he had seen, something that had shaken him. There had been four or perhaps five figures, and they'd simply been walking in his direction. The figures had been green, as though they were wearing suits or uniforms. They hadn't been doing anything sinister or threatening. They hadn't shouted at him, or shot at him.

Nevertheless, there had been something disturbing about the way they were advancing: slow, steady, relentless, utterly untroubled by the snow. He'd never seen anything as simple as *walking* look scary before, and that was saying something, because he'd seen Cybermen march. Cybermen moved with chilling, machined discipline. The way they walked matched the way they thought, and that was the terrifying part about them: the clinical precision.

The figures Rory had just seen had been lumbering. They had displayed a relentlessness born not out of mechanical rhythm, but brutal, unwavering, physical determination.

They'd been big people, whoever they were. Stupidly big. For a second, Rory wondered if they were wearing extensive and heavyweight cold-weather gear. He thought he caught a flash of red from goggles or a visor. But even cold-weather gear wouldn't have explained their size. They were towering, bulky humanoids, broad-bodied and slope-shouldered. They reminded him unpleasantly of the proper bruisers that were taken into A&E on a Saturday night, veterans of fights in pub car parks and brawls with doormen. Those blokes weren't athletically large: no broad shoulders and round biceps, like the Hollywood idea of a super hero. They were always *real* world big: thick through the chest and waist, with forearms like hams, and wrists as wide as their fists. Their flesh was dense. They had a scary, unglamorous strength, a genuine power, bred not from a gym and a personal trainer, but from graft and life. Those were the ones you were wary around when you were on shift, the sullen ones who loomed, and looked at you from under drink-lowered eyelids, the ones who could suddenly turn and cripple you with a punch.

Rory knew, simply knew as a certainty, that the men he had seen were to be avoided. His first thought of hiding had been dashed. The plodding figures were too close. If they hadn't seen him already, they would be about to, and he had no desire to cower behind a tree while they caught up with him. He'd started to run instead.

Besides, if there were things like that, giant things like that, blundering around in the woods, Rory would prefer they were chasing him rather than bearing down on Amy and the Doctor.

He could draw them off, perhaps, and then circle back to look for his friends… And then get the hell out of there.

CHAPTER 4
THOUGH THE FROST WAS CRUEL

'Someone's coming!' hissed Amy.

The Doctor's sonic screwdriver had been poised over the cage door's lock. He quickly put it behind his back.

Bel Flurrish came down the shadowy steps into the lamplight. She stared at them through the bars. 'Where is my sister?' she asked.

'We don't know,' the Doctor assured her gently.

'You *do* know,' said Bel, approaching the bars. Her expression was fierce.

'We don't!' Amy insisted. 'How's about you let us out of this stupid cage?'

'I *know* you know,' said Bel. 'How else would you have a picture of her?'

'A picture?' asked Amy, baffled.

'In that wallet!' Bel exclaimed. 'That wallet full of conjury! I saw it!'

Amy looked at the Doctor.

'Psychic paper,' murmured the Doctor. He turned to face Amy. 'Awkward. One of the drawbacks. It keys into the thing you most want to see, the thing you'll find most compelling or convincing. Sometimes a strong emotion

39

can imprint, with rather unfortunate consequences.'

'She saw her sister because she's worried about her?' asked Amy.

'It's all she can think of,' the Doctor replied. 'Plus, she suspects us of being involved somehow because we're strangers, so that boosted the subliminal response. Plus—'

'There's another plus?'

'Yes,' said the Doctor. 'I think there's a general level of tension here that's heightening emotional resonance.'

Bel was watching their rapid conversation with increasing amazement.

'You know she's standing right there and she can hear every word we're saying, don't you?' Amy asked the Doctor.

'Yes, I had noticed.'

'And you're aware her general level of freak-out is going to sky-rocket if we keep talking like this?'

'Indeed I am,' said the Doctor.

He turned back to face Bel through the bars of the cage. He smiled.

'Listen,' he said. 'Arabel – it is Arabel? – Arabel, we really want to help you. We really do. We didn't harm your sister or take her away. We didn't even see her. But we'd like to help you find her. What's your sister's name, Arabel?'

'Why would I tell you that?' asked Bel.

'So that we can help you?'

'And why would you help me?'

'To be honest,' said Amy, 'we're in a bit of a fix here. If we can do something to help you, maybe we can prove to your...' She hesitated, then gestured up the stairs behind Bel. '... to your community that we're nothing to be afraid of.'

'Indeed,' said the Doctor. 'Let nothing you dismay. We

come in peace. Besides, no one deserves to be lost in weather like this.'

'No, they don't,' agreed Amy, shooting the Doctor a significant look.

'So what's her name?' asked the Doctor.

'Vesta,' said Bel cautiously. 'Harvesta Flurrish.'

'And when did you last see her?'

'Last night, before bed. She was gone this morning.'

'Do you know where she might have gone?' asked the Doctor.

Bel shook her head. 'But she took her boots and her coat.'

The Doctor glanced at Amy, and then looked back at Bel. 'Arabel,' he said, 'it's not supposed to be this cold, is it?'

'Is it not cold where you come from?' Bel asked.

'Not this cold,' said the Doctor. 'It's getting colder each winter, isn't it? Every year, a little worse. How many years has it been going on?'

'Three or four.'

'And the reverse is supposed to be happening, isn't it?'

'Of course,' said Bel. 'That is the goal of all Morphan work. As you should know.'

'I was just thinking aloud,' said the Doctor.

'Guide tells us,' said Bel, 'that patterns may worsen in the short term while the greater changes take effect. So the Elect teaches.'

'That's true,' said the Doctor. 'Sometimes. With major projects, that's certainly true, sometimes. You're dealing with continental weather systems. Global climate. But I'm not sure. That's why you haven't done anything drastic, isn't it? You've been telling yourself it's just a symptom of short-term climate change.'

'What's this all about, Doctor?' Amy asked. 'Why are you talking about weather?'

'Look at her clothes,' said the Doctor. 'Her everyday clothes are well made but worn from long use. Her overcoats, and shawls, her boots… they're all new. The people here are not used to winters this cold.' He looked back at Bel. 'Will you let us out, Arabel?'

Bel glanced nervously at the stairs. 'I should not. It is against the word of the Elect.'

'If you let us out, we will help you,' said the Doctor.

Bel wavered.

'But I do not have the key!' she declared.

'Arabel, tell me why people are so worried about conjury?' asked the Doctor.

'It's a Cat A crime,' said Bel. 'We are taught we may only do what Guide tells us to do. If it is unguidely, then it is forbidden.'

'Arabel,' said the Doctor calmly, 'just for a moment, you're going to have to accept that Guide has told me how to do things that may not have been mentioned to other people.'

Bel Flurrish blinked and then narrowed her eyes. 'What do you mean?'

The Doctor took the sonic screwdriver from behind his back. He adjusted it, ratcheted open the pincers, and aimed it at the cage door's lock. It glowed as it warbled softly. The lock sprang with a click.

The Doctor opened the cage door.

Bel stared at him.

'Let's go and find your sister,' he said.

They slipped up the stairs of the compter, the Doctor

leading the way. The sound of voices drifted from the assembly hall.

'They will be talking for hours,' Bel whispered.

One of Duggat's men was watching the doorway, leaning on the handle of the shovel he'd been carrying as a weapon. He was watching the council debate through the half-open door. A strong, cold draft was coming down the side corridor. Arabel indicated that direction with a tilt of her head.

Hugging the chilly stone of the wall, they crept past the guard, and hurried down the corridor to the rear gate. Bel struggled a little with the heavy bolt. The Doctor helped her. Amy kept glancing over her shoulder. She was certain the guard was going to hear the screech of the bolt withdrawing.

The Doctor managed to pull it silently. He ran his finger along the bolt.

'The same metal as the nails,' he whispered.

Amy glared at him.

He gauged her reaction. 'No? Not the time for that?' he asked, still whispering.

She shook her head.

They scuttled outside, into a little snowy yard behind the assembly. Amy carefully latched the door as quietly as she could.

Bel stepped up to the Doctor and put her hand flat against his chest, pushing him firmly against the yard wall.

'I am only doing this to help my sister,' she said. 'I will not have her die too.'

'Of course,' said the Doctor.

'If you play me for a fool…'

'I won't, Arabel. I promise.'

*

'This is our house,' said Bel, closing the door behind them. No lamps had been lit, and no heat stoked up either. Bel had left the Flurrish house early in her search for Vesta. The house ached with cold. Daylight leaked in through the snow-dusted windows.

'We won't be disturbed here,' said Bel.

'It's splendid,' said the Doctor. 'We just need somewhere to think, just for a minute. There's no sense in running around the countryside looking for Vesta in this weather. We need to work out where she might have gone.'

'I'll raise some heat,' said Bel, heading for the stove.

Amy was rubbing her hands together briskly. As Bel moved away, she leaned close to the Doctor.

'Really?' she asked quietly. 'No sense in running around the countryside? Not even to, I don't know, *get away from here?*'

'We're safe enough.'

'And not even to *look for my husband?*'

'Rory's safe enough too,' said the Doctor. 'He's probably sitting in the TARDIS right now, making a cup of tea.'

'I don't believe you sometimes,' said Amy.

'Trust me, Pond,' the Doctor replied, flashing an impish smile. He began to look around the spare and simple room. 'Something's going on here, and it requires attention.'

Bel returned from banking up the stove. A rumour of heat began to infuse the room.

'Everything's hand-crafted,' mused the Doctor, looking at the furniture and the construction of the house itself. 'Beautifully made, but old. A lot of wood. Local timber, I'd guess, and expertly cut and finished. And the nails and handles, you see? The screws?'

'Shipskin,' said Bel. 'Not much of that left now.'

44

'Shipskin,' the Doctor echoed. 'Of course it is. Shipskin.' He looked at Amy. 'Hull metal,' he said, 'salvaged from the vessel that brought the Morphans here.'

'Earth before and Hereafter,' Bel said.

'And how long have you lived here, Bel?' asked the Doctor.

'All of my years,' she said.

'I meant, how long have the Morphans lived on Hereafter?'

'Twenty-seven generations,' she replied. She paused, and stared at the Doctor. 'Guide help me, why would you ask that?' she said. 'You cannot be a Morphan and not know that, but there is no one else on Hereafter who is not a Morphan.'

'There is now,' said the Doctor. 'Arabel? Bel? I know it's a lot to grasp, but you have to keep trusting us. Think of it this way. Guide sent us to help when you needed us most. Tell me this, Bel, why were the men who found us armed?'

'They were searching for Vesta,' Bel began.

The Doctor shook his head.

'The Morphans have no weapons, no firearms or anything,' he said. 'They had to grab makeshift weapons… axes and pitchforks, that sort of thing. Why would men do that to go looking for a missing girl? Why would they arm themselves when they're not even used to bearing arms?'

'They…' Bel began. She stared down at the old kitchen table as she thought about her answer. 'We… we have lost livestock. Just this winter, never before. Something has been feeding on sheep and goats. We think maybe it is a dog that has got out and run feral. Maybe from another plantnation.'

'It would have to be that, wouldn't it?' said the Doctor.

'Because there are no other animals here. Only the ones that you Morphans brought with you. Hereafter has no indigenous animals that could kill a sheep.'

'I don't know what that word means,' said Bel, 'but the men took staves and axes because they were afraid that…'

'That whatever's doing the killing might have gone after bigger prey,' said the Doctor.

Bel nodded. Her lip trembled.

'How long has there been trouble here, Bel?' asked Amy.

'Life here is always hard,' said Bel, with forced lightness. 'But three years ago, the winter started going white, and worse each year. Then we really started to struggle. Not enough food, not enough fuel to get by. We used to see people from the other two plantnations quite regular, particularly at festival time, but not since travelling got hard. It's not just that the winters are cold, it's what the cold winters mean.'

'They mean it could all be failing,' said the Doctor. 'The entire terraforming programme.'

'The Terra Firmers will never fail,' said Bel emphatically. 'It's part of our duty to maintain them. Our plantnation is called Beside because it is beside the Firmers. That is the great task Guide has given to us.'

'Now, you told me,' said the Doctor, 'that Guide tells you that can happen sometimes. That sometimes the winters get worse before they can get better.'

Bel nodded again. 'That is what Guide says.'

'But you don't believe it, do you?'

Bel shrugged. 'We must trust in the Elect and the council, but I don't think Bill Groan believes it either. It is hard to trust that things will get better when they get worse.'

'There's more to it, though, isn't there?' asked the Doctor.

'There have been signs. The livestock dead. And some say they have seen people in the woods around the plantnation. The shadows of tall men, watching us. No one has seen them clearly, but they are big. And they cannot be men, because all men from Beside are accounted for.'

She looked at the Doctor.

'Until today,' she said.

'Yes, but I came and said hello, so it can't have been me,' said the Doctor.

Bel sat down at the table and rested her nose against her clasped hands as though she was praying.

'I told Vesta not to go about alone,' she said quietly. 'I told her. She said there were no giants in the woods, and she could scare off any rogue dog. But I had seen the stars, and she had not.'

'The stars?'

'It was the other sign. Stars that go by at night, overhead. They make no sound. I've seen them, and a few others have. Old Winnowner says that the stars are an omen. The worst of all the signs. They warn us that the world is in turmoil, and that despite all our patience, the Morphan effort is in danger.'

'You said something just now,' said Amy quietly.

The Doctor and Bel looked at her.

'You said you were only letting us out to help your sister, because you didn't want her to die too. Who else has died?'

'Our mother died years ago,' Bel replied. 'Then we lost our dad four years ago to a fever. I won't lose another Flurrish, I swear to Guide, I—'

She stopped abruptly.

'Oh Guide help me!' she cried, looking at the Doctor and

Amy in dismay. 'I think I know where she went! I think I know!'

'Where?' asked Amy.

'I had forgotten the day,' said Bel, scraping back her chair and getting up. 'Vesta remembers these things, I don't. It's the anniversary of our father's death. She… she would have gone out early to lay flowers on his grave. She would have gone up to the memory yard before the start of labour.'

'Then that,' said the Doctor, 'is where we should look first.'

Out of breath, Rory slithered to a halt. He tried to get his bearings from the three mountains that the Doctor had said weren't mountains at all. He could see them through the trees, pluming steamy white clouds against the perfect blue of the winter sky.

It felt like it was past midday. The air was clear and the sun was high and bright, but it was still as cold and hard as glass.

Rory had a stitch, and his legs ached from bounding through the snow. Panting, he turned in a full circle, checking the trees around him.

He heard a sound. A crunch of snow. A footstep biting into the soft fall. Surely, after all that running, he'd outdistanced those dreadful lumbering figures?

He edged forward, listening intently. The woodland clearing was silent, the light bouncing off the snow so bright it made him squint.

Another crunch.

He took another step, his heart beating very fast.

A figure stepped out in front of him. He was big, but he looked scared too. He was holding an axe.

Rory recoiled. 'Oh, hello,' he said in surprise.

'Who are you?' the man asked, his voice thickly accented. He took a step forward and the axe rose a little.

'Listen,' said Rory, 'listen to me. There's something in the woods. These… figures. Very, very big figures…'

He glanced from side to side. Other men dressed like the bearded man with the axe were emerging from cover, surrounding him. They carried an assortment of picks, mattocks and pitchforks.

'Have you seen the Doctor at all?' Rory asked hopefully.

'Where are you from?' one of the men demanded.

'Um… Leadworth?' Rory tried.

'What kind of unguidely answer is that?' asked one of the others.

'I don't know his face,' said the man with the axe.

'I'm a friend! I'm friendly!' Rory declared, holding up his hands.

'He's a stranger,' said a man with a pick.

'Where is Vesta Flurrish?' the man with the axe asked Rory.

'Is it… *near* Leadworth?'

'Take him,' said the man with the axe. 'Bind his hands. The council can decide what to do with him.'

'There's really no need for any of that!' Rory cried. 'Why don't I just come with you? Without any need for binding of any sort? Why don't I just come along with you?'

Despite his protests, they grabbed him. They were strong, they pinned his arms behind his back and turned him around, steering him by the shoulders.

Then they all stopped.

Something had walked into the clearing behind them. It stood gazing at them through glinting, red, triangular eyes. It was green, the colour of moss on the underside of a stone, and its thick skin was whorled and ridged like the hide of an alligator. A faint rasping, hissing wheeze of respiration was coming from its barrel-thick chest.

It was at least two metres tall and built like an oak tree.

'Told you,' said Rory.

CHAPTER 5
THE HOPES AND FEARS
OF ALL THE YEARS

The green thing hissed out a breath and took a step. Rory flinched. The man with the beard let out a great howl of fear and fury, and swung his axe.

The axe was a good one, with a head fashioned from shipskin. It struck the green thing square in the centre of the chest, and actually bit into the crocodile skin bulge of the scaled armour.

The green thing didn't even jolt. It was as though the bearded man had buried his axe into an ancient and unyielding tree.

The axe was stuck fast. The bearded man tried to pull it out for another swing. The green thing made a grunting hiss and lashed out with its left arm. A massive, pincered hand caught the bearded man on the upswing and hoisted him into the air. The impact was an ugly, bone-cracking sound that made Rory flinch again. The bearded man flew backwards and upwards, particles of snow fluttering off his legs, and tore into the low canopy of the trees. He crashed back down onto the snow, bringing broken branches, twigs and a heavy fall of snow-gather with him.

Once he had landed, he stopped moving.

The other men registered a moment of shock at the sheer force that the upswing had communicated. A single swipe had propelled their leader metres through the air. Chastened, they hurled themselves at the green thing, raining blows with picks and mattocks and other stout farm tools.

It was brave. It was a terrible mistake. The blows rebounded ineffectually. The green thing threw out its right pincer and knocked a man sideways into a tree. The impact jolted snow out of the branches. Taking another step, the green thing reached up, grasped the haft of the axe buried like a handle in its belly, and pulled it out. Then it swung the axe, catching another man in the face with the back of the axehead. The impact lifted the man clean off his feet. He landed on his back in the snow with his mouth open, dead or profoundly unconscious.

A man with a pitchfork rushed the green thing, trying to run the tines through its deep torso. He yelled as he charged. The green thing tossed aside the axe, which disappeared through the trees, spinning end over end and making a slow *whupping* sound like a ceiling fan, and raised its left pincer. The movement was fast and oddly precise for something so stiff and ungainly. The pincer neatly caught the thrusting pitchfork between the tines and blocked it. The man lurched and stumbled as his pitchfork stopped moving. The green thing tightened its clamping grip and snapped the head of the pitch fork off its wooden shaft. The man holding the pitchfork jabbed the broken end repeatedly against the thing's ridged torso. The green thing pointed its right pincer at him.

There was a small tube attached to its forearm. It was a weapon of some kind. The discharge made a nasty, throbbing sound, and the air seemed to warp and bulge. Caught by this twisting, pressurised force, the man dropped dead.

Rory was running by then. In attacking the green thing, the men had entirely forgotten about him. The sheer, clinical brutality of its response had proved to Rory that his first instincts had been correct. The giant green figures were not to be bargained with. They were lethal and malicious, and they existed only to be avoided at all costs.

Rory's ears were ringing from the awful sonic discharge of the thing's weapon. Even though it hadn't been aimed at him, it had given him an awful headache and, from the blood he could taste on the back of his tongue, a nosebleed.

The other men – those still on their feet – were fleeing too. Rory gasped as he heard the sonic weapon fire a second time. The air shimmered and buckled, and a man fleeing a dozen metres to Rory's left crumpled into the snow, rolled over, and lay still.

The next one was going to be him.

There was no cover.

The next blast was definitely going to kill him.

They left Beside and followed the North Lane track up past the frozen well and out of what Bel called the Spitablefields. These large, gently sloping areas were blanketed with snow, but the Doctor and Amy could see that they had been carefully cleared and ranged into strips for cultivation like a market garden. Amy noticed lines of planting canes and frames, all edged with snow like ermine, left over from the growing season. The pathway itself, a climbing track, was screened on the settlement side by a box hedge that, snowbound, looked like a giant frosted slice of key lime pie.

Dogs barked in the village below.

'What was that?' asked the Doctor, stopping to listen.

'Dogs,' said Bel.

Amy looked back. An afternoon whiteness was beginning to hollow out the blue of the sky, and the vapour around the mountains had become more of a haze. There was a smell in the air that she associated with approaching snowfall. It was a smell she had cherished as a little girl.

'Not dogs,' said the Doctor.

They continued. Beyond the Spitablefields and the hedged track line, a stand of trees marked the edge of snow-dusted woodland.

The Doctor stopped again. He cocked his head to one side. 'Did you hear that?' he asked.

'What?' asked Amy.

'That sound. I know that sound.'

'What sound?' asked Amy.

'Just dogs,' said Bel.

'No, the other sound. It's a long way off, but it's carrying. It's distinctive. I know that sound. Where have I heard it before?'

Amy listened. 'I can't hear anything,' she began, and then stopped. 'Oh, wait,' she said. 'I heard something then. A funny noise.'

The Doctor nodded. 'A funny noise…' he echoed.

He turned around suddenly and stared at the hedge.

'I think you should come out,' he said.

A man stepped out of the shadows.

'I think you should tell me where you're going, Arabel,' said Samewell Crook.

*

Rory ducked behind a tree. Dread had a grip on him, and he desperately wished that breathing didn't make so much noise. Exertion combined with panic was making the air suck in and out of his lungs in gasps. The sound was going to give him away.

He'd heard two more of the blasts, the ear-shredding throbs of the green thing's energy weapon. The second blast had been accompanied by the agonised yelp of a man being felled by lethal, contorting air. The green thing was close. What did it want, apart from to kill them all? Was it trying to eliminate witnesses? Witnesses to what? Was it just out for revenge for getting an axe swung at it?

Was it after something else that Rory couldn't begin to imagine?

His mind was all over the place. It was hard to focus. That was shock and the panic response. He forced himself to concentrate. He needed to listen. Hiding behind the tree, the only way he could tell how close the green thing was, was to listen, but he couldn't hear anything over his own panting. He held his breath. It was a considerable effort. He held on, and listened. It felt like his eardrums were going to burst.

After a few seconds, he heard deep, crunching footfalls in the snow, the steady march of the towering monster. It was drawing level with his hiding place.

There was nowhere else to hide. Snow was all around, a white backdrop against which he would stand out, no matter where he went. Trees were no good. Sooner or later, you could walk around a tree. There were no boulders, no bushes, no holes in the ground.

He heard the crunching footsteps again, and a wheeze of respiration to go with them. It reminded him of his own need to exhale. He eased out the breath he had been holding in, trying to do it soundlessly. He so wanted to greedily suck in fresh air.

The green thing appeared about twenty metres to his left, side on to him. It emerged from between two trees and stood still, slowly scanning to left and right.

Rory, gently and ever so slowly, melted himself back around the tree trunk he was sheltering against, putting it between him and the creature.

It turned and looked his way.

How could it have seen him? He was barely moving. The thing looked like a giant, humanoid reptile. Did reptiles have acute sight? Hearing? Did they have other senses? How did they hunt? He had a feeling that he'd once read something about crocodiles having amazing night vision.

Rory realised that terror was flooding his mind with jumbled thoughts. Nothing he was thinking about really mattered. He had to find an escape route. What the Doctor would call a 'wise exit strategy'. What Amy would call a 'not at all stupid bit of proper running away'.

Amy.

Rory knew he simply had to see her again. He wasn't going to let a giant shambling lizard kill him in a snowy wood for no good reason. His wife would never let him hear the end of it.

He broke cover and started to run again, this time in a path perpendicular to his original route. A hasty glance over his shoulder told him that the green thing had spotted him. It had turned to blunder after him. Had it detected movement? Heat?

Heat made a kind of sense. He clung on to the notion.

Why wasn't it shooting? Why didn't it fire its horrible gun? It could just bring him down and save itself the effort of chasing.

There seemed to be only three possible answers to that. It had run out of shots, which seemed unlikely. That was one. The second was that he was out of range.

The third was that it wanted him alive.

'Slow down!' hissed Amy.

The Doctor was leading the way up the snowy track into the woods with the sort of indefatigable and boundless enthusiasm only he could muster. She scrambled to keep up.

'Are we taking him with us?' she asked.

They both glanced back.

Arabel was following them, with the young man in tow. Samewell was a pretty good-looking bloke, Amy had to admit. He was fresh-faced and cheerful. He seemed trustworthy. He was having an argument with Arabel as he pursued them up the lane.

'It's a Cat A crime,' Amy heard him saying. 'A Cat A crime, Bel! What are you doing with them?'

'I'm looking for Vesta.'

'But you let them out, Bel! What will the Elect say?'

'I don't know, Samewell? Are you going to tell him?'

'I ought to!' declared Samewell. 'Come on, stop and talk to me! Think about this! You're consorting with conjury!'

'I'm looking for my sister,' Bel replied. She kept walking, pulling her long skirts up a little so they didn't get trodden into the snow.

'The Elect will find Vesta,' said Samewell. 'Where is your patience?'

'Shut up, Samewell.'

'Those who are patient, they provide for all of the Plantnation,' he said.

'Don't quote Guide's words at me!' Bel snapped.

'I think we'll let him come with us,' the Doctor told Amy.

'Because if he goes back, he'll tell them where we've gone?' asked Amy.

The Doctor nodded. 'I don't think he's going to overpower us singlehanded,' he said.

'I think he'd like to overpower her singlehanded,' said Amy.

'What?' asked the Doctor.

'He fancies her,' she replied. 'It's obvious.'

'Because they're arguing?'

'Why else did he follow us? He could have just raised the alarm.'

The Doctor frowned thoughtfully and nodded. 'Keen insight, Pond. The mysterious operation of the human heart. Good job.'

He came to a halt. They had climbed quite a way into the skirts of the woods. Would Be, Bel had called it. The Spitablefields fell away behind them. They could see the village of Beside and, south of that, the glint of sunlight on the glass roofs of the heathouses.

'Would Be,' said the Doctor, looking at the shadowed trees and their bright mantles of snow. 'The original Morphans looked at this world, and imagined how it *would be*. Like a declaration of intent.'

'I thought she was saying "Wood B",' said Amy.

'She probably is,' replied the Doctor. 'That's probably all it was originally. A territorial designation. Wood B. The hospitable fields. Even the name of the settlement.

Hmmm. What's the betting?'

He turned to Bel.

'Is the third plantnation called Aside?' he asked.

'Yes,' she replied.

'How did you know?' asked Amy.

'Oh, a wild guess. Aside, Beside and Seeside. Sites A, B and C.'

'Ah,' Amy smiled. 'So Seeside isn't beside the sea, then?'

'I imagine not, though I do like to be beside it,' said the Doctor.

They walked on for a moment, not talking, listening to the breathless hush of the wood and the crunch of their footsteps and the half-audible bickering coming from behind them again.

'What is Hereafter?' Amy asked.

'It's a colony world, a human colony world,' said the Doctor. 'Late expansion, Diaspora Era. Think of the name, Morphan?'

'Like orphan?'

'Yes, but also referencing the terraforming or terra-*morphing* processes these settlers were supposed to perform. To colonise a suitable, Earth-like distant world and make it more Earth-like.'

'Earth-*ish*?'

'Indeed.'

'Where's the real Earth?' Amy asked.

The Doctor shrugged. 'Somewhere in the past. I think the Earth and the solar system are gone. The end of their natural lifespan. Humans had to find somewhere else. Think about the name Morphan again.'

'How long have they been here?' asked Amy. She had been to times when the Earth had been abandoned before, but the idea that the world no longer existed seemed especially melancholy.

'Generations,' replied the Doctor. 'Many generations. Twenty-seven, she said. Lifetimes of backbreaking toil and hard living. It takes a long time to shape and tame a world, even an Earth-*ish* one. All their labour, all their effort – the Morphans will never get to enjoy it or benefit from it. It's simply for the benefit of the future generations.'

'So what exactly is the problem?' asked Amy. 'You're worried about the snow.'

'The process has gone wrong,' said the Doctor, quietly enough that neither Bel nor Samewell could overhear. 'For some reason, the terraforming programme has abruptly failed. Hereafter is becoming less and less Earth-like. The Morphans came here to plant a nation, but now they're simply going to die out.'

'Why?'

'I don't know,' said the Doctor.

'You've got a hunch, though.'

'It could be that it was never meant to be,' said the Doctor. 'It could be that Hereafter was too difficult a world to convert. Or a fault might have developed in the main atmospheric processors. Or...'

'Or?'

'Nothing,' he said quietly.

'Or *what?*' she snapped.

'Really, nothing.'

She gave him one of her looks.

'All right,' he said. 'It could be... that there's some kind of influence at work here. I've seen... something like it before, once or twice.'

'What sort of influence?' asked Amy.

'Let's not worry about it until I'm sure,' said the Doctor. He began to stride along the snowy path between the trees with great purpose. 'Let's hope it's a glitch. A processing glitch that I can fix.'

'A glitch?' asked Amy, narrowing her eyes to look at him.

'Not even a glitch.'

'No?'

'Less than a glitch. Smaller than a glitch.'

'Glitch-*ish*?' she asked

'Exactly!' declared the Doctor. He looked back at Bel. 'Which way from here?' he called brightly.

Rory doubted he could run much further. His legs and lungs were hurting from the effort, and his heart was pounding. He could barely draw a deep enough breath. There was cold sweat on his spine under his clothes. This was certainly not the way he'd have chosen to spend Christmas.

He smelled something suddenly. It wasn't a strong smell at all, but against the clear, pure atmosphere of the woodland it stood out sharply. It was a warm smell, wet and metallic, like the linty steam of a laundrette, or the outflow of the industrial washing machines at the back of Leadworth hospital. What was that? What could possibly be warm and wet in a place so locked in by ice and snow?

He came through a stand of trees to a lip of rock. A bank fell away below him, thick with slithered snow. Below him was a river. It was quite broad, falling steeply down the rocky throat of a gorge to his right into the steep cut basin below him. The far side, steeper than the one he stood on, was densely packed with trees.

The river, once it had cleared the jumbled, snow-covered undergrowth of the gorge, was ten or twelve metres across.

It had frozen over with a thick crust of ice that had been overlaid with the previous night's snow. It looked like a broad stretch of pale concrete. The gorge clearly trapped cold air over the open stretch of water.

Rory glanced over his shoulder. The green thing was still in pursuit, trudging through the trees, occasionally raising a clamp-hand to snap branches out of its way. It was thirty metres behind him and closing. Rory had speed on his side, but not stamina. The thing just kept going. Rory knew he'd have to rest soon. He was exhausted, as if he'd run a marathon only to find there was no one waiting for him with a tinfoil blanket and a bottle of orange squash.

He made a snap decision. The density of trees on the far side of the river looked as though it offered the best chance of hiding he'd seen all day. The river was an added plus too. The green thing was big and evidently heavy. Rory doubted the ice, even though it looked like bullet-proof plate glass, would support a weight like that.

He hurtled down the bank, almost falling and rolling. He kept his footing, skidding down the snow like a downhill skier. He picked his way through the snowy rocks and boulders by the river's edge, sliding on small, trapped puddles of ice, and reached the river.

Rory knelt down, reached out, and tested the ice with his hand. He applied firm pressure. It felt rock solid. As a nurse, he'd seen plenty of people brought into casualty with hypothermia and worse after falling through ice into ponds and lakes. Going out on ice was a stupid, stupid risk to take. Then again, none of the accident victims he'd seen being wheeled in on stretchers had taken to the ice because they were being chased by a two-metre-tall, bipedal crocodile with baleful red eyes and a ray gun.

On cue, the green thing appeared at the top of the slope behind him. The afternoon sunlight flared off its pie-segment red lenses as it turned its ridged head to look at him.

Rory got up. He put a foot out onto the ice, let it take his weight, and then gingerly stepped clear of the bank. It was slippery, despite the dusting of snow. It felt like a window lubricated with washing up liquid under his feet. He took one step, and then another, arms wide for balance, teetering. The ice beneath him creaked. It made the sorts of popping, squealing protests that polystyrene packing made when you got a new TV or microwave out of its box.

He wobbled. He took another step. Another. Another.

He glanced back. The green thing was coming down the slope after him, surefootedly negotiating the deep snow. It had a clear view of him. It could shoot him now. He was an open target.

He took another step. He took another. He was almost halfway across.

The ice gave out under him.

He plunged straight down into the river as though a trapdoor had slammed open underneath him. The moment he went, he knew he was done for. Even if the shock of the freezing water didn't actually kill him stone dead, he was miles from help and medical attention. His body temperature would drop sharply, and never recover. He would seize up and die.

He went under, right under the water. He was braced for the terrible cold. It was so cold, it seemed to burn him. Then he realised it wasn't cold at all.

The water under the crust of ice, fast-flowing and brisk, was warm. The water was *warm*.

Rory floundered, baffled. He struggled for the surface. Above him, he saw daylight. The ice had given way in several places, its disintegration prompted by the hole he had caused. The warm water was eating away at the edges of the plunge-hole, like a corrosive agent at work, broadening it and creating a channel.

He struck up towards it, arms churning, weighed down by his waterlogged parka. He broke the surface and took in a lungful of air. The cold stung his face. The warmth of the water was almost like a blessed relief from the gnawing ache of winter.

Spluttering, he started to tread water, the motion of the water rotated him in the ragged space he'd made in the ice cover.

He saw his monstrous pursuer. It had reached the bank and was staring out at him. He was right there in front of it, but it didn't seem to register him properly.

Heat, he thought. Heat. It was following my heat. Now I'm in hot water, I'm harder to detect. It can still see me, but my thermal image is more difficult to isolate.

Rory took a deep breath and went under. He didn't want to be visible at all. He wanted the water to mask him entirely.

'In hot water' indeed.

He wanted the river to carry him along and hide his trail from the creature.

For a moment, almost jubilant, he considered his luck. Falling through the ice had seemed to represent certain death, until he discovered the water beneath was warm. Being cornered in the water seemed to represent a second certain death, until it became apparent that the surrounding heat was confusing his implacable pursuer.

Then Rory realised there was a downside after all. He swam underwater, borne along by the current, intending to surface for another lungful of air further downstream.

But he was under the ice again. He struck it from below, expecting it to splinter and give, but it was solid. It was as hard and firm as an oak lid on the top of the river. There was no air. There was no gap. There was no space for him to grab a breath.

He wasn't going to die of hypothermia or temperature shock. He wasn't going to be broken or blasted by a giant green monster.

He was simply going to drown.

CHAPTER 6
DEEP AND CRISP AND EVEN

In the time it had taken them to trek through the shadowed snow of Would Be, the sky had changed colour. Looking up through the trees, Amy saw an expanse overhead that looked like wet slate. There was a whisper of cloud. A moody twilight had fallen across the wood.

Snowlight. She remembered it from her childhood. A magical dusk where the ground seemed brighter than the sky, foretelling the imminent arrival of snow. It was an oddly fond memory, but in her current situation, it was not an exciting prospect.

A minute or so later, the first flakes started to fall. They came down, lazy and slow, just one or two at first, drifting like ash from an evening bonfire, or drowsy bumblebees.

'Button up!' declared the Doctor. 'Not far now.'

The snow grew a little heavier, but it was still pretty, like the picturesque flakes on a Dickensian Christmas card scene, rather than a full-on Scott of the Antarctic / March of the Penguins / 'I'm just going outside now, I may be some time' thing.

Adjusting her mittens, Amy noticed how both Arabel and Samewell were intrigued by the falling snow. Neither of them had ever seen much of it, certainly not in its most fleeting, eerie state of actually falling out of the sky.

'It's a real novelty,' said the Doctor, noticing her interest. He had plucked up the collar of his jacket and was holding it closed with one hand.

'Like a Christmas single?' she asked, smiling.

'It doesn't mean it's a good thing,' he replied.

'So, *just* like a Christmas record, then?' she asked.

She watched Bel take off her glove and hold out a hand, letting flakes alight on her pink palm. Samewell grinned, and stuck out his tongue to catch a flake.

'What are you thinking about?' Amy asked the Doctor.

'I'm thinking about the little pockets of early human beings,' he replied quietly. 'Little communities of brave and determined hunter-gatherers, delighted by the unfamiliarity of snow and not even beginning to realise it's the first traces of an approaching ice age. Not even beginning to realise that what is enchanting now will starve them and freeze them and kill them inside six months.'

He blew on his hands.

'Let's find this memory yard,' he said.

It wasn't far off. With the ghost snow falling as silently as moving stars, the clearing was hauntingly beautiful. It was also terribly melancholy. The Doctor reckoned that Would Be had been deliberately planted by earlier generations of Morphans. The little grey headstones looked like trees that had yet to flourish. Amy couldn't believe how many of them there were. They were like the rings of a tree. Add them all together, and they represented the toil and dedication that had gone into building Beside.

Bel took them to the marker of her father's grave. Though the snow was laying, it had not yet covered and hidden the jar and the little bunch of heathouse flowers.

'She was here,' said Bel. 'Only Vesta would do that.'

'You wouldn't do it?' asked the Doctor.

Bel seemed to think about replying, but didn't. She looked as though the answer was too sad or ordinary or unremarkable for her to say out loud.

'Bel would mean to,' said Samewell, 'but she's always so busy. We're all so busy. Vesta would remember what day it was.'

The Doctor walked around the grave two or three times, a thumb under his chin and an index finger crooked across his mouth.

'There are only her tracks,' he said, pointing. 'Only hers. The snow's beginning to hide them. Look, that's her. Footsteps and the brush of long skirts. Just hers. Well, ours too now, but ignore them. She came up the way we came, up the path. She came up from the plantnation. But she didn't go that way. She went off in the other direction.' He turned to Bel. 'Where else would she go?'

Bel shrugged. 'Nowhere. She'd have been late for work as it was. Guide's Bell would have rung. She would have just gone back.'

'What's this way?' the Doctor asked, following the line of swiftly vanishing footprints.

'Nothing,' said Samewell. 'If you go that way you'd eventually reach Farafield, I suppose. Firmer Number Three is roughly that way.'

'Only roughly,' said Bel.

They all squinted into the falling snow. The sky had darkened so much, it was hard to make out the gloomy shoulders of the mountains.

'She was going somewhere,' said the Doctor, leading the

way briskly. The trail took them out of the memory yard and deep into the trees. He pointed at the ground as he walked.

'Look,' he called back. 'Straight line! She wasn't wandering, wasn't strolling around. A very deliberate straight line.'

'Maybe she saw something,' suggested Amy, close on his heels.

'Saw what?' asked Bel, following along with Samewell.

The Doctor stopped suddenly. 'That's also a very deliberate straight line,' he said. There was another line of prints in the snow, crossing Vesta's path like a 'T'. It was also fading in the snowfall, but not quite as fast because of the sheer size of it.

'What made those?' asked Amy, slowly and very cautiously.

'I don't know,' said the Doctor, hunkering down to examine them. He measured one out against the side of his hand.

'They're giant,' said Samewell. There was a catch of anxiety in his voice.

'Yes,' said the Doctor, 'they are.' He got up. 'They were here first,' he said. 'She came upon the trail. Found it.'

'What are you, the last of the Mohicans or something?' asked Amy.

The Doctor looked at her.

'Baden-Powell taught me the rudiments of tracking,' he replied.

'Of course he did,' she replied.

'Chingachook merely refined some of my techniques,' said the Doctor.

'Chingachook's a fictional character,' Amy replied.

'Is he?' asked the Doctor.

'Yes, he is,' said Amy.

'Or was that just the deal Fenimore Cooper struck to get permission to write the story?'

'What are you talking about?' asked Bel.

'The real question,' Amy replied, still looking at the Doctor, 'is *why* are we talking about it, because it's a stupid conversation.'

'You started it,' said the Doctor. He turned back to the tracks. 'Look, she came up here, came across the tracks.'

'The giant tracks,' said Amy.

'The giant tracks, yes, and then she headed off back into the woods. In a hurry.'

'Scared?' asked Bel.

'Maybe scared. She didn't retrace her steps, just went off in a hurry. Come on,' he added, and started to follow the new trail in a hurry.

'Slow down, Davy Crockett!' Amy cried, following.

'Davy Crockett was a terrible tracker!' The Doctor called over his shoulder. 'Lovely man. Nice hat. Very overrated in the tracking department.'

He came to a halt again. They'd reached a small clearing close to the northern end of the memory yard.

'What is it?' asked Amy.

'Oh dear,' said the Doctor.

'What is it?' Amy repeated.

'Something bad happened here,' said the Doctor quietly.

Samewell and Bel came up behind them.

'Is that…?' asked Samewell.

'That's blood,' said Bel.

The snow was falling heavily, but it hadn't quite managed to obliterate the dark stains soaked into the ground cover.

'Yes, it is,' said the Doctor. 'And I'm rather afraid there's an awful lot of it.'

Ten seconds before he drowned, Rory managed to right himself in the fast-flowing undercurrent, just long enough to hammer his fists against the roof of ice. It was like banging against the glass of a display aquarium. The noise was as muffled as the thud of his heart. Nothing yielded.

The light was strange under the filter of the ice. There was a sickly blue-green cast. The water, so curiously warm, swirling him along in a turbulent spiral of froth and twinkling air bubbles. He bounced. He up-ended. He glanced off the ice sheet, hurting his head.

Five seconds before he drowned, he failed to hit the ice with a last, frantic punch.

Three seconds before he drowned, the water flow accelerated and smashed him through some kind of submerged gate or shutter.

One second before he drowned, he stopped drowning and breathed again.

There was no ice.

He'd surfaced, with access to the wintery air. He gulped it in, as though he was drinking it, filling his burning, about-to-burst lungs. He went under again, remembered to tread water, and came up spluttering.

Blinking water out of his eyes, he tried to get his bearings. He was in a pool, like a large mill pond. Traces of slushy ice drifted on the surface, but it was generally unfrozen.

The river had brought him downhill under its frozen crust and thrown him through a sluice gate into the pond. He still couldn't fathom why the water, deep under its cooler surface layers, was warm. It had to be some kind of artificially heated flow, surely?

Whatever the answer, it wasn't his immediate concern. The unnatural warmth of the water had spared him from a numbing death, but he was still soaking wet outdoors on a snowy day. He had to get out, get dry, find shelter.

The pool, shadowed by mature trees, was flanked by buildings. They looked like they were made of wood and stone, with plates of grey metal. The drab side-walls were patched with green moss and lichen as though they had stood for years, and some of the metal pins and bolts had corroded green. The buildings overhung the pool, and parts of them extended out into the water like dams or the gates of a filtration plant.

Rory let the gentle current of the pool, its power slackened by the sluice, carry him towards the projections. He caught hold of some metal pipework. The cold of it hurt his palms. He went down the frame, hand over hand, dragging himself through the water until he was close to a small metal jetty, then he heaved himself up out of the water. It felt like he weighed a ton.

Water streamed off him, pouring out of his saturated clothes as he stood up. Steam plumed off him. He could feel the cold biting into his skin, turning his clothes into heavy, clammy bandages.

He slopped down the jetty. The buildings were definitely water mills of some kind. The river had been directed via the sluices into the catchment pool so that it could drive turbine systems hidden in the utilitarian structures. The buildings seemed old, but the technology appeared modern. Rory had already got used to dismissing that kind of anachronism.

The sky had changed colour, as if it had soured like milk, and heavy snowflakes were starting to fall. Rory knew he had to get inside one of the buildings before he lost too much of his core body heat.

There were no immediate signs of a door.

He walked along the jetty, and then along a timber-planked service walkway between two of the structures. There was no snow here, as though internal heat had kept it from laying. If he could only get inside…

It suddenly occurred to him to look around and check for signs of pursuit. He had no idea how far the river had carried him, but even the slightest chance that the green thing was still after him made his heart skip.

He looked back up the pond towards the sluice, and towards the trees on the far bank. He saw nothing but green shadows and the snow, which was now falling quite fast.

Green shadows seemed perfect for a green thing to hide in, no matter how big it was.

He followed the walkway round. There had to be a hatch or an entrance somewhere.

He stopped. He heard something. He couldn't tell what it was. The crunch of a footstep? The creak of ice? The crack of a branch snapping under the snow's weight?

It was close. Had that thing located him again already? How had it caught up so fast? He crept a little further, encumbered by his soaked clothing. There was a hatch. Down the end of the walkway, there was definitely a hatch.

He took a look over his shoulder.

Just for a second, he saw the light reflect off red eyes. Just a glint, like the gleam of blood. Red eyes, out there in the enclosing darkness of the wood.

Red eyes searching for him.

He hurried towards the hatch. Looking back, he saw that the eyes had gone. He heard a noise. A footstep on a metal walkboard.

Something was on the jetty. Something was moving.

Rory reached the hatch. There was a recessed slot built to fit a human hand. He reached in and turned the rotator bar. The hatch unlocked. He pulled it open and went inside, not even caring what might lie within. Warmth hit him, and darkness surrounded him. He heard another footstep on the jetty, closer. He dragged the hatch shut and locked it behind him.

He looked around. He was in some kind of machine space above one of the turbines. He could hear the rush of water and the cycle of a wheel or a screw system coming up from below. It was very dark, but it was a lot warmer inside than outside.

He crouched down inside the hatch. He could hear whatever it was moving outside. He could hear it walking along the jetty and then the timber planks. He put his hand on the door bolt to stop it being turned from outside. Something came close to the hatch, went past, and then came back. He held his breath as it began to scrape and scratch at the recessed handle. He could hear a deep, rasping breath, a ragged, asthmatic wheeze.

It was trying to get in. It was trying to get in and get at him. It knew he was there.

The scraping and rattling grew worse, as if the thing outside possessed hands that were too big to fit the slot. It banged the hatch instead. The breathing became more laboured, a wet hiss from gurgling lungs.

The effort suddenly stopped. Rory waited, clasping the

inside handle. He heard a noise, almost a voice, followed by movement.

Then the hideous discharge of the green thing's weapon, a repeated burst, squealed right outside. It made him jump. It hurt his ears. There was an impact. Something fell, or collided with something else heavy. The weapon went off again.

Silence.

Rory waited for a long time, scarcely daring to move or breathe. He waited for some sign or clue from outside, but heard no further sounds.

When he had waited, unmoving, for what seemed like long enough, and then a bit longer just to be safe, he got up quietly and began to grope through the darkness to see if he could find a more secure hiding place further inside the structure.

He realised he wasn't alone in the building. He came to this realisation immediately after he managed to say the words 'Hang on', and immediately before something heavy smacked him across the side of the head and knocked him out.

CHAPTER 7
THE STARS IN THE NIGHT SKY

'Is it?' Amy asked quietly. Her voice was muffled because the snow had made her face numb, and also because she didn't want Samewell or Bel to hear her. For the same reason, she'd kept the question unspecific.

The Doctor glanced at her and shook his head. Amy knew that was Doctor Code for *I have no idea, but I intend to retain a cautiously positive approach to the situation.*

'But it could be...' she asked, trailing off before she got to 'this girl we were looking for?'

The Doctor was crouching in the middle of the clearing, examining the stains soaked into the snow. His knees were on a level with his ears, so he resembled a frog on a lily pad.

Around him, the initially picturesque snowfall had become a full-scale blizzard. The density of flakes was making it hard to see anything, and the snow was quickly covering up all of the traces on the ground. Amy hunched in her duffel coat with the hood up so that it framed her face like a funnel. Samewell and Bel were watching them from the edge of the clearing, out of earshot. Bel was stricken with concern. Samewell was trying to keep her calm.

'I don't know, I don't know,' the Doctor muttered. 'I don't know. I hope it isn't.'

'We can't stay out here much longer,' said Amy, feeling the obvious needed to be stated at fairly regular intervals lest it slipped the Doctor's mind.

'I know we can't,' he said.

'Doctor, is it what you thought it was? This… *influence* you referred to?'

'No,' said the Doctor. 'That's the thing. This is odd. It doesn't fit. My hunch was clearly wrong. I mis-hunched. I've got to go back and start again.'

'So you're attempting a re-hunch?'

'Indeed.'

'Maybe it is just a glitch, after all?'

'No, Pond. A glitch, no matter how big, doesn't rip something apart and shower blood everywhere.'

'At least there isn't a body,' said Amy, encouragingly.

'There doesn't have to be,' said the Doctor. 'Whatever bled here, it bled enough to be dead. A body could be lying close by and we'd never see it.'

He stood up quickly, snowflakes in his hair and eyelashes.

'Don't let Arabel look around,' he whispered to Amy. 'Keep her calm and keep her here. I don't want her… finding her sister.'

Amy nodded. Arabel was close by, a phantom in the falling snow, standing under one of the trees, lost in thought.

'Try to keep her occupied. Don't let her imagine the worst,' said the Doctor.

'I'll see if she knows anywhere in the area we could shelter,' said Amy.

'Good idea.'

Amy went over to Arabel. The Doctor continued to pace around the clearing, scrutinising signs and traces, as though he was in a laboratory where it just happened to be snowing.

Samewell came up to him. 'I found these over there,' he said quietly. He had some grisly objects in his hand, and he furtively showed them to the Doctor. They were almost black, like chunks of coal. They *weren't* chunks of coal. They were pieces of bone, caked in blood.

'Oh dear,' said the Doctor.

'It's all right,' said Samewell. 'It's not Vesta. These are bits of backbone from a sheep.'

The Doctor took one of the sticky lumps out of Samewell's hand and examined it closely.

'I think you're right, Samewell. Vertebrae. Ovine.'

'I know sheep. It's my labour to watch the flocks and rear them.'

'It was a sheep,' murmured the Doctor, relieved.

'It was a sheep what was killed here,' agreed Samewell. 'Like the other livestock this winter. We think it's a dog run wild, Guide help us.'

'It's been eaten,' said the Doctor. 'Devoured. Reduced to a few bones.'

'A dog would do that,' said Samewell. 'A hungry dog.'

'Yes,' said the Doctor. 'But in just a few hours? This is fresh. It's happened since last night, because the stains are still in the snow. Can even a big, hungry dog eat an entire sheep in that time?'

Samewell regarded the question with some alarm. He was also beginning to look blue around the edges.

'We need to shelter somewhere,' said the Doctor. 'This weather's getting worse by the minute.'

79

'There's a vent,' Samewell told him. 'It's about a mile from here on the skirt of Would Be.'

'A vent?'

'A herder's hut. For when we take the flocks up past the woods onto Moreland in summer. Guide knows it's closer to us than Beside.'

'OK, good. We'd better get moving,' said the Doctor.

They started walking, heads down into the blow. The snow was in their faces, hard and prickling. Samewell knew the way.

As they trudged along, the Doctor thought about the word Samewell had used. *Vent*. Another Morphan neologism, presumably derived from the word for *wind*, as in a place where a herdsman could shelter from that elemental force. In Australia, they called them watch boxes, and in Norway they called them seters. On Umonalis Quadok where, admittedly, they herded ungulate ruminant thwentilopes rather than sheep, they called them Bimbemberabemhamshighans, which the Doctor had always thought was a rather ostentatious label for a one-room shack. In the highlands of Scotland, they called them bothies.

Snow always reminded the Doctor of Scotland. It was a place he was very fond of. Many years away – not necessarily ago, because 'ago' was a clumsy concept to an inveterate time traveller – many years *away*, in a sideways direction that led to another part of his curiously structured life, the Doctor had visited Scotland and made a good friend there, a highlander called Jamie McCrimmon. Jamie had travelled with the Doctor for a while. They'd been to some places, and done some things, and on several occasions they had ended up in deep snow and deeper trouble. The thought of snow, and Jamie, took the Doctor back to his original, uneasy hunch. It was hard to shake, even though the evidence was no longer adding up.

'We should keep looking,' said Arabel.

'I can't even see my hands in front of my face in this,' said Samewell.

'She'll freeze,' said Arabel.

Samewell had his arm around her, leading her along and shielding her with his coat. 'Guide knows we won't be no use to her if we freeze first,' he said.

The Doctor stopped.

'What is it?' asked Amy. She was keeping her jaw clenched so her teeth wouldn't chatter.

'Something,' said the Doctor. He looked around. 'There's something nearby.'

It was hard to see for any distance. It was still snowing hard, and flurrying too, and Amy had a feeling evening had set in and taken over the responsibility for making things dark from the snowstorm. Constellations of snowflakes moving against the black trunks of nearby trees was about all she could make out.

'I don't see anything,' she said, wiping snow off her nose.

'Neither do I, but I feel it,' said the Doctor.

'What, like a sixth sense?'

'Much vaguer. Much, *much* vaguer. A ninth or tenth sense at best.'

He rotated on the spot again, flipped out his sonic screwdriver, scanned and then switched it off. He tapped the end of the screwdriver against his pursed lips as he thought.

'We should keep moving,' said Amy.

'We *should* keep moving,' agreed the Doctor. 'Samewell?'

'It's up this way, a bit further yet,' Samewell replied. 'We're close to the edge of Moreland now.'

There was a break in the trees, a thinning out where the snow was deeper on the ground. The snow was beginning to drift.

The Doctor stopped again and took another look around. He divined with his warbling screwdriver again. 'Let's liven things up by walking a little faster,' he said, smiling.

The smile did nothing to take Amy's chill away.

'Hang on!' Rory said, sitting up.

Of course, it's far too late to say 'hang on!' once you've already been struck around the head with a blunt object and knocked unconscious. He said it nevertheless, and then groaned as the intense throbbing in his head introduced itself and let him know it would be staying for a few days.

'Ow,' he said, resting his forehead in his hand. 'Ow. Also, owww-www.'

'Don't move,' a voice warned him.

'Fine. I really haven't got much planned except sitting here and experiencing pain for the moment,' he replied. He shook his head in an effort to dispel the pain, and it worked in exactly the same way that shaking a snow globe makes it easier to see the scene inside.

'Owwwwww,' he breathed.

'Don't you move, or I'll hit you again,' said the voice.

'Please don't do that,' said Rory.

'I didn't want to the first time,' said the voice. There was a waver of concern. 'I thought you were… *it*.'

'Really? Well, I'm not.'

'I see that now.'

'I'm glad we've cleared that up,' said Rory, 'but my head

still really hurts. What did you hit me with?'

'This,' said the voice.

The mill shed was still dark, and the turbines were humming under the boarded floor, but the gloom was softened by a small metal lamp that had been turned down very low. By its little, amber glow, Rory could see the shapes of dusty machinery around him, and a figure crouching opposite. The figure was holding a wooden mallet.

'Great,' said Rory. Even talking hurt. 'That looks like a really solid thing to hit someone on the head with. I've probably got concussion.'

'I'll hit you with it once more if you don't hush.'

'Don't do that! Why would you do that?'

'Because I think it may still be outside.'

'*It*, you mean?'

'Yes. You must've seen it too.'

Rory nodded, and then added nodding to his list of Things To Avoid Doing.

'I did,' he said.

'Those red eyes…'

'Exactly,' said Rory. He felt his scalp gingerly, and found a lump the size of a quail's egg over his left ear that was so badly bruised just touching it made him want to say things that were not good out-loud words. 'It chased me,' he said instead.

'And me,' said the figure.

Rory shifted a little to prop himself up against the wooden base of some machine.

'Don't move or I will hit you!' the voice ordered.

'I thought we'd established I wasn't *it*,' said Rory.

'I don't know what you are,' said the figure with the mallet.

'Do I look like *it*?' asked Rory.

'No, but it is an unguidely thing, most *terribly* unguidely, so it may alter its looks with conjury. It may take on a disguise of deceit.'

'Does this look like a disguise someone would choose?' asked Rory, gesturing to himself. He squinted into the gloom. The lamp was turned down so far, all he could make out was a hooded and robed shape. And the mallet.

'It doesn't seem likely,' the figure admitted.

'So could you put the mallet down?' he suggested. 'Or at least go to Defcon five with it?'

'You talk funny. What is your name?'

'Rory. I'm Rory.'

'Raw-ree? That's… that's an unguidely name, that is.'

'I'm sure it's not, but OK.'

'You're not from Beside, for I would know you. What plantnation are you from?'

'Leadworth. I'm from Leadworth.'

'There is no plantnation called that!' the figure declared.

'Do you know what? I think it's quite likely that there are some *plant-nation*-things that you haven't heard the names of.'

'That's not possible!'

'Well, you can hit me on the head with a mallet as many times as you like, but it won't change the fact that it is.'

There was a pause of indecision.

'So, wh-where is this plantnation on Hereafter?'

Rory looked at the hooded figure. 'No,' he said. 'I've answered your question, I've told you my name, and I think I've been pretty good about you hitting me on the head with a mallet, all things considered. Quite apart from anything else, I haven't had a particularly brilliant day. So

84

I think you can answer a question for me next. Who are you?'

The figure hesitated, and then pulled down the hood. The lamplight picked out a face that was small and pale, and streaked with the tracks of tears that Rory was sure were the product of frustrated anger rather than weakness.

'I'm Vesta Flurrish,' she said.

'Ah,' Rory replied, recalling the words of the men who had accosted him. 'People are looking for you.'

The snowfall eased back enough to reveal that a winter's night was setting in. Thick banks of grey snow cloud, as coarse and dense as wire wool, slumped low across the sky, interspersed with clear, cold bands of evening. The occasional early star twinkled in the clear stretches, like fairy lights behind glass.

In the twilight of the late afternoon, the snowscape had turned violet and the trees mauve. The snow was like white noise, as though reality wasn't quite tuned in. The Doctor, Amy, Arabel and Samewell trudged through the edges of Would Be, hearing only the crunch of their footsteps on the fresh snow and the puff of their breaths. Vapour trailed behind them with each exhalation. The Doctor knew they'd been out too long and had pushed too hard. They needed heat and shelter quickly. It was all very well for his Gallifreyan constitution, but human metabolisms were going to shut down very soon, with catastrophic consequences.

'You keep looking behind you,' said Amy.

'I do, don't I?' replied the Doctor.

'Why?'

'Just checking to see if it's snowing as badly there as it is in front of us.'

'Why *really*?'

'No reason.'

'What are you doing with the sonic?' she asked.

'Just re-setting it,' he replied.

'To what?'

'A different setting.'

'Why?'

'Just in case,' he said.

'In case of what?'

'Nothing.'

'Oh, I'm going to stupid well thump you if—'

'Look!' Bel cried.

They looked. She was pointing up at the sky, at a patch of clear night between cliffs of snow-bruised cloud. The stars were gleaming.

One of them was moving.

It made no sound. It was just a white light, no bigger than the other stars, but it was moving across the sky from east to west.

'I told you,' said Bel. 'Just like I saw before.'

'It's an aircraft,' Amy whispered to the Doctor.

'Too high up,' the Doctor replied. 'And besides, the good people of Beside do not possess aircraft.'

'What then?'

'Something in orbit,' said the Doctor.

'Like a spaceship?' asked Amy.

'Certainly something spaceship-*esque*,' he agreed.

She frowned at him.

'All right,' he said, 'something so much like a spaceship you may as well use the word "spaceship". My guess is, that's an interstellar craft in a distant parking orbit, but it could be some kind of lander or shuttle making a slow, shallow descent.'

'Doctor,' said Amy carefully, 'is this planet being invaded by something?'

'It's already been invaded,' the Doctor replied, 'twenty-seven generations ago, by the Morphans from Earth before. I think someone else has arrived to dispute that claim.'

Amy ignored the clever-clever nature of his answer. 'Seriously, this planet,' she said, choosing her words firmly so there could be no wiggle room in the answer, 'is about to get invaded?'

'No,' said the Doctor. 'The invasion started months ago. We're only just noticing it.'

'What are you talking about?' asked Bel, overhearing the last bit.

The Doctor stopped and held a finger to his lips. The others stopped too, looking at him. The crunching of their footsteps stopped. They caught their breath for a moment as they tried to pick up what he was hearing.

They could still hear crunching footsteps and they could still hear rasping breath. It just wasn't them. Bel's eyes widened. Samewell's jaw dropped. Amy looked at the Doctor sharply, silently demanding an explanation. The Doctor looked around, checking every direction. He was the first one to see the figures emerging through the snow.

There were half a dozen of them at least, closing from behind, and from the left and right. Grey-green shadows, they looked as tall and robust as tree trunks, except they were walking. Shambling. Trudging. There had to be a word for what they were doing, Amy was sure, but none of the ones she could dredge up seemed threatening enough.

The figures were massive. Their torsos were hugely bulky, and their fists were like pincers. Their eyes flashed red in the uncanny gloom.

Their breathing sounded like punctured bellows: long, wet, fluttering sounds.

'Turns out my hunch was right,' said the Doctor, though he didn't sound at all pleased to be vindicated.

'What are they?' asked Amy.

'They're unguidely!' Samewell cried.

'Get down!' the Doctor ordered.

'What are they?' Amy asked again instead of getting down.

'Oh, *get down!*'

'What *are* they?' Amy repeated.

'They're Ice Warriors,' said the Doctor.

CHAPTER 8
CERTAIN POOR SHEPHERDS IN FIELDS AS THEY LAY

Amy looked at him blankly. 'Should I know what that means?' she asked.

'No!' exclaimed the Doctor. 'But the basic principles of "Get down!" ought to be pretty clear, even to you!'

The four of them dropped down low in the snow. The towering green warriors had come to a halt about ten metres away, forming a semicircle. Stationary, they were entirely immobile, like statues. Snow actually settled on their sculpted shoulders and ridged craniums.

One of them slowly raised its right arm from beside its hip. There was some kind of pipe attached to the upper wrist. It pointed it at them.

The creature... the *Ice Warrior*... said something. Amy could see taut, reptilian lips move under the rim of the intimidating visor. She couldn't distinguish any words. It sounded like air escaping under high pressure from an inner tube.

'Keep down!' said the Doctor. He was frantically fiddling with his sonic screwdriver.

The Ice Warrior fired its weapon. It made one of the most unpleasant sounds Amy had ever heard, and she'd heard quite a few that featured in the Universal Top Twenty. It was a throbbing sound that she could feel in her internal organs, a pulse that brutalised the air. The blast caused a vortex in the pattern of the falling snow, whizzing flakes in a sudden horizontal spiral. A stout tree directly behind the four of them shivered and shed collected snow as the energy struck its trunk. Bark cracked and shattered. Steam wafted from the traumatised wood.

'Guide's sake!' Samewell yelped.

'It was just a warning shot!' the Doctor told them. 'They want us alive.'

As if hoping to corroborate the Doctor's statement, the Ice Warrior spoke again. This time, Amy could identify a stretched and mangled word in the fierce pneumatic hiss.

'Sssssurrenderrr…'

The Doctor sprang up to face the towering aliens. 'Not today, thank you!' he cried.

'Doctor!' Amy cried.

The Ice Warrior aimed at the Doctor and fired, but the Doctor had already activated his screwdriver. The warbling sound of the device seemed to strangle and cut short the ugly noise of the weapon.

The Ice Warrior hesitated, confused. It tried its weapon again, and this time it didn't make a sound at all. The Doctor kept his bleating screwdriver aimed at the giants. The Ice Warrior hissed a curt order, and the others of its kind took aim. They all fired.

None of the weapon tubes made a noise.

'Time to run!' the Doctor cried. 'Run away! Very fast!'

The others got up, hesitantly.

'Come on!' the Doctor yelled, still brandishing the warbling screwdriver at the Ice Warriors. 'The screwdriver's generating sound waves with the opposite polarity to the output of their weapons, cancelling the noise – oh, just run, *please*! It won't work much longer!'

They all started to run.

'The other way, Samewell!' Amy ordered.

Samewell turned and started to run with them instead of towards the Ice Warriors. Shock had rather robbed him of his wits. Arabel gathered up her long skirts to run more easily. The four of them dashed through the snow between the looming trees, the Doctor bringing up the rear, directing the output of his screwdriver behind him.

The Ice Warriors immediately started to pursue them, striding out across the snow.

'We're leaving them behind!' Amy yelled, looking back.

'Yes,' agreed the Doctor, 'but they won't get tired!'

His screwdriver suddenly went quiet and the claspers retracted and shut. The Doctor shook it and tapped it against his palm as he ran.

'That's all we'll be getting out of it for a while!' he shouted. 'Keep running, and don't let them get a clear shot!'

Behind them, they heard a tube weapon pulse. A slender tree a few metres to Amy's left exploded mid-trunk and the top half sheared away. Amy squealed, ducked, and then leapt over the fallen section as it collapsed in her path.

'Down here! This way!' the Doctor urged. Two or three more unpleasant pulses thumped out behind them. Another tree fractured. The top of a snowdrift behind Samewell went up like an explosion in an cotton wool factory.

Ahead of them, the trees were thinning out. They had reached the edge of Would Be and the start of the open grazing land beyond, the region Samewell had called Moreland.

No trees meant no cover. If they carried on, they would be sitting ducks.

'I went out this morning to put flowers on my dad's grave,' Vesta Flurrish told Rory quietly. They had turned the solamp up slightly. Apart from her voice, the only sounds were the cycle of the turbines underneath them, and the tick of ice-heavy flakes hitting the roof and wall of the shed. It was snowing hard outside.

'I meant to be back before Guide's Bell, of course,' said Vesta. 'But it is a long way up to the memory yard in this weather. The yard is in Would Be. Do you know it?'

'I'm not from around here,' said Rory.

She nodded. 'Well, I was there, and I was just leaving, and then I saw the star move.'

'A star?'

'Yes.'

'Moving?'

'Yes. A moving star. It went by in the sky. Beautiful, it was. Like a sign.' Her face fell as she thought about it. 'Like an omen. That's what they say. Bel saw it.'

'Bel?'

'My sister, Arabel. Other Morphans have seen it too. All this winter long. A star of ill omen, moving as it pleases. They say it presages the bad things that have been happening. The cold. The killing.'

'The killing?' asked Rory.

'Of livestock. Have you seen the moving stars from your plantnation?'

'No.'

'Oh,' she said. 'Anyway, I followed it for a while to see what it would do. I followed it further into Would Be, and that's when I came upon the tracks in the snow. The giant tracks. They scared me a lot. I didn't know what to make of them. I prayed that Guide might protect me, and I ran. And then...'

'Then?' Rory asked.

'I sort of ran straight into it there in the wood.'

'It?'

'That's right.'

'With the red eyes?'

'As Guide is my witness,' said Vesta.

'It's certainly a scary thing to meet,' Rory agreed.

'I was sore afraid,' Vesta nodded. 'It snatched at me, but I ran. I ran and ran and ran.'

'Did it shoot at you?' asked Rory.

'Shoot?'

'With a gun?'

'No. I didn't know it had a gun. We do not have guns in the plantnation. They are things that fire pellets, aren't they?'

'Sort of,' Rory replied. 'It shot at me.' He thought for a moment. 'Actually, the funny thing is, it didn't. I met these men who must've been looking for you, and because they didn't know me, like you didn't, they thought I was pretty suss.'

'They thought you were what?'

'Dodgy... um... they wanted to know who I was and what I was doing. Then it came along, and there was a terrible fight. It shot at some of the men. It had this horrible... *sound gun*. It was like it was firing sound. I can't explain it better. I think it hurt some of them. I think it might have killed some of them.'

'Oh save us all!' said Vesta. 'It killed people from Beside?'

'I think it might have done. I'm sorry.'

'Who were they?' she asked.

'I don't know,' Rory said, a little helplessly. 'I didn't know their names. We'd only just met. In the confusion, everybody scattered. I ran. Like you, I just ran. And it could have shot me too, but it didn't. It just chased me.'

'Like it wanted... to catch you?'

Rory nodded. His throbbing head reminded him what a bad idea that was, and he winced. 'That had occurred to me,' he said. 'It's not a nice thought. I have been wondering why. Anyway, I ran.'

'And that's how you ended up at the autumn mills?'

'Where?'

She laughed. 'Here! The autumn mills!'

'OK. I didn't know what they were called.'

Vesta's long skirts were torn and dirty. She idly smoothed them out over her knees.

'I came here because it was the closest place I could think of to hide in,' she said. 'I ran a long way just to get away from it. By the time I even thought about which way I was going, I realised I'd gone off opposite to where Beside was. I was a Cat A fool for doing that. I got my bearings and figured that the autumn mills would be the best bet for a roof and shelter and warmth.'

'Why is the water warm?' Rory asked. 'Even under the ice, there's heat in it. I know because I fell through the ice.'

'No wonder you look like a compost heap,' said Vesta. She shrugged. 'The water's warm because it flows into the streams from the Firmer. These streams, it would be Firmer Number Two, actually. It's a thermal exchange system. Guide teaches us that water is used in the Firmers for cooling, and then sent out, and the mills harvest the heat to store in the plantnation's conservator reservoir. Light and wind and water, we borrow power from all. The mills take power autumnatically from the streams.'

'How… how do they do it?' asked Rory.

'Autumnatically.'

'Automatically?'

'Say it proper! Autumnatically! Didn't you get schooled where you were raised?'

'A little.'

She peered at him, as if trying to read things in his face. Just having someone to talk to seemed to have perked her up, and reduced the trauma of what had clearly been an unpleasant day. Rory had seen that process work many times. A little chat, a chance to say things out loud.

'What labour do you do, Rory?' she asked. 'Let me guess. Are you a shepherd?'

'No.'

'Then a plantsman. That's it! A plantsman.'

'No, actually I'm a nurse.'

Vesta gazed at him, bewildered. 'A nurse? You're a nurse?'

'Yes.'

She leapt up, brushing her clothes down, her head bowed. 'Oh my Guide! I am so ashamed! So ashamed of my comportment!'

'Whoa, what?' asked Rory, getting up.

'You are an elect, an elect, and I show you no courtesy or respect! Oh goodness, and to think I struck you on the head too!'

'Calm down. Please, calm down. It's all right.'

She looked at him uneasily. 'I didn't know. Honest, and may Guide strike me down. I had no idea. You look too young, and you do not have a beard either.'

'I can understand how you made the mistake,' said Rory.

'Were you coming to visit us at Beside?'

'Yes,' said Rory.

'For the festival?'

'The festival…?' he asked.

'The winter festival.'

'Yes,' said Rory firmly, nodding. 'That's why we'd come. To celebrate.'

'You weren't on your own then?'

'What?'

'You said "we",' said Vesta.

'I did, didn't I?'

'Obviously someone as important as the Nurse Elect of a plantnation wouldn't travel alone. That would make no sense.'

'It wouldn't, would it?' asked Rory.

'So where is the rest of your party?'

'It was just a small group. Three of us… travelling from, um, afar,' said Rory. 'The Doctor and… another person. We got lost and separated.'

'How terrible, Elect,' she said. 'I hope they are all right.'

'So do I,' Rory agreed.

'We used to have wellwishers every year for the festival, but not since the winters turned white. The Morphans of Beside will be overjoyed that you have made this effort for the festival. We should go. We should go at once.'

'To Beside? Now?'

'Yes,' said Vesta. She was very earnest. 'This mill is quite secure, I suppose, but I do not wish to spend the night here, not with it out there. It is late, and it is cold, but if we go together and walk with purpose, we might make it in an hour.'

'OK,' said Rory. 'What about my friends?'

'We must hope Guide watches out for them,' said Vesta.

The Ice Warriors moved surprisingly fast for such big creatures. They weren't running, but their stride rate had increased. They pursued the Doctor and his companions out of the tree-line and onto the soft snow dunes of the open grazing. Their gait was powerful and sure-footed even on the softest snow, as though they were evolved to excel in such conditions. It felt as if they could stride for ever, and knock down anything that got in their way, and no matter how fast you fled, eventually they'd catch up with you when you collapsed of exhaustion.

'This way!' Samewell shouted, running ahead into the open ground. Lazy snowflakes billowed around him, spilling from a sky as dark as wet granite. 'Come on!'

'No! No! No!' the Doctor yelled. He was still fiddling with his sonic screwdriver as he ran. 'Not that way! Keep to the trees!'

Samewell was not going to be deterred, and Arabel was following him closely. Either he knew what he was doing, or he'd entirely taken leave of his senses, especially the one relating to direction. Given that surprise had almost sent Samewell running *towards* the Ice Warriors when they first appeared, the Doctor was not filled with confidence.

The sonic screwdriver started chirruping again. He aimed it at the Ice Warriors, neutralising the lethal blasts of their sonic weapons, and bounded on after the others.

Samewell had led them towards some kind of gully. He did know what he was doing after all.

There were some steep ditches and sunken stream beds in the slopes between the wood and the gently rising

Moreland. Snow-cover had softened them into narrow channels and defiles, blended invisibly into the whiteness. Amy and the Doctor found themselves slithering down a deep bank behind Arabel and Samewell, and then slogging along a winding channel out of view of the edge of the wood. There were a few lonely trees and coarse bushes, coated in snow, and large snow-dusted boulders jutted out of the frozen stream bed.

Arabel slipped and half-fell, but Amy grabbed her and pulled her up again. They kept running.

The Doctor's screwdriver didn't. It puttered out again. They could hear the Ice Warriors descending the bank behind them, but they couldn't see them.

Samewell led the fugitives along another channel, and then through a gentle basin where a lip of rock crowned with a gnarled tree overhung. Hard snow, driven by the wind across Moreland, blew down into their faces like sleet.

Samewell gestured urgently for them to keep following him. He scrambled up another bank, cascading powder snow in all directions, and led them back onto a raised stretch of the grazing.

There was a hut ahead of them. It was quite small, round, with a conical roof. Snow had drifted against its northward face. It was the shelter Samewell had told them about. It was the vent.

The Doctor felt an acute rush of pity. Samewell had been trying so hard. His solution to them being lost out in the snow was to lead them to the vent. His solution to them being chased by murderous Ice Warriors was the same plan, unmodified. A vent provided shelter and safety for a herder. That was the way Samewell's mind worked.

As they got closer, the Doctor rapidly revised his opinion. The vent was made of metal. The entire structure was composed out of shipskin. If they could bar the door, it might indeed protect against Ice Warriors.

'Get inside!' he shouted.

The four of them blundered into the vent. It was dark and cold inside, and smelled of straw, but it was surprisingly dry. Samewell swung the metal door shut behind them and dropped the bolt.

They looked at one another in the gloom. It was so dark, they could discern only the faintest shapes. All of them were panting and out of breath.

'Wait now,' said Samewell.

He fumbled along the wall of the vent behind the door and found a rack containing small solamps. He turned one of the lamps on. The inside of the vent was a circular chamber about six metres in diameter. There were shelves with pots and pans, a small stove, two battered sleeping cots and a chair. The floor looked like it was impacted earth covered in dried rushes or straw. It was almost cosy.

The sense of cosiness vanished the moment they heard the first mighty pincer-fist smash against the vent door. The blows came one after another, brutally hard against the metal, vibrating the door and the wall beside it. The Ice Warriors were determined to smash their way in.

'The metal will keep them out for a bit,' said Amy.

'Shipskin is strong,' said Bel.

'So are Ice Warriors,' replied the Doctor. He had taken the lamp off Samewell and was looking around, searching desperately for some kind of inspiration, some cue that might prompt invention or improvisation, anything to get them out of a small, exit-less structure that was, at best, a temporary refuge and, at worst, a hut-shaped death-trap.

'Houdini built a career out of this,' he said encouragingly as his mind raced.

'Of being trapped in a smelly shed under attack from Ice Men?' asked Amy.

'Of escaping from tight places from which there was no obvious mode of egress,' replied the Doctor. He took a cup off a shelf, looking inside it, and then gave up on that line of thought. 'And it's Ice *Warriors*.'

Amy glanced at the door, which was quivering with every dull blow from outside.

'Uh-huh,' she said. 'Is that going to matter, in the long run? Ice Men? Ice Warriors? Ice *Homicidal Freaks*, who are still going to do us in whatever we call them?'

'True,' said the Doctor. He flipped the chair over to check its underside. 'Funny thing,' he said, 'no one ever gets their name right. Not even them. I mean, as I remember it, it was a friend of mine called Victoria that first called them Ice Warriors. Then they started to refer to themselves as Ice Warriors. It's confusing. If the cap fits, I suppose.'

'You've met them before?' asked Amy.

'Several times. Not for a long while, actually. Anyway, nice to see they're still entirely Ice-ish and Warrior-esque.'

'Are they enemies of yours?' asked Arabel.

'No,' said the Doctor, getting down to look under the cots. The hammering at the hatch had grown more intense. 'Yes. Sometimes.' He shrugged. 'They are an ancient and proud culture. One of the great pan-world civilisations in this part of the galaxy. Much to be admired about them. Great code of honour. Of fairness. Then again, they are pragmatic and resolute. They fight for survival and they fight without quarter. It's very dangerous to be on the wrong side of them.'

'How many times have you been on the *right* side of them?' asked Amy.

'Oh, a couple of times at least.'

'And the other times?'

The Doctor looked at her.

'Those didn't go so well,' he admitted.

'What are they doing here?' asked Amy.

'The same thing as the Morphans, I should imagine,' the Doctor replied, standing on the chair to examine the ceiling, 'shopping for a new home. If Earth and its solar system are gone, forcing a migration of human colonists, then Mars has gone too.'

'Why does that matter?'

'Because that, Amy Pond, is where they come from,' he said.

'Mars?'

'Yes.'

'They're Martians?'

'Yes.'

She stared at him. 'You're actually, seriously telling me, with a straight face, they're green men from Mars?'

'I know,' the Doctor said. 'It's ironic, isn't it? Of course, they're not *little* green men. That would just be silly. They're nice and big.'

Amy looked at the door. The last few savage blows had actually begun to dent the metal around the bolt.

'Big and strong all right,' she said. 'Strong enough to start bashing the door in. They're buckling the metal.'

'That's shipskin!' protested Samewell. 'It's the strongest metal we have!'

'It *is*, isn't it?' mused the Doctor.

He didn't seem at all distracted by the incessant banging from the door. He stamped the heel of his right foot against the hard-packed ground, moved a short distance and did it again.

'And that's the interesting part,' he went on. 'Shipskin's the toughest material you've got. It's rare. It's a precious commodity.'

'So?' asked Amy.

'So why did the Morphans build a shepherd's hut out of it?' asked the Doctor. He stamped his heel again and began to grin.

'What have you found?' Amy asked.

'As usual, the obvious!' he announced. He dropped to his hands and knees and started to rake up the earth floor with his fingers. 'Come on! Help me! Before they knock that door in!'

They all got down and started to scrape the soil away with him. There was something under the dirt, just a few centimetres down. Something metal.

'It was surprisingly dry in here,' said the Doctor, working fast. 'That's the first thing I noticed. Dry. And made of metal. Well, made of metal was the first thing I noticed. Then I thought, why's it so dry in here?'

'You're gabbling,' Amy said.

'Sorry,' said the Doctor.

There was a particularly loud bang from the door. Part of the lip had folded in. They could see a massive green pincer clamping at the frame, trying to prise it open.

'It's obvious,' the Doctor said. 'I was over-thinking it! The Morphans don't call this a vent because it's a derivation of a word for wind, they call it a vent… because it's a vent!'

They had dug away and exposed a large hatch in the

102

floor. The Doctor brushed dust and dirt out of a latch mechanism.

'Hurry!' advised Amy looking at the door.

'This is an exhaust outlet,' said the Doctor, 'venting warm air from the underground systems. It's part of the large scale terramorphing mechanisms built under the landscape here. There are probably hundreds of them all over the countryside. The Morphans have come to use them as huts because they're usually warm and dry. They don't remember what they were originally.'

Amy looked at the doorway. Part of the door was bent inwards and a great deal more of it was bulging. Two sets of large green pincers were now visible, trying to shear the bolt away from the frame.

'*Really* hurry!' she said.

The Doctor adjusted his screwdriver, ratcheted around a setting and aimed it at the latch. It made a rather sickly and pathetic noise. He shook it and banged it against his hand.

'I drained so much power noise-cancelling the Ice Warrior weapons,' he sighed. 'It's feeling rather sorry for itself. It just wants to sit in a pocket quietly and recharge. Come on,' he whispered to the screwdriver. 'Just do this, and I won't bother you again all day.'

'Doctor!' Amy cried.

Another formidable bash from the doorway had begun to deform the bolt.

The Doctor aimed the screwdriver carefully again, clicking the base end of it with his thumb as though it was a ballpoint pen. The sonic burbled, flashed, and then maintained a steady, whirring cycle. Three green lights winked on in series across the latch unit, and the hatch released with a clank and a hiss.

They hoisted it up. It lifted on one heavy-duty hinge like a submarine's front door. It revealed a vertical metal shaft that descended into darkness. There was a metal ladder fixed down one side.

'Go! Quickly!' the Doctor urged.

'Where does it lead?' asked Arabel.

'Away from here,' replied the Doctor, 'and that's probably it's most appealing quality at the moment. Go!'

Amy scrambled onto the ladder and started to descend. Arabel followed her, and then Samewell.

The Doctor held the hatch lid up, and then followed Samewell as soon as the lad had gone down a few rungs.

Behind him, a final brutal blow broke the door in. It squealed open on mangled hinges and snow swirled into the vent. An Ice Warrior filled the doorway, staring with malevolent yet expressionless red eyes.

The Doctor clattered down the first few rungs, pulling the hatch lid down after him.

It had almost engaged in the shut position when a green pincer caught the edge of it and wedged it open.

With an exclamation of alarm, the Doctor pulled down.

The Ice Warrior pulled up.

No contest.

CHAPTER 9
THE NIGHT IS DARKER NOW

The Doctor grabbed the underside handle of the hatch with both hands, teetering on the edge of a rung. He dragged down on it as hard as he could, teeth clenched, eyes closed. Below him, climbing down the ladder as fast as they could go, Amy, Arabel and Samewell looked up and called out in dismay.

The Ice Warrior simply flipped the hatch up as easily as if he was opening the lid of a wheelie bin. The hatch went up, and the Doctor went with it. He was pulled clean off the rung he'd been standing on. He dangled for a nanosecond from the handle, his legs hanging free and driving the pedals of an invisible bicycle.

Then he lost his grip.

The Doctor dropped like a stone. The sudden release of his weight jerked the hatch out of the Ice Warrior's clamp of a hand, and it fell shut. There was a click as the latch engaged.

The Doctor was in no position to appreciate that the Ice Warriors had just been shut out. He was simply in a position of falling crazily down the vent shaft with his legs and arms waving. He hit Samewell first, knocking the young man off the wall ladder. Samewell barely had time to grunt in surprise. They were falling together when they hit Arabel, who was immediately below Samewell. The impact took her off the ladder too. She held on by one hand for a second, but couldn't retain her grip. Then she was falling with them.

All three of them, a tumbling, yelping bundle of limbs and bodies, collided with Amy, who was the lowest of the four. Her feet slipped off the rungs of the ladder, but she managed to retain her grip. The elastic strap connecting her mittens through the sleeves of her duffel coat caught on the rung for a moment, just long enough for her to plant her grip.

The Doctor, Samewell and Arabel plunged past her and vanished into the darkness of the shaft below.

'Oh my god! Oh my god!' Amy babbled, hauling herself back onto the ladder properly, and tilting to gaze down at the drop below. 'Oh my god! Doctor! Doctor!'

Her voice echoed back. There was no other sound. There was no reply. There was no reassuring answer, no *It's OK, Amy, we landed safely on this convenient mattress.*

On the positive side, there was no sound of impact either.

Amy swallowed hard, shocked by the disastrous turn of events. She called out their names again, and clambered down a few rungs. Then she went back up two steps, unhooked her mitten elastic, and started again.

There was a resounding clang from up above. The Ice Men had started work on the hatch.

Ice *Warriors*, she told herself, Ice-stupid-well *Warriors*.

She started to climb down as fast as she could. Several times she went too fast and slipped. The shaft seemed to go down for ever. They were going to be so dead when she finally reached them. It was going to be upsetting, and very messy, and then she was going to be alone with only Ice Men for company.

Warriors. *Warriors!*

She carried on down, running out of puff from the exertion. Despite the Doctor's earlier pledge that the day would be full of Christmas fun, and there'd be an absolute minimum of unnecessary shouting and running about, it had turned out to be the exact opposite. Things really had to stop ending up like this. The universe was a beautiful, amazing and enthralling place, and she wanted to travel widely and enjoy it, preferably in the alive company of her husband and her good friend the Doctor. Amy was beginning to believe that she wasn't getting the most out of the universe by touring it at speed, and viewing it in passing. There was never any time to look at things. There only ever seemed to be time to glimpse things while running away from other, more pressing, things.

Amy stopped. She closed her eyes, took a deep breath and blew it out. Her mind was in totally flippant mode because she was trying to block out the idea that she had just seen the Doctor fall to his death, along with two other people she didn't know particularly well but had good reason to believe were nice and entirely undeserving of death by high-speed ground.

She opened her eyes and started to climb down again, breathing hard, trying to bolster her confidence. The steady, brutal clanging from the hatch far above wasn't helping much.

They wanted in, and they wanted in now, did those Ice Men. Warriors. *Warriors.*

She ignored the banging and scraping, and kept going, one rung at a time, hand-and-foot, hand-and-foot, down and down. How far did this place go?

Amy became aware that there was something different about the shaft below her. It was hard to tell what at first. She grimaced and really hoped it wasn't a *decorated with splatted bodies* type of different.

Fortunately, it wasn't.

The ladder was coming to an end. The rungs ran out at a point where the whole shaft began to gently tilt to the left, like a drainpipe. It went from a straight vertical to a 35-degree drop with a very smoothly engineered bend like a joint in a piece of guttering.

She felt a distant breeze, cool and fresh coming up from below. The shaft seemed to be full of sound, sound just waiting for a chance to echo.

She stepped off the last rung and steadied herself on a sloping floor that, three metres higher up, had been wall.

'Doctor?' she called.

The echo came back to her. She edged forward.

It was quite tricky to walk on the angled floor. She struggled to keep her balance. The Ice Warriors continued to hammer and gouge at the hatch high above her.

The tube reminded her of something. She realised what it was. It was like a giant version of those water slides they had at big leisure centres, those great big, slaloming tube rides that Rory loved so much. It was just like that.

Or it was like an oversized version of those hamster playpens people bought from pet shops on the assumption that hamsters liked that sort of thing.

She wasn't convinced they did. If this was typical of the experience, it wasn't much fun and she could begin to appreciate the generally surly demeanour evinced by many hamsters.

She edged her way along. There was still no sign of the Doctor or Arabel or Samewell. They must have come all the way down and then shot off around the bend like Rory on a monster waterslide. Or a surly hamster doing hard time in a transparent plastic penitentiary.

'Doctor?' she called again, leaning forward to peer into the darkness, combing her hair out of her eyes with her fingers. 'Doctor? Give us a shout if you're OK, yeah? Doctor?'

Behind and above her, the Ice Warriors turned their sonic blasters on the unyielding latch and blew it to pieces. The awful noise of the blast reverberated down the shaft to her and made her jump. Her foot slipped. She kept her balance.

She looked back the way she had come. She heard the ruptured hatch shriek open and saw shadows move in the light shining down the vent shaft.

The Ice Warriors were in. They were Ice Warriors, and they had opened the hatch, and they were inside the shaft, and they were coming after her. There was not a single part of that summary that didn't utterly terrify her.

She had to hurry. She took another step, another, moving faster.

Her foot slipped. She steadied herself again. Then both feet slipped at once, and this time she did not keep her balance.

Amy went over on her backside.

'Ouch!' she cried. Then she realised that falling on her bum was not going to be the worst of it.

She was moving. She was sliding. She was travelling down the shaft.

She protested aloud, to no one in particular, and started to paddle and scrabble with her hands and feet. To no avail. She was picking up speed. She was sliding down the shaft as if it was a chute, on her bottom, like Rory on a monster stupid waterslide. She couldn't stop herself. She couldn't get up.

Gaining speed with every passing second, Amy rode the slide, helplessly, deeper and deeper underground.

Snow was falling. It was the blackest kind of night Rory had seen in a long while, cold and enclosing, giving nothing back. Big flakes of snow just seemed to hurtle blindly out of the darkness, zooming at him.

He was following Vesta through the snowy woods. She had brought her little solamp, but they had agreed to try travelling without it on for as long as they could. A light could attract the wrong kind of attention. Vesta had assured Rory that she knew which way to go. She knew the woods. She knew how to get them to Beside.

Rory believed she meant it, but he was still worried. They had left the comforting heat of the autumn mills – *automills*, surely? – behind them and set out into a frozen night. There was a very good chance they would die of cold before they got anywhere, and that was without factoring in the it with red eyes that was out to get them.

His clothes had dried out during their stay in the warmth of the mill. He was glad of his coat. He wasn't convinced it had been worth going back to the TARDIS for it. Maybe the day would have turned out to be rather less *energetic* if he'd stayed with Amy and the Doctor. Then again, he had no way of telling what sort of adventures they'd been getting up to. He had a fond notion that they would arrive at Vesta's village, Beside, and find the Doctor and Amy already there, already firm friends with everybody, telling stories, sitting by a hearth, eating hot food. His fond notion had a giant Christmas tree in it too, so he knew some of the details were completely fanciful, but he had hopes.

Rory was also a realist. He tried to count the number of times they had arrived anywhere, by accident or design, and not stumbled into some predicament or other. The only answer he could come up with was zero. It was inevitable, as inevitable as the wheeze of the TARDIS's console, as inevitable as the Doctor's sudden grin of insight. These predicaments, Rory believed, naturally attached themselves to Time Lords. In fact, with only one Time Lord left, there was probably a serious backlog of predicaments waiting to be attached. Danger, problems, plight, peril… He wouldn't be particularly surprised to learn there was some sort of detector circuit aboard the TARDIS that automatically drew them towards trouble. The Doctor would probably admit it one day, casually, as though he thought they already knew. 'You mean I didn't tell you about the Predicament Seek-O-Matic Module? I didn't? I could have sworn… Should I switch it off for a change? Yes, why not? I'll switch it off.'

Snowflakes continued to stream out of the darkness, become suddenly visible, and hit him in the face. They were like stars. It was like rushing through the cosmos. It was piercingly cold and blindingly dark, and all he could see were little bright white objects speeding by. It was like travelling through the universe in the TARDIS and, like the TARDIS, there was no way of knowing exactly where you were going, or how safe it would be when you got there.

*

Amy was travelling at speeds in excess of anything she was comfortable with, especially given the fact that she wasn't riding aboard anything like a bike or a skateboard or a luge or a rocket ship, and she wasn't in any way in control at all.

The lining of the tube felt frictionless, and resisted her frantic attempts to grab hold of something or stop herself. The pitch was also increasing, dropping her down a raked slide even steeper and more alarming than before. Eyes wide, hair flying out behind her, she zoomed down the tube. She realised it was the sort of ride that she might have enjoyed under other circumstances, none of which were presently operating. She also realised she was making desperate, strangled noises like 'agh' and 'eek' and 'yrk'.

Then she flew out of the mouth of a tube and landed on a bed of soft, dusty material. She bounced and came to a halt. Coughing, she slowly got to her feet. Her impact had puffed a huge cloud of dusty fibres out of the mass. She was in a small metal chamber, and the dusty material was a thick mass of leaf mould and vegetable fibres that had been sucked into the vent system and had accumulated there to rot. It had probably saved her from serious injury.

Still coughing, she glanced back up the dark tube of the vent system.

'I am *not* doing that again,' she said.

Her feet, striving for some autonomy, chose that moment to skid out from under her and prove her wrong. She slipped, fell down on her rear end again, and shot away down the next extension of the tube system, 'eek'-ing helplessly.

'Not fun!' she yelled at the top of her voice, experiencing an even sharper, steeper, faster ride than before. The tube twisted at one point and almost inverted her, before finally ejecting her into another chamber lined with deep, springy and slightly musty leaf matter.

Amy got to her feet a great deal more carefully than she had after her previous landing. She thought for a moment that she might have damaged her shoulder or back, because it was difficult to straighten up, but then discovered that this had less to do with a sprain or dislocation, and more to do with the fact that she was standing on one of her elasticated mittens.

She let the mitten ping out from under her foot, straightened up properly, and stared into the gloom around her whilst combing bits of dead leaf out of her hair with her fingers.

'Doctor?' she called. 'Doctor?'

The metal chamber, plain and grey and boxy, had several exits, all of which were further tube mouths. She edged around, making sure not to slip and plunge off on another escapade.

'Doctor?'

One of the vent tubes ran for a horizontal section, and there was a kind of fluted duct to one side that she clambered through. She was now in a hallway. It was long, metallic and dark. The air was cool but dry. A small amount of ambient light was issuing from recessed lamps in the wall. The lamps looked like smaller and more sophisticated versions of the lights the Morphans used, the devices they called *solamps*. The glow reminded Amy of the output of solar garden lights that had been on all night and were beginning to tire.

'Doctor? Hello?'

There hadn't been much opportunity to argue with where the tube was taking her, so she wondered how the

Doctor, Bel and Samewell could have ended up anywhere else.

Amy listened hard to see if a faraway voice might be answering her calls, and realised she could hear something. It was a humming, a deep resonance. She could feel it more than she could hear it. It was the sound immense machinery made, the steady industrial purr of automation, heard from a distance. It felt as if she was inside a huge factory, the biggest factory ever built, and all the machinery, whirring and chugging away, was hidden from view behind the metal skin of the walls around her.

Then she thought, *Maybe I'm inside the actual machine. Maybe I'm inside some kind of pipe or tube or channel, and it seems giant to me, but that's only because the machine's so big. Maybe it's going to suddenly fill with... water or oil or liquid waste or atomic sludge or energy. Maybe it shoots down here at regular intervals as part of the machine's operation, and I've simply arrived between those intervals, and if I stay here much longer I'm going to get drowned or washed away or burned to a frazzle or irradiated, or—*

Amy began to panic. She began to feel very, very claustrophobic. She hurried along the hallway-that-might-also-be-a-pipe looking for an exit, or a door, or at the very least something to get up onto.

She found something else instead.

A scratching sound, a skittering noise, a flash of light in the shadows, just a glint.

'Who's that? Who's there?' she asked boldly. Experience had taught her that being bold often helped. Well, not so much as bolshie. Whatever, it made her feel better anyway.

Then she saw what was making the sound. She saw the rats.

They weren't actually rats. She realised that straight off.

But rats were what they made her think of, and rats was the word that registered in her brain.

They had too many legs to be rats. Too many legs, and not nearly enough eyes or hair. Plus, they were the size of terriers, which was quite unusual for rats.

But by golly there were a lot of them.

CHAPTER 10
UNDERNEATH THE MOUNTAIN

They were going to eat her.

There was no doubt in Amy's mind about that. They were scurrying towards her along the hallway floor in a great tide of wrinkled, grey-pink bodies, with chattering teeth that looked like they were coated with metal and designed for biting through wire.

She wasn't exactly sure *why* she thought they were going to eat her. It wasn't as though they had a malicious look in their eyes, because they didn't have eyes. They just had sockets where eyes were supposed to be, sockets that looked like surgical excisions, sockets that had been emptied and then packed with brown material the texture of foam, like the covers to headphone buds or a voice mic. They had claws that resembled bird-foot articulations built from old compass and divider sets. They had tails that looked like the coating of black electrical cable stretched over bike chains.

'Oh my god, you're all completely horrible!' she exclaimed, and began to retreat very fast. They responded by accelerating towards her, rushing in a sudden flood, the larger rats pushing smaller ones aside or trampling them.

The nasty, wrinkly grey flesh on their bodies was taut enough to reveal the outlines of their ribcages.

'And you're hungry!' she yelped, finally understanding what had tipped her off. They were famished, and they were behaving the way any hungry creatures did when they detected food.

She started to sprint. They were after her. Their jaws snapped wide, ready to bite, revealing dentition that would have looked much more at home on posters for a film about memorable summers on Amity Island.

One of the rat-things leapt at her. It missed, but it nearly took a chunk out of her left calf with a snap of its teeth. Another leapt. She swatted it away with her hand. A third sprang at her and she struck at it but failed to connect, and it seized her mitten in its mouth, attaching itself to her through-sleeve elastic like a fish to a line.

'Get off!' she yelled, and swung the thing hard so that it bashed into the hallway wall. It took two fairly deliberate smacks to make it let go of the mitten and fall onto the floor.

By then, the main portion of the rat flood had reached her. She screamed in horror. What was about to happen was going to be unpleasant. About as unpleasant as unpleasant ever got.

What actually happened next *was* unpleasant, but not in the way she had been expecting. There was a shrill noise, like some kind of alarm or whistle. It stabbed into her ears like knitting needles and made her cry out in pain and stumble to her knees. It was an awful sound. It was the sort of sound that felt like it would break your ears, microwave your brain, and make smoke come out of your nose.

It actually did that to several of the rats. Some dropped

dead in their tracks. Others fell, twitching and writhing in pain. The rest simply recoiled and fled. Their frantic metal claws made skritchy, squealy, teeth-on-edge noises as they fled down the metal hallway, noises that Amy would not have enjoyed at all if she'd been able to hear them. Her ears, however, were still ringing from the monstrously shrill sound.

Shaking her head, she got up. The Doctor was standing right behind her, with Arabel and Samewell, both looking scared, behind him. The Doctor was smiling.

'————,' he said. '————.'

'What?' Amy asked.

'————,' the Doctor replied, still smiling, but looking concerned.

'Give me a clue,' she said. 'Is it a book? How many words? Why aren't you talking to me?'

The Doctor turned and said something equally inaudible to Arabel and Samewell.

'It's my ears, isn't it?' asked Amy. 'That sound knackered my ears, didn't it?'

The Doctor turned back to her. He pointed to his sonic screwdriver, and made a sad face. '————,' he said.

She could read his lips. She knew what *sorry* looked like.

Sol Farrow was a strong man, noted for his labour in the fields and heathouses. Sol was not quite as big as Jack Duggat, for Jack Duggat was the biggest of all Morphans in Beside, but he was an ox of a man nevertheless. Elect Groan had given him the task of nightwatching Beside's westgate, and offered him his choice of arms to take. Sol had chosen a fine, long-handled shovel with a shipskin tongue. He'd also taken a good sickle from the tool store, and hooked it into his belt under his heavy winter coat. Sol did not intend to be found wanting. He'd heard the stories over the past weeks, all of them: the tall figures glimpsed in the woods, the killed cattle and sheep, the stars that did not stay still. What were those things in the woods? Were they real, real giants of the forest, regarding the plantnation with evil intent? Or were they just figments of the imagination, sprites conjured by the fearful mindset of the Morphans?

Sol Farrow was a sound man, and would have normally supposed the latter. People jumped at shadows, and at sounds in the night. They saw things sometimes that weren't really there. The hard winters and the snow, well, that was a misfortune, a hardship they had to bear, but it was making people agitated, and in that agitation, their minds raced and imagined.

Now he was not so sure. There was too much that couldn't be accounted for, more than could be explained by imagination and a rogue dog.

How many men had not returned from the search today? There was no trace of them. If they'd been taken by something, like the livestock had been taken, then the population of Beside had suffered a mortal blow.

Nightwatching had not been done in his time, or his father's, or his father's father's. According to the practices listed in the word of Guide, nightwatching had been done in the early times, when the Morphans first came to Hereafter. Nightwatch had been posted around the first camps, while the towns were being raised and constructed. Back then, the Morphans had not known much about the world Hereafter, and had no idea what hid in the dark when it fell.

Bill Groan had reinstated the practice of nightwatch after the third livestock killing. He posted watchmen at the compass gates of Beside, plus another at the heathouses, another at the well, and two to patrol from the byre to the dairy. Another watchman would beat the bounds of the plantnation through the night. Bill Groan had been determined that no mad dog would get into the town and threaten the children or the old.

A precaution. That's all it had seemed at first. And a burden, because men like Sol had to stand out all hours in the cold weather.

After the day they'd just had, it seemed like a necessity.

It was bitter cold, and light snow was falling. Sol could hear the hiss and whisper of it. From his vantage, with the town at his back, he had the edge of the woods and the open land of Fairground ahead of him. To his left, he could see the slight glow of the solamps in the heathouses. To his right, like a dark and cloudy phantom behind the snow, he could just make out the bulk of Firmer Number One.

The cold was getting to him. He had a small brazier for warmth, crackling near his feet, a flask of broth, and he made sure he did not stand still for too long. Pacing kept his feet warm. He left the end of his shovel resting on the ground, supporting it with one hand, and kept the other hand tucked inside his coat for warmth. Every few minutes, he would change hands and stuff the other away.

Sol put both hands on the shovel and raised it. He had heard something. He was sure he'd heard something. Across Fairground, out near the woods. It sounded as though something had moved. He waited, listening, peering into the darkness, seeing nothing. It was probably just snow-gather building up on a branch, finally snapping it under its accumulated weight or sloughing off. Since the snows had come, that sort of odd sound, noises of slumping and fluttering as fallen snow redistributed itself, had become very common.

Sol glanced back towards Beside. Lamps were burning throughout the heart of the settlement. It looked reassuring, almost cosy. He longed to be down there, at a fireside, talking with friends and eating a good supper. That community and companionship was what life was about. The hard toil and struggle of the Morphan existence was made bearable by the simple reassurances of hot food and a hearth, and a circle of friends.

Sadly, Sol reflected, that was not why the lamps were lit in Beside tonight. The council and the community were meeting in the assembly.

Crisis talks, Cat A.

Bill Groan stood in the porch of the assembly hall under the light of a solamp, listening as Old Winnowner read out the list.

Eight names. Eight good Morphan men of Beside who had not returned at day's end. Eight fathers, eight strong labourers, part of the backbone of the community. How could eight men go missing in the snow during the daytime? A fall or other mishap might take one, two if things were really unlucky. But eight?

They were all his friends.

Winnowner read the other names on the list. Harvesta Flurrish, of course, the poor girl whose disappearance had started the search in the first place. Winnowner had reminded Bill that it was the anniversary of Tyler Flurrish's death. Perhaps Vesta had been marking that loss. Perhaps that was why she had not come for labour at the chime of Guide's Bell. It seemed a particularly cruel twist of Guide's will for her to disappear on the anniversary of her father's passing. What horrible fate had befallen her, Bill wondered. Had the dog got her? Had it cornered her and brought her down like a lamb? Or, Guide help them all, was there some truth in these stories of giants in the woods?

Arabel Flurrish was missing too. No one had seen her or Samewell Crook since the morning meeting. Bill Groan knew Arabel Flurrish well. She was one of the brightest and best, strong-willed and quick-witted. Bill had no doubt Bel would rise to a high Morphan office like Nurse Elect in her time. Vesta was sweet and kind, but Bel was strong and driven. Bill was certain Bel had gone out to look for her sister anyway, permission or no permission. It was typical of her headstrong behaviour. Samewell Crook, well he was driven by his hopeless heart and good nature. He was so struck on Arabel, if she'd told him to jump in the mill race with his boots on, he'd have done it. He'd gone with her, to help her, that was obvious too.

But they hadn't come back. By nightchime, they had not returned. Worse still, just after noon, Jack Duggat had discovered that the two strangers had vanished from the compter too. Jack had gone down to take them some food and water, and found the cage open. Had they let themselves out? If so, how? The lock on the cage was a good, strong one, and it had not been forced.

Bill suspected that Bel, perhaps in some delusion, had let them out. He would not put such unilateral action past her, especially when she was so lacking in patience and concerned for her sister. She'd been eager to question the strangers, after all. Perhaps they had promised to show her where her sister had gone in return for release?

Even so, how had Bel opened the cage? A want of patience was a true vice, and certainly one of Arabel Flurrish's personal flaws, but even she, fired up and on a mission, could not manufacture a key out of nowhere.

Perhaps the matters weren't connected. Perhaps Bel and Samewell had gone off, and the strangers had got out of their own accord.

All Bill Groan could plainly see was that in the middle of the hardest winter the Morphans had ever known, two strangers who seemed to come from no plantnation, which was the only place anyone could have come from, turned up on the self-same day eleven Morphans of Beside went missing.

'They're taking their seats, Elect,' said Chaunce Plowrite, stepping out of the assembly to speak to Bill.

Bill Groan nodded.

'We should go in,' said Winnowner. In the low solamp light, she looked older than ever. Age and effort, and the stress of the current times had shaved more years off her. Bill felt a tightness. Winnowner Cropper could be difficult and set in her ways, but he relied upon her. A doctrine of continuity had kept the Morphans alive for twenty-seven generations, and it was just as vital as the doctrine of patience. One generation learned from the last. Knowledge and skills were stockpiled and maintained. The young did not have to make the same mistakes their predecessors had done, because the results of mistakes were taught so they could be avoided. Time and effort were not wasted by learning through experience. Morphans prospered by listening to their elders and learning. Hereafter was a hard place to live and a slow place to terrafirm. It did not offer second chances, but if you paid attention to the wisdom of your elders, it reduced the chances of you needing any.

Bill could not bear to think of Winnowner going. He did not know what he would do without her. He could not imagine being Nurse Elect and not having her years and counsel to call upon. If this crisis of ice and mysteries had hastened the end of Winnowner Cropper's life, then he...

He tried not to think about it. The plantnation records and oral histories both attested to the fact that it was always a sorry time when the last of a generation passed. It always marked the end of an era, and reminded the Morphan community of the vulnerability and the sheer duration of the lifecycle they had been born into. Bill knew that Winnowner's death would be a watershed in his service as Elect, and his life too. He prayed to Guide that it wouldn't happen when they were in the midst of such an unprecedented Cat A calamity.

'We should go in,' she repeated.

'And tell them what?' Bill asked.

'Speak fairly to them,' she replied. 'There's nothing we can do tonight except keep warm and keep watch.'

'And tomorrow?'

She shrugged. 'We search again.'

Bill sighed. 'What if they are true?' he asked.

'If what are true, Elect?'

'The stories of giants.'

'There is nothing in all of Guide's words about giants,' she said.

'There was nothing about strangers either,' he said, 'but today strangers came.'

'They were unguidely, and they brought conjury with them,' she replied.

125

'I understand that,' he said. 'I do. But just because something is unguidely, just because it is not part of Guide's law, it doesn't mean we can ignore it. It could be killing us, Winnowner. Do we let it?'

'Of course not,' she said. 'Survival is the greatest doctrine of all. What is happening to us may be exceptional, and therefore not covered in specifics in Guide's words, but Guide will not fail us. We must look again. Study the passages. Guide will instruct us in ways we have not yet imagined.'

Bill Groan nodded. 'I think so too. We should start again tonight. All night, if it takes it.'

'Agreed,' said Winnowner. 'We will go in and you will say some words of consolation and comfort. Then I will open the Incrypt, and we will withdraw with the council for study.'

Chaunce Plowrite held the door for them and they entered the assembly. It was crowded. Almost every Morphan had come out, except those on nightwatch or with evening labours to perform.

Or those already lost, Bill Groan thought.

There was a hum of chatter in the room, but it died away as they came in and joined the other members of the council to take their seats. Small and very obvious knots of agitation surrounded the families of the missing men.

'What will you do, Elect?' Ela Seed asked, standing up almost at once. Her voice was clear and loud, but strained with worry. Her husband, Dom Seed, was one of the men who had not been seen since Guide's Bell had chimed middle-morning.

'I will ask Guide for direction, Ela,' said Bill Groan.

'Is that not what we have been doing for weeks now?'

asked Lane Cutter. Several of the Morphans around her uttered a rumble of support.

'It is,' said Bill.

'And what good has it done?' Lane asked, her face severe.

'Such talk is verging on the unguidely, Lane,' said Chaunce Plowrite. 'I know you are most concerned at Hud's absence, but—'

'Unguidely, am I now?' asked Lane with a brittle laugh. 'I think Guide has deserted us.'

There was a flurry of talk, some of it dismayed.

'I agree,' said Ela Seed. 'I know we must trust in Guide, and I know patience is our greatest virtue, and I know that those who are patient will provide for all of the plantnation, but we cannot just wait by for this to overcome us. My husband…'

Her voice broke. Her sister rose to steady her.

'We will consult Guide's words tonight,' said Bill. 'Winnowner is going directly to open the Incrypt. We will not rest until we have searched every passage and every section for truth and pertinence.'

'It is either that,' Jack Duggat scoffed, 'or we wait for a miracle!'

Laughter, little of it warm, rolled around the assembly.

'I think a miracle is what we might have found,' said Sol Farrow, speaking from the back of the hall. Everyone turned. He had just come in, bringing snow with him.

'A small one, at any rate,' he said, 'but it gives us hope.'

He turned and beckoned. Two people came in out of the night.

'Oh good Guide,' murmured Bill Groan. 'Vesta Flurrish?'

'I found her coming in from the edge of the woods, Elect,' said Sol.

'I am unhurt, Elect,' Vesta said. Her cold cheeks had flushed in the heat of the assembly room. She indicated the man next to her. 'This is Rory,' she said.

'Um, hello,' said Rory.

The Doctor picked up one of the dead rats by the tail and peered at it. It was heavy, and it swung slightly in his grip. 'Nasty,' he remarked. 'And purpose built.'

'What?' asked Amy. Her hearing was returning, but the world was still sounding muffled. 'Did you say purpose built?'

'Manufactured,' the Doctor said. He reached in and peeled back the dead rat's lips to reveal its metal teeth. 'It's a rat,' he said. 'Definitely a rat. Genetically, a rat. From Earth. But it's been modified. Customised. Enhanced. And on an industrial scale, given the numbers of them.'

'It hasn't got eyes,' said Amy.

'No, because the designers didn't think it needed them. These are sophisticated motion sensors.' He pointed to the foam-like filler that packed the area where an ordinary rat would have had eyes.

'Motion?'

'In space, particularly interstellar space, it's cold and often very, very dark. So motion is a much more sensible format to base your sensory function on. There are some fairly advanced acoustic sensors there too.'

'Wait,' said Amy, shaking her head and frowning. She knew it wasn't possible and she knew it wouldn't do any good, but she really wanted a cotton bud. Her ears felt like they were gummed up with glue. 'Start again. We're not in space.'

'No,' agreed the Doctor, lifting his arm so he could study

the suspended rat from below. 'We're in the terraformer. That's one of the very big machines that the original Morphans constructed to change Hereafter from Earth-*esque* to properly Earth-*like*.'

'You mean the Firmers?' asked Arabel. 'The Terra Firmers?'

'The three mountains that aren't mountains?' asked Amy.

The Doctor smiled and nodded. 'Yes,' he said. 'I think we're in Firmer Number Two, if I've been listening to Arabel correctly and my sense of direction is unerring.' He looked at Amy. 'And it is,' he grinned.

'We're underneath the mountain?' asked Samewell.

'This is what a Firmer looks like inside. Well, part of it.'

'And that factory noise?' asked Amy.

'The vast engines of the Firmer at work,' said the Doctor. 'Atmospheric processors, geo-seismic actuators, meteorological generators, seeding pumps. It's a world factory. It's changing the world. And it's been doing it for twenty-seven generations. It's an extraordinary piece of large-scale engineering performing an even more extraordinary and even more mind-bogglingly large-scale piece of engineering.'

'So returning to my original question,' said Amy, pointing. '"Blind space rats? *Huh?*"'

'Transrats is a better term,' said the Doctor. 'Like Transhumans. Re-engineering both genetically and biologically to be more rat than rat. A living tool, if you like.'

'I've met more than one of those,' said Amy.

'During the great Diaspora Era,' said the Doctor, 'when mankind was spreading out from Earth, they were quite common on bulk generation starships or hibernation arks. Those vessels are huge, like small countries in space. And they travelled for many lifetimes to reach their destinations. The human passengers would spend thousands of years in suspended animation, ready to wake when they arrived at their final colonial destination, or else they would live out lives during the travel time. Whole civilisations could rise and fall on a generation starship in the time it took to reach another star.'

'Seriously?' asked Amy.

The Doctor nodded. 'And eco-systems would develop in the ship interiors in the meantime. Pests, lice, dirt, rodents. Mankind quickly learned that the best way to keep a generation starship clean was to keep them purged. Rats eat anything. So mankind engineered rats that could survive in almost any conditions and could eat anything. Transrats lived in the dark corners of the ships, basically eating anything that wasn't supposed to be there.'

'So… these came here on the Morphans' original ship?' asked Amy.

'Well, yes and no,' said the Doctor. 'The idea of them did, the technology. But they wouldn't have lasted for twenty-seven generations. They're not immortal, and they don't breed. These were manufactured recently.'

'Meaning?'

The Doctor exhaled thoughtfully. 'Meaning there's an automated manufacturing plant for this kind of thing here somewhere, and also a genetic stockpile containing rat DNA that it could access in order to breed new rats for conversion.'

'A rat factory?' asked Amy. 'Making easy-to-build rats?'

'Flat-pack rats,' the Doctor agreed. He swung the rat he

was holding around by the tail like it was a bolas. 'Easy to build. Disposable.'

'But why?' asked Amy.

'Presumably because there's something wrong,' said the Doctor. He stopped spinning the rat, realising it was pretty undignified for both of them.

'The terraformer system has detected a loss of efficiency or some other defect,' he said, 'and it's automatically starting diagnostic procedures to address it. Transrats would be a first step. Build some, release them into the systems, clean out any dirt, or clutter, or infestation, or glitches.'

'Glitches, huh?' said Amy. She looked at the rat-thing the Doctor was holding. 'They seemed really hungry.'

'Because they're not the solution to the problem afflicting the terraformers,' said the Doctor. 'It's not a problem you can eat.'

'But if they got out,' said Bel. 'They'd attack sheep... goats...'

'They might,' the Doctor agreed. 'Hungry, and outside the system control of the terraformer, they could go on a frenzy. That would explain the livestock kills.'

'So the Ice Men haven't been killing and devouring sheep, then?' asked Amy. '*Warriors.* I meant Warriors.'

'No,' said the Doctor, 'which sorts out one of my original problems. I suspected Ice Warriors from the start. The moment I realised that something was trying to manipulate an entire planet's climate and make it colder, I immediately thought of Ice Warriors.'

'Well, who wouldn't?' asked Amy.

'Quite,' said the Doctor.

'That was your hunch? The hunch you said you'd got?'

'Yes,' replied the Doctor. 'It fitted the modus operandi of the Ice Warriors, except for one small detail. They're herbivorous.'

'So they wouldn't be eating livestock,' said Amy, 'but these rats would.'

The Doctor swung the dead rat by the tail like a conker on a string. 'Yes, if they got out. But the terraforming system should be sealed enough to prevent them escaping into the wild.'

'You reckon the Ice Warriors broke into the terrafirmer and did something to sabotage it,' said Amy, 'and you also reckon the terrafirmer detected that sabotage as a problem and built the transrats to deal with it. Makes sense that the transrats would have got out through whatever hole the Ice Warriors made to get in. That's how they got out and started eating sheep.'

'Nice deduction, Pond,' said the Doctor.

'Why would these Ice Warrior things attack the Firmers, though?' asked Arabel.

'Because they want an Earth-like planet too, but their idea of Earth-like is colder not warmer,' replied the Doctor.

Arabel shook her head. 'I don't…' she began.

'Your ancestors,' said the Doctor, 'the original Morphans, were looking for a planet like Earth.'

'Like Earth before?' asked Samewell.

'Yes, like Earth before. But the chances of them finding a world that was exactly like Earth before were slim. I mean, the variables are huge. The best chance they had was to find a planet that was sufficiently like Earth—'

'Earth-esque,' said Amy.

'Precisely right,' said the Doctor. 'If they could find a

planet that was sufficiently Earth-esque, then they could use the sophisticated terramorphing systems they had on their colony ark ship to tweak the climate and make it perfect. That's what you've been doing for twenty-seven generations. You've been watching over things while the terrafirmers tweak and fine-tune Hereafter to make it just right.'

'And these charming Ice Warrior blokes,' said Amy, 'have a very different concept of just right.'

'They need an Earth-like planet too,' said the Doctor, 'but their idea of Earth-like is not like your idea of Earth-like, it's like—'

'Way too many likes there, Doctor,' said Amy.

'OK, in broad terms you're both looking for the same sort of world, but their ideal environmental baseline is between fifty and seventy-five degrees cooler than humanity's.'

'So they're fighting against us?' asked Arabel.

'I've known them sabotage biomes before,' said the Doctor grimly. 'I've seen them doing their own terraforming. I even saw them try it on Earth once. On Earth before, before Earth before was lost. I've never seen them hijack someone else's terraforming system and recalibrate it. Typical Ice Warrior pragmatism.'

'How did you stop the rats?' Samewell asked. He copied the Doctor and picked up one of the dead rats by the tail.

The Doctor put down the rat he was dangling. He fished his sonic screwdriver out of his jacket pocket. 'I noticed the enhanced acoustic sensors,' he said. 'I guessed they'd be particularly sensitive to sonic attack. I hoped a little high-frequency burst would be enough to zap them or drive them off.'

'And deafen me,' said Amy.

'I trusted your ears wouldn't be quite as sensitive as theirs,' said the Doctor.

'Well, I'll take earache over being eaten alive by rats any day,' Amy started to say.

Samewell let out a screech of alarm. The transrat he'd picked up wasn't dead. It suddenly shivered, twitched, and woke from the fugue state the Doctor had blasted it into. Its huge jaws opened like a spring trap. Massive steel-veneered teeth gleamed in the half-light. Swinging itself by its tail, the rat started to snap and gnash at Samewell.

'Put it down!' Bel yelled.

'Don't put it down! Keep it at arm's length!' Amy shouted.

'Aaaaaaaaaahhhh!' Samewell observed.

The Doctor clicked open his screwdriver and calmly aimed it at the aggressive creature. Nothing happened. 'Ooops,' he said.

'Doctor!'

He fiddled with the screwdriver.

'I've asked too much of it today already,' he said, 'what with noise-cancelling the Ice Warriors and zapping the transrats, it's really drained. It's gone into sleep mode.'

'Doctor!'

Amy lunged and grabbed the rat's tail out of Samewell's grip. He was still yelping in alarm. The transrat snapped at her repeatedly, trying to chomp her arm or her face.

'Yeah, yeah,' Amy snarled and swung it by the tail hard into the tunnel wall. It went limp and she dropped it. 'Worked last time,' she said.

'Who is this Rory?' asked Bill Groan.

'He's my friend, Elect,' replied Vesta. 'We met in the woods. We were both threatened. He looked out for me.'

'I see,' said Bill Groan.

'I may have hit him on the head with a mallet too,' Vesta admitted.

'But that's totally not important,' said Rory.

'He's a stranger,' said Chaunce Plowrite.

'Yes,' said Vesta.

'Another stranger,' said Old Winnowner. 'That's three today.'

A hush had fallen on the assembly. Everyone was staring at Vesta and Rory. Rory felt pretty uncomfortable. In the solamp light, the faces around him were stern and unforgiving. They seemed to be searching for answers, as though they might peel back or melt away his skin to find the secrets they were looking for. There was pent-up emotion in the hall. These were people who had lived hard lives and, no matter how hard they worked, they did not expect those lives to change. Something profound mattered to them, something that threatened what little comfort and solace they had in their lives, and they wanted answers.

Despite sensing that, Rory could not help asking the question.

'These other strangers, the other two? Were they... a girl with long red hair and a tall bloke?'

Everyone around him started muttering and chattering.

'He admits to knowing them,' said Old Winnowner.

'Are they here?' asked Rory.

'They were here,' said Bill Groan. 'They escaped.'

'How could they escape?' asked Rory. 'What did they escape from? Why did they need to escape?'

'They were found to be unguidely and discovered in the practice of conjury,' said Old Winnowner. 'We placed them in the compter.'

'You locked them up?' asked Rory. 'You locked the Doctor and Amy up? That's a really bad idea.'

'They are his friends!' Vesta broke in. 'He was travelling with them. Travelling here to well-wish us at the time of festival!'

'They were miscreants sent to—' Winnowner began.

'Travelling from where?' asked Bill Groan, cutting her short.

'Rory and his friends come from a plantnation that we have not heard of,' said Vesta.

'That's not possible!' said Bill Groan.

'It's unguidely!' cried Winnowner.

'It's the truth!' replied Vesta. The voices around the hall had become quite a hubbub. 'What is your plantnation called again, Rory?'

'Leadworth. It's called Leadworth.'

'This is nonsense and it is against Guide's way!' said Chaunce Plowrite.

'Look, I don't mean to cause trouble,' said Rory, trying to impose some calm. 'Where I come from doesn't really matter. What does matter is that there's something out there. Something in the woods. And it's dangerous. You've got to prepare to defend yourselves.'

'What thing?' asked Jack Duggat.

'I got separated from my friends, and it attacked me,' said Rory.

'It has red eyes!' announced Vesta.

'It has red eyes,' Rory agreed. 'It attacked Vesta too. It's very dangerous. I ran away from it. I had to escape. That's when I met Vesta.'

'Why should we believe you?' asked Chaunce Plowrite. Several members of the congregation echoed him.

'Because it's dangerous!' said Rory. 'I saw it attack some men. I think they were from here. It attacked them. It hurt them.'

'What were their names?' asked Winnowner.

'I don't know! We hadn't been introduced.'

'What did they look like?' Ela Seed demanded.

'I… I… They looked like they came from here.'

'Was one of them my husband?' asked Lane Cutter.

'I don't know!'

'It hurt them, you say?' asked Bill Groan.

'Did it kill them?' asked Ela Seed frantically. 'Are they dead?'

The clamour was becoming quite intense. Morphans closed on Rory from all sides. They were angry and upset, reaching out to him.

'Get back there!' Sol Farrow told them. 'Mind him! Get away!'

'Leave him be!' Vesta yelled.

'Calm yourselves! Calm yourselves!' Bill Groan shouted over the din, pushing his way through the milling crowd. 'This is unseemly! Be calm now or I will have the assembly cleared! This will not do! Leave him be!'

The crowd would not be hushed. It was turning very ugly. People were pushing and shoving to get at Rory.

'You should not treat him so!' Vesta yelled at them. 'He is our guest, and a friend! You should not treat a Nurse Elect in this manner!'

Bill Groan heard her over the row. 'He's what?' Bill looked at Sol and Jack.

The two men nodded and grabbed Rory and Vesta. They began to bundle them through the angry, mobbing crowd, heading for the rear of the assembly hall. People started to protest. They threw punches and grabbed.

Old Winnowner was waiting at the back for them. She had taken out the key, which she wore on a ribbon around her neck, and used it to open the padlock to the back doors of the hall. Jack and Sol brought Rory and Vesta through, followed by Winnowner and Bill Groan. Bill and the old woman bolted the doors behind them to keep the mob back. Morphans started shouting and banging at the doors.

Rory look around. They'd come through into a large wooden antechamber behind the main hall. There were clerestory lights high up by the roof, and rush matting on the wooden floor. On the far side of the room was an ornate door made of what the Morphans called shipskin. It was set in a complex frame, and reminded Rory of some kind of futuristic airlock or submarine hatch.

'We can be calm here for a moment,' said Bill Groan.

'Where is here?' asked Rory, shaking off Sol's grip.

'It's the outer room of Guide's place,' said Old Winnowner.

'What's that?' asked Rory, pointing at the metal hatch.

'That's the door to the Incrypt,' said Vesta. 'That's where Guide's words live. Only the council go in there.'

'Stop asking questions and answer some,' said Bill to Rory. 'She said you are a Nurse. Is that true? You are a Nurse Elect?'

'Yes, I... yes. Yes, I am,' said Rory.

'Then I greet you, one Nurse Elect to another,' said Bill Groan with touching formality.

'It is a lie or a trick,' said Winnowner. 'Those others, whom he admits to knowing, said they were from Seeside, and they bore conjury to convince us so—'

'Maybe there are things we don't know about!' snapped Vesta.

The Morphans looked at her.

'I'm saying, maybe there are,' she said. 'Don't look at me so. I don't hardly know what Rory is, except that he is nice and kind, and I don't know about his friends either, but I do know there is something in the woods outside the plantnation that is most angry and dangerous, and I know it is not mentioned *anywhere* in Guide's teaching. So what do we do about it? Do we just pretend it does not exist because Guide has not spoken of it?'

'Guide gives us rules to live by for our own good, Vesta,' Winnowner said.

'The thing in the woods proves one matter, Winnowner,' Vesta told the old woman. 'It proves there are things in this world Hereafter that are more than are in Guide's words. The thing is one, Rory may be one too, also his friends and whatever plantnation they come from. I ask you, do we stand there accusing them of being unguidely, or do we do something about them?'

'We could prove it,' said Bill Groan quietly.

'What now?' asked Winnowner.

'You know that, Winnowner,' he said. 'We have both been taught it. We know Guide's doctrines, and the schema of words that instructs the Morphans. Our Guide Emanual will recognise and identify those things that belong to Guide. Only the true unguidely will remain strangers and unknown. If… Rory here is truly a Nurse Elect, then Guide will know him. Guide knows his own.'

'What are you suggesting, Elect?' asked Winnowner.

'You know what I'm suggesting,' said Bill.

Winnowner shook her head. 'Elect, this is the threshold

of the Incrypt, our most precious place. Only the most worthy and maintained of Morphan kind can pass this way and be received of Guide's words.'

'My point exactly,' said Bill Groan. 'Let Rory prove himself.'

The knocking at the doors and the clamour of voices was not abating. Winnowner looked Rory up and down.

'This isn't going to be some kind of… trial by combat, is it?' Rory asked warily. 'Or, by sharks or spiders or something? If there's a pit or a cage involved, or a choice of weapons, I'm really not up for it. Especially if there's baying and jeering going on too.'

'Nothing like that,' said Bill Groan. He walked over to the metal hatch. 'Come over here, Rory,' he said, beckoning.

Rory walked up to him in a slightly unwilling manner.

Bill Groan pointed. There was a flat panel of matt silver metal set into the hatch frame on the right-hand side. It was about the size of a hardback book and it was built in at door-handle height.

'That's the chequer,' he said. 'It knows the touch of those that are worthy and, through it, Guide knows us.'

Bill placed his palm flat on the panel. A neon glow travelled up the metal under his hand. There was a click, and then a hiss, and then the hatch opened. Clean, cool air breathed out at them. Through the open hatch, Rory could see some sort of chamber bathed in a bluish neon illumination.

'The Incrypt opens to my hand,' said Bill. He touched the panel again. The hatch closed as gently as it had opened.

'It's a palm reader,' said Rory. 'It's biometric. It's reading your handprint, or maybe your genetic pattern.'

'You try,' said Bill.

'Oh, I don't think that's such a good idea,' said Rory.

'If you're a Nurse Elect, Guide will recognise you and let you in,' said Winnowner.

'Really, I—' Rory said.

'Try,' ordered Bill Groan.

Rory placed his hand flat on the panel.

CHAPTER 11
THE MAKER
OF OUR EARTH

With the Doctor enthusiastically leading the way, they explored the deep chambers and tunnels of the massive terraformer plant.

The simple scale of it silenced Bel and Samewell, and took Amy back a bit too. The machined and engineered cavities inside the artificial mountain were bigger than any machine, factory or structure she'd ever seen on Earth. They also matched or exceeded the scale of structures she'd seen since leaving Earth and travelling aboard the TARDIS.

They followed winding tunnels lined in galvanised metal plates or slightly tarnished sheets of shipskin. They entered chambers that had been hollowed out of the hill so that the face of the rock was cut perfectly smooth and straight-edged, like set and polished concrete. Colossal machines that Amy thought of as turbines dominated these chambers, feeding whatever energies or processes they output into vast networks of gleaming metal pipes and condensers. Some of these pipes, large enough in cross-section to take two trains on parallel lines, exited into vent stacks, or swept down into stone floors, connected to other, deeper chambers and larger, stranger machines.

Sometimes, the Doctor and his companions came out of tunnels onto mesh walkways of welded shipskin that crossed, precipitously, the middle of vast subterranean spaces, delicate bridges suspended hundreds of metres above the chamber floors from which they could look up at dim ceilings thousands of metres above, or peer down into heat-exchange trenches or energy sinks or other abyssal clefts that pulsed with distant glimmers of energy, and dropped away into the planet's crust for miles. Warm updrafts touched their faces and billowed their hair.

'I've run out of words for big,' said Amy.

'None of them seem adequate, do they?' the Doctor agreed.

Everywhere they went, they could hear the whirr and hum of the giant mechanisms. Occasionally, they could also hear the scratch and scurry of transrats emanating from blind tunnels or side vents.

They entered one chamber on the level of the rock floor and found it to be the largest they had seen yet. Its dizzying space was dominated by a massive column of silvery metal that was fed by a cobweb of tubes and ducts. It looked like a huge chrome oak tree. High up, the roof of the titanic chamber was hazed by clouds of vapour, so that the branches of the giant metal tree appeared to be swathed in ghostly foliage.

'Are those clouds?' Amy asked, looking up.

The Doctor nodded.

It was drizzling slightly, like a wet autumnal day. The chamber was so big, it had its own weather system.

'That's a secondary sequence prebiotic crucible,' said the

Doctor, with the appreciative tone of a twitcher who has just spotted a very rare species. 'What a beauty.'

'What does it do?' asked Bel.

'It makes the world a better place,' said the Doctor. 'In human terms, anyway. It makes life. It's gently sculpting and shaping the ecosystem of Hereafter.'

'You said secondary,' said Amy.

'What?'

'You said it was a secondary sequence something or other.'

'Yes,' said the Doctor, matter-of-factly. 'There'll be about a hundred of these, all supporting the main sequence crucibles. I hope we get a look at one of those, because they're really big.'

Amy grinned at him. 'I don't often get to see you actually impressed,' she said.

'How could you fail to be?' he replied. 'This is human engineering at pretty much its peak. This is the point at which those little apes from Earth actually advanced so far they could rebuild and redesign whole planets. That's the mark of a great species. To be fair, it's a slow old process. It takes hundreds of years, and the people who start the process don't live anything like long enough to see the end, but still they do it. That's what I love about people. They have dreams and grand ambitions, and they start building towards them, even though they know they won't live to see them finished. That's how the pyramids were built. And the great cathedrals of the middle ages. People were prepared to invest in the future. They were prepared to donate the labour of their entire lives to a greater whole that other lives, future lives, would benefit from.'

Amy glanced across at Samewell and Arabel, who were

standing in reserved awe, gazing up at the vast machine, rain speckling their faces.

'What happens if it takes so long they start to forget what it's all for?' she asked.

'The Morphans haven't forgotten, Pond,' said the Doctor. 'They know what they're doing with their Terra Formers. They're committed to the process. They're sticking to the great plan.'

'Yeah, but even so,' said Amy. 'It's taken so long, they've started to misremember. It's taken so long... What did Bel say? Twenty-seven generations? They don't even understand the technology any more. It's all automatic. They're like the transrats living in the shadow of a machine that works all by itself. Sure, they know their routines and their jobs, and I'm sure they understand what they're part of, it's just...'

'What?'

'What happens when it ends?' she asked. 'I mean, when the job's done? Will they be ready for that?'

'It won't happen for several more generations,' said the Doctor.

'That's my point. Will the great-great-great-grandchildren of these Morphans know any better? Will they be ready? Isn't there a danger they won't know what to do with the world they've built, because all they've ever learned to do is survive during the process of building?'

'I'm sure they'll take to it,' said the Doctor.

'What did the stonemasons of Europe do when there were no cathedrals left to build?' she asked. 'What did the slaves do when the pyramids were finished? How did they feel?'

The Doctor thought about it and frowned.

'These Morphans are really good people, what I've seen of them,' said Amy. 'They're hardworking and selfless and totally serious about their lives. But it really feels to me like they only understand this, the work in progress. I don't know what they'll do when the job's finished.'

'Well,' replied the Doctor, 'that's what life and evolution is all about. The Morphans are adapting a world to fit their biology. When it's ready, when it's properly Earth-like, they'll have to adapt their minds and attitudes to make the most of living in it.'

He fell silent for a moment.

'What's the matter?' asked Amy.

'There's always the question of if they're actually going to get a chance to make a go of it anyway, of course,' said the Doctor. 'A problem that starts with Ice…'

'And ends with Warriors,' Amy said, and nodded.

'This sightseeing is all very interesting and rather uplifting,' the Doctor told her, 'but I need to work out exactly what the Ice Warriors are doing to the Firmer systems.'

'And stop them?'

'Yes,' he nodded. 'I actually have a lot of time and respect for the Martian culture, but in this instance, I'm on the Morphans' side. They have the claim here, and the Ice Warriors are essentially trying to wipe them out. We have to put things right for the Morphans.'

They started walking again, and crossed through another tunnel link into a chamber cavity that opened a giddying drop beneath their narrow shipskin walkway. Far below, magmatic forces rumbled and glowed.

'Not being funny, but how are we going to win this?' asked Amy quietly. 'The Ice Warriors are very big, very strong, and very hench. And they've got sound guns and spaceships and all kinds of freaky nastiness. On our side, we've got a bunch of farmers whose idea of a weapon is a garden rake. If it comes to a fight, it's going to be really one-sided.'

'Then we have to be clever and not let it come to a fight,' said the Doctor. 'We take on the Ice Warriors by outsmarting them.'

'Are they stupid, then?'

'No, not at all,' said the Doctor. 'They're really very intelligent. But I'm me.'

'OK,' she said, 'hit me with your clever.'

'We find out how they're sabotaging things, and we sabotage their sabotage. That's how we beat them.'

'It's that easy?' asked Amy.

'No, that's going to be ridiculously hard,' the Doctor said with a sigh.

'I thought you were super-smart?'

'Have you seen the scale and size and complexity of this system? It's going to take me a while to identify exactly what the Ice Warriors are doing, and then I've got to work out how to repair or reverse it. And I have to do all of that without mucking up any of the other systems. This is a very finely balanced process. Plus, these terraformers are automated systems. A lot of the component units are sealed because there's supposed to be no need for manual repair. A lot of them are physically inaccessible. How would you get down there if that needed fixing, for instance?'

She peered over the rail and shuddered.

'Not to mention,' said the Doctor, mentioning it, 'that I'm temporarily without a working sonic screwdriver, which makes everything a gazillion times harder.'

'It'll recharge,' Amy reassured him.

'I know,' he said, 'but we haven't got a lot of time. And my biggest concern is not to damage the terraforming systems. My normal approach, as you well know, is to fiddle and improvise, but if I attempt too much of that, I could end up doing more damage than the Ice Warriors. You know what I could really do with?'

'The Big Book of Terraforming For Beginners?' she asked.

'Yes, actually,' he replied. 'What I could really do with is the instruction manual that came with this planet cruncher.'

'It'll be in the glove box,' grinned Amy.

Bel came over to them, followed by Samewell. She was wrinkling her nose. 'What's that smell?' she asked.

The Doctor sniffed. 'Sulphur, from the mantle vents,' he said.

'No, there's something else,' said Amy.

The Doctor sniffed again. 'You're right, Pond,' he said. 'I impaired your hearing so your sense of smell has compensated. That's… decay. That's something rotten.'

'Whatever, it's not very nice,' said Arabel.

The Doctor was already moving. They followed him along the walkway, through a rock-cut tunnel, and down a metal-lined corridor that opened out into a broad, domed room that looked like some kind of store. By the time they entered it, the smell of putrefaction had become very strong.

'Ugh,' said Amy, covering her nose and mouth. 'That's rank.'

'Decaying organic matter,' the Doctor mused. 'But why down here?'

The walls of the domed room were lined with rows of plastic-fronted cupboards, each one containing a bio-hazard suit and mask, made for a human.

'This was a prep area,' said the Doctor. 'Scientists or technicians came in here to suit up. See overhead?' He pointed at banks of blue lights built into the domed roof. 'UV decontamination lamps,' he mused. 'They came in here, suited up and sterilised themselves…'

He went back to the doorway they had entered through. It was a sliding hatch, but it had already been open when they arrived.

'Look,' he said. There was a panel of silver metal in the frame to the right-hand side of the hatch. Something very hot had cut through it, fusing it. The edges of the metal cut looked like melted butter. They were blackened.

'That's a palm-scan checker,' said the Doctor. 'It operates the lock. Something cut through it from outside to get in here.'

'Something hot,' said Amy.

'I think focused sonics, actually,' the Doctor replied. He crossed to the open hatchway on the other side of the domed prep-room. That was open too. Similar damage had been done to the palm-scanner. The smell of rot and decay was much stronger on that side of the room.

'Let's see, shall we?' the Doctor suggested. He went through the open hatchway. They followed him.

On the other side, they found themselves at one end of a gallery space.

The gallery was large and very long. Very, *very* long. At least a mile long. It was immense. It reminded Amy of an industrial nursery, a massive greenhouse, except that it was underground. Banks of bright, artificial sun lamps ran along the roof, and the galvanised metal floor was lined with rows of deep metal tanks and glass vats. It seemed like something had been growing in here, a considerable crop of things.

The smell in the gallery was awful, like bins left out on a summer's day, six weeks into a garbage strike.

'What is this? Are they growing plants?' asked Amy.

'Certainly cultivation of some sort,' the Doctor agreed. 'I didn't expect this. Unless…'

He peered into one of the vats.

'Unless what?' asked Samewell.

'These cultivator units have broken down,' said the Doctor. 'There's been a malfunction and they've failed. Perhaps a deliberate malfunction. The reason they smell so bad is that it's not plant matter they're nurturing here. These were in-vitro nutrient banks for organic tissue.'

'Why?' asked Amy. She climbed up beside the Doctor and peered over into the vat. The stink that wafted up at her was frankly appalling. The vat was basically empty, but from a tide mark on the side, she could see where it had previously been full. The bottom of the tank was filled with a slimy, foul-smelling residue, like something gruesome and decomposing from a horror movie. 'Oh, that is properly disgusting,' she announced.

'Yes, but why?' the Doctor pondered, tapping a finger to his lips. 'Why tissue? I suppose this could have been some kind of storage system for organic samples. Maybe the DNA used to build the transrats was kept in suspension in this sort of thing. This may have been a genetic stockpile, a library of animal DNA, so that the Morphans could grow all sorts of strains of creature once the world was ready.'

'Really?' asked Amy. 'So this was... this *muck*... this was living tissue? Like flesh and blood?'

The Doctor nodded. 'But the vital support system has failed or been sabotaged. Sabotaged is my guess, from the way the hatches were forced. Now it's beginning to rot,' he said. 'So the genetic database is corrupted.'

He looked at Amy.

'Or,' he said, drawing out the word.

'Or what?' she asked.

'Or this wasn't a genetic library at all,' he said. 'It was an organic farm.'

'How do you mean?'

'I mean,' said the Doctor, 'that someone or something was growing meat in these tanks.'

Amy pulled a revolted face.

'Like something out of Frankenstein's lab?' she asked.

'Yes,' said the Doctor, 'but an awful lot less nice.'

The hatch to the Incrypt waited for a moment, considering the scan of Rory's palm. Rory stood with his hand pressed to the plate and a sick, fixed grin on his face, frantically working out what he would say when the hatch didn't open.

He'd just come up with an absolutely killer approach that would absolutely, without question, persuade Bill Groan and the other Morphans he was on the level, despite the non-compliance of the hatch, but then the hatch opened and he never got a chance to use it.

'You see?' he said, hoping the billion tons of relief freighting his voice at that moment would not be obvious.

'Well,' said Bill Groan.

'Guide preserve us,' said Winnowner.

'We have done you a disservice, Elect Rory,' said Sol Farrow.

'That's entirely OK and fine,' said Rory shaking his head and swallowing hard. 'I understand that you have to be careful, especially with all the... the things that are happening. Shall we?'

He moved towards the hatch.

'Well, there's no need to go in now, is there?' asked Winnowner. Jack Duggat half-blocked Rory's nonchalant advance.

'I mean,' said the old woman, 'the point was to see if you could open the door, and that point's been made. There's no need to go in.'

'Well, no, I suppose,' said Rory.

'We had resolved to consult our Guide Emanual,' Bill Groan said to Winnowner. 'The chequer has confirmed Elect Rory's worthiness. Why would we not include him in our study?'

Winnowner dropped her voice and spoke very directly and intently to Bill Groan.

'Our council,' she hissed. 'Our council, not anybody else's! This is a matter for Beside, and the council of Beside, and the word of our Guide Emanual as it is expressed to our council, not to anyone else! I'm sure Elect Rory and his council would not wish any of us to go prying into his Incrypt if we were visiting his plantnation.'

'What about a fresh eye, an alternative approach?' Vesta suggested.

'No!' snapped Winnowner.

'It's not for you to say no,' said Bill Groan.

'Nor is it for you to say yes,' replied Winnowner. 'The council must vote on it. That is all there is to it.'

Bill Groan nodded. He glanced at Sol. 'Can we get back into the hall?'

The hammering had died away. It seemed quieter in the assembly. Things had calmed down. Or things were waiting to pounce the moment the doors opened.

'Jack and I will check,' Sol replied.

'Send everyone home except the council,' said Bill. 'Clear the assembly. We need to settle this and we need to get on. If this danger is as urgent as Vesta and Rory say…'

The two men unbolted the doors and went back into the hall. Rory heard a renewed round of raised voices. He glanced at Vesta, worried. She smiled back reassuringly.

After a couple of minutes, Sol reappeared at the doors and beckoned them through. The assembly room had been emptied apart from the remaining council members. One of Jack Duggat's labourers was closing up the outer doors. Nothing had been overturned, but many of the chairs and benches in the congregation section had been pushed aside or left in disarray. The meeting had not ended happily.

'I had to bend the truth a little,' Rory heard Jack Duggat mutter to Bill Groan. 'I told them they had to return to their homes tonight because Guide needed the space. Deliberations had to be made. I told them it was Guide's express desire.'

'Guide will forgive you, Jack,' Bill replied.

'I said they'd have answers come Guide's Bell,' Jack added.

'Then we'll have to find them by then,' said Bill.

He gestured to Vesta, indicating she should take Rory to one side and be seated. There was drink and a little food set out on a sideboard. Rory hadn't realised just how hungry he was. He took some kind of soup, and some spelt bread, and watched as the council sat in discussion. Vesta ate too, with gusto, her eyes not leaving the debating council members.

'Oh,' she said suddenly, and sadly.

'What?' asked Rory. Before she could answer, he saw that Bill Groan was coming over.

'We've taken the vote,' Bill said. 'It's gone against you. I'm sorry, Elect.'

'OK,' said Rory. 'What happens now?'

'The Council will withdraw to the Incrypt and start work,' said Bill. 'I suggest you two stay here for now. Stay close by so we can talk, if we need to. Help yourself to more food. Rest a while.'

Bill walked back to the council members, who stood and followed him through the doors into the Incrypt. Jack Duggat went with them, leaving Sol Farrow behind to keep an eye on them. Sol closed the back doors, and then shrugged at Vesta and Rory, acknowledging that he shared their helplessness. Then he ladled out a bowl of soup and went to sit by one of the firebuckets.

Rory sat while Vesta and Sol continued to eat. He listened to the crack and pop of the embers in the firebuckets. A soft but steady tapping on the panes of the assembly windows told him it was snowing hard again.

He realised that, despite the dangers and alarms of the day, waiting was perhaps the worst thing of all.

'Can we leave this place now?' Amy asked. 'Because it pongs.'

'Uh-huh,' the Doctor nodded. She could tell he wasn't really listening. He was too deep in thought. She could almost see the cogs going around.

'Shall we go out the way we came in?' she asked, gesturing to the door that led back into the prep room.

'Mm-hmm,' he said. She still didn't have his attention properly. He was just making sounds in response to her sounds, encouraging, non-specific sounds that created the illusion of an actual conversation without him having to engage in one.

That worried Amy. When the Doctor got side-tracked and lost in thought, it meant that there was a lot at stake. There was clearly a big problem on Hereafter, a proper, serious life-and/or-death problem. She'd worked that much out for herself. But the Doctor seemed to be troubled because, on top of the problem, there was a mystery as well.

She knew the Doctor quite liked problems. It didn't matter how big, or difficult, or scary, or intractable, or galaxy-crushing, or *tal-king-like-this-in-a-ras-ping-mon-o-tone-ro-bot-voice-and-u-sing-words-like-ex-ter-min-ate* a problem was, the Doctor relished them. He could confront them. He could take them on. He could solve them. He could usually say something quite pithy and off the cuff while solving them.

Mysteries, on the other hand, nagged. They festered and itched. They got him distracted and made him fidgety. A problem and a mystery at the same time was a body blow, because the Doctor could only get on with solving the problem once he'd explained the mystery.

The mystery here had various elements: the complexity and scale of the terraformer, the machinations of the surly and relentless Ice Warriors, and the seriously terrible weather. Amy thought that, if it was up to her, she might choose to add a complete and utter lack of Christmas to the list, but that seemed unfair. However, there were other elements. Something to do with this giant greenhouse stacked with tanks of rotting meat, for a start. She didn't really get the significance of that, but it seemed to trouble the Doctor greatly. It didn't seem to fit with the other things he was worried about. It was odd. It was inexplicable.

Still, a bad smell was a bad smell, and a bad smell would have come as a welcome and fragrant breath of fresh air compared to the honk in the gallery. They'd been obliged to stand around in that place, surrounded by those reeking vats, for far too long as it was.

'We'll go back out then?' she prompted.

'Mm-hmm.'

He wasn't even looking at her. He was pacing up and down, his finger to his lips.

'We'll come back out through that prep room with all the suits, then?' she asked. 'Find something else to look at?'

'Uh-huh.'

She turned to Bel and Samewell.

'Come on,' she said. 'If we start walking, he'll follow us.'

They started walking back along the row of vats towards the exit hatch. Sure enough, the Doctor followed them, though he was still so deeply submerged in thought it looked like he needed an idea snorkel.

They went out through the domed prep room with the Doctor tagging along behind.

'Maybe we'll find a nice spot for a picnic?' Amy called out over her shoulder.

'Mm-hmm,' the Doctor responded.

'He's not listening to us,' Amy said to Samewell and Bel. 'His mind's gone walkabout. He's going into thinky overdrive.'

'Does he get like this often?' asked Arabel.

'Yeah,' said Amy. 'Check this out.' Still walking, she called out over her shoulder, 'I see the walruses are very big this season.'

'Mmmmm.'

'They're flowering very early.'

'Mm-hmmm.'

'Nice to see them playing glockenspiels, though, eh?'

'Mmmmm.'

With her eyes and mouth open wide in mock dismay, Amy shook her head at Samewell and Bel, and made them both laugh.

Suddenly, the Doctor was right beside them. He was staring straight ahead. He was alarmingly alert.

'We've got to go back,' he said quietly.

'What?' Amy asked.

He forced them to stop walking by sticking his arm out in front of them, and craned his head, listening.

'What?' Amy repeated.

'We've definitely got to go back,' he said.

'Into the stinky room? Why?'

'Shhh!' he said. 'Can't you hear that?'

Amy couldn't hear anything.

'We've got to go back,' said the Doctor. 'Or at the very least, we've got to *not* go this way.'

Then Amy heard it too. It was far away and coming from up ahead. It was the sound of footsteps. Heavy, regular, lumbering footsteps.

'Stay!' the Doctor whispered to them, as though his raised index finger would freeze them to the spot. He edged forward until he could peer down the corridor ahead.

The footsteps were getting closer. He saw movement

first, then a shadow, cast on the corridor wall by a row of solamps.

There was no mistaking the silhouette.

He turned to them.

'Ice Warriors,' he said. 'Coming this way. Run.'

'Regular running or run for your life running?' asked Amy.

'What do you think?' the Doctor replied.

They ran.

They ran back through the prep room and into the organic gallery, ignoring the smell. The Doctor skidded to a halt in the doorway, checking the door panel to see if there was any way to close and lock the hatch behind them. Whatever had bored through the mechanism to open it had fused the hatch motors. The hatch was wedged open.

'Keep going!' he yelled, running to catch up with them. They were running down the length of the vast gallery, following the grilled metal pathways between the stinking vats and the glass tanks clotted with slime.

'How do you know there'll be an exit at the far end?' Amy shouted at the Doctor.

'I don't!' he replied.

'Then what?'

'We don't have a lot of choice!' he replied.

Amy glanced back. Always a mistake, but she did it anyway.

She could see the entry hatch fifty metres behind her. The first of the Ice Warriors had appeared. There were three of them. They were so big, they had to come through the hatchway one at a time. There was something flat and expressionless about their faces. The overhead light banks reflected off their red lenses. They walked like hit-men, hired killers wearing expensive shades.

At least, she thought, the rows of vats and metal tanks would provide a little shelter and cover if the Ice Men started using their guns. Warriors. *Warriors.*

One last glimpse behind her showed her they weren't packing guns at all.

They were carrying swords. Dirty great, double-handed, barb-hilted broadswords.

'Oh *great!*' she said.

CHAPTER 12
BRIGHTER VISIONS
BEAM AFAR

The Doctor heard Amy's strangled expression of alarm, and glanced back at their pursuers as well. He saw what she had just seen. The brutal, medieval weapons that the Ice Warriors were carrying with such brutal, medieval intent put an extra spurt of vigour into his pace. He began to lead the way, urging Samewell and Bel after him.

'Swords?' screeched Amy, lengthening her stride to keep up. 'Swords? Honestly? For *really real?*'

'I have no idea what that's about!' the Doctor yelled back at her.

'Yes, you do!' Amy objected. 'You always do!'

'Well,' the Doctor shouted over his shoulder, sprinting hell for leather, 'I suppose I could speculate that the Ice Warriors are an ancient and martial society that takes great pride in preserving and maintaining the traditions of weapon-craft honed by their ancestors, and that the use of ancient, bladed combat weapons suggests an intent to ritually slaughter or ceremonially execute! But I didn't think that would be a particularly cheerful thing to say while they were chasing us!' he added.

At least half a dozen Ice Warriors were doggedly

following them down the length of the gallery. Still more had appeared at the hatch. The nearest Warriors seemed to be calling out to them. They were making strange, guttural noises, at least, perhaps uttering warnings, or issuing orders for their fleet quarry to halt or surrender. It was hard to tell. Each bark sounded less like words, and more like the pneumatic spit of a torque wrench driven by compressed air.

Arabel was lagging behind the Doctor, Samewell and Amy. Her long and heavy winter skirts were seriously encumbering her.

'Come on!' Samewell exclaimed, grabbing her by the arm and propelling her ahead of him. He looked around in time to see Amy trip over the lip of a deck plate and sprawl headlong.

'Go!' Samewell yelled to Bel, and darted back to help Amy.

She had winded herself. He hauled her to her feet.

'Come on!' he begged.

'O-OK!'

'Are you hurt?'

'I banged my knees,' Amy said, fighting to draw a breath.

'You've got to keep running!' he insisted.

They looked back.

An Ice Warrior was just twenty metres away. It came around the end of a row of vats, saw them, and raised its sword in a braced, two-handed grip, hilt high, the blade tipped down, like a ninja with a katana. Or whatever those swords in the kung fu movies Rory liked were called. Katanas? Kanteenas? Katonas?

The Ice Warrior didn't break stride. It seemed to accelerate, as if it was charging them.

162

Amy and Samewell fled, his hand clamped firmly around hers.

Leading the furious escape, the Doctor spotted an exit hatch in the end wall of the farm gallery. It was exactly the same as the hatch they'd entered the gallery by, except that it was shut.

It was the only way out.

He ran up to it, shoe-sliding the last few steps so he slammed into it. The hatch was sealed tight, but there was another palm-checker built into the frame. It hadn't been tampered with or bored through. It was in full working order.

The Doctor slapped his right hand flat against the plate. A neon glow travelled up the metal under his hand. Then red lights began to flash in all four corners of the door and an angry klaxon sounded repeatedly.

The door did not recognise his print.

It wasn't going to open.

'Ah,' said the Doctor. For a split second, he started to reach for his sonic screwdriver. Then he remembered that it was a waste of time. The Ice Warriors were far too close.

Arabel arrived beside him, and Amy and Samewell were just behind her. The Doctor turned to the terrified Arabel, grabbed her by the wrist, and jammed *her* right hand against the palm-checker. A neon glow travelled up the metal under her hand. There was a click, and then a hiss, and the hatch opened.

The Doctor bundled Arabel into the hatch, and then grabbed Amy and Samewell as they ran up, and shoved them through too. He turned in the open doorway, and took one last look at the advancing Ice Warriors. He grinned.

'Warriors of the Tanssor clan!' he cried out to them. 'Warriors of the Tanssor clan line of the Ixon Mons family, inform your warlord that the *Belot'ssar* greets him!'

They stopped in their tracks and stared at him. He threw a cocksure salute, stepped backwards through the hatch and pressed the palm-plate. The klaxon sounded again, and the red corner lights flashed. The hatch did not shut with the dramatic flourish he'd been going for.

'Still got to sort that part out,' he acknowledged, pointing to the lock mechanism. The Ice Warriors started forward with renewed determination, raising their blades.

Amy reached past the Doctor and pressed her hand against the plate. A neon glow travelled up the metal under her hand. There was a click, and then a hiss, and then the hatch clanged shut in the faces of the Ice Warriors, locking them out.

The Doctor looked at Amy. They were nose to nose.

'How did you know that would work?' he asked.

'I didn't,' she said.

'Good thing it did, though, eh?' he pointed out.

'I would think so,' she replied.

They both jerked back a step as several echoing blows were delivered to the other side of the hatch.

'That'll keep them out for a moment,' said the Doctor.

'What if they cut through the lock like they cut the other ones?' Amy asked.

'Oh, they will,' said the Doctor. 'But now we have a head start. And it's because you're human.'

'What?' asked Amy.

'It's because you're human,' the Doctor repeated.

'And for those of us who aren't fluent in non-sequitur?' Amy asked.

'You could operate the hatch,' explained the Doctor, 'because the palm-checker recognised your genetic code as human. It's the same reason that Bel could open the door. Humans built this, so human gene-codes work the locks.'

'Even human genes as old as mine?' asked Amy.

'Gene-code is gene-code,' replied the Doctor.

'Wait,' said Arabel, flustered and looking at the Doctor, 'if you can't open the lock, doesn't that mean you're not human?'

The Doctor glanced awkwardly at Amy. 'Ah, yes. How do I explain that best?' he began.

Before he could answer, Amy shrieked, 'Samewell!'

Samewell's outstretched hand was hovering above the palm checker. At Amy's protest, he snatched it back.

'I just wanted to see if it would work for me too,' he said. He pouted.

Several more dull but herculean blows landed on the other side of the hatch and made him recoil.

'I'd best try it on another door, though, eh?' Samewell added.

'I think that would be healthier for all of us,' the Doctor said.

He looked around, and took stock of where they had ended up. It was a service room, full of metal shelves and hoppers. The shelves were racked with tools and equipment that looked part surgical and part horticultural. The hoppers were packed with mechanical spare parts wrapped in plastic. He picked up a few items and examined them.

'We can't really stay here, Doctor,' Amy said.

'No, we can't,' said the Doctor.

To reinforce her point, the banging on the hatch ceased, and was replaced by a high-pitched and very unpleasant wailing noise. It was like a dentist's drill with the volume turned up.

'No, we *really* can't,' said the Doctor. 'That's a focused sonic drill. They'll be through that hatch in two shakes. Two shakes if we're lucky. Probably more like *one shake*. Let's get going.'

They hurried away from the painful noise to the end of the service room. There was another hatch, shut tight.

'Now you can try it, Samewell,' said the Doctor.

Samewell put his hand on the plate. The hatch opened.

Samewell looked extremely pleased with himself.

Passing through the hatch, they entered a gloomy corridor lit by a line of blue overhead lights. It stretched away in both directions. From the left came the roar of heavy turbine machinery. The Doctor took them to the right. He got Samewell to close the hatch behind them.

'That's two barriers they've got to get through,' the Doctor remarked.

Feeling a little more secure, they walked briskly down the corridor.

'What was that you were saying to the Ice Warriors before we slammed the door in their faces?' Amy asked.

'Oh, you know. Saying hello.'

'How do you say hello to an Ice Warrior?' she asked.

'Um, "Hail, Ice Warrior"?'

'You're not as funny as you think you are,' said Amy.

They reached another hatch. This time, Amy opened it.

The room on the other side was dark, but quickly woke up as automatic lights flickered on. The air smelled stale and slightly dusty. It was a large room, lined in pale white shipskin, with a wide, flat floor covered in odd patterns. The patterns were circles and spirals, inlaid in a fine, contrasting metal filament. There was another hatch at the opposite end of the chamber, and one side of the space was fitted with complicated workstations and consoles. There were also two chairs facing the console station. The chairs had high, padded backs and raised armrests. The area looked like the cockpit of a spaceship.

The Doctor walked over to the workstation area. He seemed intrigued by the control systems. 'Go and see what's behind the next door,' he said to the others. 'Don't go too far.'

'What are you going to be up to?' Amy asked.

'I'm going to look at these,' he said, leaning over the consoles. He ran a speculative finger along the fascia above a line of touch-sensitive pads. Dust came away on his fingertip. 'I think I know what this is,' he said. 'In fact, I'm *sure* I know what this is.'

'Really?' asked Amy.

'Give me a moment,' said the Doctor, investigating further. He gestured over his shoulder. 'Look at the floor, Pond. Look at the patterns on the floor. Where have we seen that before?'

'Uh, I don't know?' Amy said.

'Think about it. We've seen it recently.'

'Really? I don't know.'

'Then hang on a minute,' he said. He sat down in one of the high-backed chairs, laced his fingers together, and cracked his knuckles. He had already pressed a few switches at random. Several indicator lights had come on. The consoles began to hum with power. 'Allow me to show you what this is.'

'Have we really got time to stop and play around, Doctor?' Amy asked.

'We've got time to stop and play around with this,' said the Doctor. 'If,' he added, 'this is what I think it is. And, as I believe we established, it is.'

Arabel and Samewell returned from their examination of the next door.

'It's another hallway,' said Bel, 'and then some rooms beyond that. We didn't go too far.'

'Good,' said the Doctor. He adjusted some more controls.

'What are you doing?' asked Samewell.

'He's showing off,' said Amy.

'I'm not,' said the Doctor. 'I'm bringing these long-dormant systems back online, and juicing them up to operational power.'

'Yeah, but he's not telling us why he's doing that, or what it is he's doing it to,' Amy said to Bel and Samewell, 'and the reason is because that way it'll be more impressive when it *finally* does whatever it's going to do.'

'No harm ever came from a bit of dramatic anticipation,' said the Doctor. 'There is an art to the building up of suspense. A prince from Denmark told me that.' He gently tinkered with a few more settings, and then picked up a chunky remote-control device that slotted into a socket in one of the consoles. He stood up.

'Come on,' the Doctor said to them. 'Come over here. Into the centre of the room. Hurry now.'

Power was building. They could all hear the ambient tone. Light levels in the room were starting to increase too.

'What have you done?' Amy asked.

'It's safe, I swear,' said the Doctor. He made a tiny adjustment via the remote control.

The hum of the mounting power levels turned into a lazier throb, like a slowly cycling energy pulse.

'OK,' he said. 'Ready? Hold on to your hats.'

'I don't have a hat,' said Samewell.

'You should get one,' replied the Doctor. 'Hats are cool.'

The Doctor pressed an activator on the control pad.

The light in the room around them altered quite dramatically. Not only did it shimmer and dim, the actual quality of the light seemed to change, becoming softer and less intense. It was like a scene change in a West End play. The effect was so odd, Arabel, Samewell and Amy all murmured in surprise.

Then they realised what they were looking at. They blinked. They saw what the chamber around them had very suddenly turned into. Their second murmur of surprise was much louder and more appreciative than the first.

The Doctor grinned.

They weren't in the same room any more.

They were somewhere else entirely.

Rory wondered if he ought to risk some more soup. He didn't really want any more soup. It was good soup, but he was full. However, having some soup was about the only thing to do apart from just sitting there, and he was fed up doing that. At least having some soup was doing something. It was an activity.

The assembly hall was very quiet. Vesta was snoozing. Sol Farrow was watching the flames crackling in the nearest firebucket. Sol had already been back for seconds and thirds of soup, and Rory was worried there might not be much soup left if Sol decided to go for fourths. Then there *really* wouldn't be anything to do to pass the time except sit around and be bored.

The night wind was picking up outside, driving the snow against the windows. Rory could hear it pattering like grains of sand. It was a proper blizzard out there. Things were warm enough close to the firebuckets, but there was a wickedly cold draft blowing in under the main doors of the assembly, and odd, fluting wind sounds were coming from the chimney vents up in the eaves.

'They're taking a long time,' said Rory.

'Guide's answers are often hard to find,' replied Sol. He cleared his throat and leaned forward to warm his hands at the fire. 'Particularly when… you know.'

'It's a problem you've never met before?' suggested Rory. Sol nodded.

'Have you really never seen winter until now?'

'Not until these last three years,' said Sol. 'We knew what winter was, of course. Knew what it had been like on Earth before, because of the records. And it always got a bit colder this season, regular. But we'd never seen white and ice before.'

'Right.'

'Vesta tell you that, did she?'

'Yes,' said Rory.

'They have winters where you come from, then?' asked Sol.

'Yes, actually,' said Rory. 'Where I come from, they have them quite often. We're used to them. But this is pretty fierce. It's a bad winter. And, obviously, any winter's going to be a bit worrying if you're not supposed to have them.'

He got up and looked over at the doors that led into the Incrypt.

'Maybe I should just go and see how they're doing?' he suggested. 'I'm sure I could help.'

'It's not allowed,' replied Sol. 'The council voted.'

'What are they looking at exactly?' asked Rory.

'Well, the words of Guide, of course,' said Sol, sitting up and looking at Rory with a frown. 'The covenant that Guide provides for us, as is held in the Incrypt. Guide knows an awful lot. More than any of us, and it usually takes quite a time and a lot of cleverness to sort of sift out what Guide is telling us.'

'This is your Guide Emanual?' said Rory.

'That's right,' said Sol. 'Surely you have the same in your plantnation?'

'We've got tourist information points and a weekly free paper.'

'What?' asked Sol.

'Never mind,' said Rory. He paced a little. 'I wish I knew where Amy and the Doctor were. I hope they're OK. The Doctor always knows what to do. I keep trying to imagine what he'd say or do if he was here.'

'Hello! Hello? Can anybody hear me?' the Doctor's voice suddenly boomed out across the assembly.

Sol and Vesta both leapt up in considerable dismay.

The voice seemed to come from directly behind Rory. He turned around very slowly.

The assembly hall was bathed in a soft yellow radiance, warm but bright, that was somehow shining out of the floor, the walls, and the ceiling. Glittering traceries of energy had appeared along the circular metal patterns inlaid in the wooden floor, and up the seams in the hall's beams and roof posts.

The centre of the hall was no longer the assembly room at all. It appeared to have become, in the blink of an eye, part of a very modern-looking white chamber. The row of benches in front of the council rail had turned into what looked like a computer workstation complete with two high-backed chairs.

Rory was standing halfway inside the assembly hall, and half in the new, white room.

The Doctor, beaming from ear to ear, was right in front of him, along with Amy and two young Morphans that Rory didn't recognise.

'Doctor!' Rory cried.

'Rory!' exclaimed the Doctor in delight. 'Rory Williams Pond!'

'Not my actual name,' smiled Rory.

'I was confident we'd make contact with someone,' the Doctor said excitedly. 'I didn't dare hope it would be you!'

Dumbfounded, Amy rushed towards Rory so that she could hug him. He spread his arms wide to meet her.

'How did you get here?' Rory laughed.

The anticipated hug didn't go according to plan. Much to their mutual surprise, Rory and Amy passed through each other like ghosts. They stopped in their tracks, turned and looked back at each other.

'What just happened?' asked Rory.

'Why can't I touch Rory?' demanded Amy. 'What's going on? It's spooky! I just went right through him. How can I not touch him if we're in the same room?'

'Well, because you're not actually in the same room at all,' said the Doctor.

Amy reached out her right hand to feel Rory's face. She succeeded merely in pushing her hand through his head.

'Um, OK, stop doing that,' Rory told her.

'That's so freaky!' Amy exclaimed.

'Yeah, still, stop it,' said Rory.

'You must be in the assembly in Beside,' said the Doctor. 'Well done, Rory. That's exactly where I needed you to be.'

Rory gave a *no problem* shrug as though he'd planned it all along. 'Where are you?' he asked.

'We're in Firmer Number Two,' replied the Doctor, 'which is one of the big mountains you would be able to see from the window if it wasn't night-time. Actually, we're deep inside it, so you wouldn't see us anyway.'

He was speaking rather too loudly and rather too clearly, as though he was using a telephone with a poor connection.

'Remember the mountains, Rory?' he asked. 'The strange ones that I didn't think were mountains?'

'I do, Doctor,' said Rory.

'Well, they're *really* not mountains. They're giant machines called terraformers, or terramorphers, or whatever you want to call them. They've been set up to change this world. To re-engineer its climate and make it more Earth-like.'

'Earth-*esque*, surely?' smiled Rory.

'Touché, Mr Pond,' laughed the Doctor. 'So, it'll take years to do. Centuries. It's a long-term project. Anyway, we're inside one of them.'

'OK…'

'Specifically,' the Doctor said, 'we're in a telepresence communications chamber. We found it by accident. It's part of a communications network that probably once linked all the Morphan communities.'

'It's like you're here,' said Rory, still not quite believing his eyes.

'It's conjury!' Sol Farrow murmured. He and Vesta were rigid with fear. Their eyes were very wide.

'Who's that?' asked the Doctor.

'That's Sol Farrow,' said Rory. 'And this is Vesta.'

'Vesta Flurrish!' the Doctor cried. 'Alive and well! How fantastic is that? Very pleased to virtually meet you, Vesta. As you can see, I've got your sister and Samewell here with me. They're perfectly safe. Well, they're relatively safe. Well, they're here with me.'

Vesta and Bel stepped forward and gazed at each other.

'I was so worried about you,' said Bel.

'You look like you are made of light,' said Vesta.

'She is!' cried the Doctor. 'To you, she is! The telepresence system generates a live hologram field. It's like 3D. I *love* 3D! Especially the cardboard red and green glasses. Anyway, it creates a hologram of you, where you are, here with us, and vice versa, so we all seem to be in the same room.'

'It's really freaky,' said Amy, poking her fingers into Rory's face.

'Again, stop it,' he said. He looked back at the Doctor. 'What's going on, Doctor?' he asked. 'There's something really bad happening in this town. There's this thing—'

'With red eyes!' Vesta blurted.

'Yes, red eyes,' Rory agreed.

'That would be an Ice Warrior,' the Doctor nodded, suddenly more serious. 'I'm sorry to say, there's more than one of them around. It *is* a real problem, Rory. They're a threat to the Morphans, to all human life on Hereafter. We've got to work together to stop them. Throw a spanner in their works.'

'How?' asked Rory.

'First things first. You need to get the Morphans ready,' the Doctor told him. 'The Ice Warriors are mobilising. They could strike at any moment.'

'Is Elect Groan there, Vesta?' asked Bel. 'Can you fetch him? Any other members of the council... Chaunce, Old Winnowner, anyone? They have to hear about this.'

'They're all in the Incrypt, consulting the word of Guide,' said Vesta.

'Now that is very interesting,' said the Doctor.

'Go and fetch them, Vesta!' Bel urged. 'Hurry now!'

Vesta nodded, and darted away. Sol was still staring in wonder at the luminous figures.

'Doctor?' said Rory.

'Yes, Rory?'

'I – hang on. Amy, *seriously*, stop poking your fingers through my nose. Doctor, why are you talking so urgently?'

'Am I?' asked the Doctor.

'Yeah,' said Rory. 'It's almost like... you haven't got very much time.'

'Well, there's no time like the present!' the Doctor enthused. He really wasn't very good at lying sometimes.

'Doctor...' said Rory, a cautioning note sounding in his voice. His *take me seriously* voice.

'What?' ask the Doctor.

'What's that high-pitched noise?' asked Rory.

In the hologram field deep under Firmer Number Two, the Doctor looked back at the shimmering, life-sized image of his friend and shifted uncomfortably.

The noise of the focused sonic drill was steadily getting louder.

'Hang on, Rory,' the Doctor said. 'Stay right there.'

He walked out of the glow of the hologram field and over to the open hatch. The noise was echoing down the corridor. The Ice Warriors were already cutting through the

175

second of the hatches that the Doctor and his companions had locked in their path.

'Samewell?' he called.

The young man ran over to join him.

'Keep watch here,' the Doctor told him. 'As soon as the Ice Warriors appear through that door down there, yell out so we know about it, and then lock this hatch. It'll slow them down again.'

'Guide is my witness, I understand,' Samewell said.

'As soon as you've done that, I want you to take Amy and Bel out the other way, out the way you scouted. Got it?'

'Yes, Doctor.'

'It's important.'

'Cat A. I understand. Where will you be while this is happening?' Samewell asked.

'I'll be right behind you,' the Doctor said. 'But I need you to lead the way so you can open the doors with your hand.'

'Ah,' said Samewell, nodding. 'Right. Got you.'

The Doctor left Samewell standing watch at the door and walked back into the hologram field.

Amy and Rory were face to face, looking at each other.

'I was really worried about you,' Rory said to her.

'And I was worried about you,' she replied. 'You only went back for a coat. How hard is that?'

'Uh, I think *you* got captured while I was getting a coat,' said Rory, 'so this whole series of disasters started with you.'

'It started with the TARDIS missing Christmas by about a bajillion years, actually,' replied Amy.

'Well, I was really worried anyway,' said Rory. He raised his hand, palm open, fingers slightly spread, as though he was pressing it against a window pane. Amy echoed the gesture with her left hand, so they could 'touch' hands through the holographic medium. An elasticated mitten dangled from her cuff.

Their hands passed through one another. They both stepped back sharply, shaking their heads.

'I thought that would be, like, really sweet,' said Rory, disappointed. 'I thought it would be a proper moment, like in those films when the hero's in jail, and the girl visits him, and they put their hands up on either side of the glass partition of the visitor's cubicle? You know, like that?'

'Yeah,' she said.

'But it was just a bit creepy,' he said.

'It really was,' she agreed.

Rory saw the Doctor reappear.

'What is that noise, Doctor?' he asked.

'Nothing to worry about,' said the Doctor cheerfully.

'He's just saying that so you won't worry,' said Amy.

'What *is* that noise?' asked Rory.

'The Ice Warrior Men are drilling through doors to get at us,' Amy told him.

'What?' Rory asked, very alarmed.

The Doctor looked at Amy. His shoulders drooped and he sighed sadly.

'It's not even like it's a difficult name to remember, like Jagrafess or Castrovalva,' the Doctor said to her. 'I mean, a friend of mine just *made it up* on the spot. Ice Warriors. It's simple. It's not hard. Why are you having such trouble with it?'

'Probably the stress of the situation,' Amy snapped.

'Is she telling the truth?' Rory asked the Doctor.

'Not at all,' replied the Doctor. 'The word "men" has never had anything to do with their name. They're just plain Ice Warriors.'

'God help me… Are they drilling through the door, Doctor?' asked Rory insistently, trying his best not to shout.

'They *are* doing that,' the Doctor admitted.

'Doctor! You've got to get out of there!' said Rory.

'Has Vesta gone to get the council?'

'Yes,' said Rory.

'Well, we haven't really got time to wait for them to come back,' said the Doctor thoughtfully. 'Listen, Rory, it's actually all very simple. The Ice Warriors want this planet. They want to conquer it and colonise it. They want to take it from the Morphans. But they need it to be colder. Tons colder. They don't want the Morphans warming it up to make it all Earth-like. Their idea of Earth-like isn't like the Morphans' idea of Earth-like, and—'

'Skip that part, Doctor,' Amy advised.

'OK, Rory,' said the Doctor, focusing. 'The crucial point is that the Ice Warriors have sabotaged the terraformer systems. They've reset them to plunge Hereafter into an ice age.'

'Hence the sudden winters,' said Rory.

'Exactly,' the Doctor agreed. 'An ice age will suit the Ice Warriors just fine, but it will wipe the Morphans out. I'm not prepared to allow that. So… I'm going to sabotage the Ice Warriors' sabotage, Rory. I'm going to undo what they've done, and accelerate the global warming processes of the terraformers. I'm going to make Hereafter a *very* uncomfortable place for any Ice Warriors to be.'

'OK,' Rory nodded.

A sudden bang reverberated down the corridor outside.

'They're through, Doctor!' Samewell yelled from the door.

'Close that hatch, Samewell,' the Doctor shouted back, 'and get everybody through into the next room like I told you to!'

'Yes, Doctor!' Samewell replied. He put his hand on the palm-checker and the hatch slammed shut.

'Sorry. Really running short on time,' the Doctor said, turning back to Rory. 'Like I said, I need to reset the terraformers, but they're a huge and very complicated set of systems. I don't want to cause a global disaster by, you know, fiddling around. I need plans or schematics to work from. Rory, all the Morphans I've met keep mentioning "Guide". Guide, as I understand it, has principles that they live by. Instructions. I think they're actually referring to a *real* guide, to codified information that the original colonists left behind to cover all the details of operating and maintaining the systems.'

'I reckoned that too,' Rory agreed. 'It's such an important part of their lives, they treat it as a sort of holy text. I've heard them calling it "Guide Emanual".'

'Emanual, or e-*hyphen*-manual?' the Doctor asked, intrigued.

'Exactly,' said Rory. 'E-manual. An electronic manual. I think it's stored digitally. There's a place adjoining the hall called the Incrypt. That's where they keep it.'

'I need a copy,' the Doctor said.

'Well, they won't let me in there,' Rory replied.

The high-pitched dentist's drill whine had started howling on the other side of the hatch. The Ice Warriors were right outside.

'Come on!' Samewell said to Amy and Bel. 'We've got to go! Right now! Doctor says so!'

'Doctor?' Amy said to the Doctor.

'Rory, I need the e-manual,' the Doctor said.

'I understand that,' Rory replied, 'but they won't let me near the Incrypt.'

'You've got to try, Rory,' said the Doctor.

'OK.'

'Rory, I mean it,' the Doctor said. 'We can't stay here. It's not safe any more. We've got to go. I'm going to try to find another telepresence terminal like this one. Soon as I can, I'll contact you again. Please, have the e-manual ready for me then!'

'I'll do my best, Doctor!'

'I know you will,' the Doctor said.

'Doctor, we've got to go now!' Amy yelled.

'Amy!' Rory called out, trying to see her past the Doctor. 'Please be careful! Just be careful!'

'You know me,' she called back, waving to him as she tried to pull the Doctor away. She hoped he couldn't see the tears in her eyes. It wasn't fair she could see him but not touch him. It wasn't fair that they were going to have to say goodbye and start running. It wasn't fair that she might not actually get to see him properly ever again.

'Go! Go!' the Doctor told Amy. 'Get Samewell and Arabel out of here and run!'

'Not without you!' Amy protested.

'Oh my god!' cried Rory, utterly powerless to act. 'It's not a choice. *All* of you run!'

'I've got to disable this terminal so the Ice Warriors can't access it,' the Doctor said. 'Amy, go!'

Reluctantly, Amy ran across to the far door where Samewell and Arabel, both trembling with fear, were waiting. 'Come on, Doctor!' she yelled.

The Doctor was adjusting the remote control, resetting

the systems of the main console. 'See you later, Rory Williams Pond,' he said, grinning at Rory's holographic image.

'Please, Doctor, go!' Rory said to him, looking anguished and helpless.

Something exploded. It made a loud noise like a gunshot. A sudden stench of burning metal filled the chamber. The drill had bored all the way through the lock.

The hatch shunted open and two Ice Warriors shoved their way into the telepresence chamber. One had a broadsword. The other had an ornate battle-axe, the haft and blade all forged from one gleaming piece of metal.

Arabel screamed.

'Doctor, run!' Rory and Amy both yelled at the same time.

The Doctor turned, and saw the Ice Warriors bearing down on him. Two more had come into the room behind the first pair. The Doctor threw the remote-control handset at the Ice Warriors in an attempt to distract them, and then made to dart away sideways to reach Amy and the two Morphans.

The Ice Warrior with the axe hurled his weapon with extraordinary strength and grace. Superb martial skill sent the gleaming axe spinning through the air, making a chopping, swishing sound as it flew. It was thrown wide, not to kill the Doctor, but to force him back and cut off his escape.

The Doctor recoiled with a cry of alarm as the axe whooshed past him. It struck the console and buried itself, blade first, in the control bank. The impact blew out the power systems. The holographic image of the assembly hall, of the frantic Rory and the speechless Sol, blinked, flickered and vanished. A hot shower of sparks blew out of the console in a small explosion that knocked the Doctor to his knees.

Amy wailed, 'Doctor!'

The Doctor tried to get up. A massive green pincer clamped his right wrist. He cried out in pain.

'Go! Amy, go!' he yelled, struggling to pull free.

She was in the hatchway, staring at him in utter horror. Samewell and Arabel were trying to pull her out of the room, but she was fighting them off.

'Doctor!'

'Get out of here!' the Doctor bellowed back.

'Not without you!'

'Lock the door and get away! Save Bel and Samewell! Run!'

The other Ice Warriors were advancing on the doorway. In another few seconds, they would have her, and the door would be wedged, and they'd all be prisoners of one of the Doctor's most implacable adversaries.

'Please, Amy,' the Doctor cried. '*Please.*'

His eyes met hers. One last look.

One last communication that was beyond words.

Amy cried out in despair, and finally allowed herself to be dragged back through the hatchway by the two young Morphans. She rammed her hand against the palm-checker, and the hatch slammed shut in the faces of the Ice Warriors.

It closed with such force, a single woolly mitten on a severed strand of elastic fell onto the deck.

CHAPTER 13
BRIGHTLY SHONE THE MOON THAT NIGHT

The Doctor got to his feet. This was not an entirely voluntarily action. The Ice Warrior holding him by the wrist raised its arm, and the Doctor had no choice but to follow. It was either that or have one of his four favourite limbs snapped off.

The Ice Warrior that had hurled the axe plodded over to the smouldering console and wrenched the weapon out. A spatter of sparks, like the spill of a foundry bucket, followed it and fizzled on the deck. The other Warriors formed a loose and menacing semicircle around their prisoner.

'Hello, everyone,' the Doctor said, trying to seem friendly and open to any options. 'Why don't we go around the room so that everyone can introduce themselves? You start.'

The Warrior with the axe returned and faced the Doctor. He raised a large pincer fist and shoved the Doctor in the chest. With a grunt of surprise, the Doctor was driven backwards into one of the padded chairs.

'Sit?' the Doctor gasped, the air having been rather compressed out of his lungs. 'Excellent idea. Excellent. I've been on my feet all day.'

The Ice Warrior brought the axe down across the Doctor's middle. It came so close to cutting him in half, the Doctor yelped and breathed in hard. The axe blade bit into one of the chair's arms so that the handle was fixed across the Doctor's body, like a solid metal seat belt. The Doctor was pinned behind it. He wriggled his arms back behind the haft so he could press his palms against it and keep it at bay. There wasn't much room for movement.

'What, um, happens now?' asked the Doctor, looking up at his towering captors. Impassive red-lensed eyes glared down at him.

'Oh dear. I have this horrible hunch that it's going to involve killing me, or lopping bits of me off,' said the Doctor, 'and if that's the case, I just want to say, you know, that's not necessary. Or cool. I'm a reasonable sort. I'm sure we can talk about this—'

'Wordsssss!' hissed the Ice Warrior who had pinned him in place with the axe. The pronouncement was arctic. It was as though every single letter had been chipped out of glacial ice and then forced from the Warrior's downturned slit of a mouth by a blast of polar air.

'W-words?' asked the Doctor.

'Your elimination isss inevitable,' said the Ice Warrior, 'but firssst, there will be an exchange of wordsss.'

Each syllable of the statement could not have been any colder if the Warrior had personally fetched them from a walk-in freezer. They seemed to smoke in the air like dry ice. The sibilant lizard-hiss of the Warrior's voice sounded like the scrape of a blade being worked on an oiled whetstone.

'You're… proposing to have a conversation with me?' asked the Doctor.

'The conversssation will not be conducted by me,' hissed the giant.

'Oh, interesting! Who do I get to talk to, then?' asked the Doctor.

A figure had entered the chamber behind the half-ring of Warriors. He was not as tall or as broad as any of them, but he was just as imposing.

The Ice Lord wore a regal, form-fitting body suit of titanium mesh. It was the colour of verdigrised brass pipework or pellucid green sea-ice. His armoured mantle and long storm cloak were of a darker green, as though they had been woven from the needles of an evergreen tree. His sharply domed helm was like the nose of a burnished artillery shell. It was made of gleaming white steel with a faint threadwork of pale green. It looked as though it could have been sculpted out of the finest Pentelic marble. The eye slots were lensed with jade glass.

The Ice Lord came and stood in front of the Doctor.

'You talk to me,' he said. His voice was deeper than the wheezing, hissing tones of the bulky Ice Warriors. It reminded the Doctor of a distant rumble of thunder, like a ferocious ice storm lurking below the horizon of a bleak antarctic waste.

'Great!' declared the Doctor. 'Let's start! What shall we talk about? I think the weather's always a polite topic of conversation. Shall we discuss the weather? Been a bit chilly of late, hasn't it? Real overcoat weather. What do you think?'

'Tell me about the new weapons you have arrayed against us,' said the Ice Lord.

'I don't know anything about any weapons,' answered the Doctor, 'new or otherwise.'

'Disinformation is not a good strategy to employ,' said the Ice Lord. 'New weapons have been produced and used. Account for them. Explain them.'

'I can assure you,' replied the Doctor firmly, 'I have no knowledge of any weapons deployed against you. My only participation in your business today has been trying to prevent you from killing me and my friends.'

The Ice Lord stared down at the Doctor for a long time, longer than any human would have held a silence. He didn't seem to be having any difficulty comprehending the remark. It was more as though the Ice Lord believed that, if he waited long enough, he would get the answer he was waiting for.

This, the Doctor knew, was entirely typical of Martian psychology. As a result, he did not respond. He fixed his gaze directly on the jade eye slits and waited. You didn't win an argument with an Ice Warrior by arguing. You won it by staying silent for longer.

Behind the jade lenses, black eyes gleamed like oiled obsidian.

'This is disinformation,' the Ice Lord said at last. 'In the surface woodland earlier tonight, you evaded one of my combat echelons. You, and three other mammals.'

'That could have been anyone,' replied the Doctor.

'It was you. Heatprints do not lie. It is verified.'

'They were chasing us,' said the Doctor. 'They didn't seem all that friendly. We were obliged to run.'

The Ice Lord remained silent for another over-long moment.

'When you refused to surrender,' he said eventually, 'they fired upon you. You withstood their sonic disruptors. I return to my original question. Tell me about the new weapons that have been arrayed against us. New weapons that can repel sonic attack.'

'Oh, that?' said the Doctor. He tried to appear relaxed, leaning back and attempting to casually cross his legs. The axe wedged across his chest rather cramped his style. After a couple of tries, he was forced to put his leg back down and pretend he'd only been trying to pick lint off his coat. 'I wouldn't characterise that as a weapon. It was an improvised defence against your unprovoked and lethal assault.'

'Make an account of it,' the Ice Lord growled.

The Doctor sighed. 'I can show you,' he said. He shrugged helplessly against the axe that caged him in the chair. 'Can I get to a pocket?'

The Ice Lord looked at the attending Warrior and nodded. The Warrior reached forward, grasped the axe and plucked it out of the chair.

The Doctor breathed out, smiled, and fished around in his coat for his sonic screwdriver. He took it out and showed it to the Ice Lord.

'A simple multifunction tool,' he said. 'Not a weapon. Attacked by your cohort, I adjusted it to generate a noise-cancelling field that blocked the effects of their disruptors. Passive resistance. Do you understand me? Not a weapon.'

'Demonstrate.'

'I can't. Fending your warriors off pretty much exhausted this device. It is non-functional.'

There was another long pause.

'On the other occasions,' said the Ice Lord, 'were devices such as this employed?'

'What other occasions?' asked the Doctor.

'Do not evade.'

'I'm not,' said the Doctor. 'What other occasions?'

'This conflict is escalating,' the Ice Lord said. 'The latest advance gained by your side is a resistance to our sonic weapons. It has required us to re-equip with blade weapons. Are you the architect of this tactical advantage?'

'Oh, come on,' said the Doctor. 'I block your sonic blasters during one skirmish in the woods – a frantic improvisation, I might add – and you revise your entire combat strategy? You dump your high-tech guns in favour of ritual blades? Seriously, I'm impressive, but I'm not *that* impressive.'

'Your arrival in this theatre coincided with the sudden negation of our sonic arsenal. Can you deny that you are the architect of this tactical improvement?'

'You are misreading the facts,' said the Doctor.

The Ice Lord did not reply. At an almost leisurely pace, he crossed to the other high-backed chair, rotated it to face the Doctor, and sat down.

'Where have you and the other new arrivals come from?' the Ice Lord asked.

'We arrived yesterday,' replied the Doctor.

'All of you?'

'Yes.'

'How?'

'In my ship,' replied the Doctor.

The Ice Lord paused again. 'We have not detected a ship. Orbital surveillance is continuous and comprehensive. We have not detected a ship, certainly not a ship large enough to contain all of you.'

'Well, there you are,' said the Doctor. 'I'm telling the truth. Your instruments must be wrong. So, you're monitoring the human population on Hereafter?'

'Of course.'

'How do you distinguish between the existing population and any new arrivals?'

'Heatprints do not lie,' said the Ice Lord.

The Doctor nodded. 'Ah, yes, right. Everyone's thermal image is as unique as a gene-scan or a retina,' he mused. He turned his head and took a wistful look at the hatch that Amy had sealed behind her. The woolly mitten was on the deck where it had fallen.

'Or a palm-print,' he added, ruefully. He looked back at the Ice Lord. 'All right. This is interesting. You detected heatprints that didn't match any on your database, so you despatched troops to find and identify the new arrivals.'

'Precise monitoring must be maintained,' replied the Ice Lord. 'Constant threat evaluation and analysis keeps us ahead in this war.'

'This *cold* war,' the Doctor said. He sat back. 'How long have you been here?'

'Ten Earth years.'

'But only in these last few weeks or so have you revealed yourselves?'

'Alterations made to the climate engines were sufficient at first. We were waiting for the effects to manifest. However, we have been forced to become more proactive.'

'Your plan has run into difficulties?' pressed the Doctor.

'It has turned into open war.'

'Has it?' asked the Doctor. 'Has it indeed? Again, and I'm sorry if I offend, you are simply misreading the facts. You are traumatically altering the climate of this planet and, as a direct consequence of that policy, you are going to exterminate a sentient population. Progressive genocide. I'd say that puts you in a difficult place, morally speaking, just to *begin* with. Then I arrive, and get caught in the middle, and my actions are misinterpreted as your victims fighting back. Now, in your eyes, it's a war? You are simply misreading the facts.'

'And you know more than you claim to know,' replied the Ice Lord. 'In this complex, just a short time ago, you addressed my Warriors as you fled from them. Ssord, repeat the words the prisoner used.'

The Ice Warrior with the axe took a step forward. In a compressed air-hiss, he said, 'The captive ssspoke thusss: "Warriorsss of the Tanssor clan line of the Ixon Monsss family, inform your warlord that the *Belot'ssar* greetsss him."'

'Explain how you know these things,' the Ice Lord said to the Doctor.

'It's obvious,' replied the Doctor. 'You are of the Tanssor Clan. The characteristic pattern of scales and ridges on your breastplates and helmets is unmistakable. The emblem on your pectoral confirms that your clan allegiance is to the Ixon Mons family, which is one of the most code-honourable families on Old Mars. It's a simple matter of observation.'

'And also a simple matter to conclude that you have encountered my species before,' said the Ice Lord.

'I never claimed I hadn't.'

'Your knowledge of our culture is considerable. You know how to fortify against our weapons. You understand the lineage and hierarchy of our bloodlines. You distinguish the polymorphic traits of our physiology, a habit seldom known in other races. And you know words in our language. Belot'ssar.'

'Indeed,' smiled the Doctor. '*Belot'ssar*. I was wondering when we'd get to that.'

'As I was wondering why you used the term.'

'It means *cold blue star*,' said the Doctor.

'Curiously enough, I know what it means,' replied the Ice Lord. 'Why did you use the phrase in, so it seems, reference to yourself?'

'Because that's how I'm known to your people,' replied the Doctor. He looked quite pleased with himself. 'Traditionally, I mean. Your people, particularly the Ixon Mons family, know me as *cold blue star*. It's a reference to the ship I travel in. The title is an honorific. It shows me to be a true and lasting friend to the Ixon Mons dynasty, but also a fair and daunting adversary.'

The Doctor rose to his feet. The Ice Lord stood to face him. The Doctor drew himself up, narrowing his eyes to look at the Ice Lord. He was fearless. The gloves were off. It was time to play his ace.

'I have been a friend to the dynasties of Mars,' said the Doctor, 'but I have also been a foe. I have fought them many times and I have won *every* time. Ice Lord Azylax, warlord of the Tanssor, personally named me the *Belot'ssar* as a mark of respect, so that future generations would know me and tread carefully. The situation on this planet will end. You will disengage, and you will cease your prosecution of the human population. That's your final warning. I am everything your ancestors warned you about. I am the *Belot'ssar*.'

The Ice Lord stared back at him. There was no expression.

'Never heard of you,' he said.

'What?' asked the Doctor.

'I am Ixyldir, warlord of the Tanssor Clan,' said the Ice Lord. 'There has never been a warlord called Azylax. We know nothing of a respected foe known as the *cold blue star*.'

'But…' the Doctor began.

'Hang on…' he floundered.

'That's just not…' he added.

He sat down and rested his forehead on his hand.

'Time travel,' he murmured. He slapped his palm against his forehead repeatedly, scolding himself. 'Lets you down *Every! Single! Time!* I have *got* to learn to set my watch!'

He looked up at Ixyldir and the Ice Warriors.

'All that,' he said, gesturing vaguely into the space where he had just been standing, as if to encapsulate his bold and defiant performance. 'All of that showy-offy stuff, could we just pretend that never happened? I can see from your faces that we can't. You're going to kill me.'

'You were going to die anyway,' replied the Ice Lord.

'Yes,' said the Doctor, 'but now I'm going to be really annoyed when it happens.'

'We've got to go back!' Amy raged, fighting against the firm grips both Samewell and Arabel had on her.

'And do what, precisely?' Arabel asked.

'Save him!' Amy blurted. *'Rescue him! Poke the Ice Men in the eyes with sticks! I don't know!'*

'Ice Warriors,' Samewell corrected her.

Amy turned on him. 'Oh, really? *Really? Now* is the time to focus on that? *Is* it, Samewell Crook? Is it *really?*'

Arabel pulled Amy away from the cringing Samewell. 'You're upset,' she said.

'Damn right!' Amy cried. 'We just left the Doctor to die! We left him trapped there, surrounded by the giant green lizard things! That's just… just…'

'Just what?' asked Bel.

'It's not how I do things!' Amy declared.

She turned away from them. She was breathing hard, trying to control her anger. They'd been running for a few minutes, following an access corridor into a warren of tunnels that had finally led out onto the walkway where they were now standing.

In the vast gulf of the rock-cut cavern below them, huge turbines pumped and rumbled. There was an amber cast to the light. Vapour rose up around the suspended mesh walkway that supported them.

'He's always there for me,' Amy said quietly. 'He's always got my back. He's crossed time and space to save me, more than once. And I just ditched him.'

She turned to face them. Samewell and Arabel were watching her with great concern. Amy held up one baggy sleeve of her duffel coat.

'Also, I lost a glove,' she sniffed, 'which I know is a completely different scale of things to be upset about, but it's annoying, you know?'

'He will be all right,' said Bel.

'How do you know that?' asked Amy.

'Well,' said Bel, 'I haven't known your Doctor for anything like as long as you have. I realise that. But just in the short time I've been around him, I've been filled with a confidence. He knows what he's doing. I've… I've never met anyone who seems so capable.'

'Bel's right,' said Samewell. 'The Doctor wanted us to go. He told us to. He was quite plain about it. It was the only way.'

'Those things, they had us cornered,' said Bel. 'He wanted us to escape.'

'That won't be much consolation to him when he's dead,' said Amy.

'But it might be consolation to him as he's dying,' replied Bel.

Amy breathed out hard. She turned away, gripped the metal handrail and stared down into the pit where the mighty terraforming engines were performing their slow toil.

'He always has more than one plan,' she said quietly.

'How do you mean?' asked Bel.

'He wanted us to escape,' said Amy, turning back to face them. There was a new expression on her face. 'I mean, of *course* he did. He was trying to save us, and he'd lay down his life for anyone. But I know the Doctor. He's like one of those chess grand masters, you know?'

They both shook their heads.

'They plan their moves way in advance,' said Amy, carrying on anyway. 'They know what they're going to do long before they get there. It was all getting a bit frantic back in that room, and he definitely wanted to save us... and I know there was a lot of improvising going on as well, because I've seen what he looks like when he does that. But he always has more than *one* plan.'

'So?' asked Bel.

'He stayed there so we could get away,' said Amy. 'You said it yourself, Samewell, he told us to. He needs us to do something. He needs us to carry on with the plan while he keeps the Ice Men busy.'

She checked herself and glared at Samewell.

'*Don't* correct me,' she advised.

He shrugged and raised his hands.

'Sabotage their sabotage,' Amy said. 'That's what he said he was going to do. Sabotage whatever sabotage the Ice Warriors had caused. Get the Firmers working again. We need the Guide to do that, to set things right. Rory's going to get that for us.'

'If he can,' said Bel.

'My husband won't let me down,' said Amy. 'So the first thing we need to do is find a way to regain contact with Rory.'

She seemed galvanised and ready for action, as if she'd got her mojo back.

'I think that's the second thing we need to do,' said Samewell.

'Why?' asked Amy. 'What's the first?'

Samewell pointed. Four Ice Warriors had appeared on another walkway high above them. The Warriors looked down, spotted them, and then began to search for the nearest route down.

'I think getting away from here might be number one,' said Samewell.

'Amy! Amy! Doctor!' Rory yelped. He clamped his hands to his forehead in hopeless panic, and turned in a full, bewildered circle. The centre of the assembly hall had become the centre of the assembly hall again. There was no sign of the polished white room with the fancy console and the high-backed seats. There was no scintillating bleed of light coming out of the metal seams inlaid in the floor and the beams. There was no sign of the Doctor or Amy.

There was no sign of the axe-wielding Ice Warriors.

'I don't believe this!' Rory exclaimed.

'Where...' Sol began. He frowned. 'Where did they go? They were just here. Where did they go? Come to that, where in Guide's name did they come from in the first place? That's conjury, that is! Cat A conjury!'

'Oh, get over it!' Rory moaned. 'Did you see? Did you see what was happening? Those things! Those Ice Warrior things! They were right there! They were going to capture them!'

He looked at Sol. A flicker of true and terrible realisation crossed his face.

'They could be dead already,' he murmured.

'What happened? What happened?' Vesta asked, rushing back into the room. Bill Groan and the rest of the council followed after her.

'Rory, where did it all go?' Vesta asked, grabbing him by the arms.

'Never mind,' Rory said.

'I will strike you on your sorry head with a mallet again, so I will!' she declared. 'Where did it all go?'

'It got cut off,' Rory told her. 'Just cut off. The Ice Warriors got them.'

'The Ice Warriors?' asked Vesta.

'Yes, the thing from the woods!'

'With the red eyes?'

'Yes!' said Rory.

'Oh, Guide preserve me, they got Bel too?' Vesta asked.

'It was hard to tell,' said Rory. 'But it didn't look good.'

Vesta looked like she was going to burst into tears.

'Explain this commotion to me now,' Bill Groan insisted. 'Vesta came banging on the Incrypt door raving about a window into another place, with people in it!'

'What unguidely horror have you perpetrated?' Winnowner asked Rory.

'Do me a favour!' Rory snapped, rounding on her and the other muttering council members. 'Give it a rest with the *unguidely* this and the *conjury* that, OK? OK? It's not helping! My wife, and my friend, and *her* sister –' Rory pointed at the anxious Vesta – 'and some other bloke, just got captured by the same creatures who are messing your world up and trying to kill you off. Captured… or worse.'

'What did your friend call them?' Vesta asked quietly.

'Ice Warriors,' said Rory. 'The Doctor said they were called Ice Warriors.'

'But how,' Bill Groan asked, struggling, 'did this happen here in the assembly?'

'It was a technological link,' Rory explained. 'Transmitted hologram images. A communication system. Do any of these phrases mean anything to you?'

'Some of them are words that we know from our Guide Emanual,' said Chaunce Plowrite nervously.

'That is true,' admitted Winnowner.

'It was like they were here!' declared Vesta.

'It was, Elect,' said Sol Farrow. 'I would not have believed it except I saw it with my own eyes. As big as life, here in the hall. They spoke to us, and could hear us and see us. It was Arabel and Samewell, and the strangers from this morning, the odd fellow and the girl with the red hair.'

'What did they say?' asked Bill Groan.

'I swear I did not understand much of it,' said Sol. 'He speaks fast, the odd fellow does, and uses words I haven't the notion of. But it was clear to me that it was Cat A urgent.'

'I understood what it meant,' said Rory. 'These things are called Ice Warriors—'

'These things with red eyes, like we both saw in the woods?' asked Vesta.

'That's right,' said Rory.

'I said they was monstrous,' Vesta said, nodding and

looking earnestly at Bill and the council. 'Most ferocious thing I have ever seen, it was. I barely escaped with my life.'

'The Ice Warriors have their sights set on Hereafter,' said Rory. 'That's how the Doctor explained it. They want to colonise the planet themselves.'

'They are invading our world?' asked Jack Duggat.

'They are,' Rory agreed. 'They're going to wipe the Morphans out. This plantnation… *all* of the plantnations. They want this world to be colder, to suit them. But that means that the Morphans will die out, because it will be too cold to survive.'

'They cannot have our world,' murmured Bill Groan in horror. 'We have worked so hard for it. So many lifetimes have gone by, toiling to shape Hereafter. They can't have it.'

'The Ice Warriors have got into your Firmers, Elect,' said Rory. 'They've mucked up the way they work. They've… sort of made them do the reverse of what they were built to do in the first place.'

'They're making everything colder?' asked Chaunce. 'Our own Firmers?'

'That's why the white has come,' said Bill. 'That's why winter has claimed us.'

'Exactly,' said Rory.

'We will stop them,' Bill Groan said firmly.

'That gets my vote,' said Rory.

'What did the Doctor say we should do?' Bill asked him.

Rory shrugged. 'He said that your Guide Emanual had the answer,' he replied.

'Of course it does!' said Winnowner.

'The Doctor said that if he could consult the Guide, use it, he could reset the Firmer systems to undo the damage the Ice Warriors had done.'

'And how would this be achieved?' asked Bill Groan.

'He wants me to look at the Guide,' said Rory. 'He wants me to access it, and be ready for him when he communicates again. *If* he communicates again. Look, he said he was going to find another part of the communication system to use, to talk to us. Of course, that was before he got captured... Look, the Doctor's pretty amazing. He won't let us down. Let's get the Guide ready for him when he links through again. And if he doesn't, then we come up with some other plan.'

Bill Groan thought hard and then, grudgingly, nodded.

'You're proposing to let this stranger into the Incrypt?' Winnowner asked Bill incredulously. 'You're suggesting we let him read direct from our Guide Emanual and show it to others?'

'This man is a Nurse Elect!' Vesta exclaimed.

'I don't care what he is,' replied Winnowner. 'This cannot be permitted.'

'If our world is under attack,' asked Bill Groan, 'and our way of life also, and this is the only way to save it, then who are you to say that it cannot be?'

'Who are you trusting, Elect?' Winnowner asked. 'Guide have mercy on us all, you're trusting the word of these strangers! We have only their say that there are any of these menacing *Ice Warrior* things! None of us have seen them.'

'I have, actually,' said Sol Farrow.

'Rubbish, Sol!' said Winnowner. 'You can't even say what it was you saw!'

'I have too, Winnowner Cropper,' said Vesta firmly.

'You were frightened by something in the dark woods, child,' said Winnowner. 'I ask you all, in Guide's goodness, we don't know what we face here. But we do know there have been three strangers come among us from afar. A new star moves through the heavens, and then they show up, unannounced, claiming to be well-wishers come along in the dead of a winter's night.'

She glared at Rory.

'Maybe *they* are the real Ice Warriors,' she said. 'Did *that* occur to any of you? If they hope to damage our Firmers, and make winter come for ever, and so wipe us out, then maybe this is their conjury trick to get their hands on our Guide Emanual! What's *wrong* with you all?'

'Winnowner is right,' said Chaunce Plowrite. 'If this man and his friends are our enemies, then we should not let them near Guide's words. We'd be handing them the very secrets that they crave. We'd be giving them the means to destroy us.'

Everyone looked at Rory, even Vesta.

'Oh, come on,' he said. 'Please. *Please*. Do I look evil? I can't do evil. I can barely pull off dangerous. This is one of those moments when you've just got to trust something. I'm on your side.'

'I believe him,' said Vesta Flurrish. 'I honestly do. What about you, Elect?'

Bill Groan had bowed his head. He was gazing sidelong at Rory as though that might make it easier to see some kind of answer or eternal truth.

They waited for him to reply.

The main doors to the assembly burst open, letting in a wall of icy chill. Able Reeper, one of Jack Duggat's men, hurtled in along with the bitter cold, lugging his scythe. He was extremely agitated.

'Elect! Elect!' he shouted. 'You must come quick now! You must come and see!'

'What's the commotion, Able?' Bill Groan asked.

'Hurry, Elect!' the man replied. 'Come and see!'

They all followed him outside into the snowy yard. It was bitterly cold. Rory inhaled, and the air stabbed into his lungs like a frozen knife. Able Reeper strode off across the town yard towards the Back Row and the hedges that ran along the perimeter of the Spitablefields. He kept beckoning them to follow. A lot of other Morphans were out too, roused from their beds. They were flocking in the same direction, some carrying solamps.

It was surprisingly bright anyway. The blizzard had stopped, leaving the world under a deep blanket of snow, a thick white layer that flowed like a soft duvet over the roofs and trees and tops of walls. It looked like the deepest, richest royal icing that had ever decorated a Christmas cake.

With the snowfall stilled, the sky had cleared. It was like black glass overhead, a polished darkness that sucked the heat out of every breath and made brief, trailing clouds. The sky was so clear, it seemed to Rory that he could see every single star that there had ever been. The spiral pattern of a galaxy filled half the sky, a trillion, trillion winking points of light. The moon was up, huge and bright, a dazzling silver disk low in the sky. The moonlight was intensely bright. It was bathing the entire landscape with a radiance that meant they could all see for miles. The snow cover was reflecting and amplifying the glow.

Some of the stars were moving. Rory could track at least three of them, very high up overhead, moving in formation.

A fourth was descending.

It was growing brighter by the second. Its descent was

steady and level, perfectly controlled, but it made no sound. The Morphans came to a halt and gazed up at the star as it moved directly overhead and then swung to the east until it seemed to hang above Would Be. It looked as large and as bright as the moon. The light shining from it picked up the slopes of Firmer Number Two, making the sleeping darkness of the mountain stand out against the night sky.

It wasn't a star. Rory knew that. If you squinted against the light, you could see faint details of the structure behind the lights, vast and sleek.

'A star has come loose and fallen down the sky,' said Vesta.

'That's a spaceship,' said Rory.

The Morphans of Beside, almost every single one of them, stood in the snow and looked up at the vast, bright shape suspended in the eastern sky.

'What is that sound?' asked Bill Groan suddenly.

They listened.

Noises were echoing up the valley from the direction of Would Be. Similar noises could be made out coming from the Spitablefields, Farafield and the Fairground beyond the heathouses. They were ugly, ragged noises, the sound of fierce blows being traded by formidably strong opponents. They could hear the blunt force of weapons cracking armour and breaking bone. They could hear grunts of effort and cries of fury, metal striking metal, the crash and shiver of objects colliding with snow-laden trees.

They couldn't see it, but there was some kind of battle going on in the woodland, a vast, medieval-style battle involving close quarters, hand-to-hand violence.

'Who's out there?' asked Bill anxiously. 'Who's fighting?'

'Some of our men?' Jack Duggat ventured. 'The patrols? The nightwatchers?'

'It sounds like hundreds of them!' Bill exclaimed. He turned, pale in the moonlight, and faced his assembled community.

'Morphans of Beside, listen to me. If the fighting moves this way, we're in danger. We have to fall back and protect ourselves.'

'How do we protect ourselves from a star, Elect?' someone shouted out. Some of the community's children were sobbing.

'Just do as I say, for Guide's sake,' Bill replied. 'Come back into the plantnation. The barns and the grain stores are the most strongly built. Take the children there to make them safe. Sol, get guards up to protect the cattle sheds and the stockhouses. Jack, gather a force of men and form a line here and halt whatever comes our way.'

People started to move, obeying his orders, but many simply wanted to linger and stare at the hovering star. Rory edged back through the crowd a little. He was no longer prepared to wait for permission, nor was he going to rely on his powers of persuasion. Everything was about to get very confused and busy. He was going to head directly back to the Incrypt and get access to the Guide. The Doctor was counting on him.

He was about to slip into the shadows of the hedgerow and risk running when things suddenly got worse.

Several long, slicing beams of energy speared down from the hovering ship. They made a keening, screaming noise that split the air. Where the beams struck, large plumes of fire belched up inside the wood. Rory, aghast, saw the black skeletons of trees silhouetted by each vivid fireball. The sounds of the blasts – gritty, ground-shaking roars of fury – echoed back to them. The ship was firing its main weapons at ground targets.

Total panic gripped the Morphans. Screaming and shouting, some carrying children, they began to scatter in every direction.

Rory watched the ship bombard the wood with its battery weapons for a few moments. People ran past him. He could feel the overpressure of the distant concussion as a gusting wind against his face. The ship seemed intent on devastating the entire landscape.

He made his decision.

Rory didn't stop running until he'd reached the assembly. There was no one inside. He could hear the panic and commotion in the streets of the plantnation. He could hear the crump and boom of the bombardment. Each blast vibrated the ground and made the building tremble.

'Where are you going? Rory? Where are you going?'

He turned and saw Vesta in the doorway.

'I have to help the Doctor,' Rory said.

'What is happening, Rory?' she asked, coming forward. 'Is it the end of the world?'

'Not if I can help it,' he replied.

'Is it the Ice Warriors?' she asked. 'Have they begun to kill us?'

'I think they might have,' he said.

'Do they intend to blow us asunder with fire from the sky?' she asked. 'Guide have mercy on us, I thought they would rather rip us apart with their teeth and talons first!'

'Well, they don't really have those, do they?' asked Rory. 'More sort of big green clamps for hands.' He mimed them.

She frowned at him.

'What big green clamps?' she asked.

'Like pincers.'

'Who do?'

'The Ice Warriors! Come on, Vesta. The big, green, scaly thing in the wood? With the red eyes?'

She stared at him, bewildered.

'It had red eyes, right enough,' she said slowly, 'but the thing I saw was not green or scaly.'

'Oh,' said Rory, his shoulders sagging. 'All this time, I don't think we've been talking about the same thing at all.'

CHAPTER 14

BORN TO RAISE THE SONS OF EARTH, BORN TO GIVE THEM SECOND BIRTH

Ssord, the Ice Lord's axe-wielding lieutenant, handed a communicator pad to his master. Ixyldir studied its compact display.

'Does he have an axe because his name is Ssord?' the Doctor asked, sitting in the high-backed chair with his chin in his hand. 'I'm just saying, it might get confusing if Ssord had a sword. Is that why you gave him an axe?'

Ixyldir tilted his head to regard the Doctor. 'For a mammal that is about to be put down, you are remarkably talkative,' he said.

'Oh, but that's precisely why!' the Doctor enthused, jumping to his feet.

The Ice Warriors around him tensed slightly, thinking he was about to attack their clan lord. Ixyldir briskly raised an armoured hand to call them off.

'You intend to kill me anyway, so I don't believe it really matters what I say,' said the Doctor. 'It's a very liberating feeling, in fact. I could insult you to your face, couldn't I, lizard-lips? It's not going to make a lot of difference. I mean, it's not going to make things worse. Death is death.'

'There are things worse than death,' said the Ice Lord.

'Really? Name one.'

'Dishonour.'

The Doctor threw back his head and laughed. 'I *knew* you were going to say that,' he chuckled. 'I love it when Ice Warriors talk about honour and dishonour. It's all so terribly serious and profound. My old buddy Warlord Azylax was forever banging on about it, all the time. I would just roll my eyes. You Ice Warriors can be so pompous on the subject.'

'There is no Warlord Azylax,' said Ixyldir.

'No, unlucky for me,' the Doctor agreed. He sighed. 'No, there *isn't*. At least, there isn't going to be for about another 9,000 years. I realise that now. I got my Galactic Migration Eras mixed up. I didn't know if I was coming or going. Or if you were coming or going. Anyway, my timing's bad, and that sucks for me, because there isn't a single Ice Warrior on this world or any other who can vouch for my credentials.' He looked squarely at Ixyldir. 'But you *will*, by the time we're done here,' he said, and winked. 'I promise. You will have acquired respect for me. As a friend, or as a foe. Which one of those it turns out to be depends entirely on you, Lord Ixyldir of the Tanssor clan.'

'By the time we are done here,' replied the Ice Lord, 'this world will be an ice-locked haven, and you will be a headless corpse rotting in one of the vile meat vats in this facility. You do not impress me, or scare me, *cold blue star*.'

'Then let's talk about dishonour some more,' suggested the Doctor. 'I mean, it is such a popular topic with your kind. You take it so seriously, yet it is so malleable to you.'

'Malleable?' echoed Ixyldir.

'It means pliable or easy to reshape.'

'I know what it means.'

The Doctor looked at the other Ice Warriors. 'Honour is a code you live by… until it becomes inconvenient,' he said.

Ssord raised his axe.

'Stop!' the Ice Lord ordered.

'You see?' said the Doctor. 'Your man here was going to chop down an unarmed prisoner, just because that unarmed prisoner happened to say something he didn't like. How is that the action of an honour-bound warrior?'

'We are principled,' said Ixyldir. 'We are also pragmatic.'

'Yes, you are,' the Doctor agreed. 'But isn't it about time you started to balance those aspects of your culture? You're searching for a new home because Mars has gone.'

'Our home world, along with all the planets in our solar system, has been rendered uninhabitable by the maturing expansion phase of our star.'

'The Morphans of Earth are in the same boat, so to speak,' said the Doctor. '*And* they got here first. *And* this world is more like their home world than yours.'

'It is still generally compatible with our needs,' said the Ice Lord.

'So you're just going to take their planet from them and wipe them out? How is that honourable?'

Ixyldir growled something, a hint of anger under the surface. 'Our primary requirement is the establishment of a new home world for our clan so that we may begin rebuilding our civilisation,' he said. 'We have no particular issue with the human refugees. No malice. It is simply a competition for resources.'

'Tell *them* that,' said the Doctor. 'You're killing them.'

'At the moment,' replied Ixyldir, 'it appears to be a two-way process.' He showed the display of the communicator pad to the Doctor.

The Doctor leaned forward, frowning deeply as he made sense of the data he was being shown. 'You deployed one of your ships into a low atmospheric holding position. You're... firing at surface targets. Ixyldir, you've committed forces to an open ground offensive!'

'And why might I have done that, *cold blue star?*'

The Doctor blinked. 'I don't... Wait, how can that be? You're fighting something. You're fighting something that's fighting back!'

'Your emotional nuance is interesting,' said Ixyldir. 'I am no expert in mammalian micro-expression, but your surprise seems quite genuine. I imagine, however, that this is because you are a trained spy and infiltration agent. I offer you one last opportunity to cease your constant disinformation. I agree to make your death rapid and painless. Tell me the location of your ship.'

'My ship?'

'Where is it concealed? How many more military operatives are you carrying aboard it?'

'Wait,' said the Doctor. 'Wait, wait, wait, wait, *waitaminute!*' He started to pace, disconcerted. 'You said you were maintaining a watch on the planet. You've been monitoring the human population on Hereafter since you arrived ten years ago?'

'Yes.'

'Logging them all individually by their heatprints?'

'Yes.'

'Roughly speaking, in that time, what has the population of Hereafter been, Lord Ixyldir?'

Ixyldir paused, considering the pros and cons of

tendering the information. Finally, he answered: 'Combined, the three human settlements represent a global population of around 19,000.'

It was the Doctor's turn to pause. His mind was racing. 'But just recently,' he continued, 'the nature of the struggle has changed? It's forced you out into the open?'

'Yes.'

'You've detected new arrivals, like me and my friends?' asked the Doctor.

'Yes,' growled Ixyldir, growing impatient.

'And you distinguish between the pre-existing population and the new arrivals by heatprints?'

'Heatprints do not lie,' said the Ice Lord.

The Doctor sighed. 'Bear with me for one moment more, Lord Ixyldir,' he said. 'We're about to have a really crucial exchange of information. Everything that happens from now may hinge upon it. I'll start by telling you something, in the spirit of a free and frank debate. I arrived here, in my ship, with two companions. That's it. A total of three new arrivals. We got here yesterday.'

Ixyldir turned his head slowly and looked at Ssord. Then he looked back at the Doctor.

'Lord Ixyldir,' said the Doctor. 'According to your scans, how many new heatprints have appeared in addition to the existing human population here?'

The Ice Lord permitted himself a glacial pause before replying. 'One hundred and fifty,' he replied.

'Down here!' Amy yelled.

She was leading the way, her duffel coat flying out behind her. Samewell and Arabel were running to keep up.

'They're coming after us, Amy!' Bel cried.

Amy looked back. Thirty-five metres behind them, two Ice Warriors had appeared on a gantry platform and were following the three humans onto the grilled shipskin bridge that arched across a vast turbine chamber. In the past five minutes, Amy and her companions had been chased through four large compartments just like it. Each time they had emerged onto a platform or bridge at a different level. Each time, they believed, briefly, that they might have finally shaken off their pursuers.

But each time, the Ice Warriors had appeared, relentlessly searching and hounding.

The bridge they were currently crossing spanned a large chamber at a particularly high level. Several other walkways criss-crossed the chamber at different levels below them. Far below the bridges, at the bottom of the yawning drop, there was a huge cavity that looked like the bowl of an active volcano. Molten fire seethed and roiled down there, an abyssal well of flames. They could feel the heat rising through the space of the compartment. High overhead, unfurled like sails, titanic thermal vents were arranged to conduct and direct the heat.

'We can't run for ever!' Samewell yelled.

'Watch me!' Amy cried.

Arabel let out a shriek of despair. 'Look!' she yelled.

Amy skidded to a halt. They were about halfway across the long, railed walkway. Three more Ice Warriors had just appeared at the other end of the span. Ice Warriors were closing in from both sides.

They were trapped in the middle of the bridge. There was nowhere to go.

'What do we do?' asked Samewell.

'We surrender, don't we?' Arabel said.

'No!' said Amy firmly. 'They won't take us alive.' She looked around. She looked up. She grabbed the guard rail, leaned out, and looked down. 'We jump,' she decided.

'Are you mad?' asked Samewell.

'To kill ourselves so they can't capture us?' asked Arabel.

'No!' replied Amy. 'What do you take me for? I'm not going to stupid well kill myself! We jump down onto that!'

She pointed.

The closest of the bridge spans beneath them was only a few metres below. They were almost directly above the point where two bridges intersected.

'We'd never make it!' objected Arabel. 'We'll jump and miss!'

'We won't miss!' replied Amy. She started to hoist herself up over the rail.

'It's too far!' Samewell cried.

Amy got her heels on the edge of the walkway, holding the handrail against the small of her back. She stared down. It did look far too far. It looked *ridiculously* too far. It was like jumping off a tightrope and hoping to land on another tightrope.

'We can do it!' she insisted.

She looked at them. Arabel and Samewell were clutching each other and staring at her in dread.

'Come on!' Amy yelled. 'Look how close they're getting!'

Bel and Samewell looked around. The two Ice Warriors behind them were approaching rapidly. The three coming the other way weren't so close, but there wasn't a lot in it.

'Any better ideas?' Amy yelled. 'No? Then come on! Now!'

Uttering moans of reluctance and fear, the two Morphans scrambled over the rail next to her.

'It is so high, I fear I shall faint,' said Bel.

'Try your best not to,' said Amy. 'OK. OK. I'll go first. I'll show you how it's done. OK.'

Perched, they looked at her.

'OK, I'm going,' said Amy. Her hands didn't seem to want to let the handrail go. It really was a very, very long way down. What had she been thinking? She couldn't make *that*. It was crazy. It was crazy, crazy talk. Even if she *did* jump, and didn't miss the bridge, she'd break a leg, or a neck, or something else that she was fairly unwilling to damage.

'A-Amy?' Bel said. Her voice was trembling. 'Amy, are we going to do this?'

'Yes. We are. Hang on. OK. OK, I'm… OK. Ready? I'm ready. OK. Here we go.' Amy swallowed hard. 'Actually,' she said, 'I think it might be a bit too far after all.'

She looked around at Bel and Samewell, in time to see an Ice Warrior reaching a huge, green pincer-hand out to grab them.

'Geronimo!' she yelled.

And jumped.

'Rory?' Vesta asked. 'Rory, what are you doing?'

Rory didn't reply immediately. He was moving around the assembly hall, shifting benches and knocking on wooden wall panels.

'Not green?' he asked. 'The thing you saw? In the woods? "*It*"? It wasn't big and green?'

'It was a monster,' Vesta said. 'A big monster with claws and red eyes, but it was nothing at all like the green thing you described.'

Rory tapped his way along a panelled wall, listening.

'It's fair to say,' he said, 'that I haven't been entirely up to speed on this situation since I arrived. But now I *really* don't know what's going on. I mean, I don't have a clue. Is it possible that we're in the middle of some sort of war that we didn't previously know about?'

'I don't know, Rory,' said Vesta. Every flash and boom from outside made her jump and look towards the windows. The night sky was underlit orange with flame from burning woods. The noises of battle were getting closer.

'What are you doing?' she asked again.

'I'm looking for…' Rory began. He dropped his hands and stood back from the beam he'd been examining. He shook his head. 'I don't know what I'm looking for,' he said. 'The Doctor turned this room into some kind of communications station. A receiver. I just thought that… if he could turn it on from *his* end, I should be able to do the same here. There should be controls, hidden somewhere, I suppose. Perhaps boarded up or panelled over because the Morphans didn't know what they were for. I thought I might be able to find them.'

Vesta shrugged. 'Guide only knows,' she said. She cleared her throat. 'Rory,' she said. 'I think that I want to go and hide in the barns with the others. I think that's the safest place.'

He looked at her. 'Yes, that makes sense,' he said. 'You should do that. Do you want me to take you there?'

'No, I can find my way. Will you be all right?'

'Yes, I…' Rory's voice trailed off. He looked at her with such intent, she laughed and shook her head in confusion.

'What?' she asked.

'I said I was looking for the controls, and you said…?'

215

'I don't know, Rory!' she said.

'You said, "Guide only knows."' He grinned. 'I'm not thinking straight. I wanted to try and get this place running, so that once I had got the Guide, I had a way of sending it to the Doctor. But I can kill two birds with one stone. Your Guide Emanual will *tell* me how to operate this station. It stands to reason.'

He turned and walked towards the rear doors of the assembly hall. Vesta ran after him, her skirts gathered up.

'Are you really going in?' she asked. 'Into the Incrypt?'

'Yes,' he replied.

'Even though you are not one of the Beside council, and permission was expressly denied to you?'

Still walking, Rory gestured towards the hall windows and the rumbling flash of the onslaught.

'Hello?' he said. 'Bigger picture?'

'But—' she began.

'Vesta, I think that the solutions to all the many and troubling problems plaguing us right now are in that room. The Doctor thinks so too. So I'd better get on and find them, because the alternative isn't really very pretty.'

Rory reached the double doors. Old Winnowner, the keeper of the key, had padlocked them shut. He started to rattle and push at them, but they were very solidly made and securely fastened.

He put his shoulder against them, and rammed.

'Ow,' he said, rubbing his shoulder. 'That's not going to work. I need something else. An axe, or a crowbar.'

He turned from the doors and found himself nose to nose with the business end of Jack Duggat's hoe.

'Whoa!' he said, recoiling.

'You was trying to break into the Incrypt,' said Jack,

holding the farming implement like a rifle with a fixed bayonet.

'It's really important I get in there,' said Rory.

'It really is, Jack!' Vesta agreed.

'It is Cat A vital you do not,' replied Jack emphatically. 'Look what I found!' he called out over his shoulder. 'Just as you feared.'

Old Winnowner came in through the main doors of the hall behind him. She was out of breath from hurrying through the snow. 'I see,' she said.

'Good thing you sent me here direct,' said Jack, not relaxing his grip on the hoe.

'Vesta Flurrish, I'm surprised at you,' said Old Winnowner as she hobbled over to them. 'Betraying everything we've worked for.'

'Give him the key and let him within, Winnowner Cropper,' said Vesta firmly. 'Can you not see he's a friend?'

'I have no proof of that,' Old Winnowner replied.

'Then can you not see what is happening outside?' asked Vesta. 'Fire from out of the sky! Falling stars! The world's end! A ruin and disaster the like of which we have not even imagined! Will you just watch it happen or will you try to stop it?'

'It is being stopped,' said the old woman. 'That is all there is to it. It is in Guide's hands. Now, Jack, bring them. We'll take them to the barn with us.'

'I'm not going anywhere!' cried Rory.

'Really?' asked Jack.

Rory backed off. 'Put like that, and with such a large hoe involved in your answer, perhaps I am,' he agreed.

Jack and the old woman marched them out of the assembly. The cold clear night outside was bright orange from the flames. The ship, still hovering, was continuing its merciless prosecution of ground targets in the hills. They could smell smoke from the burning trees.

In the town yard, the snow was trampled. The fires were casting long, twisting shadows across the broken snow. The sounds of battle were closer. It appeared that some of the town's outbuildings down by the heathouses were now on fire.

'Quickly, get them to the barns,' Winnowner said.

'I think you're placing excessive faith in the protective properties of agricultural storage,' said Rory.

Vesta yelped.

On the far side of the town yard, two Ice Warriors had appeared. Both were brandishing swords. Ignoring the four humans outside the assembly hall, they strode across the yard as though they were pursuing an unseen adversary through the lanes of the houses opposite. They disappeared from view behind the granary.

'Oh, Guide!' said Vesta. 'Were they those things?'

'Ice Warriors,' said Rory. He could see the fear on the faces of the Morphans. Even Winnowner's resolve had been checked by a glimpse of the towering aliens.

'Are you going to start believing me?' Rory asked.

Winnowner didn't answer. There was a sudden and terrible mauling sound from the direction of the granary. It was the noise of bodies slamming into wooden wall boards, of timber splintering, of armour denting.

'Get them back inside, Jack,' said Winnowner. 'Hurry now.'

Before they could turn, something appeared on the roof of the granary. It had leapt up there in a bound, like a big cat. It prowled down the thick slump of snow on the building's roof, moving on all fours, and then sprang down into the yard and started to come directly towards them with a lithe, loping stride.

Its eyes flashed red in the firelight.

Rory, Vesta, Winnowner and Jack all backed away until they felt the assembly doors behind them.

'Oh, Guide! Oh, Guide!' Vesta babbled, stricken with fear. 'That's it. That's what I saw in the woods. That's *It!*'

Amy landed, on her feet, in the middle of the bridge walkway. She made a resounding clang that shivered the metalwork of the entire structure. Slowly, she opened her eyes, waiting to see if there were any clues like, for example, excruciating pain, that could tell her if she'd broken anything significant or killed herself.

She seemed to be intact.

'Oh my god, it worked,' she marvelled.

Another loud clang shook the bridge and almost knocked her off her feet. Samewell had landed beside her. His landing wasn't quite as clean as Amy's. He went sprawling as he hit, and nearly rolled off the walkway under the lowest bar of the guard rail. Amy squeaked and grabbed him, dragging him back.

'Don't fall! Don't fall! Don't fall!' she yelled.

'Am I safe? Have I landed?' Samewell asked, entirely flummoxed by the whole experience.

Amy looked up in time to see Bel falling towards them. Her long skirts billowed out as she dropped, almost like a parachute canopy.

Arabel missed the walkway. She had jumped a little too short.

Amy cried out in horror as Bel bounced off the outside

of the guard rail and went over backwards, plunging away into the fiery depths.

She stopped falling with a violent lurch. Her skirts had caught up on the rail. Bel was hanging upside down off the side of the bridge by her winter skirts, her arms thrashing.

'Grab her! Pull her up!' Amy shouted. She and Samewell rushed to the rail and leant over, each of them reaching down with both hands trying to snatch and grasp at Arabel's inverted form.

There was a long, slow and ominous sound of cloth tearing.

'Arabel Flurrish!' Samewell yelled. 'If you fall and die, I'll kill you!'

'Grab my hand!' Amy shrieked. 'Bel, grab my hand!'

Arabel's skirts tore. Unhooked from the brief suspension of the guard rail, she fell.

Amy and Samewell both grunted out air as they took her weight, straining to hold on. Samewell had both his hands wrapped around Bel's right hand. Amy had one hand locked around Bel's left. Arabel was hanging by her arms the right way up.

But Samewell and Amy were leaning out so far, Bel was in danger of pulling them both over the rail.

'*Get her up!*' Amy bellowed.

'I– *can't!*' Samewell gasped.

'Get her up now! Now! Before we all go over!' Amy told him, snorting with effort. 'On three! One… two… three!'

They hauled.

Bel came up in a rush, and all three of them tumbled backwards over the guard rail and ended up piled on the walkway in an untidy heap.

'I am *not* doing that again,' said Bel.

Amy got up. The thwarted Ice Warriors were glaring down at them from the bridge above.

'Come on!' she urged the two young Morphans. 'Get up and get going!'

Samewell helped Bel to her feet, and they both followed Amy along the span towards the exit hatch. The metal walkway rang under their feet.

Suddenly, it did more than ring. It shook as though the bridge had been hit by a wrecking ball. The violent shiver made all three of them stumble.

Amy looked back.

An Ice Warrior was slowly getting up out of a crouched position on the walkway behind them. It had jumped from the walkway overhead, and landed roughly where they had landed.

There was something completely terrifying about the giant green thing's unexpected display of agility.

It rose to its full height, and reached its right fist up to its left shoulder to grasp the hilt of the sword secured across its broad back. It drew the sword, raised it, and started to pursue them all over again.

'You know that thing I keep saying?' Amy yelped.

'What, run, you mean?' asked Bel.

'Yeah,' said Amy. 'Can we just save me some time and take it as read from now on?'

A second Ice Warrior plunged like a boulder from the bridge above. It landed behind the first, missing the main platform, but impacting, as Arabel had done, against the guard rail. Pincer clamps snapped shut around the rail to prevent it from toppling backwards into the drop. The metal railing was buckled and twisted by its collision.

Slowly, clumsily, it clambered over the bent guard rail

and onto the bridge. There, it unfastened the battle-axe anchored across its back, and set off after the first.

Amy was just a short distance from the safety of the hatch. She reached out her hand so she could touch the palm-checker plate as soon as she arrived and open the door. If they could get through and close the hatch again, the Ice Warriors would have to stop to drill the lock out, and that would buy them a little more time.

The hatch began to open. She hadn't touched the plate. Something on the other side had activated the lock system.

Amy slid to a stop, and Bel and Samewell cannoned into her from behind. All Amy could think was the Ice Warriors had somehow learned how to work the locks.

Something came through the hatch and out onto the bridge facing them.

It wasn't an Ice Warrior.

The three of them screamed anyway.

'Do you know what I'm going to do?' the Doctor asked Ixyldir. 'I can't believe I'm saying this, but do you know what I'm going to do?'

'What?' asked the Ice Lord.

'I'm going to help you,' the Doctor replied.

'Help me?'

'Help you all. There's a level to this situation that neither of us really anticipated.'

'I do not believe you can be trusted,' Ixyldir replied.

The Doctor shook his head, and snatched the communicator pad out of the Ice Lord's grip. Ssord and two other Ice Warriors reacted to stop him, but the Doctor did a little duck and weave to avoid them as if they were the least of his worries. He was busy examining the pad's display.

'You're taking a pasting, Ixyldir,' he said, reading data. 'Your slow, cold war has turned into a fast, hot one. This is not what you were expecting at all, is it?'

He looked at the Ice Lord.

'Is it?' he repeated. 'I'm not saying that you're not prepared to fight. You're Ice Warriors, for goodness sake. But this isn't the scenario you were expecting when you began your offensive ten years ago. Is it?'

'No,' said the Ice Lord.

'Escalation,' said the Doctor. 'You said it yourself. I can help you, but only if you start cooperating with me quickly. I mean very quickly. We don't even have to trust each other completely, but if we don't get this situation under control, there are going to be an awful lot of deaths. Morphan, Ice Warrior. Unnecessary deaths. This world laid waste, possibly to the point where it is of no use to either colonial effort. Come on, Lord Ixyldir of the Tanssor clan! Be smart!'

The Ice Lord seemed to take an eternity to reply.

'What form would this cooperation take?' he asked.

The Ice Warriors behind him swung their heavy heads to glance at one another.

The Doctor grinned.

'That's the spirit, Ix! That's the spirit! You're starting to thaw, pardon the pun! This could be the start of a beautiful friendship, Ix! Can I call you Ix?'

'Most certainly not.'

'We'll work on that, then. Here's what I need first. We have to find another facility like this, this telepresence communication centre.' The Doctor gestured to the chamber they were standing in. 'Ssord's handy axe-work rather ripped the stuffing out of the systems here,' he said.

'I could fix it, but it would frankly take more time than we have at our disposal. There must be another. You've been working your way through this complex for years, cutting open doors. You must have found another one or two by now. Preferably, a more significant control room than this. This is just a secondary station. Do you know of any primary command and control rooms?'

Lord Ixyldir looked at Ssord.

'Level sssix,' the Ice Warrior hissed.

'Let's go!' the Doctor cried. 'Lead the way, Ssord. Lord Ixyldir, we'll walk and talk.'

Ssord led the way out of the chamber. The other Ice Warriors fell in around the Doctor and Lord Ixyldir as an honour guard escort.

'Walk as fast as you can!' the Doctor urged. He looked at Ixyldir. 'I need to know the details of your operation,' he said. 'It's vital. On several other occasions, I've known your people to instigate terraforming processes on target worlds. You're pretty good at it.'

'When our migration fleet entered this quadrant, this planet revealed itself to be the most likely candidate for adjustment,' replied the Ice Lord. 'Long-range observation confirmed it met the majority of our colonisation criteria. We resolved to achieve orbit, to commence climate engineering, and then wait for the process to be completed by entering hibernation on our ships.'

'Were you planning to use seed technology to bring about climate alterations?' asked the Doctor.

'You are familiar with the technique?' asked Ixyldir, surprised.

'I've stopped it more than once, actually,' the Doctor said. 'It's very efficient, though. The destabilisation of carbon dioxide levels is often all it takes to induce a global arctic phase on an M-class world.'

They left the gloom of the tunnels and followed a broad, railed walkway around the edge of a plunging turbine cavern.

'Once we were in orbit,' said the Ice Lord, 'we realised that a human colony was already established on the candidate planet. It had been here for some time and, though comparatively small, it had constructed terraforming processors of significant size and effect. This process had been under way for several generations, and was already beginning to induce change.'

'So you thought, "Why bother setting up our own terraforming programme to work in opposition? Why not just repurpose the one that's already there?"'

'This was deemed to be the most viable option.'

The Doctor shook his head sadly. 'This is where you and I will be forced to disagree, Lord Ixyldir. That was a pretty underhand gambit. You decide to steal a planet out from under these settlers, you co-opt their terraformers to do the hard work for you, and you essentially consign them to a generation or two of long, slow, bitter extinction. You signed their death warrants, Lord Ixyldir, but you let the snow and ice do the actual killing for you. You didn't have enough respect for your adversary to pull the trigger yourself. Dirty pool, Lord Ixyldir. That's dirty pool.'

'I do not understand your reference,' replied the Ice Lord.

'It's not very honourable, is it?' replied the Doctor. 'That's what I'm saying. Theft, on a planetary scale.'

'This was not the humans' planet either. They selected it and claimed it. We were merely doing the same.'

'But they were here first, Ixyldir. It's a bit of a school

225

playground *he said, she said* argument, I know, but do you know what? Most honour systems are built on very simple, basic concepts of ownership, or respect, or prior claim, or of precedence. The humans were here first, Ixyldir. You decided they were in the way, and you decided to steal their technology to eradicate them. Don't talk to me about honour.'

'It was a matter of survival,' objected Ixyldir.

'Ah yes, the famous pragmatism of the Ice Warriors. You didn't mean to hurt anybody, but you were obliged to in order to survive. Lord Ixyldir, the deliberate and systematic eradication of an entire population is called genocide, and it's not regarded as especially honourable either. Not where nice people come from.'

'We had to survive! This was a viable planet—'

'You had a fleet of ships, Ice Lord. You could have gone somewhere else. The humans did not have that option.'

Ixyldir did not reply. For a few minutes, as the group continued to walk, entering a long, metal-lined hallway, the only sound was the tramp of feet and the rumble of the world-building engines.

'Anyway,' said the Doctor at length. 'Let's not dwell on your *not-really-very-honourable-at-all* decision-making process. You started to tinker with the terraformers. This was ten years ago. You knew it would be a gradual process that would take a long time, but you've got plenty of that, haven't you? Hibernation systems on your starships. Lifetimes that are naturally three or four times those of humans. You could afford to play the long game. The Morphans, you know, they talk about patience a great deal. It's a fundamental quality of their culture. Not an easy, sleep-through-it-all patience like yours. I'm talking about the patience required to live and work every day, generation after generation, for a future ideal that will benefit your descendants. It's admirably selfless. Don't you think so?'

'It is… worthy of respect.'

'It is, isn't it?' the Doctor said. 'They just work towards the future. They make their contribution. They get no reward. They're just investing the effort of their lives for the good of other people they're never going to meet.'

They came out into another turbine hall, and Ssord led them up a broad metal staircase towards an upper level.

'So, your tinkering?' said the Doctor. 'You employed seed technology first?'

'Modified seed cultures were introduced to the primary terraformer systems. Initial results were positive.'

'But you reached a tipping point eventually,' said the Doctor. 'Eventually, as the winters began to get colder, the automatic monitoring systems governing the terraformer systems began to notice there was a problem. They performed self-diagnostic reviews and identified alien properties in the system. They needed to resolve the problem, so they accessed the DNA libraries, reopened the flesh banks, and grew a brand new batch of transrats to flush out the system.'

'Vermin was our first problem,' Ixyldir acknowledged.

'Transrats are resilient,' said the Doctor. 'The more you killed, the more they made. That must have become a bit of a war. A guerrilla war, going on underground in the mountains, where the Morphans couldn't see it.'

'We prosecuted the vermin. The problem took about a year to control.'

'You used standard sonic disruptors, and you were

forced to destroy some of the DNA banks and flesh farms so that the terraformers simply couldn't produce as many replacement transrats?'

'Yes.'

'And that still wasn't enough, was it?' the Doctor asked. 'They're resilient, as I said. Eventually, you must have realised that you couldn't beat the transrats. You had to find a way around them so they were no longer an impediment to your schemes?'

'We were forced to select alternatives to the processes we had originally put in place,' replied Ixyldir, 'the processes that the vermin had disabled. Seed technology was no longer viable, because the vermin simply devoured it.'

'You started to actually convert the terraformers themselves? Recalibrate their systems?'

'Yes.'

'And that's when things really escalated, isn't it?' asked the Doctor.

'In here!' Ssord said abruptly.

The Doctor followed the Ice Warriors through a large hatch, noting that the palm-print reader had been drilled through.

They entered a massive, well-lit control room. There were several banks of consoles like the one in the telepresence chamber, each with a row of high-backed chairs. The chamber itself overlooked one of the secondary sequence prebiotic crucibles through a vast plate-glass wall. The Doctor paused to enjoy the view of the giant chrome tree. Drizzle from the cloud systems swirling the ceiling of the crucible chamber pattered against the glass wall like light summer rain.

'Yes,' the Doctor nodded. 'This will do the trick nicely. A

central operation nexus. Would have taken me ages to find this, especially with you lot chasing me.'

'What happens now?' asked Ixyldir. 'If you have tricked us into revealing the location of this facility to you, I will kill you myself.'

'I would expect no less,' replied the Doctor. He sat down at one of the workstations and began to play with the controls, lighting up banks of indicator functions and small hologram read-outs.

'You see, Ixyldir,' he said as he worked, 'what I think has happened is this. You tampered with the terraformers. The system detected you, and manufactured transrats to solve the problem. So you started tampering in a different way to get around the transrat problem, and the system detected that too. It hadn't got many options left, so it had to do something quite radical.'

The Doctor turned to look at the Ice Lord.

'It built something else, Ixyldir,' he said. 'Something bigger and nastier. With what was left of its flesh farms, it manufactured something else.'

'Like what, *cold blue star*?' Ixyldir asked.

The Doctor shrugged.

'The next effective stage beyond transrats. Something *Transhuman*, is my guess. And that's what you're fighting now.'

CHAPTER 15
NOW IN FLESH APPEARING

The thing prowled out onto the bridge. It was making a noise in its throat that was part growl, part purr. Its metal claws clinked on the grilled walkway as it took each step.

Amy, Bel and Samewell backed away from it, almost forgetting that a pair of Ice Warriors was closing on them from behind.

It was a monstrous thing. It was almost a man, a huge, lean, well-muscled man, in the same way that a transrat was almost a rat. It had been seriously bio-engineered. Its feet and hands were cybernetic implants that extruded huge steel talons. Amy realised, with rising disgust, that she could see where the bones of the hands were fused into the metal sheathing. Flexible armoured cables corded its skin like external arteries, and its scarred, baby-pink flesh was puckered with grafting scars, and covered with sockets and surgical plugs. It was moving on all fours like a giant cat. There was a disturbing hint that its human DNA had been blended with that of a major predator, like a leopard or panther, altering its spine, hips and legs so that it could move fluidly and comfortably in quadruped form. It smelled of meat and blood and diseased tissue. Upright, it would have been easily as big as the Ice Warriors, perhaps as much as three metres tall.

Its face was a human skull that had been reinforced with chromed steel and adjusted, like a regular road car customised as a hot-rod. The jaw was huge, and the chin pointed and prominent, in order to accommodate the gleaming set of monstrous fangs. The teeth, twice the size of even adult human dentition, were coated in steel like precise medical instruments. It had a grin full of scalpels. Lip-less, cheek-less, the teeth formed a permanent smile. The crown of the skull was covered in wires, cables and tubes that formed a long, straggly mane of thick strands.

Its eyes glowed red.

It pounced.

Amy, Bel and Samewell ducked instinctively. The thing went clear over them anyway. Leaving a deep, throbbing growl in the air behind it, it crashed into the Ice Warriors.

Still cowering low, Amy turned to see what was happening. The red-eyed monster was taking both of the Ice Warriors on. The glinting steel claws of one forepaw ripped around and tore a deep gouge through the scaled chest plate of one of the Ice Warriors, driving him backwards. The Warrior hissed in pain. His companion swung in, wielding the ornate broadsword with both pincers. The first stroke missed. The red-eyed monster was ridiculously agile and fast. It somehow slipped under the Ice Warrior's next stroke, and turned as it rose behind him, burying both sets of front claws in the Martian's back. Green battle armour shredded. Individual scales twinkled like stars as they showered into the air. Amy flinched as the red-eyed monster lunged its huge jaws forward and ripped into the back of the stricken Ice Warrior's neck.

The other Warrior had regained its footing. As the red-eyed thing savaged his comrade's throat, he swung the axe. It struck the monster squarely in the right shoulder. Ugly, unhealthy-looking blood sprayed from the wound. The monumental impact smashed the red-eyed thing off its prey and clean through the guard rail. It fell.

It did not fall far.

With extraordinary gymnastic skill, it snagged the struts on the underside of the walkway, and swung under the bridge, somersaulting up, free, on the other side. It landed on the Ice Warrior with the axe from behind, knocking him over, face-first, into the half-broken guard rail. Entangled, they fought brutally with each other, each one trying to break the other's grip. The red-eyed monster tore away first, but only so it could pull back and put all its inhuman strength into a driving hook that ripped across the Ice Warrior's face, shredding his visor.

The Ice Warrior, mortally hurt, staggered backwards, hissing like a punctured tyre, and toppled over the torn rail. He dropped away into the flaming abyss below.

The other Ice Warrior, bleeding from his jagged wounds and ruptured scale-armour, came at the red-eyed thing, swinging his sword. The thing evaded the first two strokes, and then drove at the Ice Warrior, catching the side of the razor-sharp blade with its cybernetic hand. It plucked the sword out of the Ice Warrior's grip and threw it away. Then it went for the Ice Warrior's throat. The Ice Warrior clawed at it, grabbing it by the neck and shoulder with his powerful clamps. Locked together, they wrestled ferociously for a few seconds.

The Ice Warrior, understanding that he was weakening and bleeding out, understanding that he was up against an adversary who was stronger, faster and essentially superior, understanding that he was effectively beaten, did what all dedicated warriors do as a last resort. Gripping the red-eyed thing that was busy killing him, so tightly that it couldn't break free, he lurched off the walkway too. He took his red-eyed tormentor to its doom alongside him.

They vanished from view in the fires far below.

Amy, trembling, looked at the two young Morphans.

'Let's get out of here,' she said. 'You know, before something else really, stupid well insane happens.'

But it was too late. There were more of them, more of the red-eyed things.

They were stalking out of the hatch and onto the bridge, advancing towards the three, defenceless humans.

Rory, Vesta, Winnowner and Jack Duggat backed into the assembly hall, trying not to make any hasty movements. Jack still had hold of his hoe, but not in any way that suggested he was likely to wield it.

The red-eyed *It* that Vesta had seen in the woods prowled in after them. Gazing at them, it padded through the snow like a leopard on all fours, frost glinting on its matted mane of tubes and wires. It smiled an eternal, unintentional steel smile.

It entered the wood-panelled hall, and looked around, as though sensing something familiar. It returned its crimson gaze to the four terrified humans and stared at them. Then it rose on its hind legs and stood upright like a man, an adjustment that was somehow even more distressing.

'Oh, save us,' whispered Winnowner. 'What has Guide wrought?'

'Guide,' the thing echoed. It was a horrid, sticky sound, a

rumble that was part growl and part phlegm. Its fearsome teeth made normal speech impossible, but it gurgled the word out of a small, cybernetic vocal implant that they could see in its throat, now that it was standing upright.

It was so frighteningly tall.

'Guide…' it repeated. 'I… am assigned to secure and protect… the Guide system.'

'The Guide?' asked Winnowner.

'The Guide system… must not fall… into enemy hands. Aggressors have been detected… tampering has been detected… purge now under way.'

It raised one gnarled, part-metal fist and wiped droplets of blood off its awful teeth.

'I… am assigned to secure and protect… the Guide system. It is… here.'

'What are you?' asked Rory.

'Transhuman sixty-eight of one hundred fifty… woken and refitted for this Category A emergency…'

'Woken?' asked Rory.

'From… the cryo-store,' it replied. 'Stand aside… I am assigned… to secure and protect… the Guide system.'

They wavered.

'I am… sanctioned to slay… anything that stands in opposition to my task…' it said.

They got out of its way. It dropped back onto all fours and padded past them.

'I never asked for this!' Winnowner said. 'I just asked for help! I never expected that any of the patients would be woken!'

Rory looked at her sharply. 'Wait, you said "woken" too! What do you know?'

'Only what I must know!' Winnowner snapped. 'The

secret that passes from one generation to the next, through the last in each line. The secret that I must pass to Elect Groan before the end of my time.'

'I think you should share it with the room,' said Rory, 'because your time could be up any second now.'

'No!' Winnowner said.

'What is this?' asked Vesta. 'Winnowner Cropper, what is this?'

'Winnowner?' Jack urged.

'I will keep Guide's secret. It is not my place to tell.' Winnowner's voice dropped low. 'I will keep it to the end, for the good of all Morphans.'

'I don't think that's anything like good enough right now,' said Rory.

'Tell us what this thing is and what it wants!' Vesta demanded.

'Be silent!' the red-eyed thing growled, turning back to them and rising up again. 'Or I will... silence you.'

'I don't think that would be very friendly at all,' said the Doctor. 'Especially not as you're all supposed to be on the same side.'

Light levels in the assembly had shifted. The shimmering effect of the holographic telepresence field was rising like mist from the metal circle patterns inlaid in the old wooden floor. The Doctor was in their midst, sitting in a high-backed chair, facing a white control console. He got up and walked over to face the beast.

'Sorry I couldn't get here earlier. I was trying to tune in,' he said. 'Very difficult, when you haven't got a reliable Guide.' He glanced at Rory. 'Everything OK, Rory?' he asked.

'Oh, you know, Doctor,' Rory shrugged. 'Apart from the

Ice Warriors, and the spaceship shooting the place up, and that thing there, everything's dandy.'

The Doctor nodded and looked back at 'that thing there'. It growled softly.

'A Transhuman construct,' he said. 'Advanced martial model. Part of an emergency protocol. A last resort. If the terraformers are threatened. The plantnations don't have any actual weapons. They don't have guns or anything. This is what the system manufactures if a weapon's really needed.'

'If the Morphans are threatened,' said Winnowner.

The Doctor shook his head. 'Sorry, no, actually. They don't really care about you. You're just… the help. In the long run, you're expendable.'

'Winnowner said she had a secret,' said Rory.

'I'm sure she does. Last of her generation. The dark and murky legacy. The sort of secret that would make life unbearable for the Morphans if they knew about it. The sort of secret that makes you oh-so protective of your Guide Emanual. You had to pass the secret on eventually. Who were you going to tell, Winnowner? Bill Groan?'

'Mind your own business, you unguidely—'

'Listen to me, Winnowner Cropper,' said the Doctor, 'I've figured it out. It took me a while, because I didn't have a Guide to show me the shortcuts, but I figured it out.'

He wandered back to the console.

'The Morphans don't matter,' he said sadly. 'They are not building Hereafter for their descendants. They're building it for their ancestors. There are around a thousand human beings sleeping here in the mountain, in suspended animation.'

'What?' asked Vesta.

'It's been misremembered over the years,' said the Doctor. 'Patience is such an important virtue to you Morphans. "Those who are patient will provide for all of the plantnation." Well, "the patient" are right here. *Patients*. Lined up in hibernetic capsules under the Firmer. I'm pretty sure they represent the elite of Earth before. The most powerful and influential people. People who were convinced that they deserved to live. People who believed they were so special they had to have a brand new world made just for them.'

He looked at the lurking shadow of the Transhuman.

'People, in fact, who weren't prepared to toil away their lives building a new world. They just expected the boring work to be done for them by common and disposable labourers.'

'Th-that's not how Guide explains it!' cried Winnowner.

'I'm sure Guide puts it a great deal more delicately,' said the Doctor. 'But that's the size of it. And only this, only the interference of the Ice Warriors, rival colonists, is a crisis major enough to force the system to wake some of them up. A Catagory A crisis. It was enough to wake them up, and arm them for war.'

He stared at the Transhuman.

'You're a frightening thing,' he said. 'And I thought Ice Warriors were dangerous. It takes a lot of fuel to keep a metabolism like that going, doesn't it? You're essentially a carnivore. I thought the transrat swarms were getting out and killing the livestock, but it was you lot, wasn't it? The first of you to be woken and released?'

'There was… a fuel requirement,' it growled.

'Because the Ice Warriors had disabled most of the flesh farms that were designed to feed you during their cull of the transrats,' replied the Doctor. 'You and your kind needed huge hits of high calorific intake to get going.'

The Transhuman walked back into the light of the hologram field and faced the Doctor.

'You have... no authority,' it said. 'The system... does not recognise you. This crisis... is almost resolved. The alien enemy... is virtually routed. Equilibrium will be... restored.'

'Good, good,' said the Doctor. 'But why don't you tell the nice Morphans what will happen to them when you finally wake up for good? Even Winnowner doesn't know that, does she? Tell them. In a few years' time, another generation or two, when the terraforming is finally finished, and Hereafter is properly Earth-like, the Patients will *finally* wake up.'

'This is... the plan,' the Transhuman said. 'The colonial scheme.'

The Doctor looked at Vesta and Jack and Winnowner. 'When the Pilgrim Fathers went across to the New World, they took livestock with them. That's all you are. Livestock. Doing all the hard work in the meantime, so they don't have to. And when they wake up in Eden, you know what? They're going to be really hungry. Really, *really* hungry.'

'No!' cried Winnowner.

'Meat is meat,' said the Doctor. 'Isn't that right, Mr Transhuman?'

'Survival requires... certain practicalities,' it growled.

'Oh, everyone's saying that today!' the Doctor grinned.

The Transhuman lashed out. Its claws passed through the holographic Doctor.

'Temper, temper,' the Doctor chided. 'You can't touch me. I'm not really there at all.'

'You have spoken... too much and for too long,' said the Transhuman. It purred a grotesque approximation of a laugh. 'Your location has been traced and identified. Terraformer Two, operations management command C, level six.'

The Doctor turned from his console in the gleaming command chamber, ignoring the hologram figures being generated around him. He'd seen something reflecting in the vast plate-glass viewport in front of him.

Behind him, three Transhuman killers were padding towards him from the hatchway on all fours, smiling their eternal smiles. A fourth followed, walking upright, herding three, rigidly frightened captives ahead of it.

Amy, Samewell and Bel.

'You will cease... your interference,' it snarled.

'Ah,' said the Doctor.

'Don't do it!' Amy said, as bravely as she could manage.

'If I don't, Pond, it will kill you,' replied the Doctor sadly.

'It's going... to kill you all *anyway*,' it growled.

CHAPTER 16
GUIDE US TO
THY PERFECT LIGHT

'Oh well,' said the Doctor, 'if you're going to be like *that*. I think it's time to act with a little honour.'

'What?' asked the upright Transhuman.

'He was talking to me,' hissed Lord Ixyldir.

The Ice Lord leapt out of hiding and swung his war sword at the towering cyborg beast. The stupendous blow hit it in the neck and it lurched sideways. The Transhuman uttered a strangled, drawn-out gurgle of pain and outrage as it toppled.

Bel screamed.

Before Ixyldir's blow had even landed, his squad of Warriors had joined the assault, lumbering like tanks from their concealment behind pipework and workstations. Ssord led the charge, swinging his barbed axe wide.

The Transhumans howled and sprang forward to meet the attack, claws and fangs bared.

'Amy!' the Doctor yelled, beckoning to Amy, Samewell and Bel. 'Get out of the way!'

The cyborg monsters were too busy with the Martian assault to bother about the three humans. Amy, Samewell and Bel rushed over to the Doctor at the workstation.

'Get down!' the Doctor cried. 'Get into cover!'

'I thought we were dead in all sorts of different ways then!' Amy cried.

'We still could be!' the Doctor replied. 'Get behind the console! This is going to get nasty!'

The battle was already a savage and hideously brutal mêlée. The Ice Warriors put all their cold-blooded fury into every strike and hack of their blades.

The Transhumans ripped back with claws that sliced through scaled plating. They possessed extraordinarily robust physiques. They had been built to be proof against the lethal sonic disruptors that the Ice Warriors had used against the transrats. They shrugged off all but the deepest and most savage cuts of the wicked Martian blades.

Ixyldir withdrew his sword after his first blistering attack to find that his target was already back up and attacking him. Talons lacerated his cape and punctured his pectoral and shoulder guards. Fangs bared, the Transhuman went for his face. Ixyldir smashed the creature in the side of its reinforced skull with his war sword and knocked it onto the floor. It rolled, rising again.

One of the Ice Warriors was already down, dead or dying on the floor. Another was torn and wounded. Despite being driven, determined and possessing greater numbers, the Ice Warriors were still not going to win the fight.

The Doctor turned back to the hologram.

'Rory Williams Pond!' he yelled. 'Do it now if you're going to do it at all!'

In the assembly hall, the Transhuman turned with a snarl. One of the humans, the smaller male, had slipped away while it had been occupied with the holographic interloper.

It sniffed, tracking him.

'Run, Rory!' Vesta screamed.

Rory was doing more than running. The key that Winnowner had slipped him while the Doctor was distracting the red-eyed beast had opened the padlock of the rear doors. He rushed towards the Incrypt hatch and pressed his palm on the checker.

The hatch opened. He ran into a vault lit by blue neon light. It reminded him of a really naff nightclub. There was a raised console in the centre of the floor, a white dais.

He ran to it. His palm-print woke it up.

The Guide opened. A column of digitised information erupted like a fountain from the middle of the dais. It just kept going, generating layer after layer of shimmering holograms: diagrams, data blocks, code sequences, text and picture information.

'Oh my god,' Rory mumbled, pressing keys and buttons at random. 'There's so much stuff! There's *too much* stuff! I don't even begin to know where to look!'

He thought hard, frantically. The hologram of the Doctor was back in the hall, too far away to consult. How was he going to find anything? How was he—

He thought hard. He tried to stay calm. How hard could it be? Though the Morphans had forgotten the technical aspects of the system, it was probably designed to be a user-friendly, multi-purpose device. It shouldn't be any more tricky than figuring out the basic functions of a new laptop, or the apps on a smartphone. He had a fundamental advantage over all the Morphans: he was accustomed to basic interactive technology.

He looked at the streams of overlapping data pouring out in front of him. Amongst it all, he saw a single, small icon:

?

He touched it.

It dissolved. Virtually incomprehensible 3D data continued to blossom around him, but the *?* was replaced by two more simple icons: a human hand and a human mouth.

Did he want to enter his question manually, or by voice?

He touched the mouth.

'Speak request,' said the voice of Guide.

'I need you to open access to the entire Guide database via…' Rory hesitated. Where the hell was it? What had the red-eyed thing said?

'… Terraformer Two, operations management command C, level six!' he yelled, remembering.

The Transhuman, snarling like a rabid dog, exploded through the Incrypt door behind him.

The console in front of the Doctor lit up. It made the Doctor jump. Deliciously comprehensive quantities of information were uploading into the workstation display.

'Good boy, Rory!' the Doctor cried.

'Did he do it?' asked Amy, peering out from behind the workstation. 'Did he? Did he do it?'

'Yes,' said the Doctor, 'he jolly well did. I never doubted him for a moment. I have direct access to our Guide e-manual.'

'So what's the matter?' Amy asked.

'Gosh,' said the Doctor. 'There's quite a lot of it. Enough information to… to build a world, in fact. It's a lot to take in.'

'Can you do anything with it?' she asked.

'It would probably take a normal human days just to browse this, even with a decent search tool…'

'Doctor! We don't have days!' Amy yelled.

Proving her point, one of the battling Ice Warriors flew overhead, hurled headlong by a snarling Transhuman. The Ice Warrior smashed into the plate-glass screen, cracked it, bounced off, and fell onto the deck. Lord Ixyldir had several deep notches in the blade of his war sword, and the monster he was battling was showing no signs of weakening.

'We certainly don't,' the Doctor agreed. 'But fortunately, I'm not a normal human.'

Rory yelped and tried to put the dais between him and the slavering, grinning predator that was coming for him.

It snarled, head low, back arched, ready to spring. Of all the possible deaths he'd faced in the last day or so, Rory was pretty sure this was going to be the least pleasant by quite a margin.

Vesta appeared behind it and hit it on the back of the head with a mallet. The creature roared and turned away from Rory for a moment.

'You've still got that mallet?' Rory said in surprise.

'I thought it might come in useful!' Vesta replied.

The monster, uttering a deep, throbbing growl, was now circling them both. It tensed to spring.

Roaring, Jack Duggat charged into the Incrypt and drove the blade of his hoe into the Transhuman's side. The impact smashed the Transhuman into the wall. Straining hard, the biggest of the Morphans leaned on the shaft of his implement and pinned the writhing, howling beast in place.

'Run away, Elect Rory!' he bellowed. 'Take Vesta with you! In Guide's name, run away now!'

Rory wasn't having that. Jack Duggat had just saved his life. He ran to Jack's side, adding his own strength to the labourer's brawn. They leaned on the hoe, spearing the raging, thrashing Transhuman to the wall. Vesta joined them, lending her effort too.

'We can hold it!' Rory cried. 'We can hold it!'

The sturdy shaft of the farm implement gave out under the force involved and splintered.

'Or maybe not,' Rory said, as he, Vesta and Jack backed away.

'Doctor!' Amy yelled.

With a vast, two-handed blow, Ssord had just managed to bury the blade of his axe in the skull of one of the Transhumans, killing it, but it was too small a victory, too late. Lord Ixyldir had been knocked over and wounded. The three remaining Transhumans were about to make short work of the Ice Warrior cohort.

And others – several others – had just appeared in the chamber doorway behind them. Their eyes shone red. Their smiles were steel.

The Doctor had selected a section of the Guide database and centred it on his desk display. His Time Lord mind had picked it out of the mass of data, like a needle in the proverbial haystack. Well, pretty much. He didn't want to admit to Amy that he was only fifty per cent sure it was actually the section he needed.

'Do you know what you're doing?' Amy yelled.

'Yes!' he shouted back.

'Do you, or are you just making it up as you go along?' she demanded.

'It's called *business as usual!*' he replied.

He took a deep breath, reached into his pocket and pulled out his sonic screwdriver. He blew on it and rubbed it briskly between his hands as though he was warming up a set of roulette dice.

'Come on,' he pleaded, 'you've had quite enough rest for one day! *Come on*, daddy needs a brand new planet!'

He aimed his sonic screwdriver at the display and pressed the activator.

CHAPTER 17
CLOSE BY ME
FOREVER

Nothing happened.

It only didn't happen for few seconds, but it felt to everyone concerned like an eternity. They teetered on the very edge of life or death.

Then the Transhumans stopped in their tracks. They stopped fighting. They retracted their claws. The red light in their eyes grew dim. They turned their backs on the battered, bemused Ice Warriors, and slunk away, as aloof and disinterested as cats.

In the Incrypt, the Transhuman pounced and crashed into Rory, Vesta and Jack, and knocked them flat on their backs, but it didn't kill them. They looked up to see it padding over them and walking away. It prowled out through the assembly hall, through the outer doors beyond, and began to bound away across the snow until it was lost in the darkness.

'Are you two all right?' asked Rory, getting up. Winnowner was peering in at them through the Incrypt hatch anxiously.

'I thought we were dead,' said Jack.

'Get used to it,' said Rory, 'that's how we roll.'

They walked back into the hall together. In the hologram field, the Doctor was beaming at them. Amy, Bel and Samewell were with him.

So were a surprising number of battle-damaged Ice Warriors.

'I reset their sanction,' the Doctor said. 'The Transhumans, I mean. It turned out to be quite a simple instruction in the end. You just had to find the right override.'

'You did what?' asked Rory.

'I countermanded their orders. I sent them back to deactivation. Back to hibernetic suspension. Back to sleep.'

'All of them?' asked Amy.

'All of them,' the Doctor confirmed, 'and I hope they'll stay there for a long time.'

He looked back at Rory.

'Rory, get your friends to go and tell the other Morphans that the crisis is over. I've got to have a little tête-a-tête with Lord Ixyldir here, but that should be a formality. Then we'll come down to Beside and find you. All right?'

'Yes, Doctor,' said Rory.

'And it *is* safe,' said the Doctor. 'Lord Ixyldir won't be doing any more attacking, will you, Lord Ixyldir?'

The Ice Lord took a moment to reply, but it was a regular Ice Warrior pause.

'No, *cold blue star*,' he replied.

The wounded Ice Warriors began to patch themselves up. Amy, Bel and Samewell tried to offer some help, but they didn't really know enough about Martian physiology, and they were also a little freaked out to be so close to giant green aliens who had spent most of the previous day chasing them with murderous intent.

'Why exactly should I desist from my pursuit of this planet?' Lord Ixyldir asked the Doctor.

'Because it's the honourable thing to do,' the Doctor replied. 'You have ships. Go elsewhere.'

'Because you won this battle for us?' asked the Ice Lord.

'If you like,' the Doctor replied. 'I suppose there's a mark of honour to be repaid there. A matter of respect. But before we even started this fight, I told you why you ought to leave Hereafter and the Morphans alone.'

He walked back over to the console where the Guide database flickered and cycled in a tight information swarm.

'You're trying to rebuild your civilisation, Ixyldir,' he said. 'That's good. Ultimately, the empire of the Ice Warriors is a positive force in the universe. Except for the few occasions you put a size sixteen foot wrong, or forget to do the right thing.'

The Ice Lord did not reply.

'Rebuild, Ixyldir,' said the Doctor. 'Rebuild your world, rebuild your race, rebuild your empire. Rebuild it all. But make sure you rebuild your ideals too. Rebuild the principles that made you a great and honourable galactic power in the first place. Don't prey on the weak. Don't steal from the helpless. Don't murder the innocent. Be a force for good, not a force for yourself.'

The Doctor selected some data from the Guide and pulled it up in hologram form.

'The original Morphan pioneers did a good job of surveying this galactic neighbourhood,' he said. 'I've only made a quick study of it, but it's very interesting. Very interesting indeed. They picked Hereafter because it was certainly the most Earth-like world in the quadrant. It wasn't, however, the most *Mars*-like. See here?'

He pointed to one of the stars on the chart. His fingertip dipped into the hologram as though he was writing on water.

'Atrox 881. It's about eight light years from here. Entirely unsuitable for humans. Well within range of your ships. I happen to know, Ixyldir, that in about 9,000 years' time, one of the most significant fiefworlds of the Ixon Mons dynasty will be located there. A quadrant capital. A famous centre of culture and power. It'll be run by a particularly able warlord called Azylax. If I remember my Galactic Migration Eras correctly, it's a colony that's due to be founded any day now.'

Ixyldir studied the chart.

'Atrox 881,' the Ice Lord murmured. 'From the scans, it appears to be... a cold blue star.'

'A *Belot'ssar* indeed, Ixyldir,' said the Doctor. 'Perhaps Lord Azylax was invoking something entirely different when he gave me my nickname. Perhaps he was remembering something that I hadn't done yet.'

'Will you not stay, Doctor?' asked Bill Groan.

Many of the Morphans gathered in the comforting warmth of the assembly raised their voices in hearty encouragement.

'We'd love to,' said the Doctor, glancing at Amy and Rory beside him. 'But... miles to go before we sleep, and all that.'

'We've got a long journey ahead of us,' said Rory.

'But you came all this way to well-wish us for the festival,' said Vesta. 'All the way from your plantnation. Wherever that is.'

'I think we've well-wished you more than enough

already,' said the Doctor. 'You need some time to tidy up. You've got rebuilding to do, Elect. Some people have lost loved ones. You've come through a crisis and survived, but there's a hard winter ahead. Several, in fact. The Firmers are stabilised, but it will take a few more years before they start to ease the climate back out of ice-age mode. So card wool. Knit. Collect plenty of firewood. You'll do fine, though. You always have. A bit of hard work, and you'll get through it. I know you're not afraid of hard work.'

He looked at the faces watching him in the solamp light.

'Celebrate your survival,' he said. 'And keep celebrating it. The elders of this plantnation, Bill and Winnowner, and the others, they know they have a fine new generation to pass the torch to when the time comes.'

Bel got to her feet. She was sitting in the front row between Samewell and Vesta.

'It is traditional for us to give gifts to well-wishers at the festival,' she said. 'We have not much this year, not with everything that has happened. But we wanted you to have this back at least.'

She handed the Doctor his wallet of psychic paper.

'Excellent choice,' he said. 'I always like to have some around. I have a gift for you too. For all the Morphans, actually.'

He looked at them.

'I took the liberty,' he said, 'of slightly resetting your Guide. Don't worry, Winnowner, I haven't fiddled with it. I've just tidied up the user interface so you can all access it. You'll find it easy to use. Just ask it questions. It has all sorts of information in it. It'll help you a great deal. It should make your life here, and the development of your colony, a little easier. It'll help you build and improve.'

He paused for a moment. Not quite an Ice Warrior pause, but a pause nevertheless.

'I also,' he said, 'reset the parameters of the hibernetic systems. The patients are sleeping. And they will sleep for as long as you want them to. When the time comes, when Hereafter is ready, you can decide whether to wake them up or not.'

'If it was up to me,' said Rory, 'I'd let them sleep for ever.'

'If it was up to me,' said Amy, 'I'd pull the plug.'

'It's not up to either of you,' said the Doctor. 'It's up to the Morphans. They might decide it's cruel to leave their kin sleeping. They might think it's kinder to let them dream out eternity. The important thing is, if you do decide to wake them, it will be on your terms. You will have total control. They can't wake up repurposed and armed to the teeth like this time. You can revive them, and you can show them how the new world works, and what their part in it can be.'

He shrugged.

'It's not much of a present, I know,' he said, 'but the shops were shut.'

CHAPTER 18
ABOVE THY DEEP
AND DREAMLESS SLEEP

It was about an hour before dawn. Guide's Bell would soon be ringing. The sky was almost mauve, and the stars were all out. The ghostly snow-cover was perfect for as far as the eye could see. The only blemish on the scene was the thin smoke rising from the fires that had burned out in the high woods. But Would Be would grow back in time. It would be a wood again.

At the top of the valley, the three of them stopped and turned to look back at the little town in the valley below. Its lamps twinkled in the cold air.

'It's beginning to look a lot like Christmas,' said Rory.

'Really? Christmas-*like*?' asked Amy.

'Christmas-*esque*,' said the Doctor.

They trudged up the slope to where the TARDIS was still patiently leaning.

'I notice *we* didn't get gifts,' said Amy.

'I got you gifts,' the Doctor replied.

'Did you?' asked Amy.

'What do I get?' asked Rory.

'You get to drive,' said the Doctor.

'Really?' asked Rory excitedly.

'For a little bit. With me supervising,' said the Doctor. 'I mean, it's now absolutely imperative that we get home for Christmas, or you pair will never let me hear the end of it, so I think Rory should drive. He's determined. He can find Christmas for us.'

'I can?' Rory asked.

'You're a wise man, Rory,' said the Doctor.

Rory rubbed his hands together gleefully and led the way into the TARDIS.

'So what do I get, then?' asked Amy.

The Doctor turned to her. He reached into his coat pocket, took something out and handed it to her.

It was a single mitten on a snapped piece of elastic.

'It's just what I've always wanted,' she whispered.

'Really?' he asked.

'Shut up, I'm welling up here,' she sniffed.

'Merry Christmas, Pond,' said the Doctor.

'It's not actually Christmas, you know,' she replied, following him into the TARDIS.

'Nonsense,' the Doctor replied, 'that's the great thing about time travel. It's always Christmas somewhere.'

The door closed.

After a moment there was a shudder, a creak and a groan. The light on the top of the police box began to flash like a cold blue star. With a shivering, juddering noise, the TARDIS began to dematerialise.

Far overhead, as the blue box faded and disappeared, taking its noise with it, lights glimmered in the night sky.

If they had still been standing there, the three travellers in the TARDIS would have been able to see the silent stars go by for the very last time.

Acknowledgements

The author would like to thank Justin Richards, Steve Tribe and Nik Vincent for their generous help and encouragement.

BBC

DOCTOR WHO

TOUCHED BY AN ANGEL

Jonathan Morris

To my wife, Debbie

PROLOGUE

10 April 2003

Slosh-thwack! Slosh-thwack! Slosh-thwack!

The rain splattered against the windscreen before the wipers swiped the glass clean, patting the water down into a splashy trough above the dashboard. Beyond, the car headlights picked out the narrow country lane rolling out of the darkness, the high hedges on either side giving it the feel of driving through a tunnel.

Rebecca rubbed her forehead. Another headache. Probably due to the idiot who had spent the last five miles behind her, his headlights blazing away in her rear-view mirror. Or exhaustion from driving non-stop from London. There was definitely no other reason for her headache. OK, so she'd been having them almost daily since the accident, but that was no reason to go and see a doctor, no matter what Mark said.

Rebecca felt a flush of anger. Mark should be with her now, paying the traditional bi-monthly visit to her parents in Chilbury. He had an excuse, of course; he always had an excuse. There was a crisis at work and he had volunteered to work late to sort it out, as usual.

263

Slosh-thwack! Slosh-thwack! Slosh-thwack!

The radio hissed as it lost the signal for *The World Tonight*. It didn't matter, Rebecca already knew what the news would be. It would be all about the invasion of Iraq. The television news had been full of nothing else for weeks; journalists in flak jackets reporting live from hotel rooms, interspersed with infra-red footage of green blobs flashing back and forth over a burning city. It was like watching someone commentating on a computer game.

Today's big story had been about American soldiers pulling down a statue of Saddam Hussein in some dusty town square while the reporter burbled excitedly about it being a momentous event in history. Seeing the footage of the conquering heroes draping their flag over the fallen statue, Rebecca had felt sick and ashamed. They'd be handing out chocolate bars next.

Slosh-thwack! Slosh-thwack! Slosh-thwack!

Rebecca twisted the dial for Radio 1. A plaintive piano riff emerged from the speakers, introducing 'Beautiful' by Christina Aguilera. Rebecca left the song playing; it suited her mood and wouldn't distract her from driving.

Slosh-thwack! Slosh-thwack! Slosh-thwack!

Approaching a sharp left turn, Rebecca changed down to second gear. She turned the corner, to be suddenly confronted by two brilliant shining lights bearing down upon her.

A horn blared out like a monster's roar. Instinctively Rebecca wrenched the steering wheel to the left to avoid the oncoming heavy goods lorry. The left-hand side of her car went into the hedge, leaves and brambles scraping along the side. Her heart pounding, Rebecca remembered, too late, to apply the brakes.

The front of her car smashed into the grille of the lorry and the windscreen shattered into a million beads of glass. The impact threw Rebecca forward, her seatbelt tightening so much it crushed the wind out of her lungs. Barely a second later, Rebecca found herself being thrown to the side as her car rolled over. Rebecca had a brief sense memory of being on a theme park roller-coaster ride. She had never liked roller-coaster rides.

Her only other thought was to observe with wry amusement that this was like something out of *Casualty*.

The next thing she knew, she was lying in her seat, gazing across a muddy field. Lying in her seat? Her seat had been upturned and her weight rested on her back. But if she was still inside the car, why could she feel the rain upon her face? She couldn't feel any pain, though, which was a relief.

Rebecca cursed herself. How many times had her mother moaned on the telephone about lorries using the village as a shortcut, even though the council had installed speed cameras? It was an accident waiting to happen, she'd said. Turned out she'd been right.

Rebecca wondered why everything in the field had an orange hue, as though lit by a street lamp. A second later, everything went dark, before lighting up again with the same orange hue. The lorry must have activated its warning lights. What had happened to the lorry driver? For a moment, Rebecca hoped that he'd been hurt, it would serve him right, before banishing the thought. She'd been very lucky not to be injured.

But if she was OK, why couldn't she move? Rebecca tried wriggling in her seat; her seatbelt was so tight she could hardly breathe. But nothing happened. She wanted to wipe the rain out of her eyes, but for some reason her hands didn't respond. She began to wonder whether she might've been hurt after all.

Outside the car, the orange light blinked back on.

Now that was weird. About six metres away, in the field, stood a statue, like might be found in a graveyard or a Roman museum. The statue was of a young woman with coiled hair wearing a flowing robe. It had two wings. An angel. The statue stood hunched, burying its head in its hands as though crying. To add to the effect, rain trickled from between its fingers.

The light blinked off, returning Rebecca to blackness. She thought briefly of bonfires, of Guy Fawkes Night and toffee apples. Why was she thinking about bonfires? And then she realised she could smell burning.

The orange light blinked on again. Rebecca couldn't be sure, but hadn't the statue of the angel been holding its head in its hands? Because now it was looking towards her with blank, pupil-less eyes.

There was darkness again. Then orange light.

The statue had moved closer now. Still staring at her with its impassive, stony eyes. Its mouth was now slightly open, as though drawing in breath to speak.

Darkness. Orange light.

It now stood only two metres away. It filled her view, looming over her.

Caught in the flickering glow of a fire, thick black smoke billowing around it, its expression had changed to a snarl of hunger. Its lips had drawn back to reveal rows of sharp fangs, like those of a bat. It reached towards her with outstretched hands, its long fingernails like talons.

But this was impossible, Rebecca thought. It wasn't moving. *It wasn't moving.*

CHAPTER
ONE

7 October 2011

Toby Murray was a difficult man to like. He had a pudgy, red face, he was flabby and sweaty, and he affected a very bad East End accent.

'We wanna win this one, Mark. We wanna take 'em dahn.'

Mark sighed. This wasn't _Law & Order_, this was a routine piece of contract law. He'd only taken it on because Toby's employers were one of Pollard, Boyce & Whitaker's most prestigious clients, and because Toby had, rather pathetically, insisted on dealing with a senior partner. But if Toby wanted to be fed a load of high-powered gibberish, Mark would be only too happy to provide.

'Nevertheless, I recommend we pick our battles carefully,' said Mark. 'Find as many areas of common ground as we can, because at the moment our position is about as solid as a soufflé.'

'So, what you saying? What's our next move?'

'Make an audit of every contract, all the ones that have been fulfilled, all the ones that haven't. I need points of contact, dates, emails and paper trails, everything you can give me.'

Toby nodded and stood up. 'You'll have it next Monday.'

Mark pressed the button to summon his personal assistant. 'Take as long as it takes.'

Toby glanced around the room, his eyes resting on the photograph that Mark kept on the shelf opposite his desk. Toby whistled in admiration as he picked up the photograph. 'Who's the babe?'

The photograph showed Rebecca perched on the balcony of their hotel room in Rome. The morning sun shone in her hair like a halo and gave her skin a golden glow. Her eyes were wide and impossibly blue and a contented smile curled across her lips.

'My, ah, wife,' said Mark, feeling a sudden flush of anger. 'If you could just put that back…'

'The missus? Bit young, ain't she? Well done!'

'It was taken a while ago, if you could just put it back—'

'Oh, got you.' Toby returned the photograph to the shelf. 'Former glories. Mine's the same. Second you stick a ring on their finger, they start to inflate. It's like there's a valve.'

Siobhan appeared in the doorway. 'All done, Mr Whitaker?'

'I think so,' said Mark curtly. 'Mr Murray has important business to attend to, no doubt.'

Mark offered his hand to Toby. Toby clasped it and attempted to crush Mark's fingers. Toby was one of those men who felt it important to establish he was the Alpha Male.

'Laters, mate,' said Toby, releasing him.

Siobhan guided Toby out of the office before returning and closing the door so they wouldn't be disturbed. 'Are you all right?'

'What?' said Mark, rubbing some feeling back into his fingers.

'Only I heard you mention your wife.'

'Oh. Toby was just checking out the photo of her, that's all.'

'I see,' said Siobhan. Siobhan was an attractive, dark-skinned woman in her forties, a lethal combination of a gentle smile and a no-nonsense attitude. She studied the photograph of Rebecca. 'She looks very happy.'

'She was,' said Mark proudly. 'That was taken the morning after we first got together.'

Siobhan turned to give Mark a concerned look. 'How long has it been now, since the accident? Eight years?'

'Yes,' said Mark, avoiding her gaze by glancing out of his window at the rush-hour traffic on the Croydon flyover. Grey clouds filled the gloomy sky. It got dark so quickly these days.

'Eight years. That's a long time for you to still be torturing yourself. Rebecca wouldn't want that.'

'You don't know what Rebecca would want.'

'She'd want you to be happy. Rather than using what happened as an excuse to be miserable.'

'An excuse?'

'You should get out more. Meet new people. Women. Single, *alive* women.'

'Is this about Charlotte?' Two weeks ago, Mark had gone on a date with Siobhan's friend Charlotte, an attractive, friendly woman whose idea of a good night out sadly did not extend to spending three hours in a wine bar listening to her date talk about his dead wife.

'Not necessarily,' said Siobhan. 'I have other friends. There's Susannah, Joanne—'

'Thanks, but no thanks. Was there anything else?'

'Only this.' Siobhan slid a battered, padded envelope about the size of a paperback across his desk. Mark picked it up. His name and today's date were scrawled on the front: *MARK WHITAKER. 7/10/2011.*

'Has this just come in?' said Mark, turning over the envelope.

'No. Bit weird, actually. Apparently it's been gathering dust in the archive for the last eight years, with strict instructions that it should be delivered to you on this date.'

'Eight years?'

'A mystery package, eh? Well, are you gonna open it?'

Mark ran a finger over the flap where the envelope had been stapled shut. Something about this envelope made him uneasy. His back suddenly felt as cold as a gravestone. 'No,' he said. 'If it's waited eight years, a few more hours won't hurt.'

Then he realised what was odd about the envelope. The name on the front was written *in his own handwriting*.

It had gone eight by the time he made his way down to reception. If anybody else had stayed behind in the office, they'd have thought he was working late, when in fact he'd spent the last hour playing Killer Sudokus on the computer. Putting off the moment when he'd have to step out into the wind and the rain and begin the drive back to his cold, empty flat.

'Night, Mr Whitaker, sir,' said Ron, the overnight security guard.

Mark nodded to avoid engaging Ron in conversation, because he would have to ask about Ron's children and he couldn't for the life of him remember their names.

'Lovely weather, eh?' said Ron, indicating the street outside. The windows and glass doors had misted up, making the street lights look like smudges in the darkness.

'Yeah, well, goodnight, Ron,' said Mark. But before he turned to go he glanced at the closed-circuit television on Ron's desk. Something had caught his eye. The black-and-white screen showed the reception area, facing out towards the street. Where someone stood peering in through one of the doors, their face almost touching the glass. As though waiting to come in. Mark turned to look at the door, but there was nobody there. He turned back to the monitor on Ron's desk, but it had flicked over to show a view of one of the office stairwells. When it flicked back to the view of the reception area, there was no longer a face at the door.

Ron paused as he turned the page of his *Daily Mirror*. 'Was there something, sir?'

'No, no, nothing.' Mark buttoned up his coat and headed out into the night, taking care to use a different door from the one in which he had seen the marble-white, staring face.

The rain eased off to a drizzle as Mark pulled into the petrol station. Pulling his coat tightly around him, he stepped into the freezing night and glugged thirty pounds of unleaded into the tank. He started to walk towards the shop to pay when he remembered the envelope, which he'd placed on the passenger seat. For all he knew, it might contain confidential legal documents and was not the sort of thing he should leave unattended.

Mark returned to his car and studied the envelope under the forecourt light. The name on the front definitely looked like his handwriting, but that didn't mean anything; someone else could have similar handwriting to him. But he was intrigued as to why anyone would leave an envelope with instructions for it to only be delivered eight years later. And why *7/10/2011*? What was so important about that date? Mark poked a finger under the flap and tore it open, just enough to see inside.

The envelope contained at least a hundred neatly folded fifty-pound notes, with several sheets of paper wrapped around them.

Siobhan had been right, it was a real mystery. But it would have to wait. Mark stowed the envelope into his coat pocket, locked his car and made his way into the shop.

It was one of those petrol station stops that was like a small supermarket, selling newspapers, magazines and microwaved sausage rolls. There were no other customers. Mark hurried to the counter to be served by a young Asian who didn't look up from his smartphone. 'Thirty quid.'

Mark slotted his card into the chip-and-pin and typed in his number. As he waited for the machine to respond, he glanced over the attendant's shoulder at a monitor showing the output of the petrol station's closed-circuit cameras. The screen showed a view from a point above the counter, looking down into the shop. Mark could see the attendant and himself at the counter in grainy, flickering black-and-white. And behind him, at the end of the aisle near the door, stood a statue of an angel.

That was ridiculous. If there'd been a statue by the door, he'd have noticed it on his way in. Mark frowned at the picture on the screen. It was an old statue, its surface crumbling and pitted. It stood hunched, holding its face in its hands.

Mark turned to look back down the aisle. It was empty. Where the statue had stood – where the statue should've been standing – there was just shiny, wet floor.

Mark returned his gaze to the monitor and shuddered. The statue was still there, at the end of the aisle. But hadn't it been standing further away? And hadn't it been holding its head in its hands? Because now it seemed to have moved a metre or so towards him, and had lowered its hands, cupping them as though in prayer.

He turned to look back down the aisle once more. It was still empty. No statue, nothing.

He looked back at the monitor. The statue had moved again. It was looking up, directly into the camera lens. Looking at him. With staring, blank eyes and a slightly parted mouth. And a couple of metres in front of it he could see himself, standing at the counter, looking up at the monitor, and the attendant, still tapping away on his smartphone.

The PIN machine beeped and the attendant tore off Mark's receipt. Mark mumbled some thanks and turned to go. Thankfully, the shop was still empty. His heart thudding, Mark hurried out of the shop, taking care to avoid the aisle where the statue had been standing.

He sprinted back to the safety of his car and slammed the door shut. He was just overtired, that was it. That was the only possible explanation.

It was with some apprehension that Mark checked the car's rear-view mirror. But there was nothing there, nothing sitting on the passenger seat behind him, nothing standing in the forecourt. He was alone.

After parking near his flat in Bromley, Mark headed to the high street to get some dinner. Huddling himself into his coat, he trudged down the road, his eyes fixed on the pavement to avoid the puddles. An ambulance siren whined in the distance, but apart from that, he could have been the only man alive on the planet.

Mark hurried on to the Taste Of The Orient. Inside, it was dry and warm and smelt of sizzled rice. A couple of kids sat waiting by the window, chatting. A petite Chinese girl emerged from the kitchen and took Mark's order: sweet-and-sour pork, egg-fried rice. Mark paid her with the last ten-pound note in his wallet.

Mark glanced around for something to occupy his attention. Mounted on the wall behind the counter a monitor showed the output of a closed-circuit camera. It showed the entrance of the Chinese restaurant, it showed the couple by the window, and it showed Mark.

And standing right behind him, there was the statue of the angel, the same one from the petrol station. But now it was reaching towards Mark's back with an outstretched bare arm.

Mark felt an icy shiver and, holding his breath, turned to look behind him. There was nothing there, just the rain-streaked window of the takeaway.

He turned to look back up at the monitor. The statue had taken another step closer. It was still reaching towards him. On the screen, Mark could see the coils carved for the angel's hair, the feathers in its wings and its unseeing, blank eyes. And he could see himself at the counter, looking up at the monitor. The statue's fingers were almost brushing the back of his neck.

Choking with terror, Mark lunged towards the door of the Chinese takeaway, shoved it open and stumbled into the darkness, the icy wind biting his face. Not daring to look back, he ran down the high street, running so fast his stomach ached.

He had to get home. He would be safe there, safe from… safe from whatever this thing was.

Mark slowed to a jog, his heart thumping in protest, and continued down the high street. Past the bookmaker's. Past the Halal butchers. Past the hi-fi shop—

Suddenly all the televisions in the shop window flickered into life. It had a video camera as part of the window display, a camera that was now pointing at Mark. He could see himself on the screens; the same image repeated, over and over again, of him staring into the window.

The statue was right behind him, reaching for his neck, its mouth open to reveal hideous jagged teeth.

'Don't look back. Don't turn around, don't close your eyes, and whatever you do, *don't look back!*'

The voice came from behind Mark. It sounded like the voice of a young man but with the authority of someone much older.

'What?' said Mark, frozen to the spot.

'Keep your eyes on the screen! It's vitally important you don't let it touch you.'

'And how do I do that?'

'It's quantum-locked. It can only move if somebody isn't looking at it.'

'Quantum-locked?'

'You know, the Heisenberg uncertainty principle, the very act of observation affects the nature of the object being observed. Amy, Rory. Keep watching the screens. Take turns blinking.'

'Righty-ho,' said a girl with a Scottish accent from behind Mark's left ear.

'Watch the televisions, got you, no problem,' said a young man nervously.

'And try not to blink at the same time,' said the voice of authority. 'That would be utterly disastrous. *Good.* Now, bloke-watching-himself-on-the-television, move forward. Very slowly.'

Mark swallowed and stepped forward until his nose was nearly touching the shop window.

'Good. Now take two steps to your right. *Slowly!*'

Mark took two steps to the right, watching himself on the television screens as he edged out of reach of the angel. 'What is that thing?'

'It's a kind of… temporal scavenger. Or a predator. One of the two. Or both.'

'Rory, I'm going to blink… *now!*' said the Scottish girl.

'But it's made of stone,' said Mark.

'Defence mechanism,' said the voice of authority. 'You see, you can't kill a stone.'

'Can't you?'

'Well, nobody's attempted it and lived.'

'Amy, I'm gonna blink… *now!*' said the nervous young man.

'OK, it's safe to look back now,' said the voice of authority.

Taking a deep breath, Mark turned around, to see a tall, pretty girl with long, fiery hair and a young man with a prominent nose and a woolly chullo hat, both staring attentively at the window. Beside them stood a handsome young man with angular cheekbones and thick brown hair swept up into a fringe. With his tweed jacket and bow tie, he looked like he was on his way to a fancy dress party as Albert Einstein.

There was no sign of the statue. 'But there… there's nothing here!' stammered Mark.

'No.' The man in the tweed jacket had a device like an old-fashioned tape recorder slung over one shoulder and he twirled a stubby, torch-like device in his hand like a pop star performing a trick with a microphone. He levelled the device at the window and it emitted a high-pitched drone and glowed green. 'No, this *particular* Weeping Angel has no corporeal form.'

'What does that mean?'

'It means it only exists within the televisions. Within *every* television. That which holds the image of an Angel becomes, itself, an Angel.'

'So it can't come out of the screen and get us?' said the girl with red hair. 'Rory, I'm going to blink… *now!*'

'No, don't think so. It must be very weak, running on fumes.'

'But it can still touch me?' said Mark.

'If you're being looked at by a camera, yes. It's on the screen, your image is on the screen, so it can make contact with your image, and thus… you.'

'Amy, I'm gonna blink… *now!*' said the man with the prominent nose.

'Who are you?' said Mark. 'And how do you know so much about these things?'

'I'm the man who's going to save your life. You can call me *the Doctor*.'

'The Doctor?'

'And in answer to your second question, I've met the Weeping Angels before. I detected this one using *this*.' The Doctor indicated the old-fashioned tape recorder. 'Whenever the space-time continuum goes wibbly, it lights up.' The Doctor tapped the recorder in frustration. 'Or it would do if the bulb worked. It also boils eggs. That's not a fault, it's a feature.'

'Rory, I'm going to blink... *now!*'

'Strange thing is, the Angel isn't the source of the wibbliness,' said the Doctor. 'No. It's *you*.'

'Me?'

The Doctor peered at Mark. 'It must've chosen you for a *reason*. I wonder *why*? What's so great about you?'

'Nothing,' said Mark. 'So what you're saying is, that thing's after me, and you don't know why?'

'No. Haven't the slightest idea!'

'But if it can't be killed... how do I get away from it?'

'You can't.'

'But if I run—'

'This whole street is covered by security cameras. You'd never make it.'

'Rory, shouldn't you be telling me it's my turn to blink now?' said Amy.

'What? Oh,' gulped Rory. 'Sorry, um, I thought it was my turn...'

And then Mark realised that Amy and Rory were looking at each other and not the window.

Mark turned. On all the televisions, he could see himself, the Doctor, Rory and Amy – and the Angel, frozen as it lunged towards his back, its face contorted into a grimace of rage. Another second and it would've made contact.

Panic took over. Mark stumbled backwards, turning away from the Angel, and broke into a run. He heard the Doctor and his friends shouting after him, but it was no good. He had to get away.

*

278

He'd made it. He'd actually made it. He could see the block of flats where he lived, the front doorway bathed in the glow of an electric light.

Mark gasped for breath. He'd sprinted down the high street, feeling suddenly and terribly conscious of every security camera. They were everywhere, mounted high on walls and lamp posts, all staring downwards with unblinking glass eyes. To avoid being caught, he'd taken a long route home to avoid garages and illuminated shops. He'd even hidden from a passing double-decker bus. They had cameras on buses now, didn't they?

But he was OK. Cold and wet, but OK. Mark hurried up the concrete steps to the entrance, past the garden and the recycling bins, until at last he reached the door. He dug out his keys from his coat, found the one for the door, and slid it in the lock. And then he realised.

There was a camera looking directly at him. The camera of the door's videophone.

Something as cold as marble touched the back of his neck.

For a split second, Mark could see his horrified reflection, and that of the Angel behind him, its hand on his neck, its jaws wide open and its tongue extended, as though about to bite.

And then he was gone.

CHAPTER
TWO

Rory and Amy struggled to keep up with the Doctor as he dashed through the gloomy, rain-soaked backstreets, his wibble-detector held in front of him. 'This way! Hurry!'

Rory had no idea where they were. They'd been running through identical housing estates for fifteen minutes and he'd lost all sense of direction.

'Here!' The Doctor halted, circled on the spot, and indicated a block of flats set back from the road. They looked perfectly ordinary to Rory, except that by the entrance he could see the statue of an Angel, its body hunched, holding its face in its hands.

'What's happened?' asked Rory. 'Something bad, right?'

'Quiet.' The Doctor advanced on the statue like a naturalist creeping up on a sleeping lion. Calmly and steadily, he made his way up the steps towards it.

'Careful!' whispered Amy.

The Doctor gave her a thank-you-for-stating-the-obvious stare, then stooped to examine the Angel. It didn't move. He buzzed it experimentally with his sonic screwdriver and tried covering his own eyes, as though playing peek-a-boo, but nothing happened. The Doctor tapped it on the wing. A chunk of it crumbled to dust under his fingers. 'It's safe, I think.'

'How safe?' said Amy.

'As safe as a doornail.'

'But I thought you said these things fed on, what was it, potential time energy?' said Rory as he followed Amy to the Doctor's side.

'All the life left unlived,' muttered the Doctor. 'Normally, they zap people back in time, whoosh, that's how they get their five-a-day.'

'Normally?'

'Whereas in this case, this Angel *used up* its last reserves of energy to send its victim into the past. Sacrificing itself, like a bee dying after its sting. But not like a bee at all. No, now it's more like a garden ornament.' As the Doctor spoke, one of the Angel's arms broke off, followed by both the wings, before the Angel toppled forward, smashing itself to pieces with a heavy crash.

'But why do that?' asked Amy, regarding the debris warily. 'Why kill itself rather than feed?'

'Maybe it couldn't.' The Doctor dusted down his jacket and trousers. 'Or maybe this is a new type of Weeping Angel.'

'You mean they come in different varieties now? Oh, *great!*'

'It must've been drawn to its prey… like a moth to a flame.' The Doctor's eyes widened in delight. 'Hang on! That analogy made sense. My analogies *never* make sense. I must write it down. Rory, write it down for me!'

'I'm not your secretary, Doctor,' said Rory patiently.

'No? Only there *is* a vacancy, yours if you want it.'

Rory spotted a set of keys hanging from the lock of the

door and took them for safe keeping. 'Shouldn't we be more worried about the guy it zapped? Find out where he is?'

'Not really a question of *where*,' smiled the Doctor. 'More a question of *when*.' He adjusted his wibble-detector. 'Yes! A residual time trace. Fading fast but we *should* be able to follow it. Come on!'

'Shouldn't we find out who he is first?' said Rory. 'We don't even know his name.' He jangled the keys in his hand.

'What do you suggest?' snapped the Doctor in exasperation. 'We try those keys in every door in the building until we find out which flat belongs to him?'

'Yes.'

'There isn't time.'

'I could do it, while you go off and do your time-trace thing. And then, once you know where – and when – he is, you can pop back here and pick me up.'

'That's a *terrible* idea.' The Doctor paused, lost in thought, then grinned. 'No, actually, that's an *excellent* idea. You're OK with that?'

'You know me, Doctor, anything to help.'

'I do know you, that is *absolutely* correct, but nevertheless you remain disconcertingly full of surprises. Very good. I'll be back here in exactly one hour. Come on, Pond. We have a time trace to follow!'

Amy gave Rory a sympathetic smile and a squeeze, then set off after the Doctor.

The statue had vanished. One second it had been touching his neck. The next, it wasn't there.

Mark sighed with relief and reached down to turn

the door key, only to find that had also disappeared. He checked, but his keys hadn't fallen to the ground.

Looking around, Mark noticed that it had stopped raining. In fact, the pavement and roads were completely dry. The sky, rather than being dark and overcast, had become a clear, early-evening blue, with a full moon.

Mark checked his pockets. Still no keys. Oh well, he'd given a spare to Mrs Levenson in Flat 12. Mark rang her doorbell.

'Yes?' replied a young female voice through the crackle.

'It's Mark.'

'Mark?'

'I've locked myself out. Can you buzz me in please?'

'Did you say Mark?'

'Yes. From next door?'

'No Mark next door.'

'Mrs Levenson, it's me, you can see me on the video thing.'

'You have wrong flat. No Mrs Levenson here.'

The intercom went dead. Mark swore under his breath and, taking care he'd got the right one, pressed the *12* button again.

'Go away please, you have wrong flat.' The woman had a Spanish accent, or something close to it.

'I live in number 11. Mark Whitaker. I don't know who you are, but—'

'No Mark Whitaker in number 11. Number 11 Mr and Mrs Ramprakash.'

'Look, can I speak to Mrs Levenson, please?'

'I told you. No Mrs Levenson here. Go away now, please, or I will call police.'

The intercom went dead. Mark considered trying

another flat but no one else would have a key. He'd have to call Mrs Levenson on his mobile. Which he'd left in his car.

With a growing sense of unease, Mark set off for the street where he'd parked. As he walked, he heard the sound of birds chirruping. Like on a warm summer evening.

Rory tried the key in the door of number 12 and gave it a jiggle. Nope. He moved quietly on as a burst of studio audience laughter came from the other side of the door.

Number 11. Jiggle. The door swung open to reveal a hallway. Some envelopes slithered on the doormat. Rory stooped to pick them up.

'Hello, can I help you?'

'Wh-what?' Rory gave a guilty gasp. An extremely short, round, elderly woman stood in the doorway of number 12. She glared at him through thick, pink-rimmed glasses.

'Hi, er, yes,' said Rory. 'I'm a friend of the, um, bloke who lives here.'

The woman regarded him suspiciously. 'A *friend*?'

'Yeah. From work. He asked me to pop in and get a… thing.'

'Mr Whitaker doesn't have friends.'

'Doesn't he? Right. And you call him Mr Whitaker.' Rory glanced at the front of one of the envelopes. 'Mark Whitaker. Marky. The Markster. The Markulator.' Rory straightened up. 'You might be able to do me a favour, actually. Only we're a bit concerned about Mark at work. We think he might be in some kind of trouble, but you know old Mark, plays his cards close to his chest. So, if he's mentioned anything, anything at all?'

The woman stared at Rory, sizing him up. 'You're a friend from work?'

'Look, he'd hardly give me his key and ask me to pop into his flat to get him a… thing if we didn't know each other, would he?' Rory gave her the same reassuring smile he reserved for elderly patients at Leadworth hospital. 'I tell you what. Why don't you come in with me? I'll make you a nice cup of tea, we'll have a sit down and a bit of a chat. Five minutes, that's all.'

The woman sucked her teeth. 'I suppose that would be all right… I am also worried about Mr Whitaker. He is, I think, a very lonely man.' She collected her keys and locked her door.

Rory led the woman into the kitchen of number 11 and began to search the cupboards for tea.

'The name's Rory, by the way. Rory Williams. You're?'

'Mrs Levenson.'

His car had been stolen. Or at least, it wasn't where he'd left it.

Mark was a little shaken, but after the rest of the evening's events, he didn't have the energy to get annoyed. He considered finding a phone box to call the police but something made him decide against it. That Doctor and his two friends, they had something to do with this. Something to do with Mrs Levenson not being in Flat 12. He'd find the Doctor, get him to explain.

He returned to the electrical goods shop where he'd met the Doctor, but there was no trace of him. Peering in the shop window, it took a while for him to register what was wrong about the television sets on display. They had all been widescreen and HD, but now they were the old, square type. And the shop sold video recorders! Who the hell sold video recorders these days? Mark looked up at the shop sign. *Dixons*. But there weren't any Dixons any more.

Mark kept walking, his mind a whirl, past the video rental store – wait, hadn't that been a fried chicken restaurant? The posters in the window advertised *Mrs Doubtfire* and *Groundhog Day*. The butchers were still there, and the bookmakers, but instead of the Taste Of The Orient, there now stood a greasy-spoon café.

Exhausted and hungry, Mark entered the greasy-spoon and leaned on the counter. The menu chalked on the blackboard included a cup of tea for 40p and a bacon sandwich for a quid. Mark gave his order to the café owner, a tired-looking man in his sixties, then sat down at a table where somebody had left a copy of *The Sun*. According to the front page Bobby Charlton had just been given a knighthood.

The date at the top of the page read *10 June 1994*.

'1994?'

The Doctor darted around the six-sided console, adjusting the controls as if trying to achieve a high score on a pinball machine. The floor juddered and swayed and Amy clutched at one of the railings around the console to stop herself from falling to the level below. '1994. Just over seventeen years into the past. Which is *odd*.'

'Odd, in what sense?' asked Amy.

'The Angels usually send their victims forty, fifty, a hundred years into the past,' gabbled the Doctor in a rush of enthusiasm. 'Stick them out of the way somewhere safe, where any minor alterations to the time stream will be absorbed by the established pattern of history.'

'Oh, right,' said Amy, trying hard to sound knowledgeable. 'Time can be rewritten!'

'Time *can*, as you say, be rewritten. Insignificant details can be changed, so long the big picture remains more or less the same. Imagine time as being a great big carpet. Or, on second thoughts, don't.'

'But you said this Angel was different.'

'Yes,' The Doctor peered at the central rotor, tensing his fingers in preparation for a landing. 'It's sent him back to a point *within* his own lifetime. Which I'm afraid is very, very bad news indeed.'

Mark leafed through the newspaper. There were a couple of pages on the forthcoming European elections and speculation as to whether John Prescott or Tony Blair would be the next leader of the Labour Party. As Mark read, a bass-heavy reggae track played on the radio.

Somehow he'd travelled in time. It was impossible, utterly impossible, but there was no other explanation for it. Ever since he'd felt the touch of that statue, he'd been walking around in 1994. It felt strange, almost dreamlike. And yet so *real*, so *mundane*. If it was a dream, he would hardly be able to read advertisements for washing machines, or taste the bitterness of the tea. And besides, if it was a dream, his feet wouldn't still hurt from the run to his flat.

So the next question was, what was he going to do? Would he ever get back to his own time? For all he knew, he was stuck here permanently. He'd have to get a job, find somewhere to live. First things first, he'd have to find somewhere to sleep tonight.

The café owner coughed and indicated the clock. It had gone eleven. 'Closing up, mate.'

Mark rummaged in his pockets for some change and dropped it in the saucer on the counter. 'Cheers. Thanks.'

Behind the counter was a black-and-white monitor showing the output of the café's closed-circuit cameras. On the screen Mark could see himself and the café owner, but thankfully no statue.

'What's this?' said the café owner, inspecting the contents of the saucer. 'A *two-pound* coin?'

'What's the problem?'

'*Problem* is, we don't take made-up money here. What is this, Scottish? Haven't you got anything else?'

Mark checked his wallet. He had a credit card and a debit card. For a moment he considered asking the owner if he could use it to pay, before he realised that chip-and-PIN hadn't been invented. Mark patted down his coat and his hand rested on the bulge of the padded envelope.

It wasn't his money. But if he replaced it as soon as he had the chance, that would hardly be stealing, would it? Mark opened the envelope and removed a fifty-pound note. 'Here, sorry.'

The owner held it up to check the watermark. 'You're lucky we've had a good day. Give us a minute.' He opened the till and dug out £48.60 in five- and ten-pound notes and coins, creating a pile which he handed to Mark.

'You wouldn't know of a bed and breakfast around here, would you?' said Mark.

'Not round here, mate. Your best bet's to head into London Bridge.'

'Yeah, thanks.' Mark headed to the door and paused, turning over the envelope in his hands. It was a bit of a coincidence that he'd received it on the same day as being sent back in time. An envelope containing the one thing he would need to survive in the past. It was too lucky. Too lucky to be a coincidence.

As the café owner disappeared into a back room, Mark returned to his table to study the contents of the envelope properly. Along with 120 fifty-pound notes, all dating from before 1994, there was a handwritten letter. Unfolding it, Mark saw a list of dates from 1994 to 2001 annotated with detailed notes.

It was written in his handwriting. And yet he had no memory of ever having written it.

Mark looked at the first date. *10 June 1994. Arrival.*

He checked the other side of the paper. Halfway down the page, the list became a letter:

Mark.

If I remember correctly, you should be reading this in a café in Bromley in the year 1994. Earlier tonight, you were sent back in time.

How did you get sent back through time? I can't go into that here. But you should know one thing. There is no way back to 2011. You have no choice but to live the rest of your life from this day onwards. It won't be easy, but you have the advantage of knowing the future. Out of all the people in the world, you alone know what tomorrow will bring.

I've included instructions describing what I did when I found myself in the past. Follow them to the letter. And whatever you do, make sure these instructions don't fall into anyone else's hands. Guard them with your life.

Your first step is to use the money to create a new identity for yourself. I'll leave you to decide the details. You'll have to make your own way in the world, just as I did when I found myself in the past.

But make sure you follow these instructions, Mark. Because if you do, remember this:

YOU CAN SAVE HER.
Just as I did.
Yours sincerely,
Mark Whitaker, April 2003.

CHAPTER
THREE

11 June 1994

The litter in the high street swirled, caught in a sudden gust of wind, and then, with a grinding sound, a flashing beacon appeared in mid air. A moment later the police-box exterior of the TARDIS materialised beneath it. The Doctor emerged, grimacing in frustration at his wibble-detector. Amy followed him, and sighed. 'We haven't moved.'

'Oh, but we have,' said the Doctor. 'Four-dimensionally. See *that*.' He pointed to the nearby branch of Our Price. 'In seventeen years' time, that shop – *that shop* – will sell sandwiches and Danish pastries.'

'So this is 1994.' Amy looked around. All the shops were closed, but one of them had a clock as part of its sign. 'At approximately five minutes past midnight.'

'The time trace has almost faded. He would've been transported through time, but at the same spatial coordinates. Allowing for the rotation of the Earth, its orbit around the sun, and the solar system's orbit around the Milky Way, of course.'

'Then, er, why isn't he here?'

'He was.' The Doctor approached a small café. Squinting inside, Amy could make out chairs stacked on tables. 'Under an hour ago,' the Doctor continued, shaking his wibble-detector. 'We just missed him.'

'Oh well,' shrugged Amy. 'Don't suppose he's got very far.'

'In *London*?' said the Doctor. 'He could be anywhere within a hundred-mile radius. If he travelled at a hundred miles an hour.'

'Can't you detect him with your amazing egg-boiling gadget thing?'

'No. The trail has gone cold.' The Doctor looked around as though the shops held the answers to the mysteries of the universe. 'We have to find him before he does any damage. The wrong word in the wrong ear and the whole course of human history – pffff!'

'Pffff?'

'Gone.' The Doctor clicked his fingers. 'Not with a bang but with a *pffff*!'

'What makes you think he's going to do any damage?'

'Amy. What would you do if you found yourself trapped in the past? In your *own* past?'

'I don't know,' said Amy. 'I'd... I'd probably look for someone I knew. So I could tell them what's going to happen in the future.'

'Exactly! The wrong word in the wrong ear. The first *pebble* of the *avalanche*! That's the danger with only being sent a short way into the past. If you've been sent back a hundred years, you won't know anyone, you won't know enough about the day-to-day events to make much of a difference, and even if you *do* make a difference, there's plenty of time for history to paper over the cracks. Whereas travelling back seventeen years, you'll know people, you'll know all sorts of details about future events, and any alteration in the *course* of future events is likely to have a direct, dramatic and disastrous impact upon your own personal timeline.'

'Then how do we find him? We don't know where he's going to go, we don't even know who—' Amy stopped as she realised she knew the answer. 'Rory!'

'Yes. *Rory*,' agreed the Doctor. 'He's probably wondering where we've got to.'

The Canary Wharf tower glinted in the morning sunshine. It looked odd, standing alone without its surrounding throng of towers. And out on the Greenwich peninsula, there was no Millennium Dome, just a derelict gas works. Ever since Mark had left his hotel, he had found his attention being drawn to the sights that no longer existed in the future; the tower block that would be demolished to make way for the Shard, the waste ground that would become the site of City Hall.

The most obvious differences from 2011 were the advertisements and those high-street shops which had changed their names or logos. But even the people looked different. Teenagers had their hair tousled like street-urchins or in centre partings. Men wore denim jackets and had their jeans belted higher above their waists. Women had highlights and glossy lipstick. The more Mark looked, the more differences he could see. It was like the first day of arriving in a foreign country, finding everything new, searching for the familiar amongst the unfamiliar.

Apart from the hiss of a teenager's walkman, the railway carriage was silent. It took a while for Mark to guess the reason why; nobody had a mobile phone. There were no laptops, no free newspapers. People just read magazines.

In addition to the eerie feeling of being a man out of his time, Mark's stomach fluttered with nerves at the prospect of the coming encounter. His apprehension grew as the train pulled into Blackheath station and he emerged to climb the hill to his parents' house.

Everything was just as he remembered it. The overgrown bushes that would be cropped back. The lawn that would be concreted over. His mother's Peugeot parked in the driveway.

Steeling himself, Mark strode up the driveway and pressed the doorbell.

A dog barked inside the house. After what seemed an age, a shape coalesced in the door's frosted glass. The door opened to reveal his mother. Looking younger than he'd seen her for years, her hair still dark brown, wearing her old, plastic-framed glasses.

'Hello, yes?' she said, smiling at him curiously. 'Can I help you?'

His own mother didn't recognise him. She had no idea who he was.

Amy stepped out of the TARDIS and onto the pavement outside Mark's block of flats. Nothing had changed. Rain splashed in the puddles and thunder rumbled in the distance. She followed the Doctor to the entrance where the remnants of the Weeping Angel had been blown away in the wind. 'Where is he?' muttered the Doctor impatiently. 'I said one hour. Some people are so unreliable!'

'We'll just have to wait,' said Amy, kicking her heels. 'Back inside the TARDIS?'

'No time.' The Doctor retrieved his sonic screwdriver from his pocket and levelled it at the door. The sonic buzzed, glowed green, and every single doorbell in the building rang at once. A dozen bedroom windows lit up as their occupants were roused from their sleep.

'Doctor, Amy, it's you!' crackled Rory's voice through the intercom. 'I'll be right down.' A minute later, he appeared at the door, looking relieved and breathless. 'You took your time!'

'I said we'd be one hour,' said the Doctor, tapping his watch.

'Yeah, I know,' said Rory. 'That was a week ago.'

'Is that all?' The Doctor paused. 'Sorry. Did you say *a week*?'

'I did.'

'A *whole week*?'

'Seven days I've been stuck here, waiting for you to turn up.'

'Oh,' said the Doctor. 'Must have forgotten to correct for temporal displacement. Still, could be worse.'

'Worse?'

'Could've been a month. Or a year!'

'I thought you'd forgotten about me! *Again!*'

'Never.' Amy gave her husband a peck on the cheek. 'So you've been here all this time?'

'Yeah. Seems to be what I do most of the time, wait. Though I did pop back to Leadworth to pick up the post. Just bills, I'm afraid.'

'But if you've been here for seven days, where have you been staying?' asked the Doctor.

'Mark's place. After all, I had his keys.' Rory dangled the keys in his hand. 'And Mrs Levenson next door to keep me company.'

'Mrs Levenson?' Amy narrowed her eyes.

'Old lady, neighbour, she's lovely, but… no,' said Rory hurriedly. 'She just made me cups of tea and chatted about Mark.'

'So what did you find out about him?' said the Doctor.

'Everything I could. He doesn't seem to have been one for keeping scrapbooks or photo albums, but I managed to find a copy of his CV and all the addresses of his friends and family.' Rory presented the Doctor with a folded sheet of paper. 'Not many names. Seems like he kept himself to himself.'

The Doctor read the paper in under a second and handed it back to Rory. 'Right. So, given all this, if Mark found himself in 1994… where do you think he'd *go*?'

'Must be a bit of a surprise, me turning up like this,' said Mark, taking in the living room. The television in the corner, the photos on the coffee table, everything was just as he remembered, except for all the photos of him on the mantelpiece. There were so many. His parents must have put them out when he'd left for university and tidied them away whenever he returned.

Mark sipped his tea but didn't swallow. His throat felt so tight he thought he might choke. He wanted to hug his mother and tell her everything that was going to happen over the next seventeen years, but looking at her sitting in the armchair opposite, her eyes twinkling in a way they hadn't done for years, a contented smile on her lips, he couldn't bear to break her heart.

'And your husband? Patrick, wasn't it? He's out at work?'

'Yes, I'm afraid he won't be back until late, council meeting. It's a pity you'll miss him.'

'Yes, a pity. I'd hoped to, well, say hello and stuff.'

'Particularly with you coming all this way, from, where was it again?'

'Canada.'

'Canada, yes. I didn't know we had relatives in Canada.'

'Very distant. Second cousins of second cousins, that sort of thing.'

'You must be on Patrick's Aunt Margaret's side, we don't know what happened to them.'

'Yes, that's right, Aunt Margaret.' There was an awkward pause. The family dog, a Labrador called Jess, padded in, its tail waggling furiously. It sniffed at Mark's legs before deciding to lick his hands.

'You're honoured,' observed Mark's mother. 'She's not normally so friendly with strangers. You know, you don't sound like you come from Canada. I thought they sounded American.'

'Not from the bit I'm from.' Mark struggled to think of a Canadian city. 'It's a small town, fifty miles out of… Toronto. My father was from England, I picked up the accent from him.'

'He was?'

'He um, died. Ten years ago now.'

'I'm very sorry. And your mother?'

'She's still around. Still, you know, coping. She moved out of the house, to a place by the sea. I think she finds it tough, without Dad.' Mark scratched Jess behind the ears. She yawned appreciatively.

'And what about you, are you married?'

'I used to be. My wife, um, died in a road accident back in 2003.'

'In 2003?'

'1993,' Mark corrected himself hastily.

'Oh, your poor thing. It must be so hard for you. Any children?'

'No. No, no children.'

There was another awkward pause. Jess lost interest in Mark and stretched out on the rug. 'So what is it you do for work?' asked Mark's mother at last.

'I'm a solicitor,' replied Mark. Even as the words left his mouth he regretted saying them.

'A solicitor? My son Mark's studying law at university.'

'Is he? Oh.'

Mark's mother stared at him over her glasses. 'You know, you really do look a lot like him.'

'Must be a family resemblance.' Mark took a framed photo of his younger self from the mantelpiece. 'Is this him?'

'Yes, that's him,' said Mark's mother proudly.

'You're right, there is a similarity,' said Mark, studying the photo. 'Reminds me of myself at that age.' Mark returned the photo to its place of honour. 'So, is he doing well, at university?'

'We think so. We don't hear from him all that often, a phone call every couple of weeks, but you know what they're like at that age, away from home for the first time, it's like they forget that Mum and Dad exist.'

'I'm sure that's not the case.'

'But he'll be home in a few weeks, and then we'll have him for the whole summer.' Mark's mother frowned. 'You haven't touched your tea. Is it all right?'

'Yes, it's lovely,' said Mark, rubbing the corners of his eyes to hold back the tears. He pretended to take another sip. 'What's he like, your son?'

'Oh, just like his father. Works too hard, every hour God sends.'

The phone rang. Mark's mother heaved herself out of her seat. 'Sorry, if you'll excuse me.' She bustled over to the hallway and picked up the receiver. 'Hello. Yes? Mark!'

Mark flinched, fearing he had been found out. But his mother continued. 'I was just talking about you.' She waved to Mark in the living room. 'A relative from Canada, over here looking up his family tree. Mr... um, sorry, what did you say your name was again?'

'Harry,' said Mark, grabbing at the first name that came to mind. 'Harold... Jones.'

'Harold Jones,' his mother repeated into the phone. 'Looks a bit like you, funny that, isn't it? Anyway, enough of me rabbiting on, was there anything you wanted?' There was a pause and Mark's mother reached for a pen and pad. 'Oh, I see. How much do you need this time?'

Mark watched her from the front room. She looked so happy, so full of optimism. Mark put down his cup of tea and rubbed another tear from his eyes.

'But what does this have to do with Mark Whitaker? Why go after him?' asked Rory.

'The Weeping Angel that zapped him back to 1994 did so for a reason.' The Doctor darted around the console, making adjustments to switches, levers and what appeared to be a bus conductor's ticket dispenser. 'It singled him out specifically. It was working to a *plan*.'

'What plan?' said Amy.

'We won't know the answer to that until we find Mark Whitaker. Then we have to return him to 2011 before he changes history.'

'But why's that so bad?' said Rory. 'You're always saying that time can be rewritten.'

The Doctor gave Rory a hard stare. 'It *can*. But that doesn't mean that it *should*. I can rewrite time, yes, because I know what I'm doing. Whereas a human being, blundering about—'

'Yeah, but you're exaggerating a bit, aren't you? I mean, how much difference can one man make?'

'One man, Rory, can change the whole world. You should know that by now.'

'Oh. OK, we have to stop him.'

'Quite. But we have to *find* him first.'

'So how long are you in the country for?' Mark's mother asked as he stepped out of the front door and onto the gravel driveway.

'Oh. About a week or so.'

'Then it's back to Canada?'

'Yes. You, um, must come and visit.' Mark had given his mother a fake address, hoping she wouldn't be too offended if she spent the next few years sending Christmas cards to a distant relative who never sent any back.

'That would be nice. I'm always on at Patrick to take me on holiday, this might be just the excuse I need.'

'I remember. You never had a honeymoon,' said Mark quietly.

'I'm sorry, what?'

'Nothing.' Mark cleared his throat. 'You should go, you really should, before it's too late.'

Mark's mother frowned. 'What do you mean, "too late"?'

Mark swallowed. The air seemed suddenly thin. 'Nothing.'

'No, you meant something, you wouldn't have said it otherwise. What did you mean?'

'I meant, well, my dad always promised to take my mum on holiday, but one month before his retirement, he had a heart attack. You know, it might be a family thing. You should get Dad to go in for a check-up.'

'Dad?'

'I mean, Patrick. Because it's the sort of thing where they can cure it, if they catch it early enough.'

Mark's mother considered this. His words had frightened her. 'You don't know what he's like. Stubborn.'

'My dad was the same. Please. Don't take no for an answer.'

'I'll try my best,' said Mark's mother, giving Mark a wary look.

'Sorry. Anyway. I have to go,' said Mark, putting on a brave smile. 'Lovely to meet you. And thanks for the tea.' He shook her hand. As their fingers touched, Mark's fingers tingled, like he'd received a tiny electrical shock.

'Thank you for coming. Give my love to, er, Canada.'

'Goodbye.' Mark smiled and headed down the driveway. He heard his mother call after him but he didn't dare look back. He couldn't let her see the tears dribbling down his cheeks.

The TARDIS floor lurched and whirled like a bucking bronco. Amy clung to Rory for dear life, while Rory clung to one of the stair railings. The Doctor danced around the console, his eyes gleaming with excitement and madness. 'I think,' he glanced up at the scanner, then tapped out a command on the console typewriter, 'Yes. I think I've found him!'

'Found him? Where?' said Rory.

The Doctor pulled a lever and a map of Great Britain appeared on the scanner. It zoomed in on a point north of London. A glowing green dot slid upwards, surrounded by pulsing circles. 'A source of wibbly time stuff – stop me if I'm getting too technical – is heading north-west.'

'You think that's him?' said Amy.

'A great big paradox just waiting to happen. Who *else* do you think it might be?'

'He's heading north-west?' Rory retrieved the folded papers from his pocket. 'Wait a sec. According to his CV, in 1994 Mark Whitaker was studying at university in…' He checked the paper. 'Warwick.'

'You don't think he's trying to find his younger self?' said Amy.

'I think that is *exactly* what he is trying to do.' The Doctor examined the scanner. 'Odd thing is, though, he seems to be travelling at about a hundred miles an hour…'

'Tea, coffee, sandwiches?'

'No thanks,' said Mark.

The rail steward gave a polite smile then rattled her trolley further along the carriage. 'Tea, coffee, sandwiches?'

Mark gazed out of the window, watching the fields, streams, roads and bridges rush past in a blur. Small villages and towns slid by in the distance and his reflection floated alongside the train in mid air.

He checked his watch. Another hour or so and he'd be back at university. In his head, he ran over the words he wanted to say. He had so much to tell his younger self.

Mark rubbed his right hand. The tingling sensation seemed to be getting worse. It was probably just a strained muscle but something about it made him feel uneasy. Vulnerable. Like he was being watched.

He glanced outside again. Trees rushed past and power lines roved up and down. And looking up, there was nothing but clear blue sky…

… and a wooden blue box spinning in mid air. It hovered about thirty metres above the ground, whirling and flitting erratically, but always remaining parallel with the train.

It was following him.

Inside the TARDIS, the Doctor, Amy and Rory stared at the scanner, showing the Inter City 125 zooming through the green British countryside. The Doctor adjusted the controls to bring them in closer. 'Might be a spot of turbulence. Time stuff won't let us get too close.'

The Doctor dashed over to the exterior doors and shoved them open. A blustering wind burst into the control room with a roar. Balanced in the doorway, the Doctor whooped with delight like a mariner in a thunderstorm, the breeze whipping at his hair.

While Rory remained at the console, Amy fought her way over to the Doctor, the wind causing her eyes to water. Gripping the doorframe tightly, she leaned out and looked down.

They were flying over the train. Trees and pylons hurtled past just a few feet beneath them. It reminded Amy of the scene in *Harry Potter* where Harry and Ron chased the Hogwarts Express.

'He's on board that train?' shouted Amy over the bluster of the wind.

'No doubt about it,' the Doctor shouted back. 'We're not the only ones who have found him. Look!'

The Doctor pointed down towards the last carriage of the train. Six grey figures crouched on the roof, clinging to it with their bare hands, their wings unfolded. All of them perfectly motionless, like statues.

CHAPTER
FOUR

The moment of decision had arrived. Our Graham had summarised the three prospective dates' replies, and the girl had made her selection. The audience whooped and applauded as the Two She Could Have Chosen passed by, then the divider slid back, the dates kissed, chose their holiday envelope, and the *Blind Date* theme began.

Watching the show, they'd played the usual game of deciding who they'd select for a date, with Rebecca and Sophie choosing the boys, Mark and Lucy choosing the girls, and Rajeev pointedly refusing to look up from his copy of *New Scientist*. Sophie always chose the boy who most resembled Mark, then paid close attention to Mark's selection to discover what he had liked about the girls.

'This is boring,' declared Rebecca. She uncurled herself from her position on the battered sofa and strode in front of the screen. 'We have to go out or we may actually die of old age.'

'What do you suggest?' called Lucy from the kitchen, scooping the remains of the pasta into the bin.

'I don't know. Go to the Saturday night disco at the Union or something. We can't stay in watching telly all night. That's what our parents do.'

'Well, I'm up for it,' said Lucy.

'You're always up for it. What about you, Mark?'

'Don't know,' said Mark. 'Should be getting back to work, really.'

'*Mark* has an exam on Monday,' said Sophie, threading her arm possessively through his.

'Which is a whole two days away,' said Rebecca. 'Look, it's a well-known scientific fact that if you don't take breaks from studying your brain will explode. Isn't that right, Rajeev?'

Rajeev nodded sagely, not looking up from his magazine. 'Fact-o-matic.'

'And if you're gonna be sitting in here watching telly, you might as well go out. Right?'

'*You* can go,' suggested Sophie. 'Me and Mark can just have a night in.' She cuddled up.

'I don't know,' said Mark. 'I kind of fancy getting out of the house.' He smirked conspiratorially at Rebecca, and Sophie felt a surge of jealousy. Rebecca – or Bex, as she preferred to be called – could always twist Mark around her little finger. And he always laughed at Rebecca's jokes, he never laughed at any of the jokes *she* made. Why couldn't Rebecca get herself a new boyfriend, or get back together with Dennis Nice-But-Dim?

'Yes, but we can't really afford it,' Sophie reminded her boyfriend.

'Which is why I suggested the Union,' said Rebecca. 'It may be totally lame but it's cheaper than any of the clubs in Leamington.' On the screen behind her, Michael Barrymore strutted about advertising chocolate fingers.

'OK.' Mark dragged himself to his feet. 'Union it is. Head

off in about half an hour? Bagsy the shower. Oh, and Bex, try not to use any hot water while I'm in there. Being suddenly frozen to death wasn't funny the first time, or the next five times.'

'I don't know,' smirked Rebecca. 'For me, it gets funnier.'

'Promise you won't do it.'

'OK, I promise. If it happens again, it will be a *genuine* accident.'

'But I can't go,' protested Sophie. 'Not dressed like this.' She'd be a laughing stock, going to a disco wearing a chunky jumper and jeans.

'You can always borrow something of Rebecca's, I'm sure she wouldn't mind.' Grinning to himself, Mark clomped upstairs. Whoever had designed their house had had a thing about staircases and had tried to incorporate them instead of hallways wherever possible.

'He was just joking, you know,' said Rebecca tactfully, as if it wasn't obvious that Sophie wouldn't be able to squeeze into any of Rebecca's clothes. Was Mark hinting that he'd find her more attractive if she lost weight? That she should be slim like Rebecca?

'You're welcome to any of my stuff,' said Lucy. 'Probably not your style though.'

No, thought Sophie, regarding her friend's army surplus trousers and *Shakespears Sister* T-shirt. 'It's all right, I'll cope,' she said. 'Half an hour then.'

'Flatmate outing. Party time, excellent,' said Rebecca. 'You coming, Rajeev?'

'No, I'm good,' said Rajeev. 'Not really my scene. Besides, I promised I'd phone my parents later, so that's my entire evening gone.'

'Suit yourself. Now, if you'll excuse me,' said Rebecca. 'I

have to make myself gorgeous. This is going to be a night to remember.'

Their old house, just as he remembered it. Mark had taken the bus from Coventry station to Leamington Spa, the same journey he'd made a dozen times before, and now here he was, standing outside the terraced house he'd shared with Rebecca, Lucy and Rajeev in his second year at university. Seeing it made Mark feel... what did he feel? Excited, yes. Nostalgic, like discovering an old school photo. But with a tinge of sadness, at how much he had lost.

The front door opened and Mark ducked out of sight. Three girls and a boy emerged. Mark's heart stopped. The first girl, an indomitable-looking, dark-haired Goth, was Lucy. Then there was Sophie, his ex-girlfriend, all curves, freckles and a severely cut bob of auburn hair.

And then there was Rebecca. Oh God. She looked perfect. She had long blonde hair and wore a black-and-white top with an Inca design and leggings. Her laughter echoed in the dusky air.

The boy was Mark's own younger self. Short brown hair, gelled into a parting, John Lennon-style glasses, sallow, red cheeks. Wearing his best Fred Perry shirt. He looked so young, so... innocent. Laughing with Rebecca without a care in the world.

Mark watched them go. He'd have to wait until his younger self was alone; he couldn't talk to him while the others were around. Keeping well back, but feeling highly conspicuous, Mark followed his 20-year-old self down the road.

'So what's the plan?' asked Amy as she watched Mark trail

his younger self to the bus stop. The old Mark then held back, keeping his face turned away from the group of students.

'We get to him before he gets to himself,' said the Doctor, ducking back behind the garden wall. 'Before his older self gets to his younger self.'

'You make it sound so uncomplicated.'

'And most importantly, before *they* get to either of them'. The Doctor pointed to the roof of the terraced house from which the young Mark had emerged. It took a while for Amy to realise what he was pointing at. Six stone Angels, perched high on the brickwork like gargoyles.

'But why are they after him, run that past me again?' asked Rory.

'Moths to a flame,' muttered the Doctor. 'If Mark succeeds in changing his own past, he'll create a paradox. Once you've altered your own timeline, the young you won't grow old to become the old you who did the altering. Which creates all kinds of peculiar and nasty side effects, including the release of a vast amount of potential time energy.'

'Which is what the Angels are after!' said Amy, keeping her gaze fixed on the Angels on the rooftop.

'Exactly. Look at them. They're hungry, desperate. Then somebody sounds a *dinner gong*.'

'Um, Doctor,' said Rory, indicating the bus stop. Amy turned to look – to see young Mark and his three female friends clambering on the bus, followed by old Mark. Then, suddenly remembering, Amy whirled back to stare at the building. But the six Angels had vanished.

'Come on!' yelled the Doctor, hurdling the wall and pelting towards the bus stop. Amy and Rory sprinted

311

after him, but they were too late. The bus pulled away and rumbled into the distance.

The Doctor spun on his heel, looking for inspiration. A car approached and the Doctor dived out in front of it. Amy gave a quiet scream. The car screeched to a halt moments from the Doctor, who walked to the driver's window, brandishing the wallet containing the psychic paper.

'Hello. I'm a policeman', he said, gesturing to Amy and Rory to get in the back seat. He then slid into the passenger seat beside the driver, a startled-looking vicar. 'Now, follow that bus!'

The setting sun bathed the students' union building in an auburn glow and stretched the shadows of the students milling about outside. Sophie clung to Mark's arm possessively, holding him back as Bex and Lucy led the way up the walkway to the entrance.

The security guards on the door checked their NUS cards and then they made their way into the near-darkness within.

The place was heaving. Ahead of them, hundreds of students packed the Market Place, their flushed, sweat-soaked faces illuminated by flashes of green and red from the whirling lamps. The chorus of 'Things Can Only Get Better' thumped out of the loudspeakers and the heady smell of perspiration and smoke filled the air.

They approached the fringes of the dance floor, the territory of those too cool or shy to dance. 'Drink?' said Mark to the girls.

'I'm OK,' said Bex. 'Fancy a bit of a dance first.' Without waiting for an answer, she strode onto the dance floor and started to sway in time to the music, stretching her arms above her head. Mark could only stare in admiration. He could never do that, just walk, sober, onto the dance floor, not caring what anybody else thought. It usually took him half an hour to pluck up the courage. But when Bex danced she looked self-assured and graceful. When he danced, Rebecca told him, it looked like he was wading through mud while swatting at invisible bees.

'I wouldn't mind a drink,' said Sophie, arching a disapproving eyebrow.

Oh God, thought Mark. She thought he was staring at Bex because he fancied her. Sophie could be so paranoid sometimes.

'Great, let's go,' said Mark, and together he, Sophie and Lucy squeezed their way through the throng towards the lights of the Mandela Bar.

Mark waited until his younger self had entered the building before joining the queue. He felt absurdly conspicuous. Here he was, 37 years old, surrounded by students nearly twenty years his junior. They shot him pitying glances and sniggered at his clothes.

Approaching the building, though, brought back a flood of memories. It resembled a car park that had been tipped on its side, a slanted slab of concrete surrounded by shallow terraces. It was austere and angular, but to Mark, it represented one of the happiest times of his life.

But how would he get in? The security guards had already given him some doubtful glances. He'd have to bluff it somehow; pretend to be a worried parent or something.

The crash of breaking glass interrupted Mark's thoughts. Immediately all the students in the queue rushed to the edge of the walkway. The two security guards also peered over the edge. 'What the heck!'

Mark took his chance. As the two guards trotted down the stairwell to investigate the disturbance, he walked calmly to the entrance and slipped inside.

Students! Normally they just stole traffic cones. But now, somehow, this time, they'd manage to steal a whole statue.

Trev looked in every direction for the culprits but there was nobody in sight. Which made no sense. Whoever they were, they'd managed to prop the statue against one of the windows of the union building, with one of its arms outstretched, as though it was in the act of punching through the glass. 'What do you think, Nick?' asked Trev.

'God knows.' Nick crouched beside the statue. 'I think some grave is missing its headstone.'

'But how did they get it here?' They couldn't have dumped it without being noticed. Maybe it had fallen off the roof? Trev scanned the top of the building for any signs of movement.

'Stupid idiots—' Nick gave a startled croak.

Trev turned to see what had alarmed him.

The statue had disappeared. Where it had once stood there was now nothing but a clear patch on the ground surrounded by shattered glass.

'I just turned away for a second,' said Nick incredulously. 'Where did the damn thing go?'

Amy, the Doctor and Rory jogged past the Arts Centre and across the road. Ahead of them lay the students' union building, its lower windows flashing with multicoloured lights. As they approached, the Doctor slowed, allowing

Amy and Rory to catch their breath. 'We're getting close,' he said.

'Close to what?' said Amy.

'A build-up of potential time energy. Can't you feel it?' The Doctor waggled his fingers and sniffed. 'A tension in the air. Like before a thunderstorm.'

'Yeah,' shrugged Rory. 'But I just thought that meant a thunderstorm was coming.'

'A thunderstorm *is* coming,' said the Doctor darkly. 'Unless we stop it. Look.'

A streak of lightning flickered across the surface of the building, scuttling over the concrete like a startled lizard, before fading away to a blue glow.

'What was that?' exclaimed Amy.

'The dinner gong,' said the Doctor. He straightened his bow tie and jacket cuffs. 'Now. I'll need your help. Do I look like the sort of person who goes to university?'

'Sorry. Do you *look* like the sort of person who goes to *university?*'

'Yes.' The Doctor brushed his fringe out of his eyes. He was deadly serious. 'Well? Do I?'

'A bit, Doctor. Just a bit,' Amy reassured him jokingly. 'Maybe not in this decade, but yeah.'

'Just say you're from the Maths department, you'll be fine,' suggested Rory.

'Good. Good. Because that is the *cool* department, and I look *cool*. Right?'

'Exactly,' giggled Amy. 'And for *no other* reason.' She then put her hand over her mouth and made a cough that sounded like 'geek!' Rory laughed but the Doctor seemed not to notice.

They headed down a slope to an underpass where a

security guard checked the students' IDs. Rubbing his hands expectantly, the Doctor joined the queue. From inside the building came the muffled thud of music.

The Doctor beamed at the guard and flipped open his psychic-paper wallet. 'Hello. I'm from the Maths department. And these are two of my students.' The Doctor leaned forward to whisper. 'I realise they don't look as cool as I do, but they *are* genuine students, believe me.'

'Whatever,' said the security guard, nodding them in. 'Next?'

Inside the building, the noise was all-consuming. The dance floor bobbed and swelled like a sea of arms and faces. The air felt uncomfortably hot but had an almost tangible sense of excitement. These students were having the time of their lives. Dancing, laughing, snogging, all their troubles forgotten.

The Doctor waggled his fingers expectantly. 'We have to find two people. Or rather, the same person *twice*.'

'You're going to suggest we split up, aren't you?' said Rory resignedly.

'I think…' The Doctor paused, lost in thought. 'I think… we should *split up*. Rory, Amy. You find young Mark, he's probably in there somewhere.' He indicated the heaving mass of students bouncing up and down to 'The Size Of A Cow'. 'I'll find the old one.'

'And when we find him?' said Amy.

'We have to get the two Marks as far apart as possible.'

'As far apart as possible, got it.' Amy offered her hand to Rory. 'Rory, are you dancing?'

'Are you asking?'

'I'm asking, lover-boy.'

'Then I'm dancing,' said Rory, taking her hand. Amy

pulled him towards the dance floor with a suggestive smirk.

'Oh, and one more thing,' called the Doctor after them. 'Keep an eye out for the Angels!'

Elsewhere on the dance floor, the 20-year-old Mark hopped and whirled amongst the crowd, all self-consciousness now forgotten. He had a couple of pints inside him and they were playing his favourite tunes at a deafening volume, that's all that mattered. It was the indie section of the night, where things tended to get a little raucous. Occasionally he'd be jabbed by an elbow or shoved off his feet, but that was all part of the fun.

Sophie wasn't enjoying herself. She swayed from side to side as though it was an obligation, smiling only when Mark looked towards her. Rebecca bounced around the dance floor, waving and grimacing to friends. Lucy, meanwhile, had joined a group of fearsome-looking girls near the stage. The last Mark had seen of her, she had been making overtures towards a very pretty Goth with a pierced tongue.

The fade out of 'Baby I Don't Care' gave way to the opening snarls of 'Smells Like Teen Spirit'. The song had a desperate, angry quality, and it felt odd hearing it given Kurt Cobain's recent death, but dancing to it felt like a celebration of his life. But Sophie had clearly had enough, and mouthed to Mark that she wanted to go. The rowdiness was starting to get out of hand.

'Any sign of him?' shouted Amy to Rory, whilst waving her arms in time to the music.

Rory shouted something back she couldn't hear.

Somebody jostled him, and he stumbled on one foot, not quite falling.

'What?'

Rory shook his head. 'No! You?'

Amy shook her head. 'No! Me neither!'

'Excuse me, excuse me.' Someone squeezed past Amy. Amy spun around, drawing a breath to protest. A familiar-looking young man gave her an apologetic smile before continuing to weave towards the edge of the dance floor, followed by a girl with a bob of auburn hair.

Mark. It was young Mark. Wow, he was quite good-looking in his day, if a little nerdy. The sort of boy who needed Taking In Hand. Fix the hairstyle and the glasses and you might have something.

'And I've found the other one,' said Rory in her ear. 'Look!'

Rory pointed towards the corner of the first-floor balcony where a man stood surveying the crowd. The same man they'd met in 2011. 'And, um, I think we have, er, bats in the belfry.'

Amy craned her neck to look up at the ceiling, which consisted of triangles fitted together in an isometric grid. Hanging from the ceiling, half-camouflaged against the bare concrete, lit by flashes of red and green from the disco lamps, were the six Weeping Angels.

CHAPTER
FIVE

Mark searched the crowd for signs of his younger self. He thought he'd caught a glimpse of him a couple of times, but had lost him amidst all the faces.

Watching the students, he felt envious. Envious of their youth, their joy, and all the years they had ahead of them. OK, so this disco was tame compared to some of the nightclubs in Coventry, but they were having fun. And that was what Mark envied most of all.

The smoke machine hissed and the hectic drum-and-bass intro of 'No Good' by the Prodigy filled the hall. Down on the dance floor, the indie kids flowed towards the bars while the dance kids surged in from Rolf's bar. Within seconds they were thrusting and gyrating to the beat, furiously miming big fish, little fish, cardboard box. Green lasers swiped back and forth across the crowd interspersed with bursts of strobe lighting.

Blue lightning flickered around the edge of the parapet, snaking over the edges before fading away. Strange. He'd never seen a lighting effect like that before. And the tingling in his fingers had grown stronger.

'Looking for someone?' Mark turned to see the Doctor

standing on the balcony beside him, arms folded in judgement.

'What are you doing here?'

'Looking for you.'

'How did you get here?'

'Same way as you. Well, not quite the same way. I have my own transport.'

'Your own transport?'

'Which is why I'm here,' said the Doctor. 'To take you back… to the future!' He beamed wildly. 'D'you know, I've always wanted to say that!'

'Three quid,' said the student behind the bar. Mark paid her, then collected his three pints of lager, balancing the plastic containers carefully. The slightest wrong move could cause him to squeeze one of the containers, resulting in a disastrous spillage. It took all of Mark's concentration to wind his way out of the bar area, which meant he only noticed that Sophie was talking when she stopped.

'What was that?' Mark asked her as they reached the quiet area by the change machine and he placed the drinks on a nearby ledge.

'I said I want to go home.'

'You're not having fun?'

'I am. It's just that I've had enough. And you've got revision tomorrow, don't forget.' Sophie squealed in alarm as two students pushed between her and Mark. 'Hey, watch who you're shoving!'

'Mark Whitaker?' said one of the students, a tall girl with long, red hair and beautiful eyes. She spoke with a perky Scottish accent.

'Yeah, yes?' said Mark, turning towards the other student, a friendly-looking bloke in a body warmer with unkempt hair and an apologetic grin. 'Sorry, do I know you?'

'No. At least, not yet,' said the girl. 'But that's not important right now. What is important is that you come with us.' Behind the girl, Mark could see Sophie glowering with indignation.

'What – what for?' asked Mark.

'Friend of yours wants a word,' said the friendly-looking bloke confidentially. 'In private.'

Sophie's mouth opened and closed like a gobsmacked goldfish.

'What friend?' asked Mark.

'You'll find out,' whispered the girl enigmatically. 'It's a surprise.'

'This isn't something to do with Gareth, is it?' Gareth was in the same tutor group as Mark, and had a reputation for playing elaborate practical jokes.

'If I say yes, would that make you come with us?'

'No.'

'Well, in that case, no, it has nothing to do with Gareth,' said the girl.

'That's just what he'd tell you to say. OK, I'll come with you,' said Mark, against his better judgement. In his experience, Gareth's practical jokes were best got over with as rapidly as possible. 'But if this is a rag week stunt, I'm not interested.' He took Sophie to one side. 'Can you hold on here? I'll be back in five minutes.'

'I'm not waiting for you,' pouted Sophie, giving the red-haired girl an I-don't-know-who-you-are-but-kindly-drop-dead look. 'Either you come home with me right now... or you don't.'

Mark couldn't think of anything to say. Sophie shot him a furious glance and walked away.

'I'll find you!' Mark called after her, before turning to the red-haired girl. 'OK, let's get this over with. Lead on!'

The green lasers whirled through the smoke and over the dancers, lending their faces an alien hue. The lightning bolts had become more frequent, crackling over the nearby slot machines.

The Doctor leaned on the parapet beside Mark. 'Let me guess. You're here because you want a quiet chat with your former self?'

'How do you know that?'

'It's what anyone would do in your situation. You want to tell him things to look out for, things to avoid. I don't recommend it, I've seen it tried before, it never ends well.'

'Who are you to tell me what I can or can't do?'

'I told you.' The Doctor regarded him with cool, detached eyes. 'I'm the Doctor. I'm the man who's going to save your life.'

'Save my life? From what?'

The Doctor indicated the balcony opposite. As he did so, the Prodigy track launched into its hyperactive chorus and the lights switched to the strobe effect. The flashing gave everything a jerky, film-like appearance.

On the balcony stood four of the statues, all staring directly towards him. But, by the flickering of the strobe light, they ceased to be statues any longer. They began to move along the balcony. Two of the Angels stretched over the parapet, searching hungrily for their prey, their necks twisting back and forth, while the other two continued to gaze blankly at Mark.

Something grabbed Mark's arm. He whirled around, to see it was the Doctor. 'Don't worry. They're not going to attack you. At least, not *yet*.'

Amy led Mark and Rory up another winding stairwell, refusing to admit, even to herself, that she was lost. This place was like a maze designed by a madman. Whenever she thought she was getting somewhere, she ended up back where she started. Or somewhere completely different that just *looked* like back where she started.

'Where are we going?' said Mark.

'I told you,' said Amy as they passed the offices for the *Warwick Boar* student newspaper for the third time. 'It's a surprise.'

'You don't know where you're going.'

Amy halted, at the end of her tether. 'OK. What's the nearest way out?'

'Don't ask me, I've never been around here before.'

'What about down there?' suggested Rory, indicating a corridor that branched off to the right. Leaving Mark with Rory, Amy hurried around the corner to see where it would lead.

Two Weeping Angels blocked the way ahead, both frozen in position as they lunged out of the darkness towards her, their mouths open in a vision of hatred.

Amy let out a startled scream and backed away from the Angels, remembering to keep at least one eye wide open at all times. She edged back around the corner and into Rory with a bump. 'No, definitely *not* that way.'

'Up the stairs?' Rory suggested.

Amy glanced towards Rory, to see that he had opened the door to another gloomy stairwell. She nodded as confidently as she could. 'Up the stairs it is.'

While Mark and Rory bounded up the stairs, Amy looked back down the corridor. The two Weeping Angels had turned the corner and stood with their bodies arched, reaching towards her with clawed fingers.

Keeping her eyes fixed on the two statues, and winking her eyes alternately, Amy backed into the stairwell and retreated up the stairs, as carefully and as quickly as she could.

'But I have to speak to him,' protested Mark.

'Of course you do. Never mind the consequences, you just make your *own* life better.'

'It's not like that.'

'Don't you get it? Do you think they sent you here out of the goodness of their hearts? No. They're here now because they think you're going to create a big, juicy, space-time event.'

'I don't care,' said Mark. He'd had enough of the Doctor, and all the heat and the smoke and the noise, and the ever-present prickling sensation in his hand, and those moving statues. He just wanted to be alone.

The Doctor blocked his path. 'Oh, for goodness' sake. If reasoned argument doesn't succeed, you'll leave me no choice but to resort to brute force.'

'What?' said Mark, and the Doctor thumped him in the face.

Mark followed the red-haired girl and the friendly-looking bloke through a fire door and out onto the rooftop terrace. After the heat and stuffiness of the union, it felt good to be outside in the cool night air.

TOUCHED BY AN ANGEL

'Rory, keep an eye on the door,' said the girl. 'And whatever you do—'

'Don't blink, I know, I know.' The bloke stared at the fire door behind them, frowning in determination as though expecting to see something burst through it at any moment.

Mark looked around at the empty terrace. 'You've brought me all the way up here just for this? I'm going back—'

'No. You have to stay put,' said the bloke, edging firmly between Mark and the fire door.

'Actually, Rory, I think we might be OK,' said the girl. She peered over the terrace parapet, down towards where two students were emerging from the building. No, they were too old to be students. Someone dressed as an old-fashioned professor was helping a dazed-looking man of about 40 stumble out of the entrance. From this angle, Mark couldn't make out their faces, but he could hear one of them singing 'Bohemian Rhapsody' with drunken enthusiasm.

The girl darted over to the stairs that lead down from the terrace, checking the way was clear. 'You wait here. Don't go anywhere. And whatever you do, don't follow us.'

'Follow you? As if! You're mad.'

'Yeah, that's it, we're bonkers. Anyway, got to love you and leave you.' The girl grinned and hurried down the stairs. The bloke gave him a long-suffering smile and disappeared after her.

Mark woke to find himself being frogmarched through the campus, one arm around the Doctor's shoulder. His forehead throbbed. 'Oh God, my head. My head!'

'Had a bit too much. Just taking him home!' explained the Doctor as they passed a security guard. The guard nodded. He'd seen it all before.

Mark began to remember the content of their last conversation. 'What did you do to me?'

'I punched you in the face. I'm sorry, I did it as gently as I could.'

Mark withdrew his arm from the Doctor's shoulder and was about to speak when he heard the sound of approaching footsteps. A moment later Amy and Rory emerged from the shadows, gasping for breath.

'Doctor!' shouted Amy thankfully. 'There you are!'

'Amy. Rory. What about—'

'The other Mark?' said Rory, rubbing his sides. 'We left him on the roof terrace.'

'Good, good,' smiled the Doctor. 'Now we just have to get as much distance between them as possible before—'

'Before?' said Amy.

The Doctor looked back the way they'd come. 'Oh dear. Don't look too happy, do they?' The six Weeping Angels stood about twenty metres behind them, caught in the orange glow of a street lamp. They were all snarling and clawing at the air.

'Not now you've deprived them of their dinner, no,' deadpanned Rory.

Amy gulped, reached out for the Doctor and Rory's hands, and together with Mark, they arranged themselves so they were all facing towards the Weeping Angels.

'Back pedal! Fast as you can!' said the Doctor, taking a long step backwards, pulling Amy along with him. 'And keep looking at them! Whatever you do, *keep* looking at them!'

*

326

Back on the terrace of the students' union building, the 20-year-old Mark gazed across the university campus, considering his next move. He should go and find Sophie. He could already imagine the argument they'd have. Why couldn't she just have fun? Why couldn't she be more like—

'So this is where you've been hiding,' said a familiar voice from behind him.

Mark turned to see Bex appear through the fire door. 'How did you know I was here?'

'Confession time. I followed you. Who were those people?'

'No idea. They just brought me up here and did a bunk.'

Bex joined him at the parapet. She didn't speak for over a minute, and when she did, she began with a laugh, as though what she was about to say shouldn't be taken seriously. 'While I've got you alone,' she said. 'There's this thing I've been meaning to get your opinion on.'

'Yeah?'

'Something I wasn't sure about.'

'Yeah, what is it?'

'This.'

Bex turned towards Mark and kissed him on the lips. Mark could barely contain his surprise. He'd never thought she liked him, not like that. But here she was, kissing him in a way that could only mean one thing. Her lips tasted of cherry lip balm and were warm and soft. And then, like waking from a dream, it was over.

'*That* was the thing you weren't sure about?' stammered Mark. He wasn't completely sure his feet were still on the ground; he would have to look down to check.

'I just wanted to know what it would be like.'

'And so now you know.'

'Yeah.'

'Revolting, right?' said Mark.

'Oh yeah,' said Bex. 'And for you?'

'I'm feeling a bit sick just thinking about it.'

'Probably not a good idea to do it again, then.'

'No.'

And then Mark kissed her. Longer than the first time, Mark holding her against him, gently stroking the back of her neck. Until, too soon, she released him.

'Nope, still revolting,' sniffed Bex.

'For me too. I really need to brush my teeth to get rid of the taste.'

Bex turned away in embarrassment and brushed her hair behind her ear. 'I'm sorry. I know you're with Sophie, it's just, well, I don't think she knows what she has. God, does that make me a bitch to say that?'

'Probably but I forgive you.'

'Speaking of which, you should probably go and find her,' said Bex, with a sad smile and Mark realised that the moment, whatever it had meant, had passed, and now it was time to return to reality.

'Doctor, they're catching up!' said Amy.

'Yes,' whispered the Doctor. 'Please let me know when they catch up and kill us, I'd hate not to notice!'

They'd walked backwards for what felt like a mile, bumping against walls and roadside barriers along the way. The problem was, whenever one of the Angels slipped out of sight, it would nip around the buildings in an attempt to cut them off. Now, although all six Angels were in plain view, they were so spread out it was impossible to look at more than one at a time. And there were only four of them to do the looking.

'It's no good,' said Amy. Each time she looked back at one of them, it had advanced a little closer, its mouth wide, its tongue tasting the air, its face twisted in an expression of utter evil.

She heard the sound of an approaching vehicle behind her. Its brakes squealed as it slowed to a halt, followed by a hydraulic whoosh.

Amy's back pressed against a glass window. Without thinking, she turned. She'd backed into a bus stop. A warmly lit bus waited at the kerb. Amy spun back to face the Angels. They were now only two metres away.

'Doctor. The bus…'

'OK,' said the Doctor. 'With me, three two one, *move!*'

Amy whirled and sprinted as fast as she could towards the bus. She leapt on board, followed by Rory, Mark, and finally, the Doctor. He patted his pockets while Amy dashed over to the window. The six Angels stood frozen alongside the bus, reaching towards it with outstretched hands. But she could see them all at once, just about. So long as she didn't accidentally blink.

'Hello,' Amy heard the Doctor say to the bus driver. 'You probably want money, don't you?'

Come on, Doctor, urged Amy. Come on! Out of the corner of her eye, could see that Rory was also watching the Angels, so she turned to see the Doctor dig a variety of odd-looking objects from his pockets; a banana, a squeaky rubber telephone, *The Venusian Book of Calm.*

Mark shoved the Doctor out of the way and handed the driver a banknote. 'Here.'

The driver took the note. 'Fifty quid?'

'Keep the change. It's your birthday.'

The driver shrugged, closed the doors, and the bus jerked forward. Amy watched the Angels through the window, still frozen in the same positions at the bus stop, now grasping towards nothing but empty road.

'We made it! We made it!' whooped Rory.

'We were lucky,' muttered the Doctor as he slumped into a seat. 'But the Angels won't give up.' He looked suddenly very tired, his expression grave. 'No. This has only just begun.'

CHAPTER
SIX

12 June 1994

'So what exactly are these "Weeping Angels"?' asked Mark.

The Doctor sliced his sausage and skewered it with his fork. But rather than eating it, he waved it in the air for emphasis. 'The most malevolent creatures in the history of the universe,' he said. 'Nothing gives them greater pleasure than to watch a lesser species suffer. And to them we are *all* lesser species.'

'And they feed by sending people back in time?'

'Usually.' The Doctor took a bite of the sausage. 'But these Angels are different. They feed on time *paradoxes*. The more potential *ramifications*, the better. Ramifications, love that word. Rory, could you write it down for me?'

'Still not your secretary,' Rory reminded him.

'Vacancy's still open.'

For a few moments, they all sat in silence in the hotel restaurant, the only sound an occasional clatter of cutlery from the kitchen.

'Which is why,' announced the Doctor, finishing his

331

breakfast, 'which is *why* we have to take you home, Mark Whitaker.'

'But if the Angels want a paradox,' said Amy. 'Why go to all the trouble of bringing Mark here? Why not just change history themselves?'

'Because that would make them a *part of* the paradox, they'd end up feeding on their own timelines. They need someone to do their dirty work for them. That way, they remain outside the chain of cause and effect.'

'What if I *can't* go back?' said Mark.

The Doctor wiped his lips with a napkin and leaned forward. 'What do you mean, "can't"?'

The supermarket bustled with Sunday shoppers, mothers with pushchairs and fathers with trolleys. None of them paid any attention to the blue police box parked beside the *Fireman Sam* ride. But Mark couldn't take his eyes off it. It was the same police box he'd seen flying through the air after his train. The Doctor's time machine.

'Let me get this straight,' said the Doctor, leaning proprietorially against the door. 'You received a letter sent from *your future self?*'

Mark nodded. 'I received it the day I travelled back, just before I met you, and the Angel.'

'How do you know the letter came from you?' asked Amy.

'Because my name was at the bottom.'

'Oh.'

'And it was in my handwriting.'

'In your handwriting,' the Doctor repeated, mulling over each word in turn.

'And so was the name on the envelope.'

The Doctor held out a hand. 'Can I see it? The letter, I mean. Not the envelope.'

'I-I don't have it any more,' stammered Mark.

'You *lost* it?'

'I put it in a safety deposit box. In London. Didn't want it falling into the wrong hands.'

'How very public-spirited of you.' The Doctor gave Mark a dark look. 'So what was in this "letter" written in your handwriting?'

'A list of instructions, telling me things I should do, investments I should make, and things I should do to make sure that history remained on track.'

'Such as?'

'Such as... Well, when I was 22 or 23, I went on holiday to Rome. While I was there, I lost my wallet. It had all my money in it, credit cards, everything. I retraced my steps but I couldn't find it anywhere. But when I got back to the hotel, it turned out that somebody had already handed it in.'

'But anybody could've done that,' said Rory sceptically. 'What makes you think it was you?'

'Because there was no way they could've known which hotel I was staying in! I didn't really question it at the time, I was just glad to have it back.'

'So this *letter*,' said the Doctor, 'tells you to be in Rome, on a certain street, on a certain day, so you can pick up your former self's wallet and deliver it to his hotel?'

'Yes,' said Mark defiantly. 'That's it, that sort of thing.'

'A Sally Sparrow survival kit,' muttered the Doctor, ruffling his hair. 'And if you're not there to do it, you'll be changing your own past.'

'Exactly. Which is just what you said I shouldn't do, because—'

'— because it would create a paradox.' The Doctor thrust open the doors of the police box and gestured for Mark to step inside. 'I'll take you there now in the TARDIS.' Within, Mark could see an impossibly large, orange-lit Aladdin's cave, a central altar with a glass column and stairwells leading off into vaulted antechambers. It hummed with energy. Mark was tempted to enter, but held back.

'That wasn't the only thing I had to do. There were others,' said Mark.

'What interests me,' said the Doctor, narrowing his eyes, 'is why you'd even *want* to stay here in the past.'

'Why I'd want to?'

'Yes.'

'Isn't that what anyone would do, given the chance?' Mark looked to Amy and Rory for signs of support.

'No.' The Doctor paused to examine the *Fireman Sam* ride, having only just noticed it, before continuing. 'That isn't what *anyone* would do. Oh, I grant you, everyone would like to go back into the past for a day or two. Check out some bands, see a few shows, pick up a few first editions. The past is like a foreign country. Nice to visit, but you wouldn't want to live there. So why do *you?*'

'I just do,' said Mark, pausing to decide how much he could tell them. 'Look, in 2011, I don't exactly have a lot to live for, all right? So I think I have a chance of a happier life if I stay here,' said Mark. 'It is my choice, after all.'

The Doctor leaned over the console, staring at the central column, exhaled and slammed his palm against the console in anger. 'Humans,' he muttered, then turned to Amy. 'You're the same species as him, what do you think?'

Amy considered. She glanced out of the TARDIS doors,

to where she could see Mark sitting on one of the wooden benches by the fire engine ride. 'I don't believe him.'

'And you?' said the Doctor to Rory.

'I agree with Amy. I don't trust him either.'

'Nevertheless,' said the Doctor. 'He was right. If he isn't here to fulfil all the tasks in that letter he sent himself… that would be another paradox.'

'If there even *is* such a letter,' said Rory.

'Yeah,' agreed Amy. 'He was obviously lying, it was written all over his face.'

'Perhaps… But the story about the wallet in Rome had the ring of truth about it,' said the Doctor. 'And only he knows precisely where and when to be.' The Doctor flicked a couple of switches in irritation. 'We've got no choice. He has to stay.'

The Doctor, Amy and Rory emerged from the police box, the Doctor looking subdued. 'You can stay,' he announced at last. 'Under certain conditions.'

'What conditions?'

'Number one. Only follow the instructions in the letter you sent to yourself. You are not to influence history in any way. Even the slightest deviation could be *disastrous*.'

'OK, I understand.'

The Doctor peered at Mark. 'Number two. You are not to talk to, approach or communicate with your younger self. Keep out of his way at all costs. And the same goes for any friends, relatives, colleagues or lovers. You cannot have *any* contact.'

Mark felt a twinge of guilt. 'Not to make contact. Right.'

'I mean it. Just one word, one telephone call, one postcard, and you'll alter the course of your own timeline.

No. Wait.' The Doctor groaned. 'Who was it? Who did you speak to?'

'No one.'

'No. You *must've* spoken to someone. I detected wibbliness.'

'Wibbliness?'

'It's what first attracted the attention of the Weeping Angel. Who was it?'

'I may have… visited my mother.'

'Your *mother*?' exclaimed the Doctor, opening his mouth wide in astonishment.

'Just to say hello.'

'Just to say hello?'

'Yes.'

'Well, I hope that's all you said. Because if you didn't… ' The Doctor stroked his chin. 'What I think is, you've had a very lucky escape, because whatever you said, it can't have made any significant impact. Or you wouldn't be sitting here right now.'

It took a few moments for Mark to realise the implications of the Doctor's words. What he'd said to his mother, trying to convince her to make his father get a check-up, it hadn't changed a thing. His father would still die in three and a half years' time.

'I recommend you stay as far away from your younger self as possible just to be on the safe side,' said the Doctor. 'Get out of the country if necessary. Belgium, I *recommend* Belgium. And I never thought I'd say *that*.'

'Any more conditions?'

'Condition number three.' The Doctor clapped his hands like a university lecturer warming to his theme. 'You are not to tell to anyone you are from the future. Not even as a joke. As far as anyone from this time period is concerned, you were born – how old are you, Mark?'

'Thirty-seven.'

'You were born thirty-seven years ago. You can keep the same birthday if you like. But you have not travelled in time. If anyone asks, you think the whole notion is just science fiction.'

'Right.'

'You'll need a new identity. I'll leave the details to you. Keep your head down. Don't do anything to arouse suspicion. Don't get married, don't have children.'

'I don't see why—'

'Isn't it obvious?' said Amy. 'Because if you end up getting married to some girl, you might be changing history because she *should've* got married to somebody else.'

'All right, I agree, I agree,' said Mark, so loudly that passing shoppers turned to look at the disturbance. 'Don't get involved.'

The Doctor patted his jacket pockets. 'Do you need money?'

'I have money,' said Mark. 'The envelope I sent to myself contained six thousand pounds.'

The Doctor whistled in admiration then frowned. 'Sorry, is that quite a lot?'

'Enough to last me a few months. Is it OK for me to get a job?'

'So long as it's not Prime Minister, yes,' said the Doctor, breaking into a smile. 'Speaking of which, that letter of yours. You have to remember to send it to yourself.'

'I won't forget. I'll keep it safe, and then send it—'

'No. You mustn't send the *original* letter. That wouldn't

make sense. You must make a copy, a handwritten copy, *identical* in every detail. And you send yourself the copy.'

'The copy, right.'

The Doctor tapped out a rhythm on the top of Fireman Sam's fire engine. 'Well, I think that's everything. Oh... and one last thing.'

'Yes?'

'Watch out for the Angels. As long as you behave yourself, you should be quite safe. The Angels are only going to be drawn to you if there's the possibility of a paradox. And if you *do* see the Angels, that means you're on the brink of creating a paradox, so whatever you're doing, stop.'

'You're sure they won't come after me?'

'They're not going to waste energy chasing you unless there's a meal at the end of it.'

Mark wasn't convinced but didn't want to press the point. 'If you say so.'

'Good luck.' The Doctor shook Mark's hand and waited by the police box. Rory gave Mark an encouraging slap on the back, and Amy gave him an encouraging kiss on the cheek.

'Be a good boy,' she said, before following Rory into the police box.

The Doctor lingered on the threshold. 'Don't draw attention to yourself. Don't contact your former self. And *don't*, whatever you do, *change history*.' He disappeared inside, shutting the door after him. The lamp on top of the box flashed and, with a wheezing, groaning sound, the police box faded from view.

He'd convinced them. Mark patted his coat pocket, feeling the reassuring weight of the padded envelope. He opened it and checked the list of instructions, reminding himself what he had to do. First, get a fake ID. He had ready cash, so it shouldn't be difficult.

The fingers of his right hand tingled for the first time since the previous night.

'Thanks for coming with me, Mark,' said a familiar voice. Mark turned to see Sophie and his younger self emerge from the supermarket, both laden with plastic bags full of groceries.

Mark ducked behind the *Fireman Sam* ride, keeping out of sight.

'Don't mention it, good to get out of the house,' replied Mark's younger self. 'Besides, I feel bad about abandoning you last night.'

'You're forgiven,' said Sophie. 'But don't do it again.'

'OK, cup of tea, then back to the exciting world of contract law,' said Mark's younger self.

His older self watched him walk out into the car park with Sophie.

The tingling in his hand faded until there was no sensation at all. Suddenly there was a brief flapping sound from overhead like the sound of a large bird taking off, but when Mark looked up at the supermarket roof, there was nothing there.

CHAPTER
SEVEN

2 April 1995

Mark poured the last of the white wine into the plastic cup and lay back on the rug. Above him vapour trails crossed the sky. Trees rustled in the breeze and ducks flapped and quacked on the river. In the distance, Warwick Castle rose from the woodland, imposing, and ancient.

Becky – she no longer liked to be called Bex – lay beside him, tickling his neck with a grass stem. 'So where's Sophie today?' she enquired idly, rolling over to lean on her elbows.

'Gone home to her parents,' said Mark. 'No reason.'

'What do you mean, no reason?'

'I mean, we haven't had an argument or anything.'

'Wasn't suggesting you had.'

Mark took a sip of wine. He hadn't had an argument with Sophie because in order to have an argument, you had to be speaking, and at the moment, they weren't speaking. He'd sent Sophie an apologetic email from the computer centre but had yet to receive a reply.

A couple of joggers bounced past listening to portable

CD players. 'What about Anthony?' said Mark. Anthony was Becky's latest boyfriend. He had a face that, in Mark's opinion, resembled a pink potato.

Becky thumbed idly through her battered copy of *Captain Corelli's Mandolin*. 'Rugby match. Said he might join us later, but he won't.'

'Right.' Mark stretched back, trying not to think about Anthony, or Sophie, or work, trying to lose himself in the blueness of the sky.

Becky gave up on her book. 'Forgive me, none of my business, but you're not getting on with Sophie, are you?'

'Yeah, you're right.'

'So what've you done wrong this time?'

'No, you're right that it's none of your business.'

Becky pouted. 'I don't know why you put up with her. Sorry to be blunt, but she makes you unhappy, Mark. It's like, on your own, you're quite a nice guy, but whenever you're with her, you just sit there, *glowering*.'

'Do I?' asked Mark, even though he knew Becky had hit the nail on the head. He didn't enjoy spending time with Sophie any more. It had become an obligation to be endured.

'You should find someone else. Someone you actually get on with.'

'I would, but you're taken, alas, alas,' said Mark mockingly.

'You had your chance, as I recall. That night, on the roof of the Union...'

'I remember.' Mark finished his wine. 'God, if Sophie knew I was talking to you like this...'

'What?'

'Oh, she has this idea in her head that I would rather be going out with you.'

'Well, *obviously*,' joked Becky. 'I mean, I'm sane, she's a control freak. Is that why she's always so unfriendly?'

'Yo, dudes,' said Lucy, clumping up to them with a smile and a clinking carrier bag. Despite the heat, she wore her usual black T-shirt, jeans and combat boots. Her girlfriend, a shy, bookish girl called Emma, followed in her wake. 'Did you miss us?'

17 February 1996

'Well, this is embarrassing,' groaned Becky.

Mark was lying in an unfamiliar bed in an unfamiliar bedroom. On the opposite wall hung a Monet print and a cork board pinned with Polaroids of parties, pets and holidays. A window looked out onto the cold, drizzly morning. And Becky was sitting on the bed beside him. He could see her back, so smooth and pale, her shoulder blades, her spine. Then she pulled a baggy T-shirt over her head and tugged on a pair of jeans. 'I suppose, civilised thing, do you fancy coffee? Or tea? We're out of milk.'

'Black coffee's fine.' Mark blinked, his eyes stinging as he'd slept with his contact lenses in. 'What's embarrassing?'

'What do you think? Last night.'

Mark remembered. 'Oh.'

Yesterday had been a bad day. He'd got fired from his job in telesales, a job which he loathed but that wasn't the point, he'd never been fired from a job before. After splitting up with Sophie – at long last – he'd moved in with Rajeev. While he had yet to get a placement with a solicitor since graduating, all his friends still lived in Coventry and the surrounding area. But while they studied for PhDs, he drifted from one dead-end job to the next.

He'd gone to Becky's for tea and sympathy. They'd talked for a while, about Anthony, and how Becky hardly ever saw him since he'd got a job in Manchester. Then Becky had boiled some pasta, he'd popped out to the off-licence, and they'd spent the evening curled up on the sofa watching *Cybill*, *Friends* and *Frasier*. By the time Channel 4 got to *The Girlie Show*, they'd got to the kissing and unbuttoning stage.

'What are you saying?' said Mark, feeling his stomach churn. 'You regret it?'

'Of course I regret it. Hello! Don't you?'

'No.'

'Thanks,' said Becky sarcastically as she inspected herself in the mirror. 'Thanks a lot, Mark. Make it complicated.'

'Look, I know you're with Anthony, it's just, well, I don't think he knows what he has,' said Mark, echoing something Becky had once said to him. 'Don't worry, it'll stay just between us.'

'There is no *us*. It was just a, just a silly—'

'Mistake?'

'Your word not mine. I was going to say "one-off". Let's just try to forget it ever happened, OK?' Becky whipped the duvet from the bed. 'Now I don't want to be rude or anything, but I think you should go, I've got loads of stuff to do today and don't need you hanging around.'

Mark ran the conversation over and over again in his head, trying to work out where he'd gone wrong, what he should have said. He sat alone in the kitchen, drinking instant coffee, watching *The Chart Show* on Becky's portable television. Apparently The Lighthouse Family felt 'Lifted'. Mark didn't share their optimism and turned it off.

'When you're finished,' said Becky, pausing on her way to the door in a thick coat, scarf and beanie hat, 'make sure the door locks behind you.'

'Don't you think we should talk?' said Mark.

'About what?'

'About what happened.'

'There's nothing to talk about,' said Becky. 'Goodbye, Mark.' She left, the door slamming shut behind her.

Mark finished his breakfast, washed up the mug and bowl, pulled on his jacket, and braved the outside world. Speckles of snow fluttered in the blustery air. The snow wasn't settling, though, it was just melting and making the pavement sludgy and grey.

Something had changed between him and Becky. The warm feeling of trust, of private jokes and shared confidences had been replaced by a feeling as cold as this February morning.

Mark huddled his hands into his pockets and headed for home, thinking about the fact that he'd lost his best friend in the world.

Inside the TARDIS, the Doctor cranked the dematerialisation handle and darted around the console, making an adjustment here, typing in a new setting there, all the while glancing at a folded sheet of paper.

'So that's it?' said Amy, trying to attract his attention through the glass of the central column. 'You're just trusting him, leaving him in the past?'

'Not quite,' said the Doctor, grimacing as he pulled a particularly stiff lever. 'I'm slaving the navigation systems to the contents of Mark Whitaker's CV.'

'What does that mean?' asked Rory.

'*Curriculum Vitae*. It's Latin. Would've thought you'd have known that.'

'No, what does "slaving the navigation systems" mean?'

'It means the TARDIS is going to follow Mark through the course of his life. Young Mark, I mean. Wherever he is, the TARDIS won't be far away. Multi-dimensionally speaking.'

'You're using the TARDIS to keep tabs on him?' said Amy.

'Which means that if there *are* any disturbances in his timeline, the TARDIS will put us down nearby.'

'Disturbances?' said Amy. 'You mean if old Mark doesn't behave himself—'

'Exactly.' The Doctor nodded. 'If at any point he crosses his younger self's path, or attempts to change the course of history… we'll be there to stop him.'

'But hang on,' said Rory. 'You said that whenever there's a build-up a potential time energy, the Weeping Angels will be drawn to it like moths to a flame.'

'I did,' said the Doctor, suddenly solemn. 'Which is why we have to get to him first.'

16 December 1997

'Mark!'

It took the 24-year-old Mark a couple of seconds to register that someone had called out his name. He turned, searching the shopping precinct for a familiar face. There were pensioners in heavy coats, young families with pushchairs, teenagers with Santa hats and rucksacks, all of them wielding bulging shopping bags. A brass band pumped out a festive carol.

But even with the brisk sense of excitement in the air, even with the silvery webs of lights overhead, even with the combined efforts of Slade, Wizzard and Wham!, Mark didn't feel full of Christmas cheer. He felt numb, miserable and anxious.

Until he saw Becky stride out of the crowd towards him, her face beaming. She wore a fluffy cream-coloured hat and scarf, her cheeks flushed from the cold. 'Mark!' she repeated, before hugging him. 'What are you doing here?'

Mark lifted his two bulging shopping bags. 'Guess.'

'Me too. God, Christmas is a nightmare.' Becky studied his face. 'Something different about you. What is it? Don't tell me. No, I give up, tell me.'

'New glasses,' said Mark, though they weren't new, he'd got them six months earlier.

'They suit you,' said Becky earnestly. 'Groovy, baby! Look, do you fancy going for a coffee, only I think that if I don't get out of the crowd, I might literally murder someone.'

'Yeah, sounds great,' said Mark.

Becky guided him through the crowd, past Woolworths with its cardboard cut-out Teletubbies, and past the large, stone fountain, where the rushing water glittered in ever-changing colours. She paused at the fountain, disconcerted. 'Hey, since when did they put the statues here?'

Mark shrugged. He'd never really noticed them before. Six stone statues of angels in robes, placed around the edge of the pool, facing outwards. Except they were all covering their faces with their hands.

They stepped into the steamy warmth of the coffee shop, to be greeted by the chorus of 'Never Ever' on the radio.

'Coffee?' said Becky. 'Let me remember. Black, no sugar?'

'Yep,' said Mark.

'Grab us a seat, can you, I'll get these.'

While Becky paid for and collected the two cups, Mark found a couple of padded seats in the corner by the window.

'So,' said Becky, carefully placing the coffees on the table, on top of a discarded copy of *The European*. 'News. Tell me everything.' She shrugged off her coat and took the seat opposite. Mark studied her for a moment. She looked different. She'd had her hair cut short and dyed red with a blonde streak, like the girl from *This Life*, and wore more lipstick and eyeliner.

'Not a lot, really,' said Mark. 'Still working for the housing association. Boring but it pays the rent, just about. Still looking for a practice that'll take me on. You?'

'Oh, you know, dissertation rumbles on. OK, that's work out of the way. What about everything else? Are you still with that girl, what was her name?'

'Jenny,' said Mark. 'Yeah, we're still together'. He'd met her on his first day at the Housing Association. They were both temping in the same office and found they both needed someone sane to talk to. Jenny was very… *determined*. It had been her idea for Mark to change his spectacles, along with most of his clothes. Mark sometimes wondered if she even had a sense of humour. Whenever he made a joke she would just look at him as though he had let her down somehow.

'And it's going OK?'

'Yeah, it's good. We haven't moved in together yet but it's, you know, inevitable.'

'Wow. Sounds serious. How long has it been, then?'

'Nearly a year.'

'A year? God, I'm so out of date.' Becky blew the foam off her coffee and took a sip. 'When I last saw you, you'd just started going out. She is the one with no sense of humour, right?'

'Yeah,' laughed Mark. Becky had met Jenny, very briefly, at Lucy's birthday party in March. He could still remember the argument he'd had with Jenny on the way home; it had been their first big argument. The first of many.

But while that had been the last time Becky had seen him, it hadn't been the last time he'd seen her. The last time he'd seen her, she'd been chatting with some people he didn't know at Rajeev's going-home party in July. He'd watched her from the other side of the room but for some reason he couldn't bring himself to go up to her. What would he say? After that night in February, they hadn't had a proper conversation. He always felt self-conscious and resentful, and she always gave the impression she would much rather be somewhere else.

'And what about you? Still with Anthony?'

'Oh, yeah. He's still keen, bless him. We're doing Christmas at his parents.' Becky grimaced. 'Which will be *agony*. I don't think they regard me as daughter-in-law material. What about you, what are you doing?'

'I'm going home, to spend it with my parents.'

'Oh, sounds nice.'

'Not really. My…' Then it all came out in a rush. 'My dad had a heart attack two weeks ago, he didn't die, but they've had to take him into hospital for observation, because it might happen again, and so… and so I've taken as much time off work as I can, I'm going down tonight, it looks like he's going to be spending Christmas in hospital, and so I have to be there, not just to see him, but to be there for Mum because, on the phone, she sounds like she's trying not to cry and, so, yeah, that's what I'm doing this Christmas.'

Mark picked up a tissue and rubbed it into the corners of his eyes.

'Oh my God. I'm so sorry.' Becky gave him a sympathetic smile, and suddenly Mark felt like he was with the old Bex again.

'Mum was always on at him to go for a check-up. Apparently some relative in Canada had a heart attack when they were his age. But he never got around to it, always too busy. Anyway, Christmas shopping,' said Mark, swallowing the lump in his throat. 'What a nightmare, eh?'

'Yeah,' said Becky, rubbing his fingers. 'Look, if ever you need someone to talk to…'

Mark felt the touch of metal, and looked down to see the engagement ring on Becky's finger. Becky saw that Mark had noticed it and withdrew her hand.

'"Not daughter-in-law material",' said Mark. 'I should've picked up on that. Congratulations.'

'Thanks.'

'So when's the wedding?'

'Oh, not for ages. Anthony's parents want to organise this massive do. They've actually been watching *Four Weddings* on video and taking notes. I think they're waiting on St Paul's cathedral becoming available. You're invited. Obviously. You and what's her name, Jenny. If you're still together.'

'What is it with you and trying to split me up with my girlfriends?' joked Mark.

'I just think none of them are good enough for you, that's all.'

'Yeah,' said Mark. 'Which reminds me.' He dug in his pocket for his new mobile phone and switched it on. One missed call, one new message. From Jenny, telling him to meet her at her office at four, that she loved him and not to be late, x. Mark checked the time. Half past four.

Mark finished the rest of his coffee. 'Look, I've got to go, it was lovely seeing you, Becky.'

'Lovely seeing you too, Mark. One thing you should know before you go, though.'

'Yeah?' Mark pulled on his coat and grabbed his shopping bags.

'No one calls me Becky any more. It's Rebecca.' She stood up as though to shake his hand. But instead she laughed and gave him a stiff hug. 'And what I said, about phoning me, any time, I meant it. Oh, and you left your paper.' She handed him the discarded copy of *The European*.

'Not mine.'

'Oh,' she said, taking it back. As she did, a lottery ticket slid from its pages. Rebecca examined it. 'Hey, it's for tomorrow.' She pressed it into his hand. 'You have it. You never know.' She put on the deep voice of the television advert. '"It could be you".'

Mark slipped the ticket into his pocket. 'Yeah. Anyway. Have to, you know.' He walked over to the door and out into the chilly, damp and oh-so-Christmassy shopping precinct.

But he couldn't help looking back at Rebecca, sipping at her coffee in the window. And then he noticed a tingling sensation in his right hand, the same feeling he'd had on the night they'd first kissed.

*

351

Rebecca drained her coffee, thinking about Mark. He looked like he hadn't slept for days, his eyes were red from crying and, God, those glasses really didn't suit him. She'd wanted to kiss him and tell him everything would be all right, but she'd held back.

And then she noticed the man standing at her table.

For a moment she thought Mark had come back, until she realised it wasn't him. The man looked familiar, but she couldn't place where from. He looked about 40, with a deep tan and tinted glasses. 'Forgot my paper,' he said, collecting *The European* and turning to go.

'Hey,' said Rebecca. 'There was a lottery ticket, I'm sorry, my friend took it, we thought—'

'It's OK. He probably needs it more than I do.' The man smiled and left, just as the coffee shop radio began to play the opening chords of 'Angels'.

CHAPTER
EIGHT

11 August 1998

'Mind if we join you?' asked Amy.

'No, not at all,' said Mark, sliding a chair towards her. 'I thought I might see you here.'

Rory let Amy take the seat with the most shade, while the Doctor eased himself into a chair directly in the glare of the midday sun. The narrow street baked in the heat, heady with traffic fumes and swarming with tourists. Occasionally the guttural rev of a motor scooter drowned out the chatter from the coffee bars and souvenir stalls, but it never drowned out the constant, thunderous, splashing roar of the Trevi Fountain waterfall.

'Three frappuccinos,' the Doctor told the waitress. 'Make mine decaffeinated.'

The waitress boggled at the Doctor. His only concession to the heat was a pair of sunglasses. He should have been roasting in his tweed jacket and bow tie, but showed no discomfort.

'How did you find me?' asked Mark.

'Wibbliness,' explained Rory. 'The Doctor has a special

detector.' The device lay in the Doctor's lap, bleeping intermittently.

'Oh, yes, I remember,' said Mark. 'When we first met. It seems such a long time ago.' Rory exchanged a raised eyebrow with Amy. As far as they were concerned, they'd only left Mark at the supermarket a few hours ago, yet he already looked noticeably older, his hair thinning, his skin tanned but showing deeper lines around his mouth and eyes.

'How long has it been?' asked Amy.

'Four years. I'm 41 now.' Mark sipped his tea and smiled. 'While you're not a day older.'

'So what have you been up to? Whatever it is, you're looking good on it,' said Rory, referring to Mark's finely tailored grey suit.

'Behaving myself,' said Mark with a curt smile. 'Keeping out of the way of my younger self. I've been travelling – I did spend a few weeks in Belgium – and now I have my own small business consultancy company.' He presented the Doctor with his card.

The Doctor read the card. '"Harold Jones". Your new identity?'

Mark nodded. 'Seemed to fit the bill. Nice and anonymous, nothing to provoke suspicion.'

'And what sort of "business consultancy" do you do?' said the Doctor, pocketing the card.

'Don't worry, I'm not giving them information about the future or anything like that. It's just a cover for my investments.'

'Investments?'

'I've done quite well for myself over the past few years, Doctor. Oh, I've been careful not to draw attention to myself – for each deal that makes a profit, I make sure I make another that makes a loss. So far I've mostly been dealing in internet start-ups, registering domain names and so on, but recently I've moved into property, share options, and, ah, West End musicals.'

'West End *musicals*?' exclaimed Amy.

'I'm putting some money into an ABBA thing that's coming up. I think it might do well.'

'Are you a big fan of musical theatre, then?'

'No, but I know which shows will still be running in ten years' time. It's the same for all my investments; if I know a company is still around in 2011, I buy shares in it. Surprising how easy it is to make money, if you know the future!'

The waitress delivered their chilled coffees. The Doctor waited until she had gone before resuming their conversation. 'So what about your little to-do list? How's that been getting on?'

'See for yourself.' Mark took a sheet of paper from his briefcase and handed it to the Doctor.

The Doctor absorbed both sides in under a second. 'This is the letter from your future self?'

'No, this is the copy. The original is kept in a safe in my flat.'

'Very wise.' The Doctor returned the letter. 'Already ticked two items off the list, I see.'

'Yes. I had to delay the start of one of my third-year exams, because my younger self was running late. And then last year I had to make sure he ended up with a winning lottery ticket.'

'A winning lottery ticket?' said Rory, his jaw dropping.

'Not the jackpot. Just matching enough numbers to win about sixteen thousand pounds.'

Amy whistled in admiration. 'Not bad for a day's work!'

'But how did you do it?' asked Rory. 'All the stuff with musicals and internet sites I get, but you couldn't possibly remember what the winning lottery numbers were, one week in 1997!'

'He wouldn't need to,' said the Doctor between slurps of his frappuccino.

'Why?'

'Because he *wrote them down in the letter he sent himself!*' exclaimed Amy with a grin.

'Eh?' said Rory. The more he tried to figure it out, the more confused he got. No, it was no good. A diagram would be required.

'Which brings us to item number three,' said the Doctor. 'Speaking of which, here they *are*... bang on schedule!' He lowered his sunglasses to peer towards the fountain.

Rory followed his gaze – to see young Mark, in a T-shirt and a floppy white bucket hat, wandering through the crowd with a girl in a summer dress. Even from this distance, Rory could tell she was stunning.

So could Amy, who gave Rory a look which in no uncertain terms reminded him that he was now a married man.

For the first time in what seemed like years, Mark felt at peace. The sky was blue, the air was balmy and breezy, and he was with Rebecca. They'd spent the morning exploring the Castel St Angelo, the Piazza Navona, the Pantheon, winding through endless streets, never hurrying but always excited at what was around the next corner. It had been the most perfect day ever.

Of course, he wasn't *with* Rebecca, not in the boyfriend-girlfriend sense. They were on holiday as friends and nothing more, that had been agreed in advance. Although they shared a bed, they shared it with a pillow between them, and were changing into their night things in the bathroom to avoid embarrassment.

How had he ended up in Rome with Rebecca? If he'd known in January how things would turn out… it wouldn't have made it any easier. His father hadn't lasted into the new year, and he'd ended it with Jenny a few weeks later. He just wanted to be a good son to his mother for once. They talked about Dad, Mark hearing stories he'd never heard before, about how they'd first met, and how his father had rushed out of a council meeting to see his newborn son, and how proud he was of him, how he always told everyone he met how proud he was of his son.

He'd remained in contact with Rebecca, talking almost daily on the phone. And she had been great. She always listened, asking questions and making suggestions, even making him laugh.

In April, it was Mark's turn to be the shoulder to cry on. Rebecca had discovered that her fiancé Anthony had been having a relationship with one of his colleagues from work, and that it had been going on ever since he'd moved to Manchester. When she confronted him about this, Anthony begged forgiveness, but Rebecca couldn't forgive him. She could barely look at him without feeling sick.

But she had already booked a holiday in Rome and now had no one to go with. It hadn't been Mark's idea to offer to take the spare ticket. It had been his mother's. She reminded him how his father had never found the time to take her to Paris, and that he'd always regret it if he let this opportunity slip through his fingers.

Mark plucked up the courage to ask Rebecca if she'd mind if he went with her. She laughed and told him that she'd been waiting for ages for him to get the hint. He insisted on paying for his half of the holiday; after all, after his win on the National Lottery, he could afford it.

He'd come so far in the past six months, out of the darkness and into the light. And as though she knew what he was thinking, Rebecca took his hand, and together they squeezed through the crowd towards the Trevi Fountain.

And Mark's right hand began to tingle.

The couple reached the terrace at the top of the steps leading down to the turquoise pool, then paused as the boy took the girl's photograph. Rory, the Doctor, Amy and Mark watched from their table, peering out from behind their menu cards.

'You think you lost your wallet here?' said the Doctor.

'That's what I remember. According to the letter, it should happen any second now.'

Rory edged forward to get a better look. He could see the wallet bulging in the young man's back pocket. But he couldn't see how it could accidentally fall out. Until he noticed a thin, seedy-looking teenager sidling through the crowd, the only person there not to be gazing in wonder at the statue of Oceanus. Without breaking his stride, the teenager lifted the wallet from young Mark's pocket and walked casually away. Towards where they were sitting.

The Doctor gave Rory a nod. In a few seconds the thief would be within reach. Rory psyched himself up to grab him. But then the thief noticed that they were looking at him. He launched himself into a run, shoving them both out of his way.

Rory turned to see the teenager skidding down a side street. Without thinking, Rory sprinted after him, giving a yell of 'Stop! Thief!' Around him, the tourists gawped on in bemusement.

Rory turned down the side street to see the teenager knocking aside any bystanders that impeded his progress. Ahead of him a Fiat blocked the entire width of the street. The teenager didn't slow down. He simply leapt onto the car's bonnet, ran across its roof and jumped to the ground, making his escape. Without pausing to think, Rory scrambled over the car after him, trying his best to ignore the blasts from the horn and the barrage of insults from the driver.

The teenager darted down another side street, glancing back to see if he'd lost his pursuer. He hadn't. After landing heavily on the tarmac, Rory redoubled his speed, ignoring the stitch in his side. He chased the teenager through a number of increasingly narrow alleyways, if not by sight then by the sound of the teenager's heels.

The next alleyway ended at a flight of steps. The teenager had already climbed twenty or so of the steps but Rory didn't give up. Groaning with the effort, Rory raced after him. The steps were incredibly steep, rising up over the rooftops, and just when Rory thought they might go on for ever, they ended at a car park.

The teenager dashed over to a motor scooter, but before he could turn the ignition, Rory lunged at him, knocking both the thief and his scooter to the ground. In the struggle that followed, Rory prised the thief's fingers apart and wrenched the wallet out of his grip. Then the teenager shoved Rory aside and, shouting expletives, scurried into the distance.

Rory lay on the tarmac, his chest heaving, until he heard the Doctor jogging up the stairs after him.

'Well done,' said the Doctor, helping him to his feet. 'You've just saved the entire space-time continuum.'

'Great,' said Rory with little enthusiasm, handing him the wallet.

The Doctor examined it and shook his head. 'But I'm afraid it's the wrong wallet.'

'Wh-what?'

'Only joking,' beamed the Doctor. 'It's the right wallet. Your *face*!' The Doctor adjusted his bow tie, feeling terribly pleased with himself. 'Now, we have to deliver it to Mark's hotel…'

It had been one of the best mornings of his life, only to be followed by one of the worst afternoons. Somewhere between the Pantheon and the Trevi Fountain, Mark had lost his wallet. The wallet containing all his money, his credit cards, his travel insurance, everything.

They spent the next hour retracing their route, Mark scanning the gutters whilst cursing his own stupidity. He knew Rebecca didn't have enough cash to pay for both of them. They wouldn't be able to go out, or visit the museums, or see Hadrian's villa at Tivoli. The more Mark thought about it, the more furious he got.

As they reached the Pantheon, Mark slumped against a wall. 'OK. That's it. I give up.'

'Oh well,' said Rebecca. 'Never mind.'

'I don't get you. I'm going out of my mind here, and you're just taking it all in your stride.'

'I'm on holiday. It's not as if Rome is going anywhere. And anyway, what's the point in me worrying when you're stressing out enough for both of us?'

'So you're not angry with me?'

'Of course not. Look. Let me buy you an ice cream.'

'We can't afford it.'

'OK, let's… let's walk back to the hotel, I might still have some traveller's cheques in my suitcase. We can at least work out how much money we have left.'

'Yeah. I suppose that's a plan.'

'It's a brilliant plan, because I thought of it,' said Rebecca, teasing a smile out of him. 'And don't worry. So you lost your wallet. It's not the end of the world.'

The Doctor twirled the wallet in his hand like a magician with a playing card before handing it to the hotel receptionist.

'Look, here's a thing. I found this wallet lying in the street and I think it might belong to somebody staying in this hotel.'

The receptionist opened the wallet, then looked at the Doctor as though he should be arrested for interrupting her day.

'Mark Whitaker,' said Amy clearly and helpfully. 'His name was on his credit card.'

'Yes,' said the Doctor. 'So if you could put it aside, for when he gets back. That's all. And if he asks about me, just say it was some… handsome stranger.' The Doctor adjusted his bow tie proudly.

Amy tugged the Doctor away from the receptionist before he embarrassed her further, to join Rory and Mark in the street outside.

'Well, that's that finished,' said Rory as Amy placed a congratulatory arm around him.

'Yes. Another one to tick off your list, Mr Whitaker.' The Doctor squatted on the ground, opened his leather satchel and took out his automatic wibble-detector. 'Except…'

'Except what?' said Mark.

The Doctor held the device above his head, like someone trying to get a better phone signal. 'I'm still getting wibbliness. You see that dial?'

Mark peered at the machine. 'The one that isn't actually moving?'

'Yes. The fact that it isn't actually moving means that the course of history is still in flux.'

'But we delivered the guy's wallet,' protested Rory. 'What else do we have to do?'

'There's nothing else in my letter,' said Mark.

'Then it must be something else,' said the Doctor, waggling his fingers. 'Something *else* that happened on this day. Something with lots of… what was the word, Rory?'

'Ramifications?' sighed Rory.

'Ramifications! Yes. Something with lots of *ramifications*! So, Mark, what was it?'

'You can't expect him to remember,' laughed Amy. 'As far as he's concerned it was, like, fifteen years ago!'

Mark ran a hand through his hair, smiling at a reawakened memory. 'Oh no, I remember like it was yesterday.'

'But it's not yesterday. It's *today*.' The Doctor gripped Mark by the shoulders and looked directly into his eyes. 'So tell me, after you recovered your wallet… what did you do next?'

CHAPTER
NINE

The disembodied heads of long-dead Roman Emperors lined the hallway, each one made of smooth, white marble.

'And this one is,' said Rebecca, reading the plaque beneath it, 'Tiberius. On a scale of bonkersness from one to ten, he was about an eight.' She continued down the Hall of Emperors, her footsteps clicking on the marble floor.

It was nearly closing time and the Capitoline Museum was deserted. Mark relaxed, breathing in the refreshingly cool air, scarcely able to believe they were here after all the traumas of the day.

When they'd finally made it to the hotel, the receptionist had greeted him with wide-eyed excitement, waving and shouting his name. She had his wallet and it still contained all his credit cards and money! According to the receptionist, it had been handed in by some 'handsome stranger'. Mark thanked her effusively, promising her that when he got home he'd tell everyone he knew that Italians were the most honest people in the world.

What it didn't contain was any details about his hotel. So how could they have known where to hand it in? Mark was too relieved to question his good fortune. He and Rebecca bought a celebratory pizza and resumed their tour, visiting the Colosseum, the ruins of the Roman Forum and the Palatine Hill, before climbing the steps to the Capitoline Hill. As they entered the museum, they persuaded a Korean tourist to take a photo of them beside Constantine's *Monty Python*-esque foot before entering the palatial interior.

'Weird,' said Rebecca, interrupting Mark's thoughts. 'Don't look very Roman, do they?'

Rebecca indicated six statues standing in a line against the wall. They were statues of angels, their arms crossed over their chests, their eyes staring worshipfully upwards. With their robes and nest-of-vipers hair, they resembled the statue of a Wounded Amazon from the Great Hall. But their wings looked anachronistically Victorian.

'What do the labels say?' said Mark, giving each statue no more than a cursory glance.

'There aren't any,' said Rebecca. 'Guess they must be new.'

Young Mark and Rebecca inspected the statues for a few more moments before disappearing through the doorway at the far end of the hall.

'Weeping Angels,' sighed Rory.

Gesturing to Rory, Amy and Mark to stay crouched behind a bust of the Emperor Hadrian, the Doctor approached the statues, holding his eyes open with his fingers, his steps not making a sound. 'Yes. That proves it.'

'Proves what?' whispered Amy.

'They're waiting for a paradox to happen.' Blue lightning crackled across the ornate ceiling.

'What sort of paradox?' shivered Rory. 'I mean, caused by what?'

The Doctor turned to Mark. 'When you were here before, did anything happen that was unusual in any way? A stroke of fortune, a coincidence that set you down a particular path?'

Mark thought back. He remembered visiting the museum before, and seeing the Angel statues had jogged a memory of having seen them before, but after that, he couldn't recall anything apart from the conversation he'd had with Rebecca on the balcony overlooking the Forum.

'Nothing springs to mind,' said Mark, then he slapped his cheek. 'Oh! Except there was one thing. We got locked in.'

'You got *locked in*?' said the Doctor.

'Er... Doctor,' said Amy quietly. 'You're not looking at the Angels.'

'I thought you were,' said the Doctor. 'Do I have to tell you to do everything?'

'I am. *Now*.' said Amy, staring, wide-eyed, in the direction of the statues. Mark followed her gaze. Three of the statues were caught in walking poses, heading for the doorway after young Mark and Rebecca. The other three had been frozen as they stalked towards the Doctor, their arms outstretched like sleepwalkers, their features calm and blank.

'They're trying to get between us and the young Mark.' The Doctor walked towards the Angels, beckoning to Amy, Rory and Mark with a finger behind his back.

'You keep an eye on the ones near us, I'll keep an eye on the others,' whispered Mark.

With Amy and Rory treading silently behind him, he crept after the Doctor, keeping his eyes fixed on the Angels heading for the doorway, resisting the urge to turn towards the ones only a few metres away. Slowly but surely they made it past the statues to the doorway. The moment they were all through, the Doctor slammed the door shut behind them and secured it with his sonic screwdriver.

'So, Doctor,' said Rory with a sigh of relief. 'What exactly is it we have to do?'

'Isn't it obvious?' said the Doctor with a wild-eyed grin. 'We have to lock young Mark in!'

'Five minutes, no more, OK?' said the museum guard, barely sparing Mark and Rebecca a glance before he disappeared into the toilet with an urgent shuffle.

They were in the underground tunnel that linked the two halves of the museum, and which led to the Tabularium, the ancient Roman record office. They wandered through a hall filled with altars and burial slabs into a rough-walled tunnel which opened onto a cloister overlooking the remains of the Forum below, the toppled Corinthian columns, and, in the distance, the Colosseum. All bathed in the coppery glow of the setting sun.

Rebecca rushed over to the balcony, sighing in awe. 'What a view!' She turned to Mark and smiled. 'I'm glad you came along in the end. This wouldn't have been half as much fun without you.'

'You call watching me panic for an hour *fun?*'

'Well, entertaining,' she smirked.

Mark snapped a photograph of the view. 'Come on, we should be heading off.'

'Let them chuck us out. I want to see what's down here first.'

Several passages littered with temple fragments branched off from the cloister. Rebecca ran off to explore the first while Mark glanced back down the tunnel to the Tabularium. For a moment he thought he'd seen a movement in the corner of his eye, as though they were being followed, but there was nobody there.

'That was close,' whispered the Doctor. They all stood flat against the tunnel wall, as still as statues, the Doctor and Mark on one side, Rory and Amy on the other. Rory could feel the clammy bumpiness of the stone wall against his back.

When the young Mark had slipped out of sight, the Doctor relaxed and stepped forward. 'If your younger self sees us…' He pulled a face to indicate an unspecified calamity.

They proceeded towards the narrow doorway that led to the cloister. 'Is this it?' asked Rory.

Mark nodded. 'Yes, I remember, we were locked out on the balcony, just through here…'

'Right, well, suppose we'd better get on with it then,' said Rory, reaching for the heavy, iron door. 'I would ask how we're supposed to lock it without the key, but—'

'Sonic,' said the Doctor, rotating his screwdriver in the air.

'Yeah, always the sonic.' Rory began to heave the door when an angry shout came from down the tunnel.

'Hey, what you doing?' The security guard waddled towards them, a tanned man in his fifties with a bushy moustache and the uniform of a much slimmer man. 'That's my job.'

'Sorry, sorry,' said the Doctor genially. 'Just worried about *security*. Can't be too careful.' He swept his sonic screwdriver through the air as though trying to locate invisible thieves.

The security guard squinted at Mark. 'I thought there was two of you?'

'There were,' said Amy perkily. 'But now there are four of us. What of it?'

The guard snorted and heaved the door shut with a bang. He locked it with a set of heavy iron keys before turning to direct them down the tunnel with his thumb. 'Closing time now. Way out is on right, you go up stairs, you go home, I go home, bye bye.'

'Yes, excellent plan,' said the Doctor, clapping his hands. 'Well done. Thank you very much, you have been *magnificent*. Come on, Mark, Rory, Amy. Nothing more for us to do here…'

'Well?'

Mark shook his head. 'No. We're locked in.' The fingers in his right hand tingled, presumably the result of him slamming his fist against on the door.

Rebecca regarded him with amusement. 'Not really your day, is it?'

Mark didn't know whether to laugh or cry. On the flight out, he'd had this insane fantasy that something might happen between them on this holiday. That she might see him as something more than just a friend. But today she had only seen him at his worst, at his most irritable and incompetent. His one chance to impress her and he'd blown it.

'I'm sure someone will find us,' Rebecca reassured him. 'There are worse places to be locked in. And worse people to be locked in with.'

'That was it? That was all we had to do?' said Amy, strutting after the Doctor.

'I think so, yes.' The Doctor checked his wibble-detector as they climbed the stairs into a gloomy hall lined with statues of mythical figures. 'I'm losing wibbliness. The future's no longer in the balance.'

Mark noticed the tingle in his hand had started to fade. He'd almost forgotten it was there.

'Um, Doctor,' said Rory warily. 'If that's the case, aren't the Weeping Angels gonna be a bit cheesed off?'

'Very,' said the Doctor, as they passed down the hall, their footsteps echoing in the darkness. As the hall had no windows or skylight, the only illumination came from the electric lights. 'So keep an eye out for them.'

Amy looked around, apprehensively studying each statue in turn. Of all the places for a statue to hide, it would have to be a museum filled with statues. 'But we're safe, so long as we see them before they see us?'

'You're never *safe* where the Weeping Angels are concerned,' muttered the Doctor darkly.

'Behind us,' cried Rory, pointing.

The six Weeping Angels stood at the top of the stairs at the end of the hall. All frozen in the process of lowering their hands from their faces.

'Everyone look towards the Angels,' said the Doctor. 'We'll be absolutely fine so long as…'

K-chunk! K-chunk!

The electric lights at the end of the hall flickered and went out. Rory yelped in surprise.

'You had to say it, didn't you?' muttered Amy sharply to the Doctor. 'You had to say it!'

K-chunk!

'Keep moving,' said the Doctor. 'Just keep moving!'

369

Amy and the others slowly backed away as the lights in the middle of the hall went out. Now the only remaining lights were those behind them. In front of them, Amy could make out the sinister, shadowy shapes of the statues of centaurs and nymphs, knowing that somewhere in the blackness the Angels were lurking, waiting for the final set of lights to go out.

K-chunk!

The final set of lights went out. It was as if Amy had closed her eyes. Somebody grabbed her by the wrist and she gave a tiny scream, until she realised the hand belonged to Rory. A moment later she heard a high-pitched buzzing sound and the Doctor's sonic lit up with a green glow.

The Doctor swung the sonic ahead of him like a torch, revealing an Angel as it lunged out of the darkness towards them. The Doctor flashed the light to the left, to halt another Angel as it reached out with scratching fingers. And another, its mouth wide in a silent scream. He flitted the green light between the Angels, trying to hold them back, but each time he lit one up, it had taken another step towards them.

'Amy, Rory, Mark! Move! Move!' yelled the Doctor. 'I'll hold them off for as long as I can.'

'What about you?' cried Amy

'I'd be extremely grateful if, on your way out, you could get someone to turn the lights back on.'

Amy felt Rory squeeze her hand and, together with Mark, they backed down the hall, watching the feeble green light as it darted back and forth between the enraged faces of the Angels. Then they reached the next room and broke into a run.

*

'Sorry about all this.'

'What are you apologising for?' said Rebecca, still enchanted by the view. As the sun had set, the colour of the ruins had shifted from orange to a dusky red. The air smelt of ancient ruins and pine trees. 'Besides, how many people get to see this? Luckiest thing, being locked in.'

'It's been a lucky day, overall,' said Mark, joining Rebecca at the balcony. From here, there wasn't a single modern structure in sight. No office blocks, no street lights, nothing.

'Yeah,' laughed Rebecca. 'Must be fate.'

'Can I ask you a question?'

'Go for it.'

'All the stuff that's happened today, anyone else would've been mad at me, but you… you were OK about it. Why?'

Rebecca swept back her hair while she considered her answer. 'Seriously? The way I see it, after what happened with Anthony, I could've got all paranoid and bitter. But then he'd have won, he'd have changed me into a worse person. And after hearing you talk about all the stuff you've been through, with your dad and everything, it kind of put my woes into perspective. Life's too short to be miserable, basically. If you can be happy, then *be* happy.'

'Seize the day?' said Mark.

'Exactly. Seize it, baby.' Rebecca turned towards him with an expression he'd seen once before, on the terrace of the students' union.

His stomach trembling, Mark leaned forward and kissed her. Rebecca responded, kissing his lips as he kissed hers, gently, precisely, before finally pulling away.

'That's not quite what I meant,' she said.

'No?'

'No. But it's a good start.' Rebecca gave him a conspiratorial smile. 'You know, we could very easily be locked in here all night…'

Back in the hall of statues, the Doctor was fighting a losing battle. No matter how rapidly he alternated the light of the sonic screwdriver between the Angels, they continued their advance, their arms reaching forward, forcing him to back away. And because the rest of the hall was in complete darkness, he had no way of knowing how long he had left before he backed himself into a wall.

'OK, I'm getting that you're not happy,' said the Doctor placatingly. 'But can't we sit down and discuss this like reasonable people? Cup of tea, jammy dodgers, comfy chairs?'

The Angels did not respond. Their eyes remained blank. Their jaws remained open.

'Look. I can—'

The Doctor slipped on the marble floor, lost his balance and landed heavily on his back. For a moment he found himself in total darkness, until he remembered he still had his sonic screwdriver in his hand. In one movement, he activated it and swung it upwards.

Its green glow illuminated the faces of the six Weeping Angels, all looking down at him with expressions of pure malice. They had him surrounded.

'Ah now, you've made a mistake, you see,' said the Doctor. 'Because I can see all of you at once. So the question now is… which one of us will blink first?'

As they reached the museum entrance, Amy grabbed the

security guard, the same guard who they'd spoken to in the tunnel. 'You've got to turn the lights back on!'

He shrugged quizzically. 'I did not turn out lights.'

'Well somebody did!' yelled Amy. 'There's still somebody in there. In the dark!'

The security guard snorted and walked slowly over to a switchboard. Rory and Mark caught up with Amy, Mark red-faced with the exertion, Rory wearing his usual worried expression.

'Hurry up!' urged Amy.

The security guard made a 'tch' noise then flicked down a succession of switches. The hallway behind them flickered into yellow light.

'Thank you,' said Amy, muttering under her breath, 'at last.' With the security guard leading the way, they hurried back through the brightly lit museum.

Returning to the hall with the statues of mythical figures, they discovered the Doctor lying on the floor, the Weeping Angels encircling him, locked in position as they prepared to strike.

'Doctor!' Amy rushed over to him and helped him slide out from beneath the scrum of Weeping Angels.

'I've been trying not to blink for the last minute,' said the Doctor. 'Harder than you'd think.' While Rory and Mark kept a careful watch on the Angels, the Doctor brushed himself down, straightened his jacket and tie, and approached the security guard.

'Hello.' The Doctor put a friendly arm around the guard's shoulders. 'You're probably wondering where those six new statues have come from.'

The guard nodded dumbly.

'Well, I shouldn't worry about them if I were you, they

won't be here in the morning,' said the Doctor. 'But until we're all safely out of the building, let's not let them out of our sight, eh?'

Mark coughed to get the Doctor's attention.

'Oh,' said the Doctor, remembering. 'But first you might like to pop down to the Tabularium. I think there might be two people locked in down there…'

12 August 1998

Mark lay in bed, woken by the morning sunshine. He pulled on his glasses and the rest of the room fell into focus. The pillow from the centre of the bed lay on the floor where he'd thrown it the night before.

Rebecca perched on the balcony in a summer dress, gazing out into the street whilst thumbing through her copy of *The Beach*.

'Rebecca?' said Mark.

'Oh, you're awake now, are you?' she said, putting down her book. The morning sun shone in her hair like a halo and gave her skin a golden glow.

'About last night.'

'Yeah?'

Mark swallowed. 'Just checking. It wasn't another mistake, was it? Another "one-off"?'

Rebecca raised an eyebrow. 'Is that what you want it to be?'

'No, no, I don't,' said Mark hurriedly.

'Me neither,' said Rebecca. 'In fact, I hope it's going to turn out to be the complete opposite.'

Mark climbed out of bed, his feet slapping on the tiled floor. He wanted to rush over and kiss Rebecca, but looking at her sitting in the window, he changed his mind. 'Wait there.'

'What?'

Mark picked up his camera and focused on Rebecca. 'Hold on, don't move, I just want to capture this moment.' As she turned to gaze out into the street with her impossibly blue eyes, he pressed the button and the camera shutter clicked.

CHAPTER
TEN

29 October 1999

Now 42 years old, Mark paused outside the office block and gazed up at the familiar concrete facade. This was where he'd worked for over ten years, starting out as a junior assistant, gradually taking on more and more responsibilities until eventually they'd made him a partner. Or rather, this was where his younger self would be working for the *next* ten years.

The reception area was just as he remembered; OK, so the walls were a different colour, and the sign above the desk read 'Pollard & Boyce', but Ron sat at the desk leafing through a copy of the *Daily Mirror* as usual. The only difference was that he now had a full head of hair.

Mark approached the desk. 'Harold Jones to see Mr Pollard, five o'clock.'

Ron nodded and informed the relevant office on the phone. 'They're sending someone down.'

A minute later, the internal door opened and Siobhan emerged. 'Mr Jones, nice to meet you at last,' she said, shaking his hand.

Mark couldn't help but smile. Siobhan was still in her early thirties, bright-eyed and fresh-faced.

Siobhan took him up the stairs to Pollard's office. Mark caught a glimpse of his reflection in the glass door. He'd taken great care not to look like his younger self. He'd grown a beard, dyed his remaining hair black and, as a finishing touch, wore a pair of tinted sunglasses.

Although he'd spoken to Frank Pollard on the phone numerous times, this would be the first time they'd met in person. Over the last year Mark had divided his time between New York and Edinburgh but now he'd decided to move to London, and had purchased a flat in Highgate. He wanted to be nearer to his younger self. Oh, he wouldn't try to speak to him or anything like that, but it wouldn't hurt to keep an eye on his progress, from afar. And, more than anything else, Mark longed to see Rebecca again.

'Mr Pollard is ready for you.'

Mark discovered Frank Pollard at his desk, beaming with pride. Even he looked younger than Mark remembered, his cheeks plump and ruddy with health.

'Harold, Harold,' said Frank. 'Overjoyed to finally make your acquaintance, in the flesh, as it were.'

'You too,' said Mark, taking a seat. 'I would've visited earlier, but my business keeps me out of the country.'

'Understand entirely.' Frank helped himself to a boiled sweet. 'Why visit Croydon when you could be basking in the manifold delights of "the big apple", so to speak? Can I get Siobhan to make you anything? Coffee? Tea?'

'No, I'm fine thanks. You're probably wondering why I've come to see you.'

'I must confess to being a little intrigued. Your last "electronic mail" was most mysterious.'

'I'm here to ask a favour.'

'A favour?' Frank leaned forward onto his desk. 'And what variety of favour might that be?'

'I believe you've recently advertised a vacancy, for a junior assistant.'

'We have.'

'But you haven't filled the position yet?'

'We have not, as yet. We have whittled the candidates down to a shortlist, as it were.'

'I was wondering if I might make a suggestion. A recommendation. You see, I'm, er, *acquainted* with one of the applicants, and would be extremely grateful if you'd consider giving them the position.'

'Hmm. That is quite a favour to ask.'

'I realise that.'

'May I ask the name of this person with whom you are, shall we say, acquainted?'

'Mark Whitaker.'

Frank opened a file on his desk and skimmed through the papers. 'Mark Whitaker. Mark… Whitaker. Ah, here he is. We interviewed him earlier this week. A personable enough young man, if a little lacking in confidence, but not really in the same league as the other candidates.'

'But I think if you were to give him a chance, he'd prove himself more than capable.'

'Hmm,' said Frank, inspecting the application. 'I *suppose* he may have *potential*.'

'Look, I'm not asking you to take on someone who can't do the job. I'm just asking you to take him on for a trial period. If it doesn't work out, then you're free to get rid of him. And I'm not suggesting you do him any special favours. Treat him exactly as you would any other member of staff. And in return I'll continue to put as much business your way as I can.'

'This is most unorthodox. But bearing in mind how highly we regard you here at Pollard & Boyce, it would be injudicious, if not unprofessional, of us to overlook such a… glowing character reference.'

'So you'll give him the job?'

'Yes. For a *trial period*.' Frank made a note on Mark's application with a dramatic flourish.

'There's one other thing.'

'Yes?'

'My involvement in this has to remain confidential. As far as Mark Whitaker is concerned, he got this job entirely on merit.'

'I *see*.'

'You mustn't mention my name to him. It's vitally important he never finds out about this.'

'Discretion is, of course, assured,' said Frank. 'This lad, is he a relative of yours?'

'Something like that. Let's just say I have great expectations for him.'

'With you cast in the role of Magwitch?' chuckled Frank. 'Was there anything else?

'No. That's everything.' Mark made his farewells and left, having ticked one more item off the list.

31 October 1999

'No milk I'm afraid,' said Mark, handing Rebecca a mug of tea. She was too tired to care. Her back ached, her fingers ached, her feet ached. But at least it was all over.

Well, the actual *moving* part of the move was over. In

terms of furniture, all their new front room had to offer was a battered leathered sofa, an Ikea chair and Mark's portable television. Cardboard boxes filled the floor, piled four high, leaving only a narrow route from the sofa to the door. They'd all have to be unpacked, but that could wait. For now, Rebecca just wanted it to be over.

Oh, it was exciting. Not just moving to London's glamorous Camberwell, but moving in with Mark. It made things official in some way. For the last year they'd basically been living together anyway, but then she'd got the job at Imperial College, so since September she'd been sleeping on a futon at Lucy and Emma's, with Mark coming down at the weekends to go flat-hunting.

And now here they finally were. Drinking black tea in their own flat. Rebecca leaned back in her chair as she watched Mark fiddle with the aerial. It was the last episode in the second series of *Cold Feet*, and it was vitally important they didn't miss it.

Mark's mobile phone bleeped. 'Hello, yes? … Yes, that's right.' He winced apologetically to Rebecca. 'No, it's fine, I wasn't in the middle of anything. Um…' He fell silent as the person on the other end of the line spoke for several minutes. 'Thanks. Thanks for letting me know… Yes, and you too. Goodbye.' He switched off the phone and looked at Rebecca.

'What was that?'

'I got it,' Mark replied at last. 'I got the junior assistant job, with Pollard & Boyce.'

'You *got it*?'

'I'm on a trial period for the first three months, but… yes.' Mark sounded like he could hardly believe his good fortune. 'I start on the eighth.'

Despite all her aches, Rebecca hauled herself off the sofa and hugged him. 'I knew it, I *knew* they'd take you on. What did I tell you? Oh ye of little faith. Well now we have a *second* reason to celebrate!' Rebecca headed into the kitchen and opened the fridge. It was empty apart from the bottle of champagne she'd placed there earlier. She couldn't find any glasses so she rinsed out a couple of chipped mugs before returning to the living room. 'Champagne in mugs, I'm afraid. Truly we live the life of decadence.'

'Start as you mean to go on,' observed Mark drily.

Rebecca peeled off her jumper, wrapped it around the bottleneck and popped the cork. Then she chugged the wine into the mugs and passed one to Mark. 'There you go,' she said, lifting her mug. 'To our new flat, and your new career as a top-flight city lawyer.'

'Hardly that,' said Mark. 'God. Our new flat! Moving in together.'

'Yeah. Serious stuff.' Rebecca sipped the champagne, feeling the tickle of the bubbles on her tongue. 'All grown-up and everything.'

'We'll be getting married next,' said Mark light-heartedly.

Rebecca snorted with laughter. 'What?'

'Well, it is, isn't it? The next logical step.'

'Is this you proposing to me?'

'No,' said Mark. He took a small box out of his jacket pocket and knelt before Rebecca on one knee. He opened the box to reveal a glinting diamond ring. '*This* is me proposing to you.'

A section of the TARDIS console exploded in a shower of sparks. The floor jolted and shuddered, threatening to throw Amy to the ground. 'Doctor!' she yelled, holding on for dear life. 'What's happening?'

They'd only left Rome ten minutes earlier, and had barely taken off before the TARDIS had started making a warping, grinding noise and everything in the control room that wasn't fixed in place fell over.

'More wibbliness in the space-time continuum, right?' suggested Rory, picking himself up.

The Doctor danced around the console, flicking switches, his forehead furrowed in concentration. 'More wibbliness. Yes. The fourth of November. The year 2000.'

'Another one of the items on Mark's list?' suggested Amy.

'There wasn't an item on his list for November 2000.'

'But that means...' said Rory.

'It *means* our friend isn't behaving himself.' The Doctor banged the console and whooped as it began to make the familiar materialisation sound. 'Trouble, here we come!'

CHAPTER
ELEVEN

4 November 2000

Pressing her lips together to remove any excess lipstick, Rebecca studied her reflection in the mirror one last time, looking for flaws. She couldn't find any. Amanda, the beautician, stood behind her, smiling proudly. 'Oh, you look *perfect*.'

Rebecca checked her hair, which had been painstakingly curled into ringlets and pinned, then, as though balancing a book on her head, she stood up. She desperately wanted to take a deep breath, but the corset of her wedding dress wouldn't allow it. Everything had been squeezed and tightened for maximum effect.

She turned to look at Lucy and Emma in their identical, peach-coloured bridesmaid outfits. She'd rather enjoyed the idea of forcing Lucy into something feminine for once.

There was a knock at the door. 'Respectable?' called Rebecca's father.

'No, but come in anyway,' replied Rebecca. Her father walked in with an embarrassed smile, resplendent in his morning suit, and paused as he took in his daughter's transformation.

'My little girl,' he said. For a moment she thought he was going to say how proud he was of her, but in the way he was looking at her, there was no need. 'Feeling nervous?'

'No. I'll be glad when it's all over, though, if only because then people will stop asking me that. Because if there's one thing guaranteed to make you nervous, it's people asking you if you're nervous all the time.'

'I won't pay any attention to that,' said her father. 'That's just the nerves talking. The, um, cars are outside, if you're ready?'

'Here goes, then,' said Rebecca. Once again she wished she could take a deep breath. She turned to go, then halted in the doorway. 'Bouquet!' She grabbed the bunch of lilies from the dressing table. 'Would've been a complete disaster if I'd forgotten that.'

A harsh wind blew across the graveyard, whirling up the leaves as it went. Fearing it would damage his meticulously tousled hair, Mark retreated into the church porch.

Mark's task, along with his best man Gareth, had been to greet the wedding guests as they made their way up the path to the church. It had been very disconcerting to see his colleagues from work, his friends from university and his mates from the pub quiz all in their finest suits and dresses. It felt like he was starring in a romantic comedy.

'Wassup?' said Gareth, slapping Mark on the back. 'Still not too late to do a runner.'

'Very funny,' said Mark, wishing, not for the first time, that he'd chosen a different best man.

Gareth checked his watch. 'Twenty minutes. Time you

were heading inside, just in case they get here early.'

'Yeah,' said Mark, rubbing the fingers of his right hand. They were beginning to tingle.

'Well?'

'He's here, Amy,' said the Doctor, absorbed in his wibble-detector. '*Somewhere*. Somewhere close and getting closer all the time.'

Amy brushed her hair out of her eyes. The TARDIS had brought them to Chichester, a well-preserved city with enough Georgian buildings, Roman walls and leafy parks to look picturesque; every other shop seemed to sell antiques or cream teas. Despite the gusty weather, the pavements bustled with shoppers, mostly families and slow-moving pensioners. It reminded Amy of Leadworth, but with more traffic.

The Doctor halted, spun on his heel, then ran back the way they'd come, bounding towards the cathedral, bounding like a gazelle with rubber legs. 'Quick!'

Amy and Rory exchanged glances and chased after him. The Doctor stopped again, shook the detector, then gawped at the approaching traffic. An SUV sped down the street towards them. It took Amy a few seconds to recognise the driver; it was Mark, his face half-hidden behind a beard and sunglasses.

'Stop!' yelled the Doctor, striding into the road in the path of the car, his hands raised. The SUV screeched to a halt. This was followed by a second screech, a loud crash and the tinkle of broken glass as another vehicle slammed into the back of the SUV.

Old Mark emerged from the car, slamming the door angrily behind him. 'What the… what are *you* doing here?'

'I could ask you the same question,' said the Doctor. 'In fact, I *am* asking you the same question. What are you doing here?'

'Driving along quite happily until some maniac ran out in front of me.'

Amy studied Mark's face. He looked like he was hiding something. 'We're here because the Doctor detected wibbliness. Are you trying to make contact with your younger self?'

'No,' protested Mark. 'No, of course not.'

'Interesting,' said the Doctor. 'Because the wibble-detector never lies. Unless it's malfunctioning, which is always a possibility. But not in this case. I can feel the build-up of potential time energy. Makes all the hairs on the back of my neck stand on end. And tastes of *lemons*.'

'So where *were* you going?' asked Rory.

Before Mark could explain, the driver of the car behind him walked up to them. He was an overweight, colonel-ish man dressed in a chauffeur's regalia. Behind him Amy could see a limousine with shattered headlights and a crumpled bonnet.

'What the hell do you think you're playing at?' yelled the driver.

'I'm sorry,' said Mark. 'It wasn't my fault, this—'

The doors of the limousine opened and out stepped a man of 60 in a grey morning suit with neatly combed white hair, followed by the blonde girl Amy had seen in Rome, now impeccably made up and wearing a stylish bridal gown.

The bride marched towards them, huffing with the effort, holding her high-heeled shoes. 'I don't believe it. I don't *chuffing* believe it!'

'What? What's the matter?' the Doctor asked her, then his eyes widened. 'Wait! Are you getting married?'

'Of course I'm getting married! This is my wedding day! Or at least it was meant to be before it turned into an episode of the *Chuckle Brothers*.'

The Doctor took Mark to one side and whispered. 'Oh, no. You weren't. Your *own wedding*. The list you showed me, of all the times you could intervene in your past? *This wasn't on the list!* Do you know what you've done? You've gone off-list!'

'I wasn't going to *intervene*,' protested Mark. 'I only wanted to stand at the back and watch.'

'Stand at the back and watch?' The Doctor waggled his fingers in frustration. 'What have I told you? Paradoxes! Angels! *Ramifications!* Why do humans never do as they're told? Someone should replace you all with *robots*. No, on seconds thoughts, they shouldn't, bad idea.'

'Sorry to interrupt,' said Rebecca unapologetically. 'Did I just hear you say you were on your way to a wedding?'

'Yes, that's right,' said Mark. 'Saint Stephen's, in a village called Chilbury. It's for a couple, Mark Whitaker and Rebecca Coles…'

'But that… that's *my* wedding,' exclaimed Rebecca. 'You're on your way to *my* wedding?'

'*You're* Rebecca Coles?' said Mark, feigning surprise. 'What a coincidence!'

'Well, there we are, small world.' The Doctor clapped. 'So if, um, *Harold* here could move his car, you can be on your way, and get married, just as you should.'

'Not gonna happen.' The chauffeur shook his head, indicating the damaged limousine. 'Can't drive with it like this, the insurance won't cover it.'

'Oh, *fantastic*,' said the Doctor, slapping his palms on the bonnet of Mark's car. 'Fantastic!'

'Look,' said Mark. 'Since I'm going there anyway… maybe I could give you a lift?'

'A lift! It gets better!' cried the Doctor to the heavens.

'I don't suppose I have any choice,' said Rebecca. 'If I'm not going to be late.'

'Oh, I'm sure a small delay won't hurt,' said the Doctor hurriedly. 'Bride's prerogative. Make him sweat. What's fifteen minutes in the grand scheme of things?'

Mark took the Doctor, Amy and Rory to one side. 'But she *wasn't* late,' he said firmly.

'What?'

'She arrived bang on time.'

'Are you sure?'

'I remember my *own wedding*!'

The Doctor paused, weighing up the situation. 'Right! Everyone into… *Harold's* car. No time to lose, we have a wedding to attend! You're the father of the bride, I take it? Isn't she beautiful? I'd marry her myself, given half a chance! In you go!'

Mark opened the side doors of his car, and Rebecca and her father piled inside.

'Sorry, what are we doing?' said Rory. 'Isn't this changing history?'

'No. If Rebecca is late for her wedding, *that's* changing history,' explained the Doctor. 'We have to get her to the church on time!'

'So, if you don't mind me asking, but who are you?' said Rebecca, her shoes in her lap. There was something strangely familiar about the four strangers. Particularly the guy in the driver's seat. Take away the beard and twenty years or so and he'd have been a dead ringer for Mark.

'A relative,' he said. He even *sounded* like Mark. 'On Aunt Margaret's side. From Canada.'

The young man to her right with the large nose and gormless expression groaned for no apparent reason. 'You're from *Canada*? All of you?' asked Rebecca.

'Yes.' said the guy in the driver's seat. 'A small place, about fifty miles north of Toronto. I'm Harold Jones, this is the Doctor, Amy, and Rory.'

Rebecca considered. Mark's mother had mentioned something about having relatives in Canada. It would explain the resemblance.

'You don't, um, sound very Canadian, if you don't mind me saying,' said Rebecca's father.

'No, but that's just it, you see,' said Amy. 'We Canadians often don't. It's one of the most interesting things *aboot* us.'

'So who exactly invited you to my wedding?' said Rebecca.

'We just happened to be in the country and Mark's mother invited us, as a last-minute thing,' said Harold. 'Not a problem, is it?'

'No. In fact, it's lucky you were here. Although, thinking about it, if you hadn't been here, I wouldn't have crashed into you in the first place.'

'Funny how things work out,' said the Doctor as the car came to a halt. At the junction ahead the traffic lights were on red. 'How are we doing for time, Mar – marvellous Harold?'

'Five minutes to one. We're not gonna make it. Not in this traffic.'

'Leave that to me.' The Doctor dug into his jacket and

pulled out what appeared to be a large electric toothbrush. He leaned out of the window and aimed it at the traffic lights. It buzzed and in an instant the traffic lights turned to green.

'Well, what are you waiting for?' grinned the Doctor manically. 'Drive!'

Mark sat between his mother and Gareth on the front-row pew. The air in the church smelt of stone and furniture polish. He stared at his shoes, so shiny he could actually see his reflection. 'What time is it now?'

'Five minutes to,' said Gareth. 'God, I hope she hasn't done a runner.'

Mark's phone beeped. He had a message from Lucy and Emma, saying they'd been caught in traffic, but they'd be there in five minutes, followed by four exclamation marks and a smiley.

Mark's mother took his hand and she gave it a squeeze. 'Don't worry. She'll be here on time. I feel sure of it.'

Mark pulled up in the country lane outside the church, right behind Lucy and Emma's limousine. The Doctor, Amy and Rory jumped out of the car, instantly regretting it as they landed in deep puddles. Rory gallantly helped Rebecca onto the grass verge. 'Careful. It's seriously muddy out here.'

Mark couldn't take his eyes off Rebecca. She looked so *perfect*. How many times had he summoned up the memory of her on their wedding day? And now here she was, living and breathing, a memory made flesh. He'd even talked to her. Hearing her voice for the first time in fifteen years, seeing her so full of hope and excitement, Mark felt both an immeasurable joy and an immeasurable sadness. Every second he fought the urge to tell her who he really was and what would happen to her one night in April 2003. But that would have to wait.

He climbed out of the car to join them, taking care to avoid the puddles. How many times had he come to this church? Once to rehearse the wedding, once for the wedding itself, and then countless times to visit Rebecca's grave. From the roadside he could see the empty patch of grass where it would one day lie, in the shade of an old, gnarled yew tree.

Rebecca's father passed Rebecca her shoes and, leaning on the lychgate, she twisted her feet into them. 'All done. What time is it now?'

'Fifteen minutes past,' said her father, indicating the clock on the church tower. 'But don't worry, it's not as if they're going to start without you.'

'Fifteen minutes?' said Amy. 'But I thought…'

The Doctor licked a finger and held it to the air. 'History is shifting course,' he announced grimly as a blue light flashed across the gravestones. The same kind of light Mark had seen in Rome and the students' union. There was a tension in the air, like before a thunderstorm, and was it his imagination or was it getting dark?

'So you were telling the truth,' said the Doctor. 'She did arrive at the church on time.'

'What are you talking about?' said Rebecca. 'I'm only fifteen minutes late, it's not the end of the world.'

'I wouldn't be so sure of that.' The Doctor reached a decision. 'Desperate situations require desperate solutions. Wait here, all of you, I'll be back before you know it.' He clambered into the driving seat of Mark's car, revved the engine and accelerated into the road. Seconds later he disappeared from view.

'What does he think he's doing?' said Rory, flabbergasted. 'Thanks, Doctor, leaving us in the lurch outside the... church! Y'know, Amy, I think he's really flipped this time.'

'Look, you can stand here if you like, but I have a wedding to go to,' said Rebecca, taking her first determined steps toward the church. 'I think I've kept my future husband waiting long enough...'

'Wait!' said Mark. Rebecca paused. The leaves on the path swirled upwards as though caught in a gust of wind, and, with a grinding, whinnying sound, the Doctor's blue police box appeared on the path directly in front of her.

The door creaked open and the Doctor emerged. 'Well, what are you waiting for? Get in!'

'What's going on?' said Rebecca, staring at the Doctor and his blue box in disbelief. 'What is that thing? And what is it doing here?'

'Just a short hop,' beamed the Doctor, patting the police box like it was an old friend. 'Same place, twenty minutes ago. Oh, and don't worry, there's plenty of room for all of us.'

'I'm sorry,' said Rebecca. 'Are you saying that's some sort of *vehicle*?'

'I assure you there's nothing to be scared of. Do I look like the sort of person who would kidnap a bride, on her wedding day, in a police box?'

'Yes.'

'It's all right,' Amy assured her. 'You can trust the Doctor.'

'But I'm *late* for my own wedding—'

'Just take a look inside,' said Rory. 'I mean, if you're already late, what difference does one more minute make?'

The Doctor stepped out of the way to let Rebecca see into the police box.

'But... but that's impossible,' stammered Rebecca in awe. 'It's like there's a whole *house* in there...'

CHAPTER
TWELVE

Mark, Rebecca and her father stepped into the TARDIS control room, looking around in awe.

'*This* is your transport?' said Mark.

Rory sympathised with them. It wasn't the easiest thing in the world, to step from the normal world into a time machine housed in another dimension. The Doctor's choice of decor didn't make it any easier; the centre of the chamber being taken up with a cross between an avant-garde brass sculpture and a child's activity centre.

The child in this case being the Doctor. He darted around the console, entirely in his element. Rory had a theory that at least half the buttons on the console didn't actually do anything and the Doctor only pressed them because they made an interesting noise.

'You know,' said Rebecca to her father. 'I don't think these people actually *are* Mark's relatives.'

Rebecca's father nodded. 'I wouldn't be surprised if they weren't from Canada at all.'

A grinding sound filled the chamber, the central column of the console came to a rest and the Doctor bounded down the steps to throw open the main doors. 'Here we are!'

Rory followed the Doctor, Amy, Rebecca and her father outside. The TARDIS had landed on the village green opposite the church. They'd moved about a dozen metres.

The Doctor checked the clock tower. 'Five minutes to one.' He grinned at Rebecca. 'A little bit early, but now you'll be able to make it to the church, bang on schedule.'

'Sorry? You're saying we've gone *back in time*?' asked Rebecca.

'Only a little bit,' said the Doctor, leaning casually against the TARDIS. 'It'll hardly notice.'

'Er, Doctor,' said Rory. 'Are you sure this isn't cheating?'

'No.' The Doctor looked offended. He straightened his tie. 'It's the opposite of cheating. It's enforcing the rules. That's what I do. That's my *thing*.' He clapped, then returned his attention to Rebecca and her father. 'Well, no time like the present, in you both go.'

Rebecca was about to cross the road when suddenly a heavy goods lorry thundered down the lane, its horn blaring. Rebecca stepped back onto the village green but, as the lorry passed by, its wheels sluiced up the puddles, splashing muddy water all over her dress.

Everybody waited until the lorry had gone before speaking. 'Whoops,' said Amy sympathetically. 'I'm sure it'll dry-clean off.'

Rebecca looked down at her mud-spattered skirt. She breathed in as much as she could, and said, 'I'm *supposed* to be getting married! In *three minutes'* time!'

The Doctor took Mark to one side. 'I don't suppose, by any chance, when she turned up at the wedding she was like this, was she?'

Mark shook his head.

'Sort of thing you'd remember?'

Mark nodded.

'Right!' declared the Doctor. 'All of you, wait here, don't move an inch.' He ruffled his hair, then darted back into the TARDIS, slamming the door behind him. The lamp on the top of the police box flashed, and with a whirl of wind, it disappeared from view. Only to reappear a second later. The door swung open to reveal the Doctor holding up a brand-new wedding dress, identical to the one Rebecca was wearing.

'Took me a while to find the shop where you'd bought the dress and get them to run up an exact copy, but I got there in the end. Thinking about it, I really should've asked you which shop it was before I left. Ooh, that Samantha does go on, doesn't she? Anyway, there you go.' The Doctor offered Rebecca the dress. 'Problem?'

'Yeah, slightly,' said Rebecca through gritted teeth. 'Firstly, if you think I'm changing into it standing here in the road you've got another think coming.'

'Oh, I'm sure you've got nothing to be embarrassed about,' smiled the Doctor benignly. 'No. That came out sounding wrong. What I meant to say was, you're welcome to change in the TARDIS.' He held open the doors of the police box.

'And secondly, I'm supposed to be getting married in *two minutes* and it took me *half an hour* to get laced up into this thing.'

'Half an *hour?*' The Doctor was aghast. 'Half an hour? Right! Back in you go.' He ushered Rebecca, still clasping her new wedding dress, back into the TARDIS. 'And you too, Amy, you know how women's clothes work.' A confused Amy followed them into the police box. Its lamp flashed and it vanished. And reappeared one moment later. The doors swung open to reveal Rebecca in her brand new, perfectly clean, wedding dress, Amy and the Doctor behind her.

The Doctor checked the road for traffic. 'OK. Safe to cross. Got everything?'

'I think so.' Rebecca turned to her father, who was regarding the proceedings with utter bafflement. 'My bouquet!' she remembered in horror. 'I left it in the limo!'

The Doctor took Mark to one side. 'And she had it at the wedding?'

'Yes,' said Mark. 'She threw it, Lucy caught it.'

'Right!' cried the Doctor in frustration, disappearing into the TARDIS. It vanished and reappeared. The Doctor emerged brandishing Rebecca's bunch of lilies. He thrust the bouquet into her hands. 'Anything *else*?'

Rebecca shook her head.

'Then let's get you *married*.' The Doctor led Rebecca, her father, Amy and Rory across the road. After they'd gone through the lychgate and were halfway up the path to the church, the Doctor stepped in front of Rebecca and her father, forcing them to stop. 'One last thing.'

'What?' said Rebecca.

The Doctor stared at Rebecca intently, touching her forehead with his fingers, and spoke in a steady, hypnotic tone. 'You will have no memory of this, of meeting me, Amy, Rory, or Harold. As far as you're concerned, you came here in your limousine, without incident.'

'We... we came here in our limousine,' Rebecca repeated hesitantly.

'Good, good,' said the Doctor. He then repeated the process with Rebecca's father.

'We came here in our limousine,' Rebecca's father confirmed.

'Excellent. Now, when I click my fingers, I want both of you to wake up, make your way into that church, and have the most wonderful day of your *lives*.' The Doctor clicked his fingers.

Rebecca twitched, blinking as though waking up. Then she saw her father beside her. He was looking around with a puzzled expression, then turned to her and said. 'Ready?'

Rebecca nodded, took her father's arm, and they headed up the path to the church.

Something wasn't quite right. As they reached the porch, Rebecca released her father's arm and glanced back at the graveyard, down the path to the road where four people stood by the gate. She couldn't see their faces, but one of them seemed to be dressed as an old-fashioned professor.

There was a squeal of tyres as a limousine pulled up outside. Lucy and Emma tumbled out in a flurry of skirts and swearing. They jiggled their shoes onto their feet and stumbled up the path towards her. 'Sorry,' said Lucy breathlessly. 'Traffic was literally insane.'

'You're here now, that's the main thing,' said Rebecca.

'I think it's time…' Rebecca's father gently reminded her, offering her his arm.

'Ready,' said Rebecca, taking one last look back at the graveyard. She'd been coming to this church ever since she was a little girl, and she'd never noticed how many statues of angels there were before.

Amy felt a warm glow as Rebecca, her father and her two peach-coloured bridesmaids disappeared into the church. Amy checked the clock. It was one o'clock exactly. They'd made it.

Mark began striding purposefully up the path to the church.

'Mark!' the Doctor shouted after him. 'Where do you think you're going?'

'I told you,' said Mark. 'To stand at the back and watch. It won't do any harm.'

'Won't do any harm?' snapped the Doctor. 'After *everything* I've told you, everything we've been through?'

'It won't do any harm, I know it.' Mark turned to continue up the path.

Two statues blocked his way. Two statues of angels, standing solemnly in front of the church, their hands cupped beneath their faces, their eyes as blank as stone.

'The Angels,' gasped Amy. 'They were here all the time!'

'Attracted by the wibbliness,' explained Rory, for his own benefit if no one else's.

'Mark!' shouted the Doctor. Mark was frozen to the spot in terror. Amy glanced away from him – to see four more statues in the graveyard, one crouched by a tomb, lowering its hands, one emerging from behind a grave, the other two rising from either side of a war memorial.

The Angels were too spread out for Amy to see them all at once. Trying her best not to blink, Amy turned to face the Angels by the church. They had moved closer to Mark, paused as they stalked towards him, hands raised above their heads, their fingers extended like claws.

Mark staggered backwards, tripping over his own feet. Amy dragged her eyes away from him to check on the other four Angels. They had advanced towards Mark as though to cut off any lines of escape, forcing him to retreat down the path towards the road.

'They're trying to *stop* him getting into the church,' said

Amy. 'Why are they doing that, if they want him to cause a paradox?'

'Yeah,' said Rory sarcastically. 'That was my major concern too.'

The Doctor dashed up to Mark and grabbed him by the arm. 'Quick!' he said, dragging Mark away from the Angels. 'Amy, Rory, keep looking at them, try not to blink!' he shouted as he guided Mark back to the lychgate. Mark's eyes were wide with fear. He'd been scared out of his wits.

And then Amy realised she wasn't looking at the Angels. And nor was Rory. She spun back to see that four of the Angels had continued down the path towards them, their bodies contorted with anger, their mouths caught in silent screams. But if she could only see four of them, that meant there were two she couldn't see...

'Into the TARDIS!' ordered the Doctor. 'Fast as you can.'

Amy didn't need telling twice. She sprinted through the lychgate, paused to check there was no traffic in the road, then splashed through the puddles to the TARDIS. Thankfully the Doctor had left the doors unlocked.

Rory, the Doctor and Mark hurried in after her. The Doctor bolted the door shut and darted over to the console. In seconds, the arduous groaning of the TARDIS take-off filled the air.

'They were *waiting* for us,' said Amy, her voice hoarse with fear. 'They were *expecting* us to be there...'

Gareth tapped his spoon on his glass. 'Groom's speech!'

Mark took one last sip of his water and stood up in front of everyone he knew.

The function room of the Grand Hotel fell silent. All of Mark's friends were there: Emma and Lucy, actually wearing dresses; Rajeev, flown over specially; Gareth, who had turned out to have unexpected depths; Siobhan from work, at a table with Mr Pollard and Mr Boyce, the two solicitors trying to outdo each other with the size of their buttonholes; Rebecca's parents, giving him approving, encouraging looks. And to his left, his mother, smiling for the first time in ages. And finally, to his right, Rebecca. His wife. Looking more elegant and glamorous than he'd ever dreamed possible.

Mark's hand trembled so much he could barely hold on to his speech. On top of that, his hand had started tingling again, like he was holding a battery. The feeling had been coming and going all day.

'Hello,' said Mark nervously. 'I've just got married. I'm a happily married man.'

There was a ripple of encouraging laughter.

'This'll be a short speech, you'll be glad to hear, because I'm sure we're all dying to find out why Gareth has set up a slide projector. But, as is traditional, I have to thank a few people.

'Firstly, I should thank my best man, Gareth, for his unwavering support and for his generous offer of a one-way ticket to New Zealand ten minutes before the wedding. I think he was joking. I *hope* he was joking. I'd also like to thank him for organising such a magnificent stag do, because unfortunately I didn't get a chance to thank him at the time due to an unexpected bout of food poisoning.

'I'd also like to thank the bridesmaids, Emma and Lucy, for making sure that Rebecca turned up, for which I will be eternally both surprised and grateful. And I'd like to thank Rebecca's parents, Olivia and Rodney, and my mother, Emily, for all their help. This day is a tribute to their kindness and generosity.

'Before I go any further, there's one more person I should mention. The person who sadly couldn't be here, who I wish was here more than anything else in the world, but who I know who is here in spirit, and that's my father, Patrick. I miss you, Dad.'

Mark paused. He could feel tears forming in his eyes. Because as he'd said those last words, it was like hearing the news of his father's death all over again, thinking of all the things he'd never get to tell him.

Looking across the room, at all the familiar faces lit up in the glow of the chandeliers, something drew Mark' gaze to the far end of the function room where a set of double doors opened onto a stairway. The doors should've been closed for his speech, but instead they were open. There was a man in the doorway, watching him. A man who looked just like his dad.

Mark glanced at his speech, then looked up. The man had gone and the doors at the far end of the function room were closed.

Mark cleared his throat. 'And finally I'd like to thank Rebecca, for everything, basically. For being my best friend, ever since I've known her. For always being there for me. For being a constant source of warmth, of inspiration, of laughter. And for doing me the very great honour of agreeing to be my wife.' He lifted his glass. 'To Rebecca.'

The night had turned cold, so they weren't likely to be disturbed in the hotel garden. The picnic tables were still wet from the rain, as Rory had discovered when he'd tried sitting on one. They were also unlikely to be seen, as the only light came from the windows of the TARDIS, parked unobtrusively in the corner, and the windows of the hotel as they flashed in time to the muffled strains of 'Dancin' In The Moonlight'.

Rory couldn't help searching the darkness for signs of a Weeping Angel. The Doctor had assured him that the moment of crisis had passed, and the Angels would now be in hiding, conserving their strength. That's why the Doctor had permitted Mark to watch his younger self delivering his wedding speech.

The Doctor gazed into the night, hands in his pockets, looking like he had all the troubles of the universe of his shoulders. 'Everything I've told you so far has been wrong.'

'What?' said Rory.

'The Angels. They haven't been following Mark in the hope of him creating a time paradox.'

'What?' said Amy. 'But they're attracted by the wibbliness, you said, like moths to a flame.'

'Yes,' said the Doctor. 'But not because they wanted him to change his past, but because they wanted to ensure that he *didn't*.'

'Eh?' said Rory. 'But I thought you said—'

'Think about it. When we met them at the students' union, they were trying to keep the two Marks *apart*. The same when we encountered them again in Rome. The same again today.'

'But why?' said Amy. 'Why do that?'

'Because they're working to a plan. Something big. Something much, much bigger than Mark just bumping into his younger self.'

'Like what?' said Mark.

The Doctor didn't reply. Instead, he looked at Mark with

all the sadness of his nine hundred years. 'You tell me, Mark Whitaker. You tell me.'

'I don't know. Honestly, I don't.'

'I let you see your wedding speech,' said the Doctor. 'But that has to be the last time. From now on, steer clear of your past.'

'Don't worry,' said Mark. 'After what happened today, if you think I'm going anywhere near my younger self again, you're very much mistaken.'

'Good,' said the Doctor, opening the TARDIS doors. 'Because if you *do* try anything, the Angels will be waiting for you.'

CHAPTER
THIRTEEN

5 June 2001

Mark went to the bookcase, slid aside the *Harry Potter* first editions and unlocked the small wall-safe behind them. He slid out the battered envelope with *MARK WHITAKER. 7/10/2011* written on the front. Crossing to his desk, he took out the letter from his future self, with its list of occasions where he must intervene in his own past. A list which he'd now completed.

Mark took a sip of freshly brewed coffee, tore a sheet of paper from a pad, placed it beside the letter from his future self, and began to copy it out, word for word, line by line.

This wasn't the first copy he'd made of the letter. He'd made a copy back in 1998, the copy he'd shown to the Doctor in Rome, which he'd shredded on his return. The one where he'd deliberately not included the final part of the message:

But make sure you follow these instructions, Mark. Because if you do, remember this:
YOU CAN SAVE HER.

Just as I did.
Yours sincerely,
Mark Whitaker, April 2003.

How many times had he read those words? Even reading them now for the hundredth time, Mark felt an ache in his heart. Rebecca need not die. It was written there in black and white, in his own handwriting.

He'd give anything just to speak to her again. Oh, he'd spoken to her at the wedding, but then he'd been pretending to be someone else. He wanted to talk to her as himself, to tell her how he felt. He longed to be with her, to hear her laugh, to hear what she thought of all the things she'd missed out on; all the films that had come out after her death, all the Christmases, Lucy and Emma's civil ceremony and their baby daughter. They had always said they'd go back to Rome for their tenth wedding anniversary. Now they could do that and so much more.

Slowly and meticulously, Mark copied out the letter. With each line, he'd pause to check that he'd reproduced the details exactly. Glancing back at the original letter, he found that the handwriting matched. There was no way of telling the two letters apart; because, of course, they were the same letter.

Mark was about to copy out *Because if you do* when he paused to glance out of the window. His reflection gazed back, a ghost suspended over a panorama of London. He could see the skyscrapers of the city, shimmering like the towers of a magical kingdom under the wine-red sunset. He could even make out the London Eye on the horizon, shining electric blue.

By now Mark was, more or less, a multi-millionaire.

This flat had been his only indulgence; a penthouse at the top of an exclusive development. All the furnishings were modern and sleek, and one entire side of the lounge consisted of a window looking out across Parliament Hill.

But spectacular views and luxury flats didn't take away the pain. Mark returned to his work, and the words YOU CAN SAVE HER.

Everything else in the letter had come true, so why did he doubt this part? Maybe it was because it was too good to be true. But also because the Doctor had warned him that he must not change history, no matter what. Saving Rebecca would certainly count as changing history. But if he was destined to save her, as the letter claimed, then surely if he *didn't* save her, that would count as changing history too.

Mark put down his pen. He would leave the rest of the letter blank until after he had saved Rebecca. Then, and only then, would he fill in the rest. That way he could be sure the message was true. And if it meant he was changing history then so be it.

Mark looked out across London. His younger self would be somewhere out there. Mark wondered what he was doing right now.

Mark's younger self was working late in his office. Everyone else had left hours ago, while Mark remained behind to prepare for a case that had unexpectedly been brought forward.

He rubbed his eyes and thought of home. Rebecca would be home by now. Mark was rarely home before ten o'clock these days. They only saw each other for half an hour before bed, when they were both too exhausted to do anything but watch television, and for half an hour in the morning when they were in too much of a hurry to talk.

But it would all be worth it. He'd been promoted to senior assistant, and in a few years he'd be in line for junior partner. Then they'd be able to afford a place of their own and could start thinking about children. But in the meantime he had to make himself invaluable, which meant volunteering to step in whenever there was a crisis. Like tonight.

Mark sifted through the case notes. The case was similar to one they'd handled the previous year, Jones versus Maxwell, and it would be quicker to see what precedents they'd used then than to start from scratch. Mark finished his instant coffee and headed into Mr Pollard's office, the neon light flickering as he switched it on.

Mark opened the filing cabinet, slid out the Jones folder and returned with it to his desk. Then he opened it, expecting to find a sheaf of notes. Instead there was a second, slimmer folder upon which was written: *IMPORTANT: NOT FOR THE ATTENTION OF MARK WHITAKER.*

Mark checked the name on the folder. It read *Harold Jones*. Someone had accidentally misfiled the wrong folder. But who was Harold Jones? And why would his folder contain something that he was forbidden to see? He'd never even heard the guy's name before. Which was odd, because Mark thought he knew the names of all of their regular clients, and going by the thickness of this folder, Harold Jones was a regular client.

Mark considered putting the folder back in the cabinet. That would be the right thing to do. If he was forbidden from reading this file, there had to be a very good reason for it. But for the life of him, Mark couldn't think what it might be.

There was only one way to find out. If there was something Pollard or Boyce didn't want him to see, Mark wanted to know what it was. He opened the folder. The first thing he saw was a copy of the CV he'd sent in when applying for the position of junior assistant. Then there was a page of notes in Pollard's handwriting under the heading *PROJECT MAGWITCH*.

Mark read the notes, at first intrigued, then with a growing sense of indignation. It turned out that this Harold Jones person was one of the firm's most lucrative clients, who had personally intervened to make sure Mark had been given the job of junior assistant back in 1999. In return, Jones would continue to use Pollard & Boyce to handle his business. It seemed that Jones's interests ranged from property development to TV production companies. Always as a sleeping partner, investing money through third parties in order to retain his anonymity, reaping the rewards by selling the shares at a profit or by receiving dividends and royalties.

Mark leafed through all the pages but could find no explanation as to why Harold Jones had intervened to get him the junior assistant job. Except for one note that Pollard had scrawled in the margin of one page: *Estranged relative?*

Whoever this Harold Jones was, Mark had to speak to him. There was an address included in the folder, a block of flats in Highgate. Mark returned the folder to the filing cabinet, grabbed his jacket and ran downstairs, not bothering to say goodbye to Ron on reception. After climbing into his car, he rang Rebecca on his mobile.

'Hiya husband,' she answered, her voice distant but cheerful.

'Hi. Look, just to say—'

'There was a crisis at work and you're going to be late?'

'Something like that, yeah. Sorry.'

'No, don't apologise. I'll just order in a curry and watch *Big Brother* on my own.'

'Can you leave me some? I had to work through lunch.'

'Was there anything else? Only I'm in the bath and I'm making the phone all foamy.'

'No, that's all. I don't know how long this will take, so don't wait up or anything.'

'I'll do my best. Bye then. Love you.'

'Love you. Bye.'

Mark tossed his phone onto the passenger seat, twisted the ignition and drove across London to Highgate, his mind racing with unanswered questions. After an hour's drive, he pulled up outside the apartment block. He was surprised by how impressive the building was; a smooth edifice of steel and glass, lit by ground-level spotlights. It looked more like a modern art gallery than somewhere where people might actually live.

Mark checked the address one last time. Flat 4-A. He headed over to the entrance and buzzed the intercom.

After about ten seconds, a voice answered 'Hello?'

'Hello. Harold Jones?'

'Yes. Who's this?'

'I'm from Pollard & Boyce. Urgent business.'

'Come up.'

The security door buzzed. Mark swung it opened and stepped into the brightly lit reception area. The lift took him to the fifth floor, where a short corridor led to the panelled door for apartment 4-A. As he approached it, the door swung open.

'Hello?'

The man standing in the doorway looked oddly familiar. For a moment, Mark thought he was looking at his own father; the man had the same watery eyes, the same thinning hairline. But this man wasn't his father, he was only in his mid-forties at most. It was the weirdest thing. It was like he was looking into a mirror and seeing his future self staring back.

'More wibbliness?' prompted Rory.

The Doctor nodded. 'A build-up of potential time energy, the biggest one yet.' He strained his eyes at the surrounding parkland. In the distance, the lights of London twinkled in the twilight. 'Mark must be interfering with his own past… irresponsible idiot!'

Amy emerged from the TARDIS, pulling on her jacket and handing Rory his. 'Any luck?'

Rory shook his head. They'd only left Mark outside the hotel about ten minutes earlier. Then the TARDIS had started wheezing like a steam engine giving birth, and the Doctor had gone into madman-in-charge-of-a-mixing-desk mode, all wild eyes and twitching fingers.

'Where are we, anyway?' said Rory. 'I mean, nice view.'

'Hampstead Heath.' The Doctor banged his palm on his wibble-detector. 'Brilliant. I can't get a fix, the signal's swamping the sensors…'

'So how are we going to find this paradox thing?' asked Amy.

Suddenly there was a flash. Rory shielded his eyes as blue lightning sizzled over a block of flats on the edge of the park. The lightning seemed to concentrate at the top of the building.

'I think we've found it,' said Rory. 'I'm no expert, but that looks like wibbliness to me…'

'You're Harold Jones?'

Mark nodded slowly. The man standing in his hallway was his younger self. It was like being confronted by an old photograph. A face he'd seen many times in the mirror, but so long ago.

'May I come in?' said Mark's younger self.

'You're from Pollard & Boyce?' said Mark.

'That's right, I work there. But I think you already know that.'

And then Mark realised the second thing that was wrong about his younger self visiting him. He had no memory of this taking place. When he'd worked at Pollard & Boyce, he'd never found out about Harold Jones. He'd certainly never gone to visit him.

'I think you'd better come in.' Mark conducted his younger self into the lounge. As he did, he felt a tingling in his right hand and noticed that his younger self rubbed his right hand at the same time. He'd felt it too. And there was an odd metallic smell in the air, the smell of dodgems and Scalextric cars. The smell of static electricity.

'Can I offer you anything? Coffee, tea?'

'No, I'm good,' said Mark's younger self. 'Can we skip the small talk?'

'If you like,' said Mark, sitting at his desk. 'So how can I help you?'

'You can *help* me by telling me who the hell you are,' said Mark's younger self aggressively. 'And why the hell you've chosen to interfere in my life.'

Amy caught up with the Doctor and Rory at the entrance of the apartment block. They were both staring up at the top floor of the building, where blue lightning flickered over the steel and glass.

'We may be too late.' The Doctor tasted the air. 'It *feels* like we're already too late.'

'What do you mean, *feels*?'

'Time running off the rails. Forging new paths, new possibilities.'

Rory looked around them warily. 'Yeah, but surely if things were going wrong, the Weeping Angels would be here too, right? Like moths to a gong and all that?'

'Oh *great*,' said Amy. 'Thanks for reminding me.'

'Oh, they'll be here,' said the Doctor. 'You can be sure of that. They've probably been lying low in the cemetery down the road, awaiting their cue.' He aimed his sonic screwdriver at the door and it swung open. 'Amy, Rory. Stay here.'

'What?' protested Amy. 'Oh no. We're going with you.'

'Hey,' said Rory, grabbing the corner of Amy's coat. 'If the Doctor says we should wait here, maybe we should do as the man says. I mean, he does know what he's talking about.'

'Amy, listen to your husband,' said the Doctor. He ran into the brightly lit reception area and bounded up the stairs.

'Yeah. Like *that's* ever gonna happen.' Amy sprinted into the reception area after the Doctor, her long-suffering husband trailing in her wake.

*

417

'You're a distant relative?'

'That's right,' said Harold Jones. 'On Aunt Margaret's side. I'm from, er, Canada.'

'Canada?' said Mark distrustfully. But the man's words had rung a bell. His mother had once mentioned a relative in Canada, a man who'd come to visit her once and who never replied to her letters or Christmas cards. And that *would* explain the resemblance…

'Did you visit my mum once, about six or seven years ago?' asked Mark.

'Yes. Yes, that's right. I happened to be in the country, for work, and I thought I'd look up some relatives.'

'Right,' said Mark. 'And that's why you got me the job at Pollard & Boyce?'

Harold nodded. 'Exactly. They handle a lot of my business, and so I thought I'd do you a favour.'

'You thought you'd do me a *favour*?'

'I recommended that they should take you on. But only for a trial period, on the understanding that if you weren't good enough they were free to let you go.'

Mark remained unconvinced. 'Really?'

'So while I may have helped you get your foot in the door, everything you've achieved since has been entirely down to you.'

'They've been keeping you updated with my progress then, have they?'

'Something like that, yes. They call it Project Magwitch.'

As Rory reached for the door of flat 4-A, the Doctor yelled out from behind him. 'Wait!'

'What?' said Rory, his fingertips inches away from the door. A moment later, blue light began to flit intermittently across its surface, and across the walls, floor and ceiling of the corridor. Rory felt the hairs on the back of his hand stand on end. 'What is it?'

'A Blinovitch limitation field.' The Doctor levelled his sonic screwdriver at the door, gradually moving closer until there was a spit and crackle. 'Nasty stuff. Not good to get too close.'

'But can we get inside?' said Amy impatiently.

'In a moment…' said the Doctor, fiddling with his screwdriver. 'Nearly there, nearly there…'

While Harold explained about 'Project Magwitch', Mark took the opportunity to look around the flat, with its huge windows and its view over London, its designer chairs, its widescreen plasma television. A blue light flashed outside, like that of an ambulance.

Harold's story made sense, but Mark still didn't believe it. 'And that's why you wouldn't let me handle any of your cases?'

'Exactly. I didn't want you to know. Look, I'm sorry. Maybe I should have told you, but—'

Harold kept talking but Mark had stopped listening. He'd noticed the two handwritten letters on Harold's desk, both of which included a list of places, times and dates going back to 1994. For 1995 he saw the details of an exam he'd taken at university. For 1997 he saw the address of a café in Coventry together with some lottery numbers. For 1998 it described the time he'd lost his wallet in Rome…

Mark suddenly remembered something Rebecca had once said to him a long time ago. About there being somebody at university who looked just like him.

'What are you doing?' cried Harold Jones as he realised,

too late, that Mark was looking at the contents of his desk. He lunged forward in a desperate attempt to conceal the letters. 'You mustn't look at them, they're, they're *confidential*—'

Mark reached for one of the letters and, as he did, the fingers of his right hand came into contact with Harold's right hand. Mark heard a loud crackling sound, like a circuit being shorted, and an agonising bolt of pain shot up his arm. For a moment he had a sensation of cramp-like numbness, and could smell something burning, and then everything went black.

Chapter
Fourteen

The Doctor forced open the door to the flat and rushed in, Rory and Amy at his heels. The entrance hallway flickered with blue light, and smoke drifted in the air. It was like stepping into a nightclub. 'Hello?' the Doctor called out. 'Anyone home?'

They made their way through the smoke into a large room with a kitchen at one end and an office at the other. All the electrical appliances in the kitchen were going haywire, switching themselves on and off, with smoke pouring from their sockets. Blue lightning crackled across the floor, the ceiling, the walls and the large, wide window that took up one side of the room.

Rory's eyes started to stream from the smoke. 'What's going on?' he coughed. 'This place is going bonkers…'

'Time-energy discharge,' answered the Doctor, advancing into the room like a prowling tiger. 'Overloads the electrics.'

The light fittings fizzled, sending out cascades of smouldering sparks. 'And what could have caused that?' said Rory.

tap-tap-tap

'I think I know.' Amy pointed towards the office, where two men lay slumped unconscious, one on the floor, the other across the desk. They both had their right arms outstretched and appeared to be giving off steam.

'Mark Whitaker, A and B.' The Doctor approached the bodies. 'Must've made physical contact, shorted out the differential.' He crouched beside the body of young Mark and took his pulse, before repeating the process with old Mark. 'They're lucky to be alive. It seems young Mark decided to pay his older self a visit.'

'So it wasn't old Mark interfering with his own past,' said Amy. 'It was young Mark interfering with his own *future*…'

tap-tap-tap

'But this shouldn't have happened?' said Rory. 'I mean, whichever way round it is, bumping into yourself's gotta be bad news, right?'

'It's not an ideal situation, no,' said the Doctor. 'We have to get them out of here. Rory, you take one Mark, I'll take the other.'

'Right,' said Rory, heaving young Mark into an upright position. While he did this, the Doctor managed to get old Mark standing and half-lifted, half-dragged him towards the doorway.

tap-tap-tap

Rory's lungs felt like they were on fire. As he struggled across the room with young Mark, all the light fittings burst into flames.

'I don't get it,' shouted Amy over the chaos. 'Why isn't the sprinkler system switching on?'

'Something's preventing it,' said the Doctor. 'Look.'

Rory followed the Doctor's gaze to the window on the far side of the room. Six stone figures stood on the other side of the glass, their hands pressed against its surface, staring inside with serene, blank faces. The Weeping Angels. All bathed in the flickering glow of the lightning.

'What are they doing?' shouted Rory to the Doctor.

'What do you think?' the Doctor yelled back. 'Feeding!'

But that was impossible, thought Rory. They were four storeys up. There was nothing for the Angels to be standing on.

tap-tap-tap

Rory couldn't keep his eyes on all of the Angels at once. Worse, with all the smoke swirling about, he could barely keep his eyes open. But that sound the Angels were making, they were tapping on the glass with their fingers…

There was a loud creaking, cracking sound. Rory caught a glimpse of the window covered in a spider's web of fracture lines emanating from the hand of one of the Angels. Then he had to blink, and an instant later there was an ear-splitting crash as the entire window shattered into a hundred pieces. The night wind roared in, fanning the flames higher and blowing the smoke towards Rory, Amy and the Doctor.

And Rory could see the Weeping Angels, never visibly moving but in the process of clambering into the room, one by one, their mouths wide as though screaming in triumph.

'Come on,' yelled the Doctor into Rory's ear. 'We have to go!'

Rory gripped young Mark by the waistband and tugged him into the hallway, through billowing smoke and surging, snapping flames. It was like they were escaping from hell itself.

*

Mark's older self came to with a retching cough. His eyes and throat stung and there was a smoky, acrid taste on his tongue. But he could smell fresh air and hear the rustle of leaves in the breeze. He was lying on the ground, he realised. Rory knelt beside him, taking his pulse. Behind Rory he could make out the Doctor and Amy, looking down at someone else laid out on the pavement, someone he couldn't see.

Then it all came back to him. The visit from his younger self. He could picture him framed in the doorway. Mark gasped deeply and suddenly at the memory.

'It's all right,' said Rory soothingly. 'You're safe, mate. Me and the Doctor rescued you.'

'You *rescued* me?'

Rory indicated the top of the apartment block. The top floor was a blaze of flickering orange flame, oily black smoke scudding up into the night sky.

'What… what happened?' said Mark, pulling himself to his feet.

'Hey, take it easy,' said Rory. 'You, um, seem to have bumped into yourself.'

Mark staggered over to the Doctor and Amy. They were tending to his younger self, who had been put in the recovery position, his suit charred, his skin smudged with soot. For one horrible moment, Mark thought that his younger self might be dead, until he groaned and breathed in a deep, sleepy breath.

Mark stared at him, then up at his burning apartment, unable to take it all in. There was something else, something he'd forgotten. 'What did you just say?' he shouted at Rory. 'I *bumped into myself*?'

'The Doctor thinks you may have, er, made physical

contact, or something. Which released a load of time energy.'

Physical contact? He could remember sitting at his desk, his younger self in front of him, and he could remember realising that his younger self hadn't been listening to him because—

'The letter!' breathed Mark. 'The letter I have to send to myself…'

'What?' said Rory.

'Where is it? Did you bring it here?'

'No. Should we have done?'

'Oh no,' said Mark. 'Oh no….' He looked at Rory, whose mouth hung open with incomprehension, then Mark turned and ran back to the entrance of the flats.

'Hey, where are you going? You'll get yourself killed!' Rory shouted after him. 'Doctor, the old one's doing a runner!'

Mark shoved open the security doors and raced up the stairwell, his chest straining with the effort. He passed some of the other residents of the block as they made their way downstairs. They called out to him, warning him not to go up there, but he ignored them.

He reached the fourth floor and slammed open the door to the corridor. A wall of searing heat hit him in the face, like he had just entered a furnace. He felt his skin prickle with sweat. The corridor ahead was clear, except for the thick black smoke that hung overhead like an indoor thundercloud.

Keeping his head low, Mark lurched down the corridor towards the door to his flat. His lungs felt like they were burning and he could hear his own ragged, desperate gasps for breath.

He made it through the door into his hallway. It was almost unrecognisable, lit a deep red by the pulsing glow of the fire. He could barely keep his eyes open. But he had to find the letter.

Mark entered his lounge to be confronted by a vision from a nightmare. The kitchen was a roaring mass of flames, a plume of fire stretched from his television up to the ceiling, and his sofa smouldered with foul-smelling smoke.

There were six figures in the room, standing perfectly still amidst the conflagration, each one holding its head in its hands, its wings folded back.

As Mark was forced to blink to clear his eyes of the smoke, the statues began to *move*. They slowly lowered their hands and turned to face towards Mark. There was no expression in their eyes. They seemed oblivious to the flames licking over their stonework.

Then, one by one, they opened their mouths, exposing their long, sharp fangs.

Mark stumbled blindly to his desk, feeling his way across the room until it banged into his midriff and the smoke cleared sufficiently for him to see the papers on his desk. As he watched, both the letters caught fire and shrivelled to black. The flames consumed both letters utterly, sending charred fragments fluttering up into the air.

Mark felt a hand on his shoulder. He turned.

'We have to go,' said the Doctor adamantly. '*Now.*'

Mark could see the Weeping Angels behind the Doctor, reaching out towards him. The sight caused Mark to freeze in terror. He couldn't speak or move.

The Doctor took him by the wrist and guided him back through the lounge, past the Angels and out into the hallway. Mark could hardly breathe and could barely see, but the Doctor kept leading him through the smoke and darkness, helping him down the stairwell and out into the clean night air.

Amy squealed with relief as the Doctor tumbled from the burning building, heaving old Mark with him. Old Mark's clothes and hair were dirty and charred, but he seemed otherwise unharmed. He sat on the pavement a few metres away from where his younger self was sleeping.

The residents of the apartment block had gathered in the car park, marvelling at the blaze as they awaited the arrival of the fire services. The fire would be visible all across London.

The Doctor squatted beside old Mark. 'What were you trying to do?'

'The letter, Doctor.' Mark took in another lungful of air. 'The letter I received from my future self, the one I had to send? It was in there. Both copies were in there!'

'Oh my God…' said Amy, her mouth falling open.

'*I saw them burn,*' said Mark wretchedly. 'So that's it. History's been changed.'

'What do you mean?' asked Rory.

'How can I have sent myself the letter, *when I don't have it any more!*' yelled Mark.

'Can't you just make another copy?'

'I can't remember every single word of the letter, can I? And if I got a single word wrong…'

'Oh. Right. Yeah.'

'Didn't you make any photocopies, or anything like that?' said Amy.

'No,' Mark replied, levelling his gaze accusingly at the

Doctor. 'Because you told me *not* to, remember?'

The Doctor frowned. 'So, so now you can no longer send the letter to yourself, and the entire course of history has changed, with disastrous *ramifications* for the entire planet.'

He paused to straighten up, lick a finger and hold it in the air. 'Unless…' He reached for his wibble-detector, which was still slung around his neck, and began to urgently twiddle with its dials. 'Oh no. Oh no no no no no…'

'Unless?'

The Doctor didn't answer. He was too preoccupied taking a reading with the detector. Then he looked up at Amy with a fearful look in his eyes. 'Unless the course of history *hasn't* been changed.'

'What?'

'Which can only mean one thing,' said the Doctor gravely. '*Mark wasn't the one who wrote that letter!*'

'What? But of course he did,' said Amy. 'You said—'

'Of course,' said the Doctor. 'It was all part of their plan.'

'Whose plan?'

'The Weeping Angels.'

'Sorry, Doctor, you're saying the *Weeping Angels* wrote that letter?' said Rory. 'The one that Mark received in the year 2011?'

The Doctor nodded. 'A list of instructions that Mark would think came from his future self, in order to make sure he obeyed them to the letter. In order to make sure that I'd *tell him* to obey them to the letter.'

'But hang on, you're forgetting something. Mark said the letter was written in his own handwriting!'

The Doctor shook his head and turned to Mark. 'You never showed me the original letter, did you?'

'No,' said Mark.

'I wish you had,' said the Doctor. 'Because I would've noticed that it was written on *psychic paper*. Write a letter on psychic paper and the handwriting will look like that of whoever reads it.'

Mark pulled himself to his feet. 'But the name on the envelope was in my handwriting too.'

'Psychic envelope,' said the Doctor. 'Same material.'

'And the Weeping Angels got hold of all this *how?*' asked Rory. 'Did they just pop down the nearest psychic newsagents?'

'The Angels are creatures of perception. To them it would be child's play.' The Doctor looked at Mark mournfully, as though he was a condemned man. 'The copy of the letter you showed me. It wasn't the whole letter, was it?'

Mark twitched. 'What do you mean?'

'There was something else. Something else the Weeping Angels wanted you to do.'

'No.'

'What was the other part of the letter, Mark?' The Doctor exploded in anger. *'Tell me!'*

'There wasn't any other part of the letter, you saw the whole thing.'

'I don't think so. Because listen to me. Whatever was written in that letter, it's not true. The Angels wrote it, because they want you to *change history*. It is something that can *never happen*. Something *you must never do.*'

'No,' protested Mark, doubling up in pain as though crushed. His chest was heaving and he kept swallowing, gasping, grimacing, as though trying to speak but unable to find the words. 'No, you're wrong,' he hissed at the Doctor. 'It can happen. I'm going to *make it* happen.'

'Mark, you can't, no matter how much—'

Mark straightened up and regarded the Doctor with cold, angry eyes; eyes filled with years of loneliness and grief. But instead of speaking, he turned away and strode towards the car park.

'Mark. Where are you going? *Stop*—'

Mark raised his key fob, aimed it at his SUV, and unlocked it with a beep. He climbed into the driving seat. The Doctor attempted to grab the car door, but he was too late; the car's engine growled into life, its headlights flashed on with blinding brightness, and it swung out into the road. Amy, Rory and the Doctor could only stand by uselessly as it accelerated into the night.

As the car disappeared from view, the wail of sirens grew louder until two fire engines and an ambulance appeared at the end of the road, illuminating everything with their flashing lights. Firemen clambered out, shouting instructions and craning their necks to assess the blaze.

Distracted by the firemen, it took a few moments for Amy to realise the Doctor wasn't with her. He and Rory had returned their attention to Mark's younger self, who was still curled up on the pavement. He regained consciousness with a wheeze and splutter, his bloodshot eyes darting around in confusion. 'Who are you? What happened?'

'You came to see a man called Harold Jones,' said the Doctor calmly. 'Why?'

'Harold Jones?' Mark frowned as he struggled to remember. 'I was working late in the office, and came across this folder… he was the reason I got this job. And he had these letters on his desk, with lists of stuff from my life!'

'It's all right,' said the Doctor gently as he placed his

fingers on Mark's forehead. Mark's eyelids drooped and his head lolled forward as he fell into a trance. 'You'll be fine. Listen to me. You will have no memory of the events of this evening.'

'No memory,' repeated Mark.

'The last thing you'll remember is working late in the office. You won't remember me, my friends or Harold Jones. When you awake, you will never have heard of him. Understand?'

Mark nodded.

'There was a small fire in your office, someone dropped a lit match into a bin, you threw your jacket over it, that's how it got burnt.'

Mark nodded.

'And when you wake up, I want you to phone your wife and tell her you'll be coming home, then go back to your car and drive straight there. You've got all that?'

Mark nodded.

'Good.' The Doctor clicked his fingers.

Mark's head lifted. For a moment he looked around, not sure where he was, then he stood up. 'Sorry, um, excuse me…' he muttered, before speed-dialling a number on his mobile phone. 'Hiya… Yeah. It's me. Just calling to let you know I'm on my way home… Love you too.' Then, without registering the Doctor, Amy or Rory, he strolled over to one of the cars parked outside the building, got into it, and drove away.

The Doctor, Amy and Rory stepped aside as the firemen located the nearest hydrant and connected their hoses.

'So that's that?' asked Amy, rubbing the soot off her hands.

'I think so,' said the Doctor. 'Mark goes home to his wife,

having forgotten all about tonight, and all about us…'

Rory's mouth fell open as a sudden, terrible realisation dawned on him. 'Wait a minute,' he said. 'Did you just say he's going home to his *wife*?'

'Yes—'

'But when I spoke to Mrs Levenson, she never mentioned anything about Mark being married!'

'No,' said Amy. 'And when I asked him a couple of days ago, he said he had no wife or children…'

'But we know he has a wife *now*, so if he doesn't have one in the future,' said Rory. 'Then that means either they get divorced, or…'

The Doctor suddenly looked incredibly old and gaunt. 'So that's it. That's what the Weeping Angels have been working towards.'

'You mean, something happened to Rebecca?' said Amy. 'Or rather, something's *going to* happen to Rebecca. Oh my God. She's going to die…'

'And Mark's going to try to stop it,' muttered the Doctor, staring into the depths of the night. 'He's going to try to save her.'

'But if he saved her,' said Rory, piecing it together. '… then he'd be changing history.'

'Not only that, but—' Before the Doctor could finish he was interrupted by a voice calling to them from down the street.

'Doctor! Amy!' A familiar figure ran out of the darkness towards them. As he got closer and slowed down, he moved into the glow of a street lamp and Amy could see his face.

It was Rory.

But Rory was standing right next to her, gawping in

disbelief at the new arrival. Amy turned from him to the other Rory, the new Rory. He approached with an exhausted look on his face.

'Thank God,' he sighed in relief, rubbing his side and wincing. 'For a minute there, I thought I'd missed you.'

'*Rory?*' said the Doctor, regarding him suspiciously. 'What are you doing here?'

The new Rory give Amy a reassuring smile, before he noticed his former self and his mouth fell open 'I'm, er, from the future, yeah?' the new Rory began. 'I mean, I was with you in the future, but then I was touched by an Angel…'

CHAPTER
FIFTEEN

21 April 2002

It had been their first major argument.

It all started when Mark suggested that Rebecca shouldn't bother to buy another car after her previous one had been written off. His point was that having a car in London was a waste of money, as she hardly ever used it except to go to her parents', and she'd said herself that driving in London was insanely stressful and dangerous.

Rebecca's response had been to accuse Mark of calling her a bad driver. Which hadn't been his point at all. It wasn't Rebecca's driving that worried him. It was everybody else's.

Rebecca had been driving to Peckham for the weekly shop when, as she turned left at a crossroads, the car on her right jumped the lights and crashed into her. She'd been lucky to escape with whiplash and a dislocated shoulder.

The argument happened the following night. They were both overtired, neither of them having slept more than a few hours since the accident. Mark still had the stress of the day coursing through his system, and Rebecca kept being woken up as her painkillers wore off. Then they had a day of dealing with the police, and the insurance. On top of that, they had to cancel their holiday in Paris which had been due to begin the following day.

That was what the final part of the argument had been about. Rebecca accused Mark of being glad that their holiday had been cancelled because it meant he could go back to work. Mark hotly denied this, but the problem was, Rebecca knew him too well. The thought of returning to work had occurred to him.

And that's why he spent the night on the sofa in the living room.

Rebecca woke as a jab of pain in her neck reminded her of her injury. Slowly and awkwardly, she eased herself into a sitting position and reached for the painkillers and water on the bedside table. She had to twist her waist to see what she was doing as she couldn't turn her head.

The alarm clock read 11:30. The other side of the bed was empty. For a moment Rebecca thought nothing of it; she often woke after Mark had gone to work, until she remembered this was the first time she and Mark had spent the night apart since their wedding.

Rebecca washed and put on a fresh T-shirt, then headed downstairs, gripping the banister with her one good hand. She'd have a cup of tea and maybe watch the news. Today she should've been exploring the art galleries and museums of Paris with Mark; instead she'd be spending it alone in a cold flat.

Rebecca stopped at the foot of the stairs. She could hear something sizzling in the kitchen, and could smell the smoky aroma of pancakes. She wandered in to discover

Mark at the oven with a frying pan in his hand, a string of garlic around his neck, a beret on his head, humming 'She' by Charles Aznavour.

'What are you doing?' said Rebecca.

'Making crêpes. This is my sixth attempt, I think I've almost got it.'

'I mean with the,' she indicated the garlic, 'and the,' she indicated the beret.

'Oh. Idea I had. For the next two weeks, I've designated this flat as French territory.'

'What?'

'If you can't go to Paris... then let Paris come to you.' Mark slid the pancakes out of the frying pan and turned towards her.

'Please take that thing off, you look like Frank Spencer.'

'I thought it made me look like Che Guevara,' protested Mark. 'I got it while I was out shopping. Couldn't get snails or frog legs, but we have croissants, *pain au chocolat*, and later you have a choice of me attempting either *coq au vin* or ratatouille.'

Rebecca noticed the five bulging supermarket shopping bags on the side.

'I also thought,' continued Mark, 'that if we're going to be stuck in the flat together for two weeks, we might need some entertainment, so I got a few DVDs and videos.' Mark indicated one of the bags.

Rebecca rummaged through it. '*Amélie. Cyrano de Bergerac. Betty Blue. Mon Oncle. Asterix & Obelix Take On Caesar.* And the first two series of *'Allo 'Allo...*'

'Can't get more French than that.'

'Very true.' Rebecca sniffed the crêpes. 'So we're spending the next two weeks stuck in the flat together, are we?'

'I mean, I could always go into work, if you'd prefer, but I thought, two weeks with my gorgeous wife Rebecca, versus sitting in a solicitor's office in Croydon. No competition really.'

'Not when you put it like that. Is this your way of saying sorry?'

Mark handed her a pancake on a plate. 'Overdoing it, do you think?'

'A bit, yes.' Rebecca broke off some of the pancake and ate it. 'But I strongly approve.' She kissed him gently on the back of the neck. '*Merci beaucoup.*'

'You're lucky. I very nearly bought an accordion.'

'You have no idea how grateful I am that you didn't.'

'And you're sure you're OK with having me hanging around, waiting on you, hand and foot?'

'I could get used to it,' said Rebecca. 'I should get into car crashes more often. No, I think if I have to be stuck in the flat for two weeks, there isn't anyone in the world I'd rather be stuck with.'

'So you're not annoyed, about not going to Paris?'

'Not any more. I mean, it's not as if Paris is going anywhere. There's always next year.'

'Is this strictly necessary?' asked Rory as the Doctor ran the sonic screwdriver over him like a customs official with a metal detector. Instead of giving an answer, the Doctor darted across the control room and repeated the process with the other Rory, the Rory from the future.

It was a weird feeling to be in the same room as your future self. That person over there, with the surprisingly large nose and gormless face, would be him at some point. Staring back at his past self, who as far as Rory was concerned, was his current self. Which was confusing if you thought about it, so Rory decided to stop thinking about it.

'Completely necessary,' said the Doctor, closing his sonic screwdriver with a flourish. 'It's now safe for you both to be in the same room together.'

'Eh?'

The Doctor went into explanation mode. 'Blinovitch Limitation Effect. Two identical versions of the same person, at different points in their timeline, should not co-exist within the same space and time. All sorts of nasty potential for paradoxes. And if they should happen to make physical contact – bang!'

'Like with the two Marks?' said Amy.

'Like, as you say, with the two Marks,' said the Doctor. 'But I've now neutralised the effect. Ask me how.'

'How?' said the future Rory.

'You couldn't possibly begin to understand. But thanks for asking.'

Rory tried to get his head around it. 'So it's now safe for me to touch my future self?'

'Yes,' said the Doctor. 'Although I would strongly advise you not to.'

'Why?' said Rory.

'Yeah, why not?' said the future Rory.

'Because it would look *odd*. Best keep your hands to, um, yourself.'

Rory and his future self exchanged indignant frowns. 'Right. Yeah. Thanks a lot, Doctor.'

'So where are you from?' Amy asked the future Rory with a flirtatious smirk. Rory couldn't help feeling jealous. 'What happened to you exactly?'

'Um, well, I'm not sure how much I can say,' said the future Rory hesitantly. 'You know, spoilers and stuff. But we were all in this field, on the South Downs, on the night of the tenth of April 2003, and the Weeping Angels were there too, and well, I got zapped.'

'Zapped?' said Rory.

'Back to 2001. Which was a bit of a head-scratcher, to say the least.'

'And then you came and found us?' asked the Doctor.

'Not *quite*. First I had to hang around for a month waiting for you to turn up.'

'What?'

'I was sent back to the first of *May*. Four weeks I've been stuck in the past waiting for you!' Future Rory sighed indignantly. 'I seem to spend half my life waiting for people!'

'Still, four weeks,' said the Doctor. 'Give you a chance to catch up on old times and stuff.'

'You try being dumped in the past with no money, no job, and nowhere to live! I could hardly go back to Leadworth, could I?'

'I'm sure you coped admirably. No need to go into the grisly details.'

'Hang on,' said Rory. 'If this is going to happen to me, I'd quite like to hear the grisly details, thank you very much. Give me some idea what I'm in for.'

'That's precisely why you mustn't know,' said the Doctor. 'And why your future self mustn't tell you. You've heard too much as it is.' He returned to future Rory. 'Let me get this straight. It was the night of the tenth of April 2003, when you were touched by the Angel?'

'Yeah.'

440

The Doctor swung the small monitor screen to face Rory. It showed the front page of a local newspaper. 'Which was the night that Rebecca Whitaker died.'

Future Rory nodded and swallowed. 'Yeah.'

'Right. Now, I need you to answer this as precisely as you can. When you were the Rory over there,' the Doctor indicated Rory, 'and your future self turned up, what did we do next?'

'What did we do next?'

'Yes. It's vitally important you remember.'

'I do, it's just that I'm not sure I should tell you. You know, spoilers.'

The Doctor let out an exasperated sigh. 'OK. Let me put it like this. I think the next thing I should do is that I should take us to the time and place where Rebecca was killed. If I were to do that, would I be changing history?'

'No,' said future Rory. 'That's exactly what I remember you doing last time.'

'Good. Then that is what we shall do.' He turned to Rory. 'I hope you're paying attention to this, I'll be asking questions later.'

'Yeah, don't worry,' said Rory, tapping his forehead. 'Committing it all to memory.'

'Good.' The Doctor advanced on the console like a concert pianist about to give a recital, but before he could start laying in a course he paused. 'You know, it could potentially get a little confusing having two Rorys about the place…'

'I'm not confused,' said future Rory.

'No, me neither,' said Rory. 'I know which one I am.'

'Yeah, and so do I,' said his future self.

'Yes,' said the Doctor. 'But nevertheless it would be useful if *I* had some way of telling you apart.'

'What, like one of us growing a moustache?' said Rory.

'Yes, but there's hardly time for that, is there?' The Doctor bit his lip as he thought. 'Future Rory. Future Rory. "F" Rory. "F" Rory… Ha! I know! I have just the thing!' The Doctor jumped down into one of the storage areas by the interior doors, pulled out a chest, and rummaged inside it before extracting a red cylindrical hat with a tassel. 'Fez Rory!' the Doctor announced. He strode over to Rory and slid it on his head. 'Future Rory, Fez Rory!'

'Er, Doctor, I'm not the future one,' said Rory. He pointed towards his future self. 'He is.'

The Doctor snatched back the fez. 'You see, I *said* you'd start getting confused.' He bounded over to future Rory and placed it ceremonially onto his head. 'There. Now, you have to keep this on. The fate of the entire universe may depend on it.'

'Really?' said future Rory. 'The entire universe? Depends on me wearing a fez? That's how these things work, is it?'

'Now, if you'll give me a moment,' said the Doctor, returning to the controls. 'The sooner I get us to 2003, the sooner we can stop having two Rorys roaming about the place!'

CHAPTER
SIXTEEN

10 April 2003

At last, after nine years of waiting, the day had finally arrived. The day Rebecca died. Except this time everything would be different.

Mark drove through the narrow lane, squinting as the setting sun flashed through the hedges that towered over the road. In the distance he could see the black thunderclouds of the approaching storm. In an hour or so it would be pitch dark and bucketing with rain. But Mark would be ready. He'd left nothing to chance.

His mouth was dry with anticipation. He'd explored every option of how to prevent the accident. He'd considered simply stealing Rebecca's car, but what if a passing policeman caught him in the attempt? He'd spend the night in the cells while she continued to her death. No. He would have to keep it simple, intervening only at the last possible moment. Only then could he be sure he would prevent the accident without being part of the chain of events that led to it.

The details of the accident were indelibly burned into

his memory. At 10.26 p.m., Rebecca was involved in a head-on collision with a heavy goods vehicle one mile from the village of Chilbury. She had just taken a blind left turn. The lorry was travelling at over fifty miles an hour. Because of the high hedgerows there was no way either of them could have seen the other. Mark had visited the site of the accident in preparation and knew every detail of the journey.

So all he had to do was to stop the lorry before it reached the fatal corner. Mark knew that the lane continued towards Chilbury, with no junctions or intersections, but about a quarter of a mile further on there lay a long stretch of road, the width of a single lane, that led uphill into the village. This was where the lorry had built up speed. This was where Mark's car would be blocking the road. The driver of the lorry would see it in plenty of time and be forced to come to a halt. And Rebecca, coming the other way, would also see the car and slow down. Only then would Mark move his car out of the way.

And then he'd have Rebecca again. All the years without her, all those long, lonely years of grief and regret, would be wiped out in an instant. They would never have happened. And if it summoned the Weeping Angels, then that was a small price to pay for the life of the woman he loved.

Almost without noticing it, Mark came to the point in the road where the accident had taken place. Would take place. Would no longer have taken place. He changed down gear, steered his SUV around the corner, and accelerated up the long, straight road to Chilbury. Then, at a small, gravelly lay-by about halfway up the road, he pulled in and switched off the engine.

He'd checked the area the week before. Even in torrential

rain there was no chance of his car being stuck in mud. He'd checked the engine, there was no chance of it failing or running out of fuel. He'd checked the police report after the accident – read it so many times he knew it off by heart. In the ten minutes leading up to the accident, there had been no other traffic sighted on that stretch of road. At 10.16 p.m., he'd move his car into the lane, then he'd be able to watch from a nearby field as the lorry approached from a distance of half a mile. He'd thought of everything.

There was a rumble of thunder and rain spattered against the windscreen.

Rory followed the Doctor and Amy out of the TARDIS and immediately he flinched from the cold and hugged his coat for warmth. Thankfully his woollen chullo hat covered his ears, as the wind blasted icy rain into his cheeks. Beside him, Amy brushed her hair from across her face and pulled her hood over her head, while future Rory tried his best to look nonchalant whilst wearing an increasingly damp fez.

Only the Doctor seemed immune to the freezing weather. 'This is the place?'

Fez Rory nodded.

The Doctor handed them each a torch which they clicked on. The beams only extended a few metres into the gloom, the lights picking out an ever-shifting curtain of raindrops. Rory could make out uneven, mud-soaked turf beneath their feet. He'd have to be careful not to trip up.

'I'm getting wibbliness on an unprecedented scale,' said the Doctor as he took a reading from his wibble-detector. 'Hard to pinpoint the exact source, but this is it. This is the tipping-point, the moment where the future hangs in the balance.' There was a sudden boom of thunder and a flicker of bright blue lightning. 'The moment the Weeping Angels have been waiting for.'

'The dinner gong?' said Amy.

'With a big, juicy, space-time event on the menu. It's time for the *feast*.' The Doctor lowered his detector and clenched his jaw, his face filled with dread, then waved the beam of his torch downhill. 'This way, I think.'

As they followed the Doctor across the muddy field, Rory strained his eyes to see anything in the gloom. It was so dark he kept thinking he saw movement, but it was only his eyes playing tricks as they grew accustomed to the darkness. But then he saw it; a pale yellow light about a quarter of a mile away, at a point further down the hillside.

'There!' said Rory. The light came from inside a car parked halfway up a steep country lane.

'That must be him.' The Doctor turned to Fez Rory. 'Am I right?'

'Um, yeah. That's his car,' confirmed Fez Rory.

'Then there's no time to lose.' Using his torch to pick out the ground ahead, the Doctor strode towards the light with renewed urgency. 'But watch out. The Weeping Angels are here. And they will try to stop us.'

Ten minutes later, Rory's shoes were soaked through and his feet were numb. From here they could see that Mark's car had been abandoned in the middle of the road. Rory couldn't tell if the SUV's engine was running; all he could hear was the roar of the wind and the occasional crash of thunder.

'What's he doing?' said Amy. 'He's just left it there? Why?'

'His wife met her death on this stretch of road,' said the Doctor. 'A collision with an oncoming vehicle. Which can no longer *be* oncoming if there's a car in its way.'

'You got all that from just a parked car?' said Rory, stamping some feeling back into his feet.

'He's left the lights on, he wants it to be seen. It's a *warning*. Best way to stop a crash between two vehicles? Put something *large* and *very obvious* between them. It's what I'd do.'

'Er, Doctor,' said Fez Rory. He indicated a figure standing about twenty metres away, between them and the car. A man in a puffy winter coat, his face ruddy from the cold. He stared defiantly into the glare of their torches.

'Mark,' the Doctor shouted to him. 'Whatever it is you think you're doing, you have to stop!'

Mark shook his head. 'Whatever I *think* I'm doing?' he shouted. 'I'm going to save Rebecca. And there's nothing you can say or do that will stop me.'

The Doctor began to slowly venture toward him. 'After everything I've told you, haven't you learned anything? You have to move your car out of the way and let history take its course.'

'No.'

'You have to do it, Mark.' The Doctor wiped his hair, out of his eyes. His face and clothes were sopping wet, raindrops dripping off his nose and eyebrows. '*Listen* to me.'

'In about seven minutes' time a heavy goods lorry is going to come down that hill. If my car isn't there to stop it, that lorry will hit Rebecca's car. And I am not going to let that happen.'

'You don't have any choice!'

'But I do. Otherwise you wouldn't be here to try and talk me out of it,' said Mark, his face lit up by a flash of lightning. 'No. This time it's going to be different. This time she lives.' There was another boom of thunder.

'She *dies*, Mark. What has happened, has to happen. You can't change that.'

'Why not?' protested Mark. He began to back away from them, down towards the road.

'Because it's a *trap*,' shouted the Doctor, walking steadily towards Mark. 'Everything that's happened, it's all been engineered by the Weeping Angels to bring you to this point.'

For a moment it looked like Mark believed the Doctor, his face twitching as he fought back tears. 'They've given me the chance to save her,' he said, his chest heaving with rage.

'The Angels don't care if Rebecca lives or dies. They're just using her, and *you*, to give them what they want. A time paradox.'

'I don't believe you!'

'Then look around you, Mark!' shouted the Doctor. 'Look around you!'

The Doctor flashed his torch towards a marble-white figure stood in the pitch blackness five metres to Mark's left. The figure had its hands held out before it, palms upwards, the rain spattering and dribbling over its stone wings and Greek-style dress.

The Doctor swung his torch to Mark's right, lighting up a second Weeping Angel in the same submissive posture.

Rory, Amy and Fez Rory flashed their torches around them, illuminating the wet grass, the shimmering sheets of rain, and four more Angels emerging from the void of darkness, two to their left, two to their right. All with their hands palms out before them, as though in greeting.

'Oh hell,' muttered Rory.

'You took the words right out of my mouth,' said Fez Rory.

'You brought them here,' said the Doctor with an edge in his voice. He took another step towards Mark. 'Just as I warned you not to.'

Mark backed away, his eyes darting between the Angels. 'No. No…'

'Don't worry,' the Doctor assured him. 'They won't stop *you*. They can't get involved directly, you see, they need the paradox to be the result of someone else's interference. But as for us… well, ha, that's another story.'

As the Doctor spoke, Rory kept moving his torchlight between the Angels. They were all still standing in the same posture, but was it his imagination or were they moving nearer? No. It wasn't his imagination. The four Angels to their left and right had closed in, to cut off any line of escape. 'Um, Doctor, about that…'

The Doctor ignored Rory, keeping his attention fixed on Mark. 'You think it's bad now?' he said. 'You have no idea what the consequences will be.'

'I know what I'm doing,' protested Mark, taking a stumbling step away from the Doctor. 'I'm going to save Rebecca.'

Rory noticed that the Angels on either side of Mark had moved closer together. They were now only a couple of metres away from Mark, trying to get between him and the Doctor, to cut them off and prevent them from reaching the car.

'And you think that will make the world a better place?' said the Doctor.

'How could it be *worse*?' cried Mark. 'How could it?

Answer me that! I've spent seventeen years without her. I don't care about paradoxes, I don't care about Angels.' Mark blinked back the tears forming in his eyes. 'I just want her back.'

'You can't have her back. She has to die.'

'Why?' screamed Mark. 'Why does *she* have to be the one who has to die?'

While the Doctor concentrated on Mark, Rory directed his torch into the blackness that surrounded them. With two Angels behind them, two to the sides and two in front, they were effectively caught in the centre of a circle.

The Doctor gave Mark a sympathetic smile, ignoring the two Angels who flanked him on either side. 'Why do you think the Angels chose you, Mark?'

'I don't know.'

'*Exactly*. It could've been anyone, they just happened to pick on you. Because everyone has something they'd like to go back and change.'

'I just want to save one person,' sniffed Mark, wiping more tears from his eyes. 'Do you have any idea what it's been like, these last nine years? All the good people who have died, where I've stood by and done nothing. How do you think I felt on September the 11th, watching all those people die? But I did *nothing*. I could've saved my own father, but I did *nothing*. I followed the rules, Doctor. I did as I was told. I just want one life. Is that too much to ask?'

'Yes,' said the Doctor regretfully. 'I'm afraid it is. You can't change the past.'

'Can't he?' said Amy. She had tears streaming down her cheeks. 'You're always saying time can be rewritten. Why not now?'

'Because this isn't about one person's life,' explained the

Doctor. 'The Angels have arranged this deliberately so that any change in the timeline will have the greatest possible impact.'

'But there's got to be some way of saving her,' cried Amy. 'There has to be something we can do!'

'No. Rebecca's death is a complex space-time event. If Mark prevents it, he won't just change the future, he'll change the past as well.'

The poor guy, thought Rory. All he wants to do is to save his wife's life. Rory thought about what he would do if he was in Mark's shoes, and it was Amy who was about to die. Would he risk everything just for the slightest possibility of saving her? Of course he would. Like a shot. Because the thought of her death, the thought of having to go on living without her, was simply too terrible to imagine.

Rory wiped the tears from his eyes and swung his torch around him again, almost grateful for the distraction. While the two Angels on either side of Mark hadn't moved, the others had each taken three or four steps closer and had raised their arms to either side. Closing off any gaps between them.

'You're lying!' cried Mark. 'You can't know any of this for sure!'

'Mark, if you save her, what do you think will happen?' said the Doctor. 'You think you'll just get to carry on from where you left off?'

'No—'

'No. You'll wipe out the events of the next eight years. All that time will be unwritten. But that's not all you'll lose. You'll lose the *past* nine years too. All the time you had with Rebecca will cease to have existed. All gone. Not even a memory. Every moment you ever spent with her will be lost without trace!'

'Why?'

'Think. You've *travelled in time*. Your past, present and future are inextricably bound up together. Think of all the times you've intervened in your own past. Would you have even got together with Rebecca in the first place if it hadn't been for your future self? No. But if she never died, you'd never have travelled back and so you'd never have got together. That whole timeline will be erased.'

'I don't believe you,' stammered Mark. 'I don't believe you!'

'You'll lose her, Mark. And the Angels will feed, and they will grow stronger. And that will be the beginning of the end of the Earth.'

'What? How do you know that?'

'Because I've seen it *before*! Do you think when the Angels are done with you that'll be the end of it? No. They'll move on to someone else. Put them through everything you've been through until they create another paradox. Then there'll be someone else, and someone else, until there isn't a single person left on this planet whose life hasn't been used by the Angels as a source of nutrition.' The Doctor raised his eyebrows and spoke softly, pleadingly. 'And I won't be able to stop them. They're weak now but they won't remain weak for long. You're just the first. But you won't be the last.'

Mark's face crumpled in pain. 'I just want to save her.'

'I'm sorry,' said the Doctor, with the sadness of centuries. 'But you've got to let her go.'

Fez Rory coughed to get the Doctor's attention. While the Doctor had been trying to make Mark see sense, the four Weeping Angels had advanced even closer. They were now standing only four or five metres away, each with their arms outstretched, their faces eerily calm. 'Er, Doctor, hate to interrupt, but we have a Weeping Angel situation here.'

'It's like they're waiting for something,' said Amy from somewhere behind Rory. 'Why haven't they attacked?'

'They're running low on fuel,' said the Doctor. 'They won't do anything unless we try to escape or get to Mark's car. They'll want to conserve their energy until the paradox takes place.'

'And then?' said Rory nervously.

'Oh, then we're all dead,' said the Doctor nonchalantly. 'It's either us or Rebecca.' He turned back to Mark. The two Weeping Angels were now between him and the Doctor. Mark stood staring at them in horror, stumbling backwards. Then he turned and broke into a run, quickly disappearing into the total darkness.

'So what do you suggest we do now?' said Rory, waving his torch between the Angels. They were getting closer all the time. Soon they'd be within touching distance.

'Rory. You know how you've always wanted to be my secretary?'

'No.'

'Well now's your chance.' The Doctor rummaged in his pockets and retrieved a notepad and pencil. He rapidly scribbled a note on the pad, before handing it to Rory along with the wallet containing his psychic paper. 'Look after this for me. May come in handy.' He flipped a card out of his sleeve like a magician and gave it to Rory. 'Psychic credit card, don't go mad.'

'Sorry, why are you giving me your stuff?' said Rory, putting the pad, wallet and card in his jacket. 'And what do you mean, "come in handy"?'

'You're going to run a little errand for me.' The Doctor raised his eyebrows at Fez Rory as though checking something. Fez Rory nodded. The Doctor nodded back, then turned to Rory and gave him a reassuring smile which only served to make him more worried. 'I need you to pop back to the TARDIS. You think you can do that?'

Rory aimed his torch at the nearest Weeping Angel, the one cutting off their route back up the hill. It reached out towards him with both arms. If he was quick, he might be able to slip past it. 'I'll give it my best shot,' said Rory. 'But you still haven't—'

'Then go,' urged the Doctor. 'Now! *Go!*'

Rory took a deep breath and hurled himself towards the Weeping Angel. All the time concentrating on keeping his torch trained on its face and not blinking.

Without warning his right foot snagged on what felt like a length of rope and Rory tripped over, landing heavily on his front. The torch rolled out of his fingers. For a moment, Rory had the sensation of being extremely cold and damp, his hands and face drenched in slimy mud. He strained his eyes to look around him but could only see darkness. He reached out, desperately trying to find the torch. But instead he felt the touch of something made of stone.

And then Rory wasn't in 2003 any more.

CHAPTER
SEVENTEEN

'Rory!' screamed Amy. 'Rory! No!'

It had happened in an instant. There hadn't been a flash or a sound. Rory had simply disappeared into the blackness like a light being switched off. Amy aimed her torch towards where she'd heard him fall. The thin light picked out an empty patch of glistening grass and a Weeping Angel, reaching down towards the ground with an outstretched hand.

Amy's heart pounded. He'd gone. Her brave husband Rory had gone. He'd been touched by a Weeping Angel.

'It's all right,' said future Rory, removing his Fez. 'He's just been sent back to 2001. Didn't hurt a bit. Though you do get this sort of garlic-y taste in your mouth which takes ages to shift.'

'You mean, that was how you ended up back there…' Amy turned and thumped the Doctor on the arm. 'You *knew* that would happen!'

The Doctor nodded, then looked up in alarm. There was another flash of blue lightning and a clap of thunder. But instead of fading, the lightning lingered, sending bright trails of light zigzagging across the grass like bouncing snakes.

'Rory,' said the Doctor. 'Did you manage to complete my little errand?'

'Little errand?' said Rory. 'Hardly *little*. Insanely complicated, more like!'

'Sorry, what errand would that be?' said Amy.

'Just before Rory went back in time I jotted down a note,' said the Doctor, his eyes darting between the six Angels that surrounded them, as though daring them to move. 'Containing instructions on what to do when he arrived in 2001. Well?'

'Yeah, I did it,' Rory sighed. 'Took me four weeks to convince the farmer I wasn't having a laugh. If I got it right, the "on" switch should be on the ground somewhere around here.'

'What "on" switch?' said Amy as the Doctor and Rory swept their torch lights over the turf at their feet.

'Here it is! Yes! You beauty!' announced Rory. The beam of his torch illuminated a thick cable twisting through the grass. It was so well-concealed, Amy would never have spotted it if she hadn't been looking for it. With a start she realised that it was this cable that Rory – the other Rory, the one who had vanished – had tripped over only a few seconds ago.

'What's that doing there?' said Amy. 'Will somebody *please* tell me what's going on!'

Rory's beam ran along the cable to where it joined several other cables at a black box with a big red switch. All very heavy-duty, the sort of thing you'd expect to find backstage at a rock concert.

'Found it!' announced Rory joyfully, before he gave a frightened yelp as his torchlight illuminated the two motionless white figures that were standing on either side of the switch, their hands outstretched, leering at him mockingly. 'Oh. Whoops.'

The Weeping Angels were between them and the black box. Whatever that red switch did, there was no way they could reach it.

His heart thumping hard in his chest, Mark paused to catch his breath as he reached the gate, drawing in deep lungfuls of ice-cold air, lifting his head to let the rain cool his face.

His SUV remained in the road, its lights on full-beam. Mark glanced up and down the lane, but found no sign of any traffic. But in a couple of minutes, a heavy goods lorry would be accelerating down that lane towards him.

Mark wiped his eyes, wet with rain and aching from tears, and glanced back up into the field. Electric torches danced in the darkness. The Doctor, Amy, Rory and the other Rory in a Fez. Except there seemed to be only the three of them now. The Angels had formed a ring around them, as though performing a circle dance.

There was another rumble of thunder and flicker of electric blue light.

The Doctor's words echoed in his ears. 'It's either us or Rebecca.' And what had he done? He'd run away and left them to die. But that wasn't his fault, Mark told himself. He couldn't save them, not from the Weeping Angels. He couldn't.

That wasn't the only thing the Doctor had said that preyed on his mind. If he saved Rebecca, then according to the Doctor he would change not just the future, but the past. He would lose not just all those long, lonely years of grief, but also all the time he'd had with her.

Because if he'd never travelled in time, everything would have been different. That night at the students' union when they'd kissed on the rooftop wouldn't have happened. He probably wouldn't have gone to Rome with her, he wouldn't have been able to afford it if his future self hadn't given him that winning lottery ticket. And even if he had gone, he wouldn't have got his wallet back after it was stolen so they wouldn't have gone to the Capitoline Museum. And they wouldn't have got together at the museum had it not been for his future self, the Doctor, Amy and Rory locking them in.

Mark thought back to all the other times he'd had with Rebecca. The most precious pages in his book of memories. All the times he'd met her for coffee to discuss their relationship troubles. The day they moved into their first flat together. Their wedding day. And the time after Rebecca had been in that accident and they'd spent two weeks in their flat together, watching videos and DVDs.

The saddest part of all was that there weren't enough memories. He wanted more. He deserved more. He regretted to the core of his being all the nights he'd worked late when he could have been with Rebecca.

He would give anything, anything in the world just to have one more hour with her. To have just one more memory. It had been that single driving wish, that burning feeling of injustice, that had kept him going for the past seventeen years.

He had to have Rebecca back. If he didn't, what was the point? What had it all been for?

But if what the Doctor said was true, then all those memories would be taken from him. And people would die. Innocent people would die, and it would all be because of him. Rebecca wouldn't want that. She wouldn't want to be the reason why that happened.

Mark looked back up the hill, to where the Doctor and his friends were surrounded by the Weeping Angels.

'I'm sorry,' choked Mark, stifling a sob as he walked over to his car. 'I'm sorry, Rebecca.'

Rory backed away from the two Weeping Angels in front of him, flashing his torchlight from one to the other. He backed into the Doctor, busy trying to keep his own two Weeping Angels at bay. 'It's no good,' said Rory. 'I can't reach the "On" switch. I messed up, and now we're trapped and are probably going to die.'

'It's not over yet, I should be able to activate it with this,' said the Doctor, deftly raising his sonic screwdriver. Which failed to light up or make any sound. 'Oh. That would've been a lot more impressive had it actually worked. No, you were right with the first thing you said.'

There was another boom of thunder and crackle of lightning. It lit up the Angels' faces. They were snarling hungrily, their jagged teeth bared, their tongues lolling, their foreheads ridged in scowls of hatred, their eyes hideous staring blank orbs of stone.

Rory held them back using his torchlight. The light grew dimmer. Rory shook the torch and banged it with the palm of his hand, but it didn't get any brighter. 'Doctor. The torches—'

'The Angels are draining the energy,' said the Doctor. 'I know. Hence my sonic trouble.'

Rory flashed the feeble beam back towards the Angels. They were now less than a metre away, reaching towards him with their long, claw-like fingers. The torchlight was now so weak he had to strain his eyes just to make out the shape of the Angels in the darkness.

'Rory,' said Amy. 'I don't think I can keep them back much—' She gave a short scream.

Rory spun around to see Amy standing perfectly still, her eyes wide with terror, a Weeping Angel's arm coiling around her neck, almost but not quite making contact with her skin. The Weeping Angel's mouth hung open lasciviously, like a vampire about to sink its fangs into her jugular.

'Don't stop looking at it, Rory', begged Amy. 'Don't look away. And please, whatever you do, d-d-don't blink!'

Rory kept his eyes glued to the Weeping Angel, but as the light from his torch faded away, it slowly but surely disappeared into the darkness.

Suddenly the roar of a car engine filled the air and Amy and the Weeping Angel were caught in the lurching beams of an approaching pair of headlights. Rory didn't dare look away from Amy, he didn't dare blink, even as he heard the car draw nearer and come to a halt, even as he heard the sound of the car door slamming and someone running towards them.

'Mark,' shouted the Doctor. 'Press the big red switch! On the ground by your feet!'

K-chunk! K-chunk! K-chunk!

There was a brilliant, dazzling light. Temporarily blinded, Rory blinked.

When he looked again, when his eyes adjusted to the brightness, he found that the Weeping Angel hadn't moved. It still had its arm wrapped around Amy, but the fact that the electric lamps had come on meant that the Doctor's plan had worked.

The Weeping Angels were still in a circle around them, all frozen in position as they lunged forward, clutching at the air. But outside the circle of Angels, about six metres away, there was a second circle of six powerful halogen lamps mounted at ground level, all shining inwards. And beside each of the lamps was a video camera, on a tripod, pointing inwards, and beside each camera was a television monitor showing six pictures from six different angles of the Weeping Angels. They were standing in the middle of a ring of cameras.

Mark was crouching beside the big red 'On' switch.

'It's all right,' the Doctor reassured Amy. 'They're not going to move.' With some difficulty, he helped her squeeze out of the Weeping Angel's embrace.

'What did you do?' asked Amy once she was free, shielding her eyes against the glare of the lamps.

'Nothing,' said the Doctor with a generous smile. 'You have Rory to thank for this.'

'*Rory?*' said Amy incredulously.

'Yeah, well, all in a month's work,' said Rory. 'Though to be fair, it was the Doctor's idea.' He pulled the Doctor's notebook out of his jacket. Flipping open the cover, he showed Amy the contents; a page of almost illegible instructions from the Doctor on what to do in 2001, along with a diagram on how to set up the video cameras.

'*What* was?' said Amy, turning from Angel to Angel, making sure that they'd stopped moving.

The Doctor pocketed his torch. 'It's quite simple. The Weeping Angels are quantum-locked, meaning they can only move if they're not being observed.'

'I know that, you have mentioned it once or twice.'

'So what we've done,' said the Doctor. 'Is to arrange

things so that each Weeping Angel is not only being observed, but is also observing itself *and* all the other Weeping Angels.'

Amy peered at one of the monitors. 'You mean this is showing the pictures from all the cameras at once?'

'And there's nowhere you can stand where you're not looking towards one of the monitors,' said Rory. 'Every direction is covered.' It had taken him the best part of a month to set it all up; travelling down to locate the exact spot, then persuading a video equipment company to not only set up a specific arrangement of lights, cameras and monitors, but to do it on a specific date, two years in the future. And then he'd had to convince the farmer who owned the land to let them do this. Rory had only managed to get everything sorted the evening before he was due to meet the Doctor and Amy. If he'd learned one thing during his time in 2001, it was this; it's amazing what people will agree to if you're prepared to pay cash in advance.

When they'd first arrived in the TARDIS, he'd been terrified that the Doctor might lead them to the wrong part of the field. But he needn't have worried; of course they would all end up in the right spot, because that's what they'd done last time. And although Rory had caught the occasional glimpse of the cameras, lamps and monitors, because he knew where to look, they were all sufficiently well hidden by the grass not to be seen by the Doctor, Amy, his former self – or, more importantly, by the Angels.

'So you led the Angels into a trap?' said Amy. 'Using us as the bait!'

'Bait and switch! They should know better than to put me in a trap!' The Doctor walked over to Mark. 'You came back,' said the Doctor delicately.

Mark nodded, blinking back tears, his breathing shallow. 'I could hardly let you die, could I?'

'Had me worried for a moment there, though,' said the Doctor.

'Doctor! The Angels!' shouted Amy.

Rory turned to see the Weeping Angels begin to flicker and fade away, like the picture on a television screen during interference.

'They're too weak to maintain their corporeal forms,' explained the Doctor. 'And as they're quantum-locked, there's only one way left for them to go…'

In a few moments they were all transparent, their stonework fizzling like static, and then, in an instant, they all vanished.

'Go?' said Amy. 'Go where?'

The Doctor nodded to one of the monitors. On the screen Rory could see the Weeping Angel, staring out at him in grainy, flickering black-and-white, its hands pressed against the glass as though it was trying to break through. Rory looked in the next monitor along. The story was the same. Each screen showed an Angel, trapped behind the glass, an indistinct grey mass.

'*Caught in a closed circuit!* This is our chance. Do what I do!' The Doctor rushed over to one of the cameras, lifted it by the tripod, then positioned it so that it faced towards the monitor to which it was connected.

'What *are* you doing?' asked Rory.

The Doctor flicked a switch. 'I'm sending them into infinity.'

The Weeping Angel on the screen gained a line of identical, ghostly Angels behind it. This then dissolved into a swirling, looping pattern of fog which rapidly faded to blackness.

The Doctor, Amy and Rory repeated the process on the remaining Angels. It was only when they reached the sixth monitor and discovered that it was blank that Rory realised something was amiss. 'Doctor. One of our Weeping Angels is missing.'

'What?'

'There were six. One of them must've got away.'

The Doctor looked briefly alarmed, but then he peered up at the night sky. There hadn't been a rumble of thunder or flash of lightning since Mark had returned. The Doctor turned towards him. 'You moved your car,' said the Doctor. 'There's not going to be a paradox. History isn't going to be changed. That's what weakened the Angels…'

Mark nodded sadly and then turned back down the hill. The headlights of a heavy goods lorry flashed out of the darkness. It accelerated down the steep country lane, past where Mark's car had been parked, and onwards into the night.

And then, just for a moment, the lorry's red tail-lights illuminated the shape of a figure at the edge of the field. 'Doctor, the Weeping Angel!' said Rory 'Where's it going?'

'The scene of the accident,' said the Doctor bleakly. He began to stride down the hill towards where the Angel had been standing. 'Come on.'

They didn't see the crash. But they could see the orange warning lights that blinked on and off, lighting up the hedges that loomed over the lane.

The lorry had come to a rest halfway up the hedge, the cabin tilted onto its side, its radiator grille steaming, its warning lights flashing. The driver was slumped unconscious on his steering wheel.

'You leave the driver to us.' The Doctor patted Mark's back. 'Be with her.'

Mark looked around in a daze, unable to take it all in, and then he spotted Rebecca's car. The force of the collision had sent it into the next field, rolling over until it came to a rest upside down. Thick smoke poured out of the engine and he could see the tell-tale flicker of flames.

Standing about six metres from the car, caught in the sickly orange glow of the warning light, was the remaining Weeping Angel.

Looking out across the field, Rebecca wondered why everything had an odd orange hue, as though lit by a street lamp. Her seatbelt was so tight she could hardly breathe. She wanted to wipe the rain from her eyes, but her hands didn't respond.

Now that was weird. About six metres away, in the field, stood a statue, like might be found in a graveyard, or a Roman museum. It was a statue of a young woman with coiled hair, a flowing robe and two wings. An angel. The statue was hunched, burying its head in its hands.

The orange light blinked off, and Rebecca thought of childhood bonfires.

The orange light blinked on again. The statue of the angel was now staring towards her with blank, pupil-less eyes.

The light blinked off and on again, and each time the statue drew closer, closer, until it filled her view, looming over her, reaching out towards her with hands like talons.

Rebecca wished that Mark was here.

And he was. The statue had vanished and Mark had taken its place. He leaned into the car and gently brushed the rain from her face. He smiled at her tenderly. She could see tears streaming down his face.

Why did he look so old? His hair was thin and flecked with grey, his skin was weathered and his eyes were lined with crow's feet. They were the sad, tired eyes of a man who had suffered years of sleepless nights. But they were still the same eyes she'd fallen in love with, and they were still full of love for her.

Rebecca attempted to say his name, but no words came. She wanted to ask him what he was doing here. He should be working at the office in Croydon, not out here in the depths of Sussex in the wind and rain with her.

She felt him take her hand and squeeze it. His skin felt so warm against hers, like fire. Looking up at him, into his sad, tired eyes, she smiled. Because Mark was here. She knew everything would be all right.

And then Rebecca Whitaker felt no more worries, no more fears, no more pain. She slipped away into death with her head cradled in her husband's arms.

Amy, the Doctor and Rory watched in a respectful silence as Mark released Rebecca from her car and placed her body on the grass a short distance away.

Amy sniffed and wiped the tears from her eyes. 'He couldn't save her.'

'He never could,' said the Doctor. 'The Angels just made him believe that, to serve their own ends.'

'So time can't be rewritten?'

'Not without people getting hurt,' said the Doctor ruefully.

'What about the Weeping Angel?' asked Rory. 'Where did that go?'

'It escaped.' The Doctor indicated a metal box perched in the hedge by the side of the road a few metres from where the lorry had come to rest. The speed camera reflected the glow of the lorry's warning lights as they blinked on and off.

'But if it's in the speed cameras, it could go anywhere...' said Rory. 'We have to find it.'

'There's no need,' said the Doctor. 'That's the Weeping Angel we encountered when we first arrived, in 2011. The Angel trapped inside a television.'

'You mean, the one that sent Mark back to 2003?' said Amy.

The Doctor nodded. 'In a desperate attempt to break the time loop. But by trying to change history, it ends up creating it. A prisoner of its own past.'

'But why wait until 2011?'

'Recharging its batteries? And it couldn't send Mark back until he'd received the letter. The letter I imagine they dropped off at Mark's office a couple of days ago.'

Another minute passed in silence, then Mark returned. His eyes were raw from tears and his breathing was shallow and weak, as though each inhalation caused him pain.

In the distance Amy could see the headlights of a car through the trees. The driver that would be the first on the scene, the one who would call the emergency services.

'Come on,' said the Doctor. 'Time we were gone.'

Mark was about to leave the office at Pollard & Boyce when his mobile rang. He checked the clock. Who would be ringing him at five past eleven at night? He pulled his phone out of his pocket. The caller ID read *Rodney Coles*.

Mark pressed answer. 'Hello, yes?'

'Mark, it's, um, Rodney. Rebecca's father.' He sounded oddly frail and distant, pausing between his words.

'Rodney. What is it?'

'It…' There was a long silence. 'There's been an accident, Mark. Rebecca has been in an accident. She was driving home to see us when…' There was another long silence, leaving Mark listening to nothing but a faint hiss.

Mark swallowed and walked unsteadily over to his desk. He felt like he was standing at the top of a very high cliff, looking down over the edge. 'She's all right, though, isn't she? Tell me she's all right.'

'I'm sorry, Mark,' said Rodney. 'She's gone. She, um, when they found her, she'd already, they said, she'd already died.'

Rebecca was dead. Mark couldn't believe it. Even saying the words in his head, he couldn't believe it. He felt like he was suffocating. His lips were dry, his heart felt as heavy as a stone and there was a terrible twisting sensation in his stomach. He felt like everything around him was suddenly distant, unreal, like he was watching someone else in a movie. Or a bad dream from which he might wake up at any moment.

But he wasn't going to wake up. Mark talked to Rodney for a couple of minutes but his mind was elsewhere. The call ended and he sat in silence, looking at the photograph of Rebecca he kept on his desk. The photograph of her sitting on the balcony of their hotel room in Rome, in her summer dress, gazing out into the street, the morning sun shining in her hair, a contented, secretive smile on her lips. The photograph he'd taken the morning after they'd got together.

Mark picked up the photograph, his hands trembling.

Rebecca was dead. He'd lost her. He'd never hear her voice again. Mark wanted to scream. He wanted to fall on his knees and beg the heavens; please, take time back. Let me go back just one hour, to before Rebecca was killed so I can save her. Anything, I'll do anything, if you'll just let me go back, and for this not to be now, for this not to be real, for this not to be for ever.

Mark held the photograph to his face to try to stop himself crying, because he knew that once he'd started, he might never stop.

Epilogue

16 April 2003

Mark stood at the lychgate, the Doctor, Amy and Rory beside him, unnoticed by the mourners at the graveside. The grave had been dug on the edge of the graveyard, in the shade of an old, gnarled yew tree. The pallbearers lowered the coffin into the ground and the vicar spoke the prayer of committal, his solemn, lilting voice carrying through the warm spring air amidst the rustle of leaves and the birdsong.

It was the same vicar who'd conducted the wedding service two and a half years earlier. He was addressing the same people as at the wedding; many of the male mourners were even wearing the same suits. There was Gareth, Mr Pollard and Mr Boyce, and Rajeev, Lucy and Emma. And there were Rebecca's parents, Olivia and Rodney, both looking so tired, so stunned and lost. And there was his mother, dabbing at her eyes with a handkerchief.

And there was his younger self. Standing at his mother's side, staring into the grave, tears streaming down his cheeks. Mark could remember standing there as though it was yesterday. He could still feel the grief, like a huge

471

weight pressing down on his chest. But as he remembered it, the day of the funeral had been a cold, grim overcast day. He hadn't remembered it taking place on a sunny day under a clear blue sky.

The service ended, and Mark turned to the Doctor, Amy and Rory, who had stood beside him throughout. Their eyes glistened with tears. It must be strange for them, Mark thought. As far as the Doctor and Amy were concerned, they had only met a few days ago. It must be strange and heartbreaking to travel in time as they do. But maybe not as strange and heartbreaking as it had been for him.

'Enough,' said Mark. 'Enough. Can I go back now?'

'Not just yet. There's one more thing you have to see.'

8 May 1993

The guitar riff of 'Two Princes' echoed out of the open doors of the Dunmore hall of residence and into the cool spring evening. Students stretched out on the freshly cut grass with folders of notes and paperback books. Everyone looked so young, so carefree.

Beaming at everyone he passed as though they were old friends, the Doctor led Mark, Rory and Amy into the student hall. For Mark, it was an unnerving experience. He'd spent his first year at university living in this building. It was both strange and familiar, as he saw so many details he'd long since forgotten. The posters on the noticeboard gave details of NUS demonstrations, of upcoming gigs, and of the opening hours of the computer centre.

A hall party was in progress. From one end of the corridor could be heard the glam jangle of the new Suede album. They squeezed past the students lining the hall and entered the communal kitchen. There, the Doctor indicated for Mark to look across the room.

To see Rebecca, leaning against the far wall, paper cup in hand, a sardonic smile on her lips. Her long hair had been dyed black and she wore an American college sweatshirt.

'Speak to her,' said the Doctor, adjusting his bow tie with a cheerful waggle.

'Are you sure? Won't I be changing history?'

'I'm not expecting you to give her a list of future presidents of the United States.' The Doctor nudged Mark forward. 'Speak to her.'

Mark took a deep breath and walked towards her, feeling as self-conscious as he had when he was a 19-year-old student. Even though he was now 46 years old.

'Hi,' he said to Rebecca. 'Do you mind if I have a quick word?'

'No, no, not at all.' She sized him up and frowned. 'Mature student, right?'

'Yeah. Something like that.'

'Interesting,' Rebecca smiled. 'So what was it you wanted to talk to me about?'

Mark told her everything. He was careful to leave out the dates, names, and time travel, but he told her all about the beautiful girl he'd met and fallen in love with twenty-seven years earlier, who, after several false starts and wrong turnings, he'd made his wife. He told her how happy they'd been together. And he told her how his wife had been killed in a traffic accident, and how, ever since, a single hour hadn't passed without him thinking about her.

Rebecca listened with intense concentration. 'She sounds great, this – what was her name?'

'Um, Rebecca, actually.'

'Spooky, that's my name.' Rebecca grimaced at the contents of her cup. 'Though no one calls me that and lives. So how long ago has it been since she died, if you don't mind me asking?'

'Seventeen years.'

'Seventeen *years*?' repeated Rebecca in astonishment. 'Whoa. Long time.'

'Not that long.'

Rebecca paused to consider her next words carefully. 'Tell me to shut up if I'm speaking out of turn, but, well, everything you've said so far has been about you, about how *you* feel. Haven't you ever stopped to consider what Rebecca would want in all this?'

'What *Rebecca* would want?'

'Would she want you to be miserable for the rest of your life? Would she want you to spend all your time on your own, wishing for what might have been? No.'

'No?'

'No. She'd want you to be happy. She'd want you to find somebody else, somebody else who makes you happy. That's what I'd want, if I was her.'

'I'm not sure I can.'

'You don't know until you've tried. That's an *order*.' Rebecca smiled at him irreverently, her eyes twinkling as she looked up at him and stroked him gently on the cheek. 'Do that for me.'

Mark stared at her for a second, struck dumb. His cheek tingled. Then he turned back towards the door, where the Doctor, Amy and Rory were waiting. 'Thanks,' said Mark. 'I will.'

'Glad to be of service.'

Mark returned to the Doctor and his friends, who looked

at him questioningly. Had he got the answer he wanted? Mark nodded.

'You'll always have the time you had with Rebecca,' the Doctor told him. 'No one can take that away from you.'

'I know,' said Mark. 'I know that now.'

'Then I think it's time to say goodbye.'

Bex watched the man leave the kitchen. He seemed like such a lovely guy, so sweet and so sad. It had been strange, speaking to him; it was like they'd known each other for years. She hoped he'd follow her advice and find someone.

Her thoughts were interrupted by a cry of indignation from the hallway. A young man she'd never seen before stumbled into the kitchen, his neck and T-shirt soaked with red wine. He looked so ridiculous, Bex couldn't help but laugh. 'Would you believe it?' he muttered in response to her amusement. 'Some stupid bloke in a tweed jacket just banged into me, making me spill red wine all over myself.'

'Yeah,' said Bex sympathetically. 'I can see that.'

'My best shirt, this is, you know. Ruined.'

'No, you should be able to get it out if you pour hot water through it straight away.' Bex indicated the kitchen sink with her cup. 'But you have to do it straight away.'

The young man sighed and pulled his T-shirt over his head. Giving Bex the chance to admire his bare chest. For a skinny little thing, he was surprisingly well-defined.

He put his T-shirt in the sink and ran it under the hot tap. While he tried in vain to remove the wine, Bex studied him. He had short brown hair, gelled into a parting, and wore John Lennon-style glasses. He was quite cute. And there was something strangely familiar about him.

475

'Hey, have I just met your dad?' said Bex.

'What?'

'I was just speaking to a bloke who looks just like you, but older.'

'Really?' said the young man. 'You'll have to point him out to me.' He inspected his T-shirt. 'Well, I think I've got most of it out. Thanks.' He turned towards her. 'I'm Mark, by the way. Mark Whitaker.'

'Bex Coles.'

'Cool name.' Mark looked at her, as though he was about to speak, but no words came. Bex tried not to laugh out loud at his awkwardness. 'Um, yeah, er. I don't suppose you fancy, you know, going out some time?'

'What sort of thing did you have in mind?'

'Well, there's this band on at the Whip-Round next week who I've heard great things about. Apparently they're going to be bigger than Suede or Blur.'

'Really? What are they called?'

'Echobelly.'

'I shall have to make a note of that, then,' said Bex. 'So you don't have a girlfriend then?'

Mark paused before answering. 'No. You?'

'No, and I don't have a boyfriend either.'

'So? Do you fancy going to this thing with me?'

'Yeah, why not?'

Bex heard someone coming in and turned to see her boyfriend Dennis McCormack standing in the doorway, dressed, as usual, in a ridiculously formal jacket that showed off just how overweight he was. 'Hi, babes. Surprise, yeah?' He glanced at Mark standing at the sink with his shirt off. This puzzled Dennis. 'Why haven't you got a shirt on?'

'Red wine,' explained Mark.

'Ah, right,' said Dennis, returning his attention to Bex. 'Anyway, turns out the debating society dinner was dead, so I thought, Dennis, doesn't do to keep the lady waiting.' With that, he kissed her on the lips and attacked her mouth like it was a lick-before-sealing envelope.

When Dennis finally allowed her to come up for air, Bex noticed that they'd been joined by a girl with an unwieldy chest and a severely cut bob of auburn hair. 'Hey, Mark,' said the girl, giving him a peck on the cheek. 'Who are you talking to?'

'Um. This is Bex,' said Mark. 'And—'

'McCormack, Dennis,' said Dennis, grabbing Mark's hand and pumping it vigorously.

'Aren't you going to introduce me, Mark?' prompted the girl.

'Oh. Yes. This is Sophie, my, um, girlfriend,' said Mark.

'Nice to meet you,' said Bex.

'Why haven't you got your shirt on?' Sophie asked Mark.

'Red wine,' explained Dennis.

'Well we can't have you standing around half-naked, can we?' said Sophie, taking Mark by the hand. 'Come on, I'll find you another shirt.' She led him out of the kitchen. Bex watched them go, thinking what a pity it was that Mark had a girlfriend and she had a boyfriend. If they'd both been single, this could've been the beginning of something.

Mark's cheek was still tingling when he stepped back inside the TARDIS. The Doctor danced around the console, flicking switches and, after a few moments, the central column began to rise and fall.

The tingling sensation spread from Mark's cheek across his face and down his neck. It prickled like pins and needles. 'Doctor…' he said.

The Doctor glanced towards him and recoiled in shock. 'Oh my,' he breathed, staring at Mark as though there was something wrong with his face.

'What is it?' asked Mark, touching his cheek. His skin felt odd. Softer, smoother. He turned to Amy and Rory, who were both gawping at him in amazement. 'What's happening?'

'Amy,' said the Doctor. 'Mirror!'

Amy fished a small hand mirror out from her coat and handed it to Mark. He lifted it to study his reflection. The face that stared back wasn't that of a man in his late forties. It was the face of a much younger man, a man growing younger all the time. As he watched, the lines around his eyes faded away, his hair grew thicker and all the grey hairs turned brown.

The tingling continued down his arms to the ends of his fingers. Mark watched as the wrinkles on his hands smoothed away. The sensation spread down to his toes, then faded.

'When Rebecca touched your face, she shorted out the time differential,' explained the Doctor matter-of-factly. 'She's given you the past nine years of your life back. You're the same age now as you were when we first met you. It'll be as if you'd never spent all those years in the past.'

'But I can still remember them.'

'Oh, they still *happened* all right,' grinned the Doctor. 'It's just that you're not a day older, that's all.'

Mark returned the mirror to Amy, barely able to believe the truth. He was young again. Well, 37 years old. And all it had taken was one touch from Rebecca's hand.

*

14 October 2011

It was a cold, drizzly evening, just like the evening when he'd first met the Doctor, Amy and Rory. The streets were dotted with puddles and thunder rumbled in the distance. They'd materialised a few minutes' walk from his flat, and just as they were turning into the street, the Doctor ordered them to stay back and keep out of sight. Peering out from behind a recycling bin, Mark soon discovered the reason why.

On the pavement stood a blue police box, and standing at the entrance of the block of flats he could see *another* Doctor, Amy and Rory. He watched as they hurried into the TARDIS. Seconds later, it faded from view with a groaning, wrenching sound.

'OK, they're gone,' said the Doctor, straightening up and wringing his hands. They walked the remaining few metres to the path leading up to entrance, then the Doctor halted. 'Well, this is where we came in, more or less. One week after you were touched by the Weeping Angel.'

'One week?' Mark patted his pockets. 'Oh. Hang on a minute…'

Rory smiled and passed him his house keys. 'Been looking after them for you. Say hi to Mrs Levenson from me, I've been, um, flat-sitting for the last week.'

'Right,' said Mark.

'Oh, and you're out of milk,' added Rory. 'And tea. And bread. And toilet paper.'

'Thanks,' said Mark, turning to Amy. 'Thanks for everything.'

'It was a pleasure,' said Amy with an affectionate smirk.

'Goodbye,' said the Doctor. 'And good luck in the, ah,

future. Where, fortunately, the rules of time mean that you can do *whatever* you want.' He beamed, patted Mark on the shoulder, and turned to go. Rory shook Mark's hand, Amy kissed him on the cheek, and then the three of them walked away, back down the street to the TARDIS.

Mark walked up the stairs to the entrance. He paused before slipping the key in the lock. Just as he had done before a week ago, nine years ago.

He was back in 2011, but now things would be different. He still owned Harold Jones's property, stocks and shares. He was still a multi-millionaire. He didn't have to go back to work at Pollard, Boyce & Whitaker, not if he didn't want to. He could do anything he wanted.

The first thing he would do, he decided, would be to go and see Lucy and Emma. He hadn't seen them for years but he knew they wouldn't mind if he turned up out of the blue and spent an evening talking to them about Rebecca. Not because he wanted to talk about her death or how much he missed her, but because he wanted to remember her and celebrate her life with friends, because the memory of her no longer made him feel sad.

He'd take her advice, Mark decided, and find somebody. But where to look? He didn't have the faintest idea. But it would be fun finding out.

Mark unlocked the door and entered the block of flats, ready to begin the rest of his life.

Acknowledgements

Thanks to Justin Richards for giving me the chance to show off; to Steven Moffat for letting me borrow his best monsters; and to the following, who made this book better: Stephen Aintree, Steve Berry, Debbie Challis, Robert Dick, Debbie Hill, Matt Kimpton, Joe Lidster and Simon Guerrier.